SOPHIA ZANE

The Lies We Whisper

The Lies That Bind Us Series Book 1

First published by Zane Books 2025

Copyright © 2025 by Sophia Zane

All rights reserved. No part of this publication may be reproduced, stored or transmitted in any form or by any means, electronic, mechanical, photocopying, recording, scanning, or otherwise without written permission from the publisher. It is illegal to copy this book, post it to a website, or distribute it by any other means without permission.

This novel is entirely a work of fiction. The names, characters and incidents portrayed in it are the work of the author's imagination. Any resemblance to actual persons, living or dead, events or localities is entirely coincidental.

Sophia Zane asserts the moral right to be identified as the author of this work.

Sophia Zane has no responsibility for the persistence or accuracy of URLs for external or third-party Internet Websites referred to in this publication and does not guarantee that any content on such Websites is, or will remain, accurate or appropriate.

Designations used by companies to distinguish their products are often claimed as trademarks. All brand names and product names used in this book and on its cover are trade names, service marks, trademarks and registered trademarks of their respective owners. The publishers and the book are not associated with any product or vendor mentioned in this book. None of the companies referenced within the book have endorsed the book.

This is a work of fiction. Any names, characters, places, organizations, or incidents are either products of the author's imagination or used fictitiously. While some real-world references appear, including Great Meadow Correctional Facility, the Federal Bureau of Investigation (FBI), the Cohoes Police Department, and pop culture titles like The Lost Boys, Supernatural, Grey's Anatomy, and Disney properties, all depictions are fictional.

Any mention of real individuals, including public figures such as Kiefer Sutherland, is used fictitiously and for narrative flavor only. This work is not affiliated with, endorsed by, or representative of any real person, agency, or organization.

All product names, media titles, and trademarks are the property of their respective owners and are used for storytelling purposes. No endorsement, sponsorship, or association is implied.

First edition

ISBN (paperback): 979-8-218-69497-5
ISBN (hardcover): 979-8-218-68798-4

This is dedicated to all those who crashed and rose.
For the ones with broken childhoods and silent scars,
told they were too much or never enough.
For those who were used, dismissed, and unloved and still kept going.
You swallowed pain, stood without applause, and finally said enough.
You are why these stories breathe.
This book is for you.
Because you didn't just survive.
You became the storm.

Contents

Preface — iv
Acknowledgments — vi
Content Warning — viii
Prologue — 1
Chapter 1 — 3
Chapter 2 — 13
Chapter 3 — 18
Chapter 4 — 23
Chapter 5 — 27
Chapter 6 — 32
Chapter 7 — 38
Chapter 8 — 42
Chapter 9 — 47
Chapter 10 — 55
Chapter 11 — 65
Chapter 12 — 72
Chapter 13 — 78
Chapter 14 — 84
Chapter 15 — 94
Chapter 16 — 101
Chapter 17 — 107
Chapter 18 — 113
Chapter 19 — 122
Chapter 20 — 128
Chapter 21 — 135
Chapter 22 — 141

Chapter 23	152
Chapter 24	156
Chapter 25	161
Chapter 26	167
Chapter 27	171
Chapter 28	176
Chapter 29	180
Chapter 30	184
Chapter 31	189
Chapter 32	193
Chapter 33	204
Chapter 34	209
Chapter 35	216
Chapter 36	231
Chapter 37	240
Chapter 38	248
Chapter 39	252
Chapter 40	261
Chapter 41	265
Chapter 42	274
Chapter 43	277
Chapter 44	284
Chapter 45	288
Chapter 46	291
Chapter 47	298
Chapter 48	305
Chapter 49	309
Chapter 50	313
Chapter 51	319
Chapter 52	325
Chapter 53	330
Epilogue	335
Family History	337

A Note from the Author	344
About the Author	345
Also by Sophia Zane	346

Preface

This story has lived in my mind for decades, a quiet whisper that refused to fade. It began in the early 2000s as scattered notes; fragments of an idea with no clear path, just a lingering sense of something waiting to be told. I didn't know where it would lead, only that I wanted to create a world with someone to root for and someone to fear. For years, it remained in the background, growing and evolving in the quiet corners of my mind, patiently waiting for its time.

Then, in 2014, I finally made the commitment to bring it to life. But progress was slow; agonizingly slow. Two to four chapters a year, hesitant steps into the unknown, never quite certain where the journey would take me. Yet, no matter how much time passed, the story never let go. The characters became more than just figments of imagination; they were voices that demanded to be heard, emotions that tangled with my own. When they cried, I cried. When they laughed, I laughed. Their struggles became my struggles, their triumphs my triumphs. In so many ways, they felt real, living and breathing within me, waiting for the moment they would finally spill onto the page.

I immersed myself in research, determined to make this world feel as authentic as possible, even within the realm of fiction. Every profession, every crime detail, every psychological nuance, I wanted it all to ring true. My notes sprawled across a board like a detective's case file, with lines connecting one thought to the next, weaving a web of relationships, conflicts, and unanswered questions. Some pieces fell into place as if they had always belonged, while others shifted and transformed, deepening the story in ways I never could have predicted.

The journey was long and winding, filled with moments of doubt and discovery. There were days I sat for hours, lost in thought, piecing together the next move like a puzzle. Ideas would spark, one leading to another, and then another. Some turned into dead ends, others into breathtaking twists that took even me by surprise. But through it all, the characters refused to be silenced. They pushed and pulled, shaping themselves with every passing day, until at last, their story was no longer just a dream waiting to be told; it was real, living on the page, exactly where it was meant to be.

Acknowledgments

Stories may begin with a single idea, but they come to life through the people who believe in them. This book would not exist without the love, support, and patience of so many.

To my daughter, Thank you for letting me interrupt your day with countless *"Hey, can you read this?"* moments, for listening patiently to my endless ideas, and for always being my sounding board. Sometimes your feedback came in words, sometimes in just a look, but every bit of it meant the world to me. Your quiet support, your honesty, and your belief in me kept me going more than you'll ever know. I'm so proud of the woman you are.

To my family, thank you for believing in me and for cheering me on even when this dream felt impossibly far away. Your love and encouragement gave me the strength to keep pushing forward.

To my friends, thank you for indulging my endless plot discussions, debating character choices with me, and standing by me through every high and low of this journey. Writing can be a lonely process, but because of you, I never felt alone. To those who endured my *"Does this part give you chills?"* questions or caught me watching, waiting for a shiver, a pause, or even just an *"It's okay," you* may not realize it, but every reaction helped shape this story. Even the "Can you read my manuscript?" You helped me more than you know.

A special thanks to Jenn Chung; your insight into character development and storytelling went far beyond feedback. You helped shape this book. Your honest perspective encouraged me to meticulously refine even the smallest details, serving as a constant reminder that a single glance, a carefully chosen word, or a fleeting gesture can convey a multitude of messages. I deeply value your friendship, and I truly don't think I would have finished this without you. Thank you for always pushing me and for enduring the countless discussions along the way. I value you more than you know.

To the man who inspired this story, your memory has never faded. Even in your absence, you've remained with me through every word and every scene.

Many of the memories in these pages are ours, frozen in time. Your influence lives in the choices my characters make and the emotions that move them. This story exists, in part, because of you. And I thank God for the time I had with you.

And finally, to every reader who picks up this book, you are the reason stories endure. Thanks for letting these characters live in your mind, even if only for a little while. I hope they stay with you the way they have stayed with me.

Sophia

Content Warning

This novel contains depictions of sexual assault, domestic violence, substance abuse, and PTSD. Some scenes may be distressing for readers. **Reader discretion is advised.**

* * *

If you need resources or support, consider reaching out to:
Sexual Assault & Trauma Support
RAINN (Rape, Abuse & Incest National Network) – *24/7 confidential support*
1-800-656-HOPE (4673)
www.rainn.org

Domestic Violence
National Domestic Violence Hotline – *24/7 support for survivors*
1-800-799-SAFE (7233)
www.thehotline.org

Substance Abuse & Addiction
SAMHSA (Substance Abuse and Mental Health Services Administration)
1-800-662-HELP (4357)
www.samhsa.gov

PTSD & Mental Health Support
National Alliance on Mental Illness (NAMI) HelpLine
1-800-950-NAMI (6264)

www.nami.org

* * *

International Support

*If you need support **outside of the U.S.**, please reach out to a crisis line in your area. Below are international resources that may help:*
Sexual Assault Resources (RAINN):
RAINN's https://rainn.org/international-sexual-assault-resources

Domestic Violence Resources:
Safe & Together International DV Resources https://safeandtogetherinstitute.com/international-domestic-violence-resources/

Prologue

July 2006

Before the silence, there was a scream. Not the kind that ever left Hanna's mouth, but the kind that stayed buried deep inside her, tangled in memory and muscle. The other kind, the ones that tore out loud and raw, were easier; they made noise that bounced off walls. Sometimes they even left bruises in the air, visible enough that someone might actually stop and notice.

This one had stayed inside her, a raw, splintered sound that no one else could hear. It began years earlier, long before prison walls and intake assessments, before the polished office, the framed degrees, and the calm expression she wore like armor. It had started in a living room where adults forgot she was there and in a bedroom where the door didn't always lock. These were memories she had tried to file away like case notes, tucked into neat folders in the back of her mind, but they always found their way back, especially when the world got quiet.

People liked to say that trauma made you stronger, but Hanna knew that wasn't true. It didn't make you tougher or braver. It made you quieter. It made you sharper. You learned how to watch, how to listen, and how to stay one step ahead. You learned to smile when you were hurting and to nod in agreement when every part of you wanted to run. It taught you how to survive, even when survival meant disappearing inside yourself.

She had learned all of that before she turned twelve.

Now she was a woman shaped by stillness. A woman who understood that not all monsters lived behind bars. Some wore wedding rings. Some carried badges. Some looked you in the eye and said, "I love you," right before they shattered everything. And sometimes, they sat across from you in handcuffs and asked for therapy.

Very few inmates ever requested a specific therapist.

But Richard Hale had. His name was printed at the bottom of the intake form in steady, deliberate block letters:

Dr. Hanna Nowack only

He wasn't her patient. He wasn't even in her unit.

Hale was high risk, housed in solitary, and always escorted by at least two guards. There was to be no direct contact. His file was long and unsettling, layered with flags for psychological manipulation, aggression, and control. He wasn't just the kind of man who craved power. He was the kind who studied how to take it from other people.

And now, for reasons he didn't explain, he wanted her.

Hanna stared at the form. The phone sat in her hand, still warm from the last call, but now it felt heavier somehow, like it already knew what was coming.

She'd been warned by others in the department to steer clear of him. They told her not to fall into his trap. Richard Hale didn't talk unless he was working an angle.

Her thoughts raced. Her gut told her to walk away, but curiosity pressed in harder than caution. She had to know why. Maybe she could get him to talk.

She dialed the Special Housing Unit extension.

"This is Dr. Nowack. I'll see Richard Hale at ten."

Hanna hung up the phone and leaned back in her chair. She had stopped fearing monsters a long time ago. She'd learned early that the real ones never looked like monsters at all.

Chapter 1

October 2006, Great Meadow Correctional Facility

The air inside the prison stung with bleach; beneath it lurked something musty, like damp stone and maybe old sweat. Hanna shifted her bag higher on her shoulder. The crisp blouse, sleeves rolled, left room to breathe; the gray slacks let her move. White sneakers, scuffed from the sidewalk, were better than heels, which they banned anyway. She hadn't come to impress anyone. She came to find something human, if it still existed in places like this.

She'd been working at Great Meadow since 2000, right after finishing her PhD. For six years, she'd observed the same truth play out in different faces: power is the real currency behind bars. And Richard Hale? He was the kind of man who never cashed out. A few months ago, he'd requested her by name. That never happened. Not unless the inmate thought he could get something. Or worse, already had.

She reminded herself of the rules she lived by: maintain objectivity, show no emotion, and never let the inmate steer. Those weren't only guidelines; they were survival mechanisms. Rapport had its limits, and empathy could be a trap.

Her eyes were still blue, but they weren't soft anymore. That wide open hue had darkened over time, sharpened by grief and grit. She didn't mind. Clarity came at a cost, but distance was a form of armor.

The security gate clanked behind her. Hanna straightened. The walk was part performance: calm gait, eyes forward, no hesitation. Never let them sense a crack.

Her sneakers squeaked down the hallway. Fluorescent lights buzzed overhead. Far off, a door slammed, a reminder that everything here echoed. It was filled with sound, pain, and fear. All of it stuck.

The door opened with a mechanical groan. The air shifted. Two guards led Hale in; shackles on his ankles echoed with each step, steady and deliberate. Like he owned the sound.

He sat across from her like he was the one holding court. His posture was relaxed but alert. His eyes, calculating.

Richard Hale wore his warmth like a mask. Most men in here looked worn down, like the weight of the place had already crushed them. But Hale? He wore the whole thing like it was temporary. None of it truly resonated with him. He viewed the moment as merely a setback, engaging in a game of patience.

His dark hair, now streaked with silver, was neatly combed, a quiet display of control amid the chaos. He trimmed his beard enough to appear deliberate, not unkempt. The jumpsuit should have stripped him of his power, but it didn't. Somehow, he still looked like the most in control man in the room.

Then there were his eyes. Behind rectangular glasses, they were brown, cold, and unreadable, yet precise. They were constantly observing and evaluating, identifying weaknesses, and assessing advantages. Even shackled, he moved with measured confidence. It was as if he had never rushed a day in his life. Men like Richard Hale didn't need speed to be dangerous because they had power. Power wasn't about movement. It was about patience and control.

He didn't say anything at first. He sat there, studying her, calculating. Then he smiled; easy, too easy. His smile seemed out of place in this particular environment. It was the kind of smile that could cause someone to forget who he truly was.

Men like Richard Hale didn't make threats. They made promises without warnings.

Hanna took her seat. The room was barren and lifeless, a place where emotions went to die. She sat straight, her clipboard resting lightly in her

CHAPTER 1

hands. Internally, she recited it again: no emotion. No disclosure. No loss of control.

He leaned back, shackles rattling enough to make her tense. His fingers tapped the armrest rhythmically, practiced. It was a calculated gesture. Just like his silence. Just like his stare. She clocked every micro movement: posture tightness, tone of breath, and twitch at the jaw. Always observe. Especially when it feels like nothing is happening.

He looked at her not like prey, but like a mirror. That unnerved her more.

"You seem different today, Richard."

He smirked, tilting his head. "Different? That's not much of a clinical observation, Doctor. Can you be more specific?"

She ignored the bait. Classic reversal attempt. "You're quieter. Less anticipatory. In our previous sessions, you spoke about control. You mentioned the excitement it brings. But today, you're sitting there, as if you're waiting on something."

Richard gave a dry chuckle, almost thoughtful. "Maybe I just enjoy our time together. You listen well. Not many people do. They hear, but they don't listen."

She said nothing. Rapport, not friendship. Boundaries, not trust. "And what do you think I hear that others don't?"

He exhaled slowly. Measured. "The parts of me I don't say out loud. The things I leave unfinished." His smile curled slowly. "You hear her in me, don't you?"

The words landed heavily. Manipulative. Too pointed to be random. Hanna straightened. "Who is she, Richard?"

He leaned in just far enough to make the restraints creak. "You already know."

Stillness pressed in. Redirect, Hanna. Don't follow his rhythm. Break it.

"You've never spoken about a woman before. Not like this. Who was she to you?"

He shifted, jaw clenching. His fingers twitched at the cuffs. Then he looked up suddenly, like something in his mind had just vanished. "She kept me… stable." His voice softened. "When she was there, the noise wasn't so loud. The need to do something... it dulled. She looked at me like she knew everything. Even the worst. And she didn't flinch."

Hanna noted the word choice: *need*, not *impulse*. The reframing was intentional and subtle. "And when she died?"

His mouth drew tight. A flicker of rage? Regret? She wasn't sure. Then it disappeared.

"I lost the one person who made me feel like I mattered. When someone cuts you loose long enough, you stop trying to find your way back."

Her pulse ticked faster. Not out of sympathy. Out of recognition. And she hated that.

She leaned in slightly. Controlled. Curious, not vulnerable. "You loved her."

He met her gaze. For a moment, something flickered. Then he buried it. "More than I ever knew was possible."

They sat in silence. Her clipboard was still in her lap, her pen uncapped. But she hadn't written a thing.

Carefully, she asked, "Is that why you dreamt of her? Because you still feel her?"

He laughed, dry and humorless. "No, Doctor. I dreamt of her because I lost her in an accident. A real one. The kind no one plans. That's what we have in common, isn't it?"

His eyes narrowed, his voice lowering to something more dangerous. "Your husband wasn't taken by accident, was he?"

The words hit like a blow. Her body didn't react, but she did grip her pen tightly.

"What did you just say?"

Richard leaned forward, his voice a whisper. "You wear grief like a second skin, doctor. You've built a life around it. Wrapped it on purpose. But tell me... does it ever stop feeling like unfinished business?"

The room chilled. The past wasn't behind her. It was sitting across from her, in chains, but still in control. For the first time in years, Hanna Nowack wasn't sure she was the one holding the line.

CHAPTER 1

***

MHU staff room

The coffeemaker hissed and sputtered. Hanna stood at the counter, both hands around a warm mug, letting the steam curl over her fingers. She stared past it, still running the session over in her head.

Richard Hale had changed today. The change wasn't in his words. It was in the delivery. His jaw tightened as he spoke. He held his breath for a moment. The subtle tension in his fingers was noticeable.

Michael Carter's voice broke through. "Hale again?"

Hanna nodded, distracted, still trapped in memory. She pictured Hale's hands, the restraint in them, and the way his shoulders shifted.

She set the mug down and turned to face him. "He felt something today."

Michael crossed his arms, skeptical. "He wanted you to think that. That's what they do."

"No," she said quietly. "This wasn't rehearsed. It wasn't part of the act."

He studied her. Something unreadable flickered across his face. "Alright, I'll bite. What was different?"

She paused. "When I asked about the woman he lost, his whole body changed. He locked up, and his breath shifted. That wasn't control, Michael. It was something that was breaking."

"You think she triggered the violence?"

"I think she was the turning point."

Michael exhaled. "And you think you can use that?"

She hesitated. She wanted to believe she could. She wanted to dig deeper. Grief transforms individuals. She knew that more intimately than anyone.

"Hanna," Michael said, voice firm.

She looked up. There was more than concern in his expression. It was personal.

He was there at the start. He witnessed her disintegration only once. He wasn't going to let it happen again.

"You can't use your grief for this."

She gasped in shock. That was indeed the truth, wasn't it? She wasn't just analyzing Richard Hale. She was chasing something. She was making an effort to comprehend him better. Trying to understand herself.

"I'm not," she said.

"You are."

She turned away, holding the cup tighter.

He didn't push. He didn't have to.

They both knew he was right. That realization scared her more than Hale ever could.

* * *

Back in her office, Hanna barely registered the hallway. Richard's words clung to her like a stain. She sat at her desk but didn't move for a full minute. Then she opened her laptop. The report could wait. But her thoughts? They wouldn't.

Maybe that's why she ended up in this career. Not only was she trying to assist them, but she was also attempting to understand herself better. Her life had always been steeped in distrust, loss, and lies. The people who were supposed to protect her had been the first to betray her.

* * *

December 1996

The baby was asleep in the nursery, the glow of the Christmas tree casting flickering shadows on the walls. Hanna sat at the kitchen table, an offer letter in her hands for an internship at Great Meadow Correctional Facility.

Brian stood by the counter, his badge and service weapon resting beside a half finished cup of coffee. He was frustrated.

"Tell me you're not actually considering this, Hanna."

She rubbed her temples. "Brian, we've been over this."

He snapped, "No, we haven't. You decided, and now I'm supposed to just live with it?"

CHAPTER 1

Hanna exhaled slowly, trying to stay calm. "It's a good opportunity. This internship is a stepping stone for my career."

Brian shook his head, his tone elevated. "What career, Hanna? You're a wife and a mother," his finger pointing down the hall at the nursery, "You have responsibilities around here."

That hit harder than she expected. He said it like it was law. Like being a wife and a mother should be enough. "So that's it? I'm supposed to stay home forever? I don't get to have something of my own? You make it sound like a degree isn't important."

Brian rubbed his face, the way he did when he was worn down to the edge. Hanna watched him, unsure if it was this fight wearing him thin or something else. The late nights. The silence. The look he got when he thought she wasn't watching. "That's not what I'm saying. You decided to pursue grad school. I told you it was a bad idea with the house, and now Caitlyn."

Hanna stood, her voice sharp with anger. "Then what are you saying, Brian?"

His eyes flicked from her to the closed nursery door, and then through his teeth, "I don't want you near those men, Hanna."

"Brian, it's a prison. There's security. It's not like I'm walking down an alley looking for criminals."

He laughed, but there was no humor in it, only fear. His voice dropped, low and sharp. "You're fucking kidding me; you don't get it, do you? Do you have any idea what kind of men end up in there? It's a max facility, Hanna, think about it."

She folded her arms, her voice even. "And you do?"

Brian froze. Then, he said sharply, "Are you fucking serious, Hanna? Hello, I'm a cop. It's my job to know. For Christ's sake, I'm the one who puts them in there."

But Hanna wasn't naive. She'd seen the late nights, the missed calls, and the look in his eyes like he was carrying something no one else could see. "Is there something you're not telling me?"

"I'm telling you you're not taking this job."

"I'm doing this, Brian."

Brian responded with finality, "No, Hanna, you're not!"

She looked at him, feeling slightly dizzy due to her rising blood pressure, and said, "I am your wife; you can't tell me what to do."

Brian turned and hit his head on the cabinets. "Fuck Hanna." Then he turned around and said in a harsh voice, "Fine, do the fucking internship, but that is it. After the internship is finished, you're done there, understood?"

She nodded, hiding back the grin.

He looked at her, annoyed, tone still rough. "How long is the damn internship?"

Hanna met his eyes. "Twelve weeks."

"You get twelve weeks. They offer you a job, and you will turn it down. Your responsibility is here. If it starts getting in the way, you quit. Understood?"

"Yes." She snapped. She hated that he sounded more like a father than a husband.

He was pacing now. He looked at the clock, then walked over to her. "I have to go."

He leaned in and kissed her. "I love you, but sometimes you really fucking piss me off."

She smiled. "That's why you love me."

He stared, stone faced. Said nothing. He was still pissed.

She watched him grab his badge and keys; he looked back at her, shook his head, and walked toward the door to the garage. When the door shut and locked behind him, she sat back and thought, "We'll discuss this again. Because if they offer me a staff position, I'm taking it."

* * *

Present Day 2006 Hanna's Office

She sat down at her desk, opened her laptop, and began her report. Hanna stared at the blank document, fingers hovering over the keyboard. Richard Hale was different today. He wasn't playing games. He wasn't performing. He had lost the smug, cocky smirk that usually indicated he was ten steps ahead of everyone else. Instead, he had sat there, still, unnervingly still. His gaze was sharper, heavier, and more calculating. Then, like all men of his kind, he turned the conversation back on her.

CHAPTER 1

She started typing.

Richard Hale. October 17, 2006. One on one therapy sessions.

Her hands hesitated. She exhaled, then kept going.

There has been an unusual shift in behavior. The behavior has become less performative and more controlled.
  Introduced personal history unprompted.
  Mentioned a past relationship as an 'anchor.'
  He said she kept him stable. Maybe losing her really was his breaking point.

Or maybe that's just what he wants me to think

Possible emotional trigger? Or is it just another tactic used for manipulation?

It should've ended there. It wasn't just that he mentioned Brian. It was the way he said it, not as guesswork, but as if he *knew*. Knew how he died. Knew what she hadn't told anyone. That was what chilled her. Hanna's fingers curled into a fist. That single moment had sent something cold down her spine. It wasn't just that Hale was aware of her husband's existence. The difference lay in the way he expressed it.

Might it eventually stop feeling like unfinished business? It is not a question or a guess but a statement. How the hell did he know? Hanna shut her laptop. She'd deal with the report later. Right now, she needed answers.

She grabbed her keys, shoved her laptop into her bag, and did a final sweep of the office.

As she was locking up, a correction officer walked by. "Don't know how you do it, Doc. I don't know if I'd want to be in their heads."

Hanna laughed, though it felt hollow. "Sometimes I wonder myself. I like to think there's still some humanity left in them."

The CO snorted. "I don't know, Doc. I work with them on the block. They're animals."

Hanna smiled politely. "Have a good night."

"You too, Doc."

She walked to her car, but her mind wasn't in the parking lot.

How did Hale know about Brian? Was he just fishing, throwing out vague statements until something stuck? Or was this different? Was this how he pulled his prey close before striking?

Was Michael right? Should she back off? Or was there more to this? She felt a deep seated need to discover the truth. She needed to learn not only about Richard Hale but also about herself.

Hanna took out her phone and called down to his block. "This is Dr. Nowack. I want Richard Hale brought back on Wednesday at the same time." She hung up, locked her office, and stepped out into the cold night air. As she started her car, her thoughts didn't leave her. They stayed locked inside that room with Richard Hale.

Chapter 2

Present Day 2006

The house was too quiet. Hanna sat at the kitchen table, her laptop open, but her mind miles away. Richard's words still clung to her, stirring memories she'd spent years trying to bury.

She twirled a simple gold band between her fingers. Brian's ring. She used to wake to the feel of it against her skin. See it when he held Caitlyn. When he touched her cheek.

Always, Hanna. It'll always be you.

The ring caught a sliver of moonlight, and suddenly, she was back there.

* * *

February 1995

Brian leaned against the doorway, still half in uniform, tie crooked, sleeves pushed back. For a moment, he stood there like the only stable thing in the room.

Hanna curled in the corner of the couch, arms around her knees. Even after seven years, he could still knock the breath out of her without trying.

His hair was damp from the weather, a few strands wild. He looked tired. not just physically, but deeper than that. He almost smiled. Almost.

"It's too much, Brian."

He rubbed a hand down his face. "Hanna..."

"The venue, the dress, and your mother's damn guest list. Over three hundred people."

Brian tipped his head back against the door frame, hands in his pockets. The uniform stretched across his chest, but Hanna forced herself not to get distracted.

"It's a wedding. Isn't that the whole point? To show off?"

"Shouldn't we get a say in it?" She snapped. "All the decisions are being made for us."

Brian kept his voice even. "Then let's just tell them the truth."

"We can't."

He crossed the room and sat on the coffee table in front of her. The air shifted. Closer now, she could see the faint crease between his brows, the tired edge in his eyes. She could smell the mix of rain and something that had always been uniquely him.

"What's really holding us back?"

"They'll lose it," she whispered. "She won't forgive us."

"She will. Eventually."

"No, Brian. She has this perfect version of you. If we tell her we eloped..."

He smiled gently. "She'll be a little mad, but she'll deal with it. It's not the end of the world, Hanna."

She shook her head. "You don't get it."

"Then explain it to me."

She looked away. "My whole life, I felt like I was never enough. I wasn't the daughter my parents longed for. I was just the reason. The reason for the marriage and the reason for the divorce. I was never as good as my brother, not worth loving."

Brian's expression softened. "You are worth loving. Trust me. Forget about them. Don't give them the pleasure of another thought. They aren't worth it."

She looked down and wiped a tear. "I just..." She took a deep breath. "Your mom she's the opposite. I don't want her to hate me or look at me the way my parents do. If she knew..."

He cut her off. "She'll still love you. She'll still love me."

"But she won't see me the same. I can't take that."

Brian reached for her hand. "Hanna, my mom doesn't love on condition. She won't stop loving you because she's mad. But if it'll make you feel better, then we don't have to tell them."

Relief eased her shoulders. "Thank you."

CHAPTER 2

He rested his forehead against hers. "Let her and your grandma have their fun. This is the only wedding she'll get to be part of, well, until our kids." He smiled.

She nodded. "Okay."

Brian kissed her. "Hanna, look at me. I love you. Stop giving them power. You're better than that."

"I know."

Then his radio crackled from the counter, shouting codes.

He looked at her. "I have to go. We'll talk more about this later." He got up, kissed her forehead, and headed for the door.

* * *

Present Day 2006

It had been three years since she'd worn the ring. Still, she couldn't bring herself to close the jewelry box. She slid the ring onto a chain, fingers trembling. But the memory stayed lodged in her chest like a stone.

A breeze stirred the curtains. Hanna looked up. The porch light flickered, casting strange shadows across the floor. A cold unease settled in her chest. She rose slowly, approaching the front window.

The movement was barely visible, but enough to catch her eye. The darkness didn't give much away. The darkness revealed only a shape. It could've been anything. Her breath hitched, her hand brushing the edge of the curtain. It jumped. She jumped back.

"A deer," she whispered.

"Mommy?"

Caitlyn's voice jolted her. Hanna turned to find her daughter standing in the hallway, rubbing her eyes, clutching a stuffed animal.

Her gray eyes were sleepy but curious. Hanna swallowed and forced calm into her voice.

"What is it, baby?"

"Bad dream."

Hanna scooped her up, holding her close. She grounded herself in the only soft thing left in her life. The child was all she had left of Brian. She saw him in her every day.

Then a knock.

Hanna froze. Her pulse spiked. She glanced at the clock. It was late. Too late.

"It's just the wind," she told herself.

"Who's at the door, Mama?"

"No one, baby."

She tucked Caitlyn into bed, kissed her forehead, and lingered a moment longer than usual.

Another knock. Softer this time. Intentional.

She stepped to the door and turned on the porch light.

Nick.

He stood in the mist, coat damp, hands in his pockets. His eyes searched hers.

"Hey," he said.

"Hi, Nick."

She let him in. When he leaned toward her, she embraced him first, warm and restrained. Not what he wanted, but more than nothing.

He saw the chain and the ring. She knew he did.

"You okay?"

"Just tired."

He nodded. "Let's sit."

She followed him to the living room. He reached for her hand. His fingers brushed the chain. He didn't say anything. That was Nick's version of patience.

"I'm going to run you a bath," he said.

It wasn't a question.

He disappeared down the hall.

And she sat there, thinking not of him but of the space Brian left behind. And how Nick, for all his trying, would never fill it.

* * *

CHAPTER 2

Great Meadow Correctional Facility

Richard sat on his bunk, flipping through papers and documents tied to Brian DeLuca. Across from him, Dom Russo watched.

"Didn't think you cared about dead cops."

Richard didn't look up. "I don't. I care about the people he left behind."

Dom narrowed his eyes. "So that's what this is about?"

Richard leaned back, smirking. "Tell me about the DeLuca's."

Dom frowned. "You don't poke them unless you've got a death wish, and that one there in that file is a guaranteed death. Don't poke into that one."

Richard shook his head. "I am in here for life. I die in here either way."

Dom shook his head. "They find out."

Richard's fingers tightened on the file. "What if one of them is already on my side?"

Then the smile returned. "Now talk."

Chapter 3

The next morning, Nick's eyes drifted to the open jewelry box on the table, the simple gold band still resting inside. A ghost from the past, a memory that never faded, always standing between them.

Why was he still competing with a ghost? Nine years had passed, yet Brian lingered in Hanna's smiles, her quiet pauses, and every hesitation. It made no sense to Nick how a man buried in the ground could still hold Hanna's heart more firmly than he ever could.

Nick forced himself to look away, determined not to dwell on it, not today. He moved toward the window, but his gaze caught on a photo stuck to the fridge: Hanna, Caitlyn, and Steve Riley at the zoo, laughing from atop a camel. Steve had been Brian's best friend, practically family, and since Brian's death, he'd quietly hovered around the edges of Hanna's life. Always checking in, dropping by unannounced, ensuring they were okay. Nick resented the effortless way Steve had stepped into Brian's role, naturally protective of Hanna and Caitlyn.

Photos of the three of them filled the house, captured moments that never included Nick. They looked like a real family, Steve filling the empty space Brian had left behind, a space Nick desperately wished was his. Yet despite everything, not a single photo of Nick existed in their home. That stung more than anything.

She should have been his by now.

***

CHAPTER 3

The smell of coffee filled the kitchen as Nick poured two mugs. Routine. Stability. That's what he offered her.

Hanna walked in, rubbing her eyes. Nick handed her a cup.

"Morning," he murmured, leaning in to kiss her cheek.

She shifted slightly, subtly avoiding him, wrapping both hands around the warm mug instead. "Morning."

She glanced at the clock. "You're up early."

"Early rounds. Six surgeries," he replied, leaning against the counter. "You?"

She sighed softly. "Prison this morning. Class after. My grandma's getting Caitlyn; they have an early dismissal today."

"Half-day again? They barely settle in before sending them home."

Hanna smirked, tired but amused. "Torture builds character."

Nick chuckled softly. "If it were later, I could've picked her up. It's been too long since we've had an afternoon together."

Hanna nodded, sipping coffee, her fingers tracing the rim of the mug.

Nick's stomach twisted. "Dinner at my place tonight? Chicken fingers and fries. Caitlyn will love it."

"Healthy choice," she teased gently. "But yeah, she'd love that. Sounds great."

Nick's gaze drifted back to the table, to the ring box, a silent third presence in their conversation. No matter how much time passed, Brian remained. Nick's grip tightened around his mug. No more waiting. He was done competing with ghosts.

Hanna caught his glance, her expression unreadable.

Nick wasn't flashy or reckless. But he was steady, loyal, and protective; he was everything a woman should want. So why didn't it feel like enough? No matter how hard she tried, she could never feel what he wanted her to feel, expected her to feel.

* * *

Hanna helped Caitlyn get ready for school.

"You're going to see Pradziadek and Prababcia today after school," she said as she tied Caitlyn's shoes.

"Am I staying the night? Are you going somewhere?"

"No, it's an early dismissal day."

Caitlyn frowned. "What's the point? I get there only to leave."

Hanna blinked, then smiled nervously. She loved that Caitlyn had such a strong bond with Nick, but sometimes she worried Caitlyn was starting to lose Brian's traits.

She looked at her, so big already. Growing fast.

The memory of her birth was still sharp in Hanna's mind.

* * *

May 17, 1996

The house was quiet except for the ticking of the old wooden clock in the hallway. Rain had slowed to a drizzle, tapping lightly against the windows. Hanna shifted in bed, trying to find a position that didn't make her back ache. At nine months pregnant, sleep had become a luxury.

Then something changed.

A sharp cramp tore through her stomach. Then warmth. Her heart pounded as she reached down.

Sticky. Wet. Blood.

"The baby."

"Grandma!" Her voice cracked as she struggled to sit up. "Grandma!"

Irene Nowack rushed in, her nightgown swaying. "What's wrong?"

Hanna threw back the blankets, revealing a crimson stain across the sheets. "Something's wrong. It's the baby."

Irene paled. "Henry! Get the car started!" She steadied Hanna. "We're going. Now."

* * *

Henry's hands trembled as he dialed dispatch. "Crystal, it's Henry Nowack. I

CHAPTER 3

need Officer DeLuca. It's urgent."
"What's going on, Mr. Nowack?"
"Hanna's in labor. There's bleeding. We're heading to the hospital now."
"I'm on it."

* * *

Static crackled over the police radio.
"Unit 211, DeLuca, be advised your wife is having the baby."
Brian smirked. "Yeah, I know. Any day now."
Then: "DELUCA, GET YOUR ASS TO THE HOSPITAL! SHE'S HAVING THE BABY RIGHT NOW!"
Brian froze. His partner choked on coffee. "Oh, shit."
Sirens wailed.

* * *

Glen Falls Memorial

The hospital smelled of antiseptic and lavender lotion. The fetal monitor beeped steadily.

Hanna lay in bed, damp curls pressed to the pillow. The plan had been induction, calm and steady. Brian, of course, had other plans.

The video camera whirred as he panned across the room, capturing the lights, the bassinet, and Hanna's scowl.

"DeLuca, put the camera away."
"You're glowing," he grinned. "I want us to remember this forever."
"I'm sweating."
"You'll appreciate this later."
"Turn. It. Off."
Across the room, Irene chuckled. "Told you, no one's safe when she's in labor."
Brian kissed Hanna's forehead. "You're still beautiful."
"Talk to me after I push a watermelon out of my body."
He took her hand, brushing her knuckles. She exhaled as another contraction

began.

***

Labor & Delivery Room

In the delivery room, Hanna gripped the rails, breath shallow, fingers aching from how tightly she held Brian's hand.

"Breathe," he said gently.

"I don't want to breathe," she hissed. "It doesn't fucking help."

Brian froze.

Even Irene stiffened.

Hanna looked ready to commit murder.

"Okay," he said carefully. "Then don't."

When the contraction passed, Hanna collapsed back onto the pillows.

"Better?" he asked, smoothing her hair.

She muttered, "Breathing helps."

He grinned. "Knew it."

She smacked his arm.

***

Later that night

Everything blurred: pain, nurses, monitors, and voices.

"One more, Hanna! She's almost here!"

Brian gripped her hand, whispering, "You've got this. I'm right here."

Then a cry.

The doctor held up their daughter. Brian laughed, breathless, forehead pressed to Hanna's. "You did it. She's here. I love you, Hanna. We have a family."

They laid Caitlyn on her chest, warm, perfect. Ten fingers. Ten toes.

Brian kissed Hanna's temple, his voice breaking. "Hi, baby girl," he whispered. "I'm your daddy."

Even in the exhaustion, even in the chaos, Hanna knew: This was everything she'd ever wanted.

Chapter 4

Present Day 2006-Glen Falls University

Today, the room was full; eighty-five students and barely enough air between them. Hanna adjusted her notes and braced herself. She pulled up the PowerPoint and displayed a familiar exchange, part of her last session with Richard, though she didn't reveal that.

"Read the interaction," Hanna told her criminal psychology class. She didn't mention it was from her last session with Richard Hale. "The patient murdered 28 women, all under the age of 27, with dark hair and eyes. For sixteen months, he showed no emotion." She paused for a moment. "Until now, the patient never opened up like this before; he was always reserved and guarded. Is the patient finally opening up, or is he faking it? We have no description of the woman he references, but we can assume she shared the same characteristics as his victims. Could she be what drove him to kill?"

She scanned the room, observing the students' reactions. "Take 15 minutes. Write down your observations, what's driving the patient, whether he's being sincere, and if this moment is a breakthrough. Don't forget your name, date, and class on the paper; otherwise, I can't grade you."

She planned to read them that night. Maybe it would help her understand Richard better or herself.

She pulled open the slide.

>   Patient: *"I lost the one person who made me feel like I mattered. When someone cuts you loose for long enough, you stop trying to find your*

way back."
Therapist: "You loved her.
Patient: "More than I ever knew was possible."
Therapist: "Is that why you dreamt of her? Do you still feel her presence?"
Patient: "No, Doctor. I dreamt of her because I lost her in an accident. A real one is one that operates without a hand guiding it. That's what we have in common, isn't it?"

* * *

Twenty minutes later, Hanna walked around the room, collecting the papers. As she picked up the last one, Kristy, one of her brightest students, raised her hand.

"Dr. Nowack, would it be okay if I shared something?"

Hanna nodded. "Of course. I'd love to hear your thoughts."

Kristy sat up slightly. "We know the patient is a serial killer who murdered 28 women, each resembling someone from his past. He claims to have lost someone important to him for the first time; he lost a woman he loved, who died in an accident. That distinction is key. He differentiates her accidental death from his intentional killings. To me, that suggests a need for control. But what really stood out was his final statement: 'That's where we're different, you and I.' It's subtle, but it feels like a challenge. He seemed to sense an emotional vulnerability in the therapist. Maybe even a shared loss."

Hanna folded her arms, intrigued. "Interesting observation. So, you think the therapist's objectivity may have been compromised?"

Kristy nodded. "Yes. The way he phrases things, he's testing the therapist. He's saying the loss of that woman caused him to spiral. It's not only grief; it's obsession. And if the therapist reacted, even slightly, the patient would've picked up on it.

She gestured to the quote. 'No, Doctor. I dreamt of her because I lost her in an accident. A real one.' That line implies he knows or suspects the therapist lost someone too, but under different circumstances. Maybe even violent ones. He flips the dynamic. Now he's analyzing them."

Josh, another student, leaned forward. "So he's in control?"

Kristy shrugged. "Not fully. But he's trying to change the situation. And if the therapist isn't aware of how they're being affected, then yes, they're losing control."

Hanna stepped closer. "Let me challenge you, Kristy. What if the therapist is unaware of the extent of their impact? What if they think they're still objective?"

Kristy blinked. "Then they're even more vulnerable. They can't see the shift."

Hanna nodded. "Exactly. I want you all to consider this question: To what extent does our past influence our perceived objectivity? When does our experience turn into a weakness rather than a strength?"

The room fell silent.

"Great discussion today. I'll see you next class."

As the students packed up, Kristy lingered. "Dr. Nowack?"

Hanna turned. "Yes?"

Kristy hesitated. "Did I touch on something real about the therapist?"

Hanna smiled faintly. "That's an intriguing question. Let's talk more next class."

She walked out, Kristy's question echoing behind her, and for the first time, Hanna wasn't sure she knew the answer.

***

Outside, the air had cooled. Hanna climbed into her car, tossing her bag onto the passenger seat. She didn't start the engine right away.

She sat there, hands on the steering wheel, staring through the windshield at nothing in particular. Her reflection in the rear view mirror stared back, worn and washed out.

Kristy's question echoed in her mind: *"Did I touch on something real?"* She had.

Richard's voice followed close behind, looping through the cracks: *"That's where we're not so different, you and I."*

It hadn't just been a line. It was a probe carefully placed, intentionally delivered. Something meant to expose her.

And maybe it had.

She should have been on her way to Nick's for dinner.

She leaned forward, resting her forehead against the wheel.

Deep down, she didn't want to go.

Part of her wished Nick would meet someone who could actually reciprocate what he felt, although having him around made life without Brian almost bearable.

With a quiet sigh, she started the car. She needed to pick up Caitlyn from her grandparents' house.

As the engine hummed , a thought rooted itself deep in her chest:

Maybe Michael had seen it before she did.

This wasn't just a case.

Richard's grief echoed her own. Different shape. Same raw edge and ache no one asked for.

Two people, left behind, still trying to crawl back to the one person who made them feel like they were enough.

She saw it too clearly.

And maybe that was what scared her the most.

Chapter 5

Later that afternoon, Hanna turned onto the long gravel drive, the tires popping and crunching beneath her. Late afternoon light slanted across the bare winter fields. As she crept forward, something moved out by the coop.

Caitlyn tore across the yard, arms stretched wide as she chased a flurry of flapping chickens, grinning like a girl on a mission. Hanna smiled. Of course. She put the car in park. Caitlyn spotted her and bolted toward the car.

"Mama! I almost caught a chicken! Pradziadek said, If I caught one, I could take it home as a pet!"

Hanna laughed, stepping out. "Did he now? I think I need to have a word with that Pradziadek of yours."

When Caitlyn was born, Hanna's grandparents insisted on using Polish great-grandparent names instead of English ones to keep their heritage alive.

She ruffled Caitlyn's curls, remembering how her grandfather had pulled the same trick on her as a kid. It was his way of burning off extra energy: send the child after a near unattainable goal and let nature do the rest.

As she walked toward the house, Nebraska plates on a car caught her eye.

Wonderful. Dad's here. So much for a peaceful visit.

Before she reached the door, Henry Nowack stepped out, hands in his flannel pockets. He pulled her in for a brief hug.

"Be nice," he murmured. "Your father's here."

Hanna sighed. "Figured. What's he doing here this time?"

Henry exhaled through his nose. "Divorce."

"Of course," she muttered, rolling her eyes.

"He's moving back," Henry added. "Transferred to the plant here. It might help me out when he's not working. Might even keep him out of trouble."

Hanna arched a brow. "Dad attracts trouble like a magnet, Grandpa. Do you believe a change in zip code will alter that?"

Henry gave her a tired smile. "Probably not. But a man can hope."

Inside, warmth hit her like a hug. Fresh bread lingered in the air, and Irene was at the sink, washing a spoon. At the table, Lee rustled through the paper like he'd never left.

The second he spotted her, a grin tugged at his mouth. "Here comes trouble."

"Nice to see you, Dad."

"So, back in town again?"

Lee shrugged. "Same ol' story. Got transferred. My stuff gets here in four days."

Hanna glanced at Irene and Henry. "A heads up would've helped. We could've figured something out."

"We told him he could build something here on the property," Irene said gently. "We'd sign the land over to him. That way, he'd have his own space."

Lee's expression hardened. "Ma, I don't need a damn handout."

"It's not a handout, Lee. We help all our kids. Just think about it."

Hanna studied him. He wasn't rejecting it outright, but tension sat in his shoulders.

"Dad, think about it. It'd be good for Caitlyn to know her grandfather."

"Yeah, yeah," Lee waved his hand. "I'll think about it." He looked toward the door. "I want a chance to know her. Make up for what I missed with you."

Hanna's chest tightened. Deep down, she wanted to believe him. But history made it hard.

Before she could respond, Caitlyn burst into the house, breathless. "Grandpa! Come help me catch a chicken! Pradziadek said I could take one home, but it keeps jumping in the air!"

CHAPTER 5

Laughter filled the kitchen. Even Lee chuckled. And for the first time in years, the house didn't feel so broken.

She looked at Lee, and it all came back how he let her down.

***

June 10, 1995—St. Mary's Catholic Church, Cohoes, NY
Her father wasn't there. He was supposed to be waiting outside the bridal suite, steadying her arm and telling her to breathe. Instead, he passed out in a barn. Drunk. Again.

Hanna stared at her reflection in the mirror, the embroidered bodice of her gown blurring as tears threatened to rise. The dress was meant to honor her heritage, a blend of Italian lace and Polish embroidery, but today, it only reminded her of everything that was missing.

The scent of roses clung to the air, mingling with faint incense from the cathedral outside. Behind the heavy doors, the pews were filled with DeLuca's and Morettis, Wojcik's and Nowack's, everyone except him.

She'd told herself not to expect him. Yet, she did. Of course, she had.

The door opened. Rachel slipped in, adjusting a pearl pin in her hair. She took one look at Hanna and sighed. "He's not coming, is he?"

Hanna's throat tightened. "Peter said he's in the barn. Drunk."

Rachel muttered a curse under her breath. "Unbelievable."

There was another knock. Elaine DeLuca stepped inside, poised and purposeful. She took one look at Hanna and crossed the room, her hands gentle as she cupped Hanna's face.

"Oh, sweetheart," Elaine whispered. "What's wrong?"

"My dad's not here."

Elaine's jaw set, but her touch stayed tender. "That's his loss." She pressed a kiss to Hanna's forehead. "Don't you dare let his absence make you question your worth."

Hanna's eyes filled. "Grandma's asking Grandpa to walk me down the aisle."

Elaine nodded. "That is a wonderful idea. I want you to remember: DeLuca women are strong. We are the heart of this family. And today? You're becoming one of us."

A soft knock followed. Henry Nowack stepped in, his expression unreadable for a moment. Hanna turned to him, and her composure broke.

"Grandpa..." Her voice wavered. "He let me down again."

Henry took a slow breath. "Then let me walk you down the aisle," he said quietly. "I've been dreaming of this day since you came into this world."

She gave a trembling laugh. "A thousand times, yes."

Five minutes later, the bridal party began to line up. The grand wooden doors of the cathedral stood closed, muffling the hum of the crowd. Hanna stood behind them, her hand wrapped tightly around Henry's arm.

Her stomach was in knots, not because of Brian, but because of everything else. Because of Lee. Because of an old ache that never quite healed, it was tough to trust.

Elaine stepped into the entryway one last time. She met Henry's eyes and reached for his hand.

"Thank you," she said simply. "For always being there for her."

Henry blinked, throat bobbing.

Elaine turned to Hanna, brushing a curl from her cheek. "You're stunning, sweetheart."

Then she slipped back inside. Moments later, the doors creaked open.

Mozart's Ave Verum Corpus filled the church, soaring through the vaulted ceilings. The bridal party moved first, then the flower girls.

Canon in D began. Hanna swallowed hard, her fingers trembling around Henry's arm. He gave her hand a gentle pat.

"You got this, princess."

She lifted her chin. Her eyes locked with Brian's across the room. He stood at the altar, tall and steady, his eyes searching hers like an anchor.

Rachel's voice echoed in her mind: *"You must be psychic. How did you know this day would come?"*

He's my soulmate, Hanna thought. *I knew it the moment I saw him in seventh grade.*

She took one step at a time, then another. Towards Brian. Toward forever.

And still, for a fleeting second, for the whisper of a heartbeat, something inside

CHAPTER 5

her hesitated.
  But she ignored it.
  Brian was waiting for me, and she loved him.

Chapter 6

Present Day 2006

Hanna eased up the gravel drive. Wind whispered through the trees. Nick's house loomed ahead, sleek, towering, and silent.

She parked and unbuckled Caitlyn's seat belt.

"Can I swim in the pool later?" Caitlyn asked, bouncing in her seat.

Before she could answer, Nick shouted, "After dinner." From the doorway

Dinner was too perfect.

Caitlyn chatted about art projects and chickens. Nick laughed at all the right times and tousled her curls like he'd done it a hundred times before.

And then it slipped. Caitlyn innocently asked, "Dad, can I have more fries?"

Nick didn't blink. He didn't correct her.

"Sure, sweetheart," he said, reaching for the fries like it was the most natural thing in the world.

Hanna's fingers tightened around her glass.

Her eyes narrowed.

She stared at him long enough that he finally looked up, smiled, and went back to eating, like nothing had happened.

This has gone too far, she thought.

Dinner continued in stiff, uncomfortable silence.

Hanna sat there, waiting for the right time to confront him.

After dinner, Caitlyn ran to the living room, humming to herself.

Hanna dried her hands on a towel and looked at Nick.

"We need to talk."

CHAPTER 6

Nick smiled, quick, almost eager. "I know what you're going to say. I was just as thrown as you were."

Hanna stared at him, thinking, *Liar.*

She kept her voice steady. "I'll talk to her. You're not her father, Nick. You never will be."

His smile flickered. His body shifted, just a little too tense, before he forced a boyish grin. "Of course," he said smoothly. "I fully understand."

Moments later, Caitlyn came running back in, breathless. "Can I swim now?"

Hanna glanced at Nick, then nodded.

Caitlyn bolted for the backyard, already tugging her shoes off.

Hanna turned back to Nick. "I left a sweater upstairs."

He nodded. "Go ahead. I'll watch her."

She offered him a thin smile and headed for the stairs, her pulse quickening with every step.

She walked up the steps, the floorboards creaking quietly under her weight.

Passing by his bedroom, she slowed, glancing at the closed door.

Then, as she reached the study, she noticed the door was cracked open.

A soft pool of golden light spilled out onto the hallway.

Curious, she pushed it open a little more and stepped inside.

Bookshelves lined the walls, heavy with thick legal encyclopedias, old textbooks, and reference volumes. On another shelf, tucked higher, were leather bound novels: The Lord of the Rings, To Kill a Mockingbird, and The Great Gatsby; all classics, worn with use.

She moved closer, her fingertips trailing lightly across the spines.

The smell of old paper and polished wood hung in the air, comforting and steady.

Then her gaze fell to the desk.

There, neatly placed under the lamplight, was a file.

She leaned closer and froze.

The tab at the top bore the clean block letters DELUCA, BRIAN.

Her heart lurched. She reached for it, her hands trembling slightly.

Carefully, she opened the folder.

Inside were police reports and photographs.

An autopsy report.

Her breath caught in her throat. An autopsy? *H*er mind raced, her pulse hammering at her temples. Why would there be an autopsy?

She flipped through the pages with shaking fingers, the cold, clinical language blurring before her eyes.

Toxicology results. Tissue samples. Organ weights.

Every word deepened the pit in her stomach.

This wasn't only a report. It was an investigation.

Her hands trembled.

Why the hell did Nick have this? Every line she read deepened the pit in her stomach. This wasn't just a file. It was an investigation.

"Find what you were looking for?"

She spun around.

Nick stood in the doorway. Calm. Patient. Like he'd been waiting. He stepped closer. "It's late, Hanna."

She clutched the file, heart hammering. "Why do you have this?"

He didn't answer. His voice stayed soft. "You should go."

She set the file down slowly and sternly "You didn't answer my question, Nick. Why do you have this?"

"Hanna, you should go."

Her eyes narrowed. "This discussion is not over. Not even close." She pushed past him, collected Caitlyn, and left without saying another word.

Nick followed and watched her leave.

Nick returned to the study.

He hadn't meant for her to find it; he'd forgotten he pulled it out.

He quickly flipped through the file, turning page after page.

Internal bleeding. The cause of death was blunt force trauma from a car accident. Cause of death: internal bleeding.

His eyes narrowed. "Matt, how did you miss this?" he muttered.

CHAPTER 6

* * *

Hanna drove in silence. The radio stayed off.

Caitlyn slept in the backseat, curled against the window.

It wasn't a long drive, but it felt endless.

"Daddy." The file. Nick's smile.

Her mind reeled, jumping from one fractured thought to the next.

She pulled into the driveway and killed the engine.

She closed the car door quietly and walked up the porch steps, unlocking the door.

She went back for Caitlyn, lifting her out carefully.

Inside, she tucked Caitlyn into bed and kissed her forehead.

She poured herself a glass of wine she barely tasted.

The house was dark and too quiet, the floor creaking under her steps as she moved down the hall.

She pushed open her bedroom door and flipped on the light.

She crossed to the nightstand and froze.

Brian's ring.

Sitting dead center, catching the light like it was waiting for her.

Her stomach dropped so fast she swayed.

It hadn't been there before.

Her hands started to shake, and she set the wine down, hard enough to make the table rattle.

Someone was in the house.

Instinct kicked in.

She knelt down, retrieved the storage case from beneath the bed, and forcefully opened it.

Her fingers found the cold weight of the gun.

She stood, heart hammering, and moved through the house, clearing one room at a time.

She grabbed the cordless phone. Almost dialed Nick, but stopped. Her gut screamed against it.

She called Tony instead. "Someone's been in my house," she whispered.

Tony didn't hesitate. "I'm on my way."

Fifteen minutes later, headlights cut across the driveway.

Tony stepped onto the porch; Hanna opened the door.

"Down the hall," she whispered.

He followed her into the bedroom.

She pointed at the nightstand. Brian's ring gleamed under the overhead light.

"You're sure it wasn't there earlier?" Tony asked, his voice low.

"Positive."

Tony scanned the room, his frown deepening.

"What is it?" Hanna asked.

He shook his head. "Nothing. Let me check outside."

Hanna stood frozen at the doorway, heart hammering against her ribs.

Headlights again, this time unfamiliar.

Tony looked at her. "Stay here."

He walked outside.

Nick got out of the car. "I need to talk to Hanna."

Hanna came running out, "Go home, Nick."

"I need to explain why I had the file."

Hanna shook her head.

Tony looked at Hanna, then Nick. "What file?"

Nick didn't say anything, and then Hanna blurted out, "Brian's."

Tony looked at him. "What kind of file?"

Hanna furious Nick was there "It looked like an investigation file."

"Hanna, it's not what you think; there are secrets."

Hanna raised her hand to him and went back into the house, closing the door behind her. She would let Tony handle this.

Tony stepped forward, his posture calm but unreadable. "What secrets, Nick?"

"You know exactly what I'm talking about." Nick moved closer, his voice

CHAPTER 6

low. "Are you always this protective? Or is there something you don't want her to know? Like the fact your son was part of a crime family?"

Tony didn't flinch. "Brian and my family aren't your business."

Nick's jaw clenched. "She deserves the truth."

"She deserves peace," Tony said, his voice like iron.

They stared each other down, the night pressing heavy around them.

Nick took another step. "You're hiding something."

Tony stepped in, crowding him back. His voice stayed steady. "No, Nick. You're just trying to win her. You don't love her. You want to *own* her. You think pretending to solve Brian's death will buy you her heart."

Nick swung without warning.

Tony caught the punch midair and twisted his wrist until Nick stumbled, gasping.

Nick yanked free, breathless. "You don't scare me, old man."

Tony's eyes hardened. "Son," he said, his voice steel cold, "my family owns yours. Don't push your luck. Does your daddy know you're here?"

Nick's lip curled. "Maybe I'll tell Hanna your family's full of gangsters."

Tony didn't blink. "You must be stupid," he said quietly. "Go home before you do something you'll regret."

Nick opened his mouth to speak but stopped.

Through the living room window, he saw her. Hanna, watching them.

His jaw tightened. "I *will* tell her. Maybe not tonight, but I will. She'll find out your perfect son trapped her into your family. Then you'll lose them all."

Tony took a step forward. "You have a death wish, don't you, boy? Are you really this stupid?"

Nick turned without another word, stormed to his car, and slammed the door. As he peeled out of the driveway, tires screeching, he shouted through the open window:

"This isn't over!"

Tony watched the red taillights vanish down the street. Then, calmly, he pulled out his phone and dialed. "I just had a run in with the youngest O'Sullivan boy," he said quietly. "I think we've got a problem."

Chapter 7

Great Meadow Correctional Facility

Richard Hale ran a hand over the worn manila folder resting in his lap, placing the photos along his mattress. Two deaths, two accidents, and two lies; only one had been an accident, and it wasn't Tony Jr.'s.

His eyes traced the ink on the pages, the autopsy reports, the crime scene photos of Brian DeLuca's mangled body sprawled across the pavement, and the supposed wreck that took his life. Another DeLuca. Another dead cop. And Hanna? She was an anomaly. She was unlike any mafia wife he had ever met. He wondered if she even knew. She always walked into their sessions with a steel spine and eyes that had seen too much. She wore pain, grief, and loss like armor. Richard respected her for it. Which made working with her dangerous.

He didn't understand people like she did. He studied and dissected them emotionally, psychologically, and eventually, physically. The woman before her? All DeLuca adjacent. Wives, mistresses, confidantes. Every one of them had blood on their hands. All 28 got what they deserved.

Except Hanna. She didn't fit the pattern. Yet, here they were. Fate, perhaps, giving them one last dance.

* * *

December 23, 1993 – Albany, NY

She was leaving. She stood at the window, arms wrapped around herself, the neon glow from the motel sign painting her in red and blue flashes. "I have to go,"

CHAPTER 7

she whispered.

Richard sat motionless on the edge of the bed, his fingers flexing. "You know he won't let you."

Her jaw tightened. "I don't care. I can't do this anymore, Richard. I can't live in his world."

His world. Tony's world. The DeLuca empire was built on blood, control, and the illusion of choice. "You don't walk away from him," Richard said carefully. "Not alive."

She exhaled sharply. "Then I'll run."

Richard stared at her. And for the first time in his life, he felt afraid. He felt fear, not for himself, but for her.

Something flickered in her eyes: hesitation, doubt. Then she stepped toward him, her voice softer. "I need to tell you something."

Richard swallowed. "Then tell me."

Before she could say another word, a sleek, black Camaro rolled into the lot; it was Tony Jr. Izzy's face went pale. "It's him," she breathed.

Richard moved instantly, grabbing her wrist and trying to pull her away from the window. "You don't have to."

She shook her head. "No. This is my fight." She gave him a quick, desperate kiss before disappearing.

Richard's pulse roared in his ears, and that was the moment he made a decision: Tony Jr. wasn't leaving this night alive.

The deep rumble of the V8 filled the motel lot before the headlights even hit the pavement.

Tony Jr.'s 1992 Camaro Z28 pulled in, slow and deliberate. The jet black car, with tinted windows and chrome wheels, gleamed under the neon glow of the vacancy sign. A car that screamed, "I own this town."

Richard watched from the shadows, jaw tightened.

Of course, Tony Jr. was always about appearances. It's always about making an entrance. Even at twenty years old, he carried himself like royalty, like Vince DeLuca himself had raised him instead of his own father, like he was untouchable.

The Camaro idled, engine growling.

Richard could see him inside, lounging in the driver's seat, fingers tapping the leather steering wheel. It would be simple; just a single cut and a brief moment of chaos would complete the task.

The car door cracked open, and Tony Jr. stepped out, adjusting his shirt. He had that signature smirk, the one that made women weak and men want to break his teeth in.

Richard moved fast; the blade sank in before Tony even registered that he wasn't alone. His breath hitched with shock, then pain. His smirk twisted into something ugly, something too late. Blood bloomed across the white fabric of his dress shirt, seeping through the expensive silk like an ink stain.

Richard ripped the door open and shoved him.

Tony Jr. stumbled back, his foot slipping onto the gas pedal.

The Camaro lurched forward. Then, a pair of headlights approached them at an excessive speed, causing a collision. The metal crunched, and glass shattered everywhere. The Camaro spun, tires screaming, and then flipped violently multiple times.

Richard barely had time to process it before the world was spinning. The deafening sound of the crash interrupted her scream. When the wreckage settled, the blood stopped roaring in his ears.

She was gone and dead. Tony Jr.'s broken body lay sprawled near the twisted remains of the Camaro, his headset down somewhere before the car made its final impact.

And her? She was trapped in the mangled mess of what used to be Tony's car. Richard couldn't move, and his knees hit the pavement; his breath became ragged.

For the first time in his life, he experienced the true meaning of loss, and upon the release of the reports, he discovered the truth: she was carrying Richard's child. The weight of it nearly crushed him.

***

Present Day 2006

Richard gripped the folder. The DeLuca's had taken everything from him. His father. His woman. His child and the biggest joke? He was one of them.

The bastard son of Little Vinny DeLuca. He was born to a mistress.

CHAPTER 7

Raised in the shadows.

Tony Jr. had laughed as he died. "Does he know? He'd kill you himself."

Richard had never known if Vince or Vinny suspected. Maybe his blood had doomed him before he even had a chance.

He looked at Hanna's file. Why did she matter?

She was different. She carried the same scars. Wore the same grief. People like them weren't built; they were forged.

And for the first time in years, Richard felt something new: not hunger, not power, but respect. It made it all the more thrilling.

"If he ever had the chance, he'd take his time with her. He wondered if she would fight. He hoped she would. It would make it sweeter. The only thing missing was Brian DeLuca watching it all crumble. They would all pay. And Hanna? She would be the perfect ending.

Chapter 8

Rain tapped against the window. Hanna stared at the ceiling, willing the knot in her chest to loosen. Her gaze drifted to Brian's ring on the nightstand, still there, unmoved, wrong somehow. The memory swept over her: a wave of smoke filled air, pulsing music, teenage recklessness, and Brian DeLuca, who had appeared like an avenging angel when she needed him most.

But it wouldn't, not after last night. Her thoughts were torn between Nick and Tony. The tension between them and the ring on her nightstand, Brian's ring.

She turned her head, her gaze landing on it again. The gold band sat exactly where she had left it, unmoved, unchanged, and yet, something was different now.

It wasn't just grief pressing against her ribs; it was unease. It was a question she wasn't ready to ask herself. Who put it there? Hanna slowly rubbed a hand over her face, willing her thoughts to settle. But they didn't. Instead, they drifted.

* * *

Fall 1987 Freshman Year

The house was too loud. Music pulsed through the walls, the bass shaking the floor beneath Hanna's feet. The air was thick with cigarette smoke, cheap beer, and teenage recklessness. Somewhere in the distance, someone was laughing too loudly. A couple stumbled past her, the girl's giggles slurring into the boy's ear as

CHAPTER 8

he pulled her toward the stairs.

Hanna hugged her arms around herself, regretting every decision that had led her here.

Rachel had convinced her to come. "It's only a party; we need a little fun," *she'd said. However, Rachel had vanished from sight. Hanna had lost her friend in the crush of bodies about twenty minutes ago. She tried to push through unfamiliar faces, but every door she opened led to something worse.*

There was a couple making out on the stairs, a group passing around a joint on the back patio, and some upperclassmen playing a drinking game in the living room.

She felt small here, almost like she didn't belong, and she wanted to leave. Turning on her heel, she started toward the door and ran straight into him. Jason Murphy. He was a senior, a football star, the kind of guy who walked the halls like he owned them. He grinned down at her, eyes hazy with whatever he had been drinking. "Hey, Nowack," *he drawled, his voice too loud, too confident.* "Didn't think you were the party type."

"I'm not." *Hanna tried to step around him, but he moved with her, blocking her path.*

His smirk widened. "C'mon, don't be like that. You're here, aren't you?" *His hand found her wrist, his grip firm, fingers pressing a little too tightly.* "Have a drink. Loosen up."

Hanna's stomach turned. "Let go," *she muttered, trying to pull back.*

But he didn't. Instead, his grip tightened, his smirk shifting into something sharper. "I don't think so," *Jason murmured, his free hand reaching for her waist.*

Then, in an instant, he vanished. One second, Jason was in front of her, and the next, Brian DeLuca had him pinned against the wall.

Hanna barely processed the movement; she barely understood what had happened.

One hand was fisted in Jason's shirt, the other gripping the collar tight enough to choke him. Brian's voice was low. Dangerous. "You touch her again, and I'll break your fucking hand."

Jason's face turned red. "D-DeLuca, come on, man, I was only messing around."

Brian didn't let go.

Hanna had never seen him like this before. She had noticed Brian before, of course. How could she not?

Jason swallowed hard. "Look, man, I"

"Apologize," Brian ordered, his voice steady and even.

Jason's eyes darted toward Hanna. "I'm sorry."

Brian held him for a moment longer, making sure he felt it, before finally releasing his grip.

Jason stumbled forward, coughing as he caught his balance. Without another word, he turned and bolted, disappearing into the crowd.

As soon as he left, Brian turned to face her. His expression softened instantly. "You okay?"

Hanna's heart was still pounding not because of Jason but because of Brian. Brian DeLuca could leave girls breathless with his presence. There was something about him, something effortless, like he belonged to a world beyond everyone else's reach.

His warm brown eyes held a sharp, playful glint, always carrying some secret only he knew. His smirk was devastating and dangerous, melting girls and making them trip over their words. His face was all strong angles and easy charm, his skin kissed by the sun, his hoop earrings just rebellious enough to make him impossible to ignore.

He didn't dress to impress, but it didn't matter. He wore a black T-shirt, easy fit jeans, and those damn yellow Converse sneakers, all of which somehow worked. Everything about him worked. People noticed his presence when he entered a room. But right now, he was looking at her. And for the first time, it didn't feel like the rest of the world mattered at all.

She nodded.

He studied her for a second longer, then exhaled. "Come on. Let's get you out of here. You hungry?"

Hanna nodded, and she followed him out the door. And just like that, Brian DeLuca had saved her. That night had changed everything.

She had told Rachel once, half joking, half serious, I'm going to marry him someday.

But that night, for the first time, she knew.

CHAPTER 8

He was hers, and she was his. No one had ever looked out for her like that before. No one but Brian DeLuca.

* * *

Present Day 2006

Hanna blinked, the memory fading back into the past.

She was still in bed and still staring at the ceiling, reaching for something she could never have again. Her fingers twitched toward Brian's ring but didn't pick it up. She closed her eyes and exhaled. She realized that Brian was no longer there to save her. For the first time in a long time, she wasn't sure anyone could.

Hanna glanced at the clock, 6:15 a.m.

She exhaled, running her fingers through her hair. She needed to get Caitlyn up, give her breakfast, and get moving. But her thoughts lingered in the past, not in the present.

It was another fun day with Richard Hale in prison. This session provided him with another opportunity to push himself. If there really was a woman, and if there was someone who kept him steady before he started killing, then she mattered, and that made her the key.

Hanna flipped open her notebook, scanning through the notes and the dates.

His first confirmed kill was in March 1994, three months after Tony Jr. died.

She checked again, and the timeline fit

A sick feeling stirred in her gut. Richard Hale didn't start killing. His first was personal, emotional, and a turning point, and then it hit her: the name of the woman. Isabelle Moreau. She had to be the one who kept him steady.

The one who died the night Tony Jr. did.

The police report barely mentioned her, a passenger from a tragic accident. She was in the wrong place at the wrong time.

If Richard was being truthful and Izzy was the woman he loved, then that night Richard lost everything.

Hanna swallowed hard. Was she Richard Hale's first kill? Was it revenge? No, it couldn't be, or could it?

Hanna's pulse pounded as she flipped through her notes again. If she was right, and Richard Hale had killed for the first time after Izzy died, then this wasn't about a serial killer's first victim. This was something bigger. It was something that had been buried for over a decade. Tony Jr. was decapitated before the crash. The words sent a chill down her spine; it was not an accident or a simple wreck.

Hanna exhaled sharply to push back the heavy weight in her chest; she needed to move.

She climbed out of bed, shaking off the chill that had settled over her skin, and headed straight for the shower.

By the time she stepped into the kitchen, the rich scent of coffee filled the air. She poured herself a mug and then went to wake Caitlyn. Today was going to be a big day. At the very least, it was going to be an interesting day.

Chapter 9

Great Meadow Correctional Facility

Hanna pulled into the staff parking lot, gripping the steering wheel a little too tightly. The morning air was sharp, her breath fogging up the inside of the windshield despite the heater blasting. Heavy clouds sagged over the prison walls, casting everything in an oppressive gray shadow.

She exhaled slowly; something felt different today. She could feel it coiled tight in her chest, running through her fingertips as she traced the edge of the worn leather bag beside her. The files inside held something she hadn't been ready for.

Her mind raced; before she could talk herself into or out of anything, there was a sharp knock on the driver's side window that made her jump.

Hanna turned, finding Michael standing outside, hands shoved deep into the pockets of his coat, a smirk tugging at the corner of his mouth.

She rolled down the window, exhaling. "Jesus, Michael. Couldn't you have waited inside?"

"And miss the chance to scare the hell out of you?" He grinned. "Not a chance."

Hanna shook her head. "You're an ass."

"Yeah, yeah." He tilted his head. "Are you ready for this?"

She didn't answer right away. Instead, she reached for her bag, adjusting the strap over her shoulder. "You're still sitting in?"

Michael's smirk faded slightly. "Yeah. I want to see how he reacts."

"Good."

She pushed the door open, stepping out into the cold. The air hit her immediately, sharp and unforgiving. Michael fell into step beside her as they walked toward the entrance.

So, he said, voice low. "You really think Hale's first kill was about Izzy?

I think he started killing after she died. Hanna kept her gaze straight ahead. Whether it was because of her, I don't know yet. But I'm about to find out."

Michael let out a slow breath. "Crap."

"Yeah."

They reached the first checkpoint, flashing their IDs to the guard at the gate. A low buzz sounded, followed by the heavy clank of the lock releasing. Inside, the security check was as slow as ever due to the large number of people present.

Michael muttered under his breath as he handed over his pager. "Swear to God, one of these days they're gonna have something better than this stupid thing."

Hanna raised a brow. "It's called a cell phone, Michael."

"Yeah, but they still don't do anything. Am I supposed to type a whole message with numbers? No, thanks."

She smirked. "It's called texting."

"It's called a waste of time."

Hanna laughed under her breath. "Give it a few years. You'll be obsessed like the rest of us."

Michael scoffed, taking his ID back from the guard. Doubt it.

The main corridor stretched ahead of them, beige walls and fluorescent lights buzzing overhead. The air was thick with the scent of stale coffee, disinfectant, and something else that had settled deep into the bones of the building. There are too many men, too many locked doors, and too much history.

Michael nodded toward the hallway ahead. "You go on. I'll be in the observation room."

Hanna swallowed, gave a small nod, and kept moving.

With every step toward the psych unit, her pulse picked up. It wasn't fear, but "anticipation." She was determined to test Richard Hale today, and if

CHAPTER 9

she was correct, he would be unable to conceal it.

***

Hanna sat across from Richard Hale, pen in hand, notepad untouched. It was too quiet, the kind of quiet that made her aware of her heartbeat. Michael was behind the one way glass, watching and analyzing. She could feel his presence as if it added weight to every breath.

Richard was too at ease today.

He leaned back in his chair, hands resting loosely on the armrests. No tapping, no shifting. Just still and intentional. As if he was waiting her out. Like he knew something she didn't.

She wasn't going to give him the satisfaction.

"You seem more relaxed today," she said finally, her voice calm but probing.

"Am I?"

"You're less fidgety."

He smiled without warmth. "Maybe I'm getting comfortable, Doctor. You make me feel at ease."

"Comfortable isn't a word I'd associate with someone like you," she said. "Not unless you're the one in control."

His smile turned sharper, more dangerous. "Maybe I enjoy our conversations."

"Richard, I believe you don't actually care what I think. I think you want to see how far you can push."

"No." A pause. "Hanna, Hanna, why would you think that? I do care; I look forward to our time together. I heard you were," he smiled, "the best. And that we had a lot in common."

Hanna didn't flinch. That was the game. He threw bait, and she didn't bite.

She flipped a page in her notebook, though she still hadn't written a single word.

"Let's talk about loss," she said.

There was a flicker, barely visible. But she saw it. The way his fingers twitched before stilling again. His expression remained composed, but the shift was real.

"Loss? So I guess we aren't going to talk like old friends? I was really hoping we could get to know each other."

She ignored the push. "You mentioned someone before. Someone who kept you stable. What did you mean by that?"

Richard tilted his head slightly, studying her like she was the subject under glass now. "Doctor, everyone has someone like that. Wasn't that your husband? What was his name again? Oh, that's right. Brian DeLuca."

She ignored it. He was being difficult today, trying to get her riled up. She wasn't biting. She reminded herself: control. Maintain control.

"Richard, tell me about this person, this woman, I presume, who kept you stable."

He said nothing for several seconds. She let the silence linger, let him stew in it.

Finally, he spoke. "Why the sudden interest?"

Hanna leaned forward a fraction. "Because people don't become what you are overnight. Let's face it together."

He exhaled. Not a sigh. Something closer to memory. "Together, Hanna? We've never been together."

"Richard, tell me about her."

"She saw me," he said quietly.

Hanna blinked. "How?"

His voice lowered. "Like you do. Soft eyes like yours."

She froze inside. Don't let him get to you. But the words sank like a hook into her chest.

"What was her name?"

He drummed his fingers once, then stopped. A calculated gesture, and then softly, "Izzy."

Hanna waited a second. "Izzy? And how long did you know Izzy?"

"What does it matter? She's dead. An unfortunate accident. Do you enjoy talking about your husband? Why make me go through the pain?"

CHAPTER 9

"Richard, I want to help you."

Richard gave her a fake laugh. "It's a little too late for that, isn't it? You come in here with your PhD, thinking you can fix everyone, but the truth is, Hanna, you can't even fix yourself. I see you. You're dying inside. You walk among the living, but you lie with the dead."

Hanna looked at him. He was pushing her. She couldn't let him know he was getting to her.

"Izzy. Who was she?"

"You already know," Richard said, his eyes narrowing. "Don't you?"

She didn't answer.

He looked at her. "You really want to know what really started it, don't you?"

Hanna leaned in. "Let's start at the beginning."

Silence stretched long enough to turn oppressive. He leaned in closer than usual. The air between them grew charged.

"Beginning? Alright, Doctor. I'll start at the beginning with you." He smiled, his voice lower, colder. "Tony Jr. didn't scream."

She looked at him. His body stiffened. Color had risen in his face.

"The best part?" he continued. "He was still alive when I took his head off. But not for long."

Hanna's throat tightened. She stared at him, refusing to blink.

Richard's mouth curled. "He bled. Oh, did he bleed. He fought until the end, even as I pushed his body from his head. Now you're wondering if he deserved it."

"Did he?" she asked.

Richard leaned back slowly, satisfaction flickering in his eyes. "Ah. There it is."

"There's what?"

"That look. The look of interest. Like a bedtime story. Every part of you wants to understand."

"I want the truth," she said.

"No," Richard said softly. "You want closure. You think understanding the monster means taming it. But you and I both know it doesn't end there."

He leaned back harshly and said. "I can't give you what you want, Hanna. You have to find that out yourself. Instead of focusing on ghosts, perhaps you should explore the lives of the living. Maybe look at those who are close to you; you might not like what you find."

He looked up at the clock. "Ah. Look at that. We're out of time." He smiled wider. "Guess we'll have to finish this later."

Hanna shifted forward. "We can continue."

Richard chuckled. "You already have enough to analyze, Doctor."

He dropped his voice again, low, velvety, and calculated. "Wouldn't want to give you more than you can handle, Hanna."

The way he said her name made her spine stiffen. Not from fear. From revulsion.

"Let's savor what we experienced today," he said. "Save a little for next time."

He stood slowly, then looked down at her, not with menace, but with intimacy, like he was seeing through her skin. "Foreplay, Doctor. Just enough to leave you wanting. So when I drive it in deep… you'll embrace it."

She didn't flinch. But she closed her notepad, not gently, not with panic. With purpose. She reclaimed the space between them.

Richard's posture shifted, coiled now, not lazy. On edge.

He nodded at the guard like this was all routine. As he was led past her, he glanced down and whispered, "Think about me."

The door slammed behind him. Only then did Hanna breathe.

She didn't move.

Didn't blink.

But the echo of his voice stayed with her.

* * *

The door flung open. Michael walked in, his face grim, and dropped into the chair across from her. "You're right," he said. "He's different. I can't shake the feeling he's setting you up for something."

CHAPTER 9

Hanna kept her voice calm. "I need more sessions with him, Michael. I need to pull on Tony Jr."

Michael's jaw tightened. "Hanna, this is going too far. Tony was your family."

"I can handle it," she said, forcing the words out. "I have to see this through."

"Hanna"

She cut him off, her voice soft but firm. "Please, Michael. He's never opened up like this for anyone else. Let me run with it."

Before Michael could answer, the door cracked open, and a correctional officer stepped inside.

"Block C is on lock down," he said, voice cold. "Davidson was attacked. He's in the med bay now."

Hanna nodded mechanically, her mind still half on Richard. She turned to Michael, forcing a thin smile. "Guess it's an early day for me."

Then she glanced back at the CO. "Is he okay?"

The officer shrugged slightly. "You'll have to check with Dr. Alden."

* * *

C Block

The cell door slammed shut behind him, but Richard barely noticed.

He sat on the edge of the bunk, elbows resting on his knees, staring at the concrete floor as if it contained all the answers.

His plan was coming together brilliantly.

First, request her. Hanna.

The right bait mattered. Not just anyone would suffice.

Then lure her in. Offer her pieces of himself, the broken ones.

Make her believe they were the same.

Next, take her down from the inside.

Chip away at her clinical distance. Blur the lines between doctor and patient until she couldn't see where he ended and she began.

Make her want him.

Finally, find a way to get his hands on her. Richard smiled, slow and patient.

Hanna Nowack was already halfway his. His mind drifted to her, the way her body would feel beneath his hands, soft and breakable once the walls between them crumbled.

He grew aroused, the sensation winding tight through his body, thickening his breath. "Yes," he murmured, savoring the taste of her surrender before it ever touched reality.

When the moment came, he wouldn't simply possess her.

He would sever her from her core, compel her to plead for him even as she crumbled, savoring every broken breath, savoring the life draining from her eyes as she slipped away.

Chapter 10

Later that afternoon, Hanna rolled to a stop at the intersection. The low hum of the engine was the only sound in the car.

Her fingers tapped the steering wheel once, then twice, before going still. She didn't notice the red light right away. Her thoughts had drifted, not to work or to Caitlyn, but to Richard.

To the way he had said her name. Slow. Intentional. "Think about me."

The words stayed with her, settling in her chest like something heavy and unwanted.

She blinked, trying to shake them loose, but another memory surfaced before she could stop it.

Her mother's voice. Not the words, just the sound of it. Tense and bitter, sharp with something old and familiar.

It wrapped around her, quiet and invasive. The ache started at the base of her throat.

She blinked again, this time with more force, but everything still felt distant. The light stayed red, or maybe she had just stopped noticing the change.

Outside, the world moved on. Cars passed, the light turned green, but Hanna stayed where she was, lost in a memory she thought she had let go.

* * *

THE LIES WE WHISPER

Summer 1990, Cohoes, NY

The house smelled like cigarette smoke and spilled liquor. Music blasted through cheap speakers, a mix of hair metal and pop that shook the walls. People filled the small space, moving in and out, laughing too loudly, and talking over one another.

Hanna hated these parties.

Her mother, Rebecca, was somewhere in the house, high, lost in a haze of pills and whatever else she'd taken that night. She wouldn't even notice if Hanna slipped away. She most likely wouldn't notice if Hanna vanished entirely.

She moved toward the kitchen, keeping her head down, hoping to make it to the back. Suddenly, a hand shot out of nowhere. Rough fingers seized her wrist and yanked her backward.

The reek of beer and sweat was suffocating. With each breath, her stomach churned. Hanna's throat tightened, and then the vomit surged up before she could stop it, just as black spots pricked the edges of her vision.

The guy was older, mid-twenties, maybe. She recognized him, Rob. One of her mother's "friends." He reeked of whiskey and sweat, his grip too tight, his smile too easy.

"Hey, where are you runnin' off to, sweetheart?" His low, slurred voice was too close to her ear.

She jerked back, but his grip tightened. "Let me go," she hissed, panic rising in her chest.

He laughed. "Relax, I only wanna talk and get to know you. Come on, come with me."

He pulled her into another room, muttering something under his breath, his hand pressing hard against the small of her back. "I only wanna talk," he murmured, dragging his lips along her neck.

The suffocating stench of beer, pot, and sweat clung to him. The closer he drew, the more difficult it became to breathe; Hanna began to experience nausea. She twisted to move, but then crack.

The slap was hard and sharp, splitting across her cheek. A sharp ringing filled her ears, drowning out the music, the voices, everything except the panic clawing up her throat. Her mind flickered, disoriented, not the first time, not the first

CHAPTER 10

time.

It was her mother's voice, and she was drunk and dismissive of what was going on. "Stop being dramatic, Hanna. Nobody likes a tease. Just let it happen. If you fought less, maybe you'd enjoy it. Do you think men won't take what they want? It's better to give it to them and not fight. If you had behaved, none of this would have happened."

Hanna was shocked and tried moving again. But he held her tighter and shut the door. "You're not going anywhere," he sneered, breath hot against her face. "We're gonna have some fun. Rebecca said the girls here liked to party, and she said you were the funniest of them all. Too bad your boyfriend's not here to see."

His fingers curled around the neckline of her shirt and yanked, moving to her neck. With his other hand, the fabric of her shirt tore, the sound nearly as loud as her own heartbeat. The room blurred, and she pushed against him, but he was too strong, too solid. She tried to shove his chest and claw at his arms, but then he hit her again, fighting his grip on her neck. Her head snapped sideways, a burst of pain shooting through her skull.

No one is paying attention. No one ever does. His smell was causing her stomach to stir; she wanted to vomit; she had to get away; he started moving faster. Then, almost instinctively, her adrenaline slammed through her veins, and raw and unthinking, she twisted, yanking her arm as hard as she could, and then she brought her knee up, striking hard.

A choked sound left his throat as he buckled, his grip loosening as he dropped to the floor. He shouted, "You bitch," coughing.

She ran as fast as she could. Her breath was ragged, panic roaring in her ears, but she ran. She stumbled through the hallway, shoving past bodies, hands grazing her shoulders. No one stopped her or even looked. Just another drunk girl running; no one would care, pushing past the laughter and shouting and the music, running out the door, into the humid summer night.

Her lungs burned. Her legs threatened to give out. She didn't know where she was going, just away. The pavement blurred beneath her feet. The streetlights flickered in her vision. She wasn't thinking, wasn't feeling, wasn't anything except motion.

She stumbled once, her ankle twisting painfully, but she didn't stop, couldn't stop; she never looked back to see if he was coming after her or if anyone was following her. She just kept running until she reached the gas station two blocks away.

Fluorescent lights buzzed overhead, washing the cracked pavement in harsh white. Hanna's hands shook as she dug for change in her pocket, shoving coins into the payphone slot.

She knew who to call. The only person who would be willing to come was Brian. The phone rang twice before he picked it up.

"Yeah?"

"Brian." Her voice broke, and she had a hard time trying to keep it together. "I-I need you to come get me."

There was silence on the line; she wasn't sure he was still there

His voice then became lower and much sharper. "Hanna, where are you?"

She gave him the address.

"I'm on my way."

He hung up.

Hanna exhaled shakily, wrapping her arms around herself, her body still trembling. Her face hurt from being slapped and punched, and her wrist ached from where Rob had held her against the wall. The tear in her shirt felt too obvious. People were staring; she felt dirty and ashamed.

* * *

Fifteen minutes later, she heard the deep rumble of Brian's car pulling into the lot.

The driver's door opened and slammed shut, and then there he was. Brian swiftly moved, his dark eyes sweeping over her entire body. His eyes moved straight to the bruises on her face, on her neck, then to the rip in her sleeve, to the way she was holding herself. His jaw locked; she could see anger and pain all at once in his face when he looked at her.

"Hanna." His voice was low and controlled, but there was something dangerous underneath. "Who did this?" It wasn't a question, more of a demand. "I am going to fucking kill the bastard." Then, his face changed; it became something darker,

CHAPTER 10

and his brown eyes turned pitch black.

For the first time, Hanna wasn't sure if she was looking at Brian or someone else. She simply stood there, staring, and then, almost instinctively, she touched his arm and softly spoke. "Brian, I am okay. Can you just please take me out of here? I feel so dirty."

Brian calmed down as much as he could, and he looked at her, his nostrils still flaring. "Did he?" *He couldn't say it; the thought of it ate at him*

Hanna shook her head no.

"Don't lie to me, Hanna," *he said, trying to sound calm, a look of concern coming over his face, his fingers flexing*

"I got away before he could do anything, I swear. I kneed him before he could do anything. Please, can we go?"

Still agitated, he forcefully said, "Get in the car." *He walked her over to the passenger side and opened the door for her to get in. She didn't hesitate. Once she was inside, the door shut with a solid thunk, and she let out a large sigh; she felt safe; she knew she was safe.*

Brian climbed into the driver's seat, gripping the wheel so tight his knuckles turned white. He didn't start the car. Instead, he stared straight ahead, his chest rising and falling too evenly; he put his head on the steering wheel and looked at her. "Tell me who did it."

Hanna swallowed. "It doesn't matter, Bry, just let it go."

Brian's head snapped toward her. "It does matter; it matters to me. I will kill anyone who hurts you. Just tell me."

Hanna hesitated, but she knew he would not let it drop, and she just wanted to get out of there. "It was my mom's friend, Rob."

Brian's grip tightened on the steering wheel, and he let out a loud exhale, trying to sound calm. "Where did this happen?"

Hanna looked at him; she couldn't say it, she was ashamed. She thought back to her mother encouraging it. Her eyes teared up. "Please, Brian. Please, take me out of here."

He looked at her, and he knew, and without thinking, "This happened at your mother's, didn't it? Where the hell was your mother?"

Hanna didn't say anything; she looked at him.

He knew the answer by the look on her face. A muscle twitched in his jaw. He stayed still for a long moment, shoulders tense, something simmering behind his eyes. It was killing him that this happened to her, that he wasn't there to stop it. He would take care of it, but for now, he let it go.

Brian pulled out of the lot, the tires crunching over gravel as he turned toward his house. "You're never going back to that fucking house," grabbing her hand.

Hanna leaned her head against the window, closing her eyes. She wanted to forget tonight ever happened; what hurt the most was that she could still smell him, still feel his hands on her skin like a stain she'd never scrub off. But what scared her most? Not the memory. Not even the shame. It was the question she didn't dare ask: would Brian still love her after this?

* * *

Elaine DeLuca took one look at Hanna and knew something had happened. Knew the girl standing in her kitchen, swallowed up in her son's oversized hoodie, wasn't just Brian's friend; she was his girl.

Hanna kept her eyes down, fingers wrapped tightly around the warm ceramic cup of tea Elaine had made her. *This poor girl has been through hell. What kind of mother lets this happen?* Elaine's throat tightened, her chest aching as she reached out, gently covering Hanna's hand with her own. Her voice softened, "You're safe here, sweetheart." Hanna's gaze lifted, uncertain but searching. Elaine's own eyes shifted to her son. Brian was pacing, hovering, his father's son through and through. The tension in his shoulders, the way his jaw clenched, and the quiet rage simmering beneath the surface were all evident. She knew that look, and that's what scared her the most.

But it was that look that also made her understand, and for the first time, she truly saw it. Understood why Brian looked at Hanna the way he did, why he never gave up on her. And it was at that moment that Elaine DeLuca fell in love with the girl her son had already given his heart to.

* * *

CHAPTER 10

Tony Jr. was pissed; he paced the room, arms crossed, face dark. "I don't care what Brian says; I should go down there."

Brian shot him a warning look. "You're not."

Tony Jr. scoffed. "And why the hell not?"

Hanna was curled up on Brian's bed with a blanket, her hair wet from a shower. "Because, Tony, I asked him not to; I want to forget it ever happened."

Tony Jr. paced. He was younger than Brian, but barely. He had that signature DeLuca smirk, except tonight, it was gone. He dropped onto the bed next to her, shaking his head. "I swear to God, Hanna, if I ever see that guy."

Brian cut him off. "It's done, Tony." Shooting him a look that let him know it was being taken care of.

Tony exhaled sharply, then flopped back onto the pillows with a groan. "I need a distraction. We're watching The Lost Boys."

Hanna blinked. "The vampire movie?"

Tony Jr. grinned for the first time all night. "Hell yeah. It's a masterpiece."

Brian rolled his eyes. "You've seen it a hundred times."

"And I'll watch it a hundred more."

Brian sighed but grabbed the VHS tape, shoving it into the player.

As the opening credits rolled, Tony Jr. leaned in, whispering, "This is the part where all the women fall in love with Kiefer Sutherland."

Hanna let out a soft laugh. For the first time that night, and maybe the first time in her life, she felt truly safe. It wasn't just comfort. It was the quiet certainty that she belonged here.

* * *

Present Day 2006

She arrived back at the prison and headed down to her office. She sat at her desk trying to write up her summary. The morning had been a whirlwind; she had a hard time wrapping her thoughts around what had happened, and her conversation with Michael just made things worse.

She thought back to Davidson's attack, then Richard's confession; when it rains, it sure does pour. What really stuck, though, was the way Tony Jr.'s name had rolled off Richard's tongue like it meant nothing, so *nonchalant*.

The cursor blinked on the empty screen, a steady, mocking pulse she couldn't match.

Hanna sat at her desk, staring through the monitor, the pen loose in her fingers.

She should be writing the session report.

Instead, she kept seeing him.

Richard, leaning forward, elbows braced wide on the table like he was staking a claim.

The slow flex of his wrists against the cuffs.

The slight roll of his shoulders, like a man preparing for a different kind of fight.

His voice was low, roughened, and almost gleeful.

Not detached or clinical, but coarse.

His eyes were sharp and greedy, tracking every twitch of her expression like it fed something inside him.

And his mouth, the way his lips curled when he talked about the kill. A sick pleasure pulling at the edges.

"Foreplay, Doctor. Just enough to leave you wanting. So when I drive it in deep, you'll embrace it."

He had said it like it was something filthy. Like he meant every twisted word.

Not seduction, but possession. His violence had always been clean, strategic, and efficient until now. Or maybe there had always been something lurking in his past, something he kept buried.

Sexual predators often turned deadly. It wasn't unheard of. And prison had a way of corroding men, wearing down the restraints, and sharpening the hungers that survived.

Maybe Richard hadn't changed, but instead he was evolving.

Hanna tightened her grip on the pen.

She needed to dig deeper. Find out if this darkness had always been there or if something inside him had finally snapped.

CHAPTER 10

***

She was so deep in thought she didn't hear the knock until it startled her.

Michael laughed from the doorway. "Are you leaving soon?"

Hanna looked up, dazed. "As a matter of fact, I'm going now."

"Good. I'll walk out with you.

Quite the day today, Nowack."

She nodded, gathering her things, barely registering his voice as they made their way through the sterile corridors toward the staff exit.

"You gonna be okay?" Michael asked quietly.

She blinked, realizing he had been watching her more closely than she realized. "Yeah," she muttered, tugging her coat tighter around herself.

Michael didn't look convinced. "You want my advice?" he said, pushing open the heavy steel door, letting her step outside first.

"No," she sighed, forcing a small grin.

"Too bad. You're getting it."

She shot him a look.

"Go home," he said. "Drink something strong and then sleep. You're unraveling, Nowack. I see it."

Hanna huffed out a dry, humorless laugh. "Thanks for the concern, Dr. Carter."

Michael smirked , but it didn't reach his eyes. "I'm serious. Whatever this is with Hale, you're in deep. And when you get like this, you don't stop until it eats you alive." He hesitated, then added, "Maybe I need to pull you off and assign someone else. This is striking too close to home. I don't want this turning into something personal."

Hanna didn't respond immediately. She stared at him, stunned, because deep down, she knew he was right. And that was the part that scared her the most. She pulled open her car door and slid into the driver's seat. "I'll be fine," she said finally, her voice tighter than she meant. "If it gets to be too much, I'll ask you to pull me off. I really want to see this through."

Michael nodded, but the concern in his eyes didn't fade. He wasn't letting it go. He waved and headed to his car.

She needed to clear her head. Which meant only one thing. She needed to talk to Elaine.

Chapter 11

Hanna walked into the DeLuca home, the familiar smell of marinara sauce and fresh bread washing over her like a memory.

Elaine didn't even need to look. She was already moving around the kitchen, setting out plates.

It didn't matter whether you were expected or not. If you entered Elaine's house, you would receive food.

"Sit," Elaine called over her shoulder. "You look like you haven't eaten all day."

Hanna smiled faintly, shrugging off her coat and draping it over the back of a chair. "I haven't."

"Then it's a good thing I made lasagna."

A minute later, Elaine set down a plate in front of her with a massive slice that looked like it could feed two grown men.

Hanna picked at the food, her appetite nonexistent.

Elaine sat across from her, arms crossed over her chest. "Alright," she said sharply. "Spill it."

Hanna blinked. "Spill what?"

"Whatever has you looking like you've seen a ghost."

She hesitated. Elaine was the closest thing she had to a mother, and somehow, that made it harder to say out loud.

But before she could talk herself out of it, the words came anyway. "Caitlyn called Nick 'daddy' last night."

Elaine didn't react right away. Her expression stayed still, but Hanna noticed the small shift, the slight tightening of her mouth, and the brief flicker in her eyes that turned sharp and cold.

"And how did he react?" Elaine asked.

Hanna exhaled sharply. "He didn't correct her. He just grinned at me, like it was something he expected."

Elaine stayed too still. "And?"

"I confronted him," Hanna said, her voice rougher than she intended. "I told him straight up he's not her father, and he never will be."

Elaine's eyes sharpened. "What did he say?"

"He lied." Hanna pushed her food around her plate. "He smiled and said, 'I was just as thrown as you were.'" She shook her head. "But he wasn't surprised, Elaine. He let it happen. He wanted it to happen."

Elaine leaned back slowly, studying her. "I don't trust him," she said flatly.

"I know."

"He's been around forever. He's been good with Caitlyn. He has shown loyalty to you. Sure." Elaine's voice sharpened. "But that doesn't mean he should take Brian's place."

"That was never the intention," Hanna whispered. "I would never."

"But does he know that?" Elaine cut in. "Because letting Caitlyn call him daddy without a word, that's not slipping into your life. That's replacing what you lost."

The words hit hard.

"I don't love him, Elaine," Hanna admitted quietly. "Not the way he deserves."

Elaine's gaze softened slightly. "Then you need to make that clear. Because men like Nick?" She shook her head. "They don't just walk away when they want something. They take it."

Hanna exhaled shakily, rubbing her hands over her face. "It's not that simple."

"It never is," Elaine said, her voice low. "But it doesn't change who he is. Stop it now, before it becomes something you can't undo."

Hanna stilled.

"Brian's been gone nine years," Elaine continued, her voice thickening. "You're allowed to move on, sweetheart. In fact, you should. But don't

CHAPTER 11

let anyone erase what he meant to you. Don't let anyone force you into something that feels wrong."

Hanna stared down at her hands. "I wouldn't."

Elaine reached across the table, squeezing her fingers gently. "I know you wouldn't do it intentionally. But it could happen. Caitlyn barely remembers Brian. If you let Nick step in now, he'll be the only father she knows."

Hanna swallowed hard. "I know," she whispered. "And I think we're already at that point."

Elaine inhaled sharply. "Then decide. Move forward or turn him loose, but don't let it drag you down."

Hanna nodded. But deep down, she never expected it to get this far.

* * *

Hanna stood to leave, Elaine's words still reeling in her head like a movie on a broken loop.

She turned to the door, then hesitated.

Her gaze caught on the framed photo near the fireplace.

Brian. He was twenty-three, smiling, his arms wrapped around her waist, alive and unbreakable in that frozen moment.

She crossed the room, reaching for it, her fingers brushing the cool glass. The photo had been taken the summer of '94. Before Caitlyn, the accident, and before, she had to learn how to survive without him.

Hanna set the frame back down carefully, but before she could turn away, her gaze snagged on another photo. One she had seen a hundred times but never really looked at. It sat half obscured by an old candle and a stack of napkins, as if Elaine had never decided whether to display it or hide it away.

A boy, no older than seven or eight, stared out from the frame. A navy blue blazer hung too large on his thin frame. A school crest stitched onto the pocket. There is a faint glint of a silver chain against the crisp button down.

Brian. But not the Brian she knew. This Brian was small and brittle.

The deep, angry bruise blooming beneath his left eye made the photo difficult to look at. But it wasn't just the bruise. It was the way he stood stiff and straight, as if someone had already taught him not to slump. His lips slightly parted mid sentence. And his eyes, God, the eyes wide and unflinching and far too old for a child.

The eyes of someone who had already learned the hardest lesson life had to offer. Hanna swallowed hard, the weight pressing against her ribs, heavy and sharp. She glanced toward the kitchen, where Elaine moved quietly, methodically. Elaine never spoke of that photo. Never explained why it sat there.

Maybe it was a reminder. Maybe it was a warning. Maybe she had been waiting for someone to finally ask. Not today. Hanna turned away. But instead of heading for the door, her feet pulled her toward the stairs. Brian's room. A time capsule, frozen in memory. She climbed the steps on autopilot. Her fingers curled around the doorknob, and she pushed it open.

The air inside was heavy, unmoving. The scent of old wood and faded cologne clung to everything. She crossed the room, hardly breathing, and laid down on the bed.

The mattress dipped beneath her weight, the way it had a lifetime ago. And just like that, she was eighteen again.

* * *

Summer 1991—DeLuca House

Rain dripped steadily against the open window. The lingering warmth of the afternoon clung to the curtains. Brian's cologne, clean and sharp, drifted from the pillows.

Brian had kicked off his shoes hours ago, stretched out barefoot across the bed, the soft blue cotton of his shirt rumpled and clinging in the heat. The sleeves strained slightly around his biceps, drawing the eye to the fresh black ink curling around his arm, a tribal design, dark and raised, still tender against his skin. He hadn't bothered to cover it. He was proud of it. It was perfect, so perfectly Brian.

Hanna lay beside him, the thin straps of her black tank top slipping over sun-kissed shoulders, her golden hair a chaotic, beautiful mess against the pillows.

CHAPTER 11

Stray strands framed her face, and her bright, restless eyes caught the fading light like they were made for it. "Let's run away," *she whispered.*

Brian smirked without opening his eyes. "Where would we go?"

"Anywhere but here."

She crawled closer, resting her chin lightly on his chest, feeling the constant rise and fall beneath her. "Just get in the car and drive. We could be halfway across the country by tomorrow."

His eyes opened, dark and thoughtful. "And do what?"

"I don't care." *Her voice was soft but certain.* "We'll figure it out."

Brian sighed, dragging a hand through his hair. "Hanna..."

She heard it in the way he said her name, the way the air thickened between them.

"You think I don't know what you're about to say?" She sat up, crossing her arms tightly.

Brian shifted, leaning back against the headboard. Looking at her. "I just..." he exhaled, frustration flickering across his features, "I don't want you to regret anything."

"What the hell would I regret?" She snapped, blinking back sudden tears.

"Me."

The word landed like a punch.

"That's the dumbest thing I've ever heard," Hanna whispered, her voice shaking.

Brian's jaw tightened. "You've never even been with anyone else, Hanna. You've never even looked at another guy. You're eighteen, for Christ's sake. What if..."

"What if nothing!" She cut him off, anger slicing through her fear. "I know what I want."

He looked away, pain etched deep into his features.

It made her chest ache. It made her furious. "You don't get to decide what I need, Brian."

He raked his hands through his hair again, frustration pouring off him in waves. "I've seen too many people rush into something and then wake up ten years later hating their life. Hating the choices they made."

"So what?" Her voice cracked. "You think I need to go sleep with some random guy to be sure? Is that what you want?"

His head snapped back toward her. "No."

"Then what?" *Hanna demanded.*

Brian's whole body tensed. "I just..." *He exhaled hard.* "I want you to be sure."

"I've never been more sure of anything in my life."

He didn't answer. The silence between them stretched, raw and splintering.

Hanna's throat burned. "Don't you love me?"

Brian's gaze locked on hers, unflinching. "You know I do."

"Then why push me away?"

His voice dropped, low and wrecked. "I don't know."

Brian sat up, folding his arms over his knees, resting his forehead against them, closed off, like he was trying to shield her from something inside himself.

It wasn't the answer she wanted. But it was the only answer he had.

And just as she opened her mouth to say more, Elaine's voice floated up the stairs, sharp and cutting through the moment: "Brian, your dad's on the phone!"

The air between them fractured.

Brian stood, rubbing the back of his neck. "I gotta take that."

Hanna didn't move as he crossed to the door. He didn't say anything.

But before he stepped out, he glanced back, and the look in his eyes told her everything she needed to know.

Hanna knew he loved her. Maybe more than he knew how to handle. Maybe more than he was ready to admit.

* * *

Present Day 2006

Hanna exhaled, pressing the heels of her hands against her eyes.

The air in the room felt heavier now, thick with memory.

She shouldn't have come here. She knew what this house did to her. She knew what this house would always do to her. Still, she had let herself get lost in the past, let herself drown in it.

She rolled onto her side, gripping the extra pillow. It still smelled like him. Hanna sat up abruptly. That wasn't possible.

Elaine had washed these sheets, hadn't she? Maybe she was imagining it.

CHAPTER 11

Maybe she was pushing herself too far.

Anniversary grief, that's all this is. She swallowed hard. *You're imagining things, Hanna. You're just tired.*

But the thought didn't hold. Not here, not in this house. Not in a room full of too many ghosts

For a moment, a breathless, fragile moment, she let herself believe it was Brian.

That somehow, he was still here, lingering, watching, and protecting her.

Tears burned behind her eyes, sudden and sharp. "Brian," she whispered, so low it wasn't even a sound.

The silence swallowed it whole. Brian wasn't here. There was only the memory of him.

Only the aching part she hadn't let go of. The part that never really would.

She wiped the back of her hand across her face, forcing herself to move. She stood, legs stiff and unsteady, the blanket slipping from her grasp.

She crossed the floor, one slow step at a time, not looking back.

Not daring to. Because if she did, if she let herself turn around, she might never leave this room at all.

Chapter 12

Nick sat in Doug O'Sullivan's office, looking at his brother, waiting for the reason why he was summoned. The dim office smelled like old books and expensive whiskey, the air heavy with something unspoken.

Nick knew why he was there. The fight with Tony DeLuca. The DeLuca's, a deal with the devil, the one his father, Seamus, made long before he was born. His father never really told them the full story, only that Vince DeLuca offered him a future, and he took it and never looked back.

Doug sat behind his desk, elbows resting on the polished wood, fingers steepled as he studied Nick like he was some goddamn *disappointment*.

He was already irritated. "You called me in, so say what you need to say."

Doug shook his head slightly. "You really don't get it, do you?"

Nick's patience was wearing thin. He leaned forward. "Why don't you enlighten me then?"

Doug didn't respond right away. Instead, he reached into his desk drawer, pulled out a folder, and slid it across the desk.

Nick hesitated before picking it up, inside Brian's file. The same goddamn file he had found in his own office. His blood ran cold.

Doug's voice was quiet. Controlled, "Tell me, Nick… What were you hoping to find?"

Nick swallowed, but his voice was calm. "The truth."

Doug let out a humorless chuckle. "That's cute, little Nicky is playing detective."

Doug leaned back in his chair, watching Nick like he was a naive kid

CHAPTER 12

instead of a grown man who had spent the last decade clawing his way to the top of his field.

"Let me make this simple for you," Doug said, voice measured. "You're done with all of it, the digging, the questions, and the late night theories. It all stops now."

Nick scoffed, "And if I don't?"

Doug's expression didn't change. "Then you'll see how much control you have over your own life."

Nick's jaw flexed. "Is that a threat?"

Doug shook his head. "No, Nick. It's a reality check." He leaned forward, his voice lower now, weightier. "You think you're different? You think you're not like the rest of us just because you hold a scalpel instead of a gun?"

Nick sat up straighter. "I don't work for them."

Doug slowly smiled "You think the O'Sullivan's have been standing on their own this whole time?" He tilted his head. "You think your cushy career just happened, fuckface? That your fancy education, your spotless record, your rise in the medical world none of that was influenced by the people who actually run this city?"

Nick's stomach turned, but he didn't break eye contact. "I earned everything I have."

Doug's smile faded. "You've been allowed everything you have."

Nick felt it then, the weight of it. The truth was pressing down on him like a slow, suffocating choke hold.

Doug sat back again, giving him a long, measured look. "Tony wanted to handle you himself, but I assured him that I could take care of it."

Nick's spine went rigid.

"But Vince?" Doug continued. "He thought maybe you needed a little reminder of who owns your future, but I assured him that one conversation with me and we would have nothing to worry about."

Nick's fists gripped. "You think they're going to kill me for asking questions?"

Doug exhaled sharply. "Jesus, Nick, seriously? You don't get it, do you?"

73

He leaned forward, his voice quieter now. "They don't need to kill you. They don't even need to ruin you. All they have to do is take away the one thing that matters to you." Doug let the words sink in. "You keep pushing, you won't just lose your career. You'll lose Hanna."

Nick froze.

Doug kept going, his voice casual, like he wasn't ripping Nick's world apart. "One word from Tony, and you'll never see her again. No late night phone calls, no casual dinners, and no weekends with Caitlyn. You'll be nothing to them, just a stranger. And when Hanna moves on?" Doug shrugged. "You'll have no one to blame but yourself."

Nick's breath came sharp now. "You can't control her."

Doug smirked. "Maybe not, but we don't have to." He leaned forward. "You think she would choose you over family? You think she goes against Tony, against Vince, against Brian?" His voice dropped, sharp as a knife. "She's never really been yours, Nick, and she never will be. You need to get your little happy ending fantasy out of your head and face the facts: she will never be yours."

Nick stared at him.

Doug sat back, satisfied. "This is your last warning."

Nick didn't move. Didn't speak.

Doug opened a drawer, pulled out a lighter, and set the file in a metal tray. He flicked the flame, and just like that, Brian's file burned.

Nick watched the edges curl, the flames devour every page, every report, every photo he had spent months trying to make sense of.

Doug let it smolder. Then, he looked up. "This conversation never happened."

Nick's jaw flexed. "And if I don't let this go?"

Doug smiled. Slow. Cold. "Then the next time you see Hanna, it'll be because she chooses not to see you, and you will watch your perfect little life crumble."

Nick exhaled, his hands shaking at his sides.

Doug watched him carefully.

Nick forced himself to breathe. "Fine." His voice was hollow. "I'll drop

CHAPTER 12

it."

Doug nodded, pleased. "Good choice."

Nick turned and walked out. As the cold air hit him, his fists clenched. For the first time in his life, he felt truly powerless, and he hated it. Almost as much as he hated being told what to do.

* * *

April 1996

The waiting room of Doug O'Sullivan's law office smelled like old books, fresh coffee, and something faintly woodsy, probably whatever expensive cologne Doug wore. The place wasn't flashy, but it carried an air of power. Influence. You didn't come here unless you were someone or unless you belonged to someone.

Nick had only stopped by to drop off paperwork. In and out, he had no reason to linger, nor did he want to.

But then, he saw her. Hanna DeLuca, she was seven months pregnant. She sat in one of the leather chairs, absently tracing her fingertips over the curve of her belly. She was wearing a simple, fitted sweater, the kind that stretched over her growing stomach, making it impossible to ignore the life she carried. Her dark curls were pinned back, but a few strands had slipped free, framing her face.

And her eyes were soft and bright. Full of something he didn't have a name for. She was glowing. Not in that cliché way people describe pregnant women. It was him, Brian.

He stood in the doorway of Doug's office, talking in low tones with his brother. Nick didn't know what they were discussing and didn't care. His focus was on her and the way she was watching Brian. Like he was the only thing that mattered in the entire world.

Like he was her home. Then Brian turned. Once their eyes met, something passed between them. It wasn't only love or affection. It was something else; it was a certainty. Like they belonged to each other in a way that no one, not time, not distance, not even death, could change.

He had never seen anything like it before. He wanted it; no, he needed it; and one way or another, he was going to have it.

It was an ugly, raw kind of jealousy, the kind that made his hands clench at his sides. He had no right to feel it. Brian was a good man and a good husband.

But it didn't matter, because at that moment, Nick knew if he could trade places with Brian DeLuca, he would.

No hesitation or second thoughts, because then Hanna would look at him like that.

And for the first time, he realized something even worse: he would never be enough for her. One way or another, he would have her, and once he had her, she would look at him that way.

***

Present Day 2006

Nick returned to his office later that day. He sat in his chair, Doug and Tony's words repeating in his mind. He opened up his drawer and pulled out a small box.

Nick turned the box over in his palm, staring at the ring nestled inside. The diamond caught the light, refracting tiny bursts of brilliance across his desk. It was classic, elegant, and, of course, timeless. The saleswoman had assured him it was the perfect choice: understated yet beautiful, sophisticated without being flashy. A ring made for a woman like Hanna.

But was it? Would it ever truly belong to her?

His fingers tightened around the box.

Tony's words echoed in his head, sharp and unforgiving.

"You love the idea of taking something that was never yours."

Was that true? Had he spent the last nine years chasing a ghost, waiting for her to come around, trying to mold himself into the man Hanna *would* want, the man she *could* love?

His jaw tensed. He wanted to believe that what he felt for her was real. That it wasn't about Brian. That it wasn't about proving something to himself, to Tony, or to *anyone*.

But deep down, a sickening thought crept in. Would she ever wear this ring?

CHAPTER 12

Or would it always pale in comparison to the one she still kept tucked away, hidden in the nightstand beside her bed? The one she refused to let go of, even after all these years. Nick snapped the box shut.

Maybe Tony was right. Maybe he was chasing something that was never meant to be his.

Nick picked up the phone and dialed Hanna's cell, straight to voicemail.

"Hey, Hanna. Look, I'm sorry about the other night. Can you see if your grandparents can take Caitlyn this weekend? We need to talk. Call me back."

Chapter 13

Hanna stepped through the front door with Caitlyn in tow and let it shut behind them with a quiet thud. She exhaled slowly, pressing her back to the door for a moment. The last few days had drained her mentally and emotionally. She needed a minute to breathe, to regroup, to figure out what the hell came next.

This week has been chaos.

She rolled her eyes and muttered under her breath, "Why can't anything ever be simple?"

***

1989

"It's not goodbye, Hanna. I'll be there for fall break."

Hanna shook her head, fighting the sting in her eyes. "Maybe I shouldn't go. Maybe I should just stay with my grandparents."

Brian smiled, brushing a loose curl from her face. "Your dad needs you. We'll talk every day."

Tears welled up, her throat tightening. "But I won't see you every day."

Brian exhaled softly and wiped away a tear with his thumb. "Distance will be good. You'll make new friends and see new places. You're getting out of this town; that's what you wanted."

"Not like this," *Hanna whispered. Her voice cracked. She was crying now.*

"You'll find someone else," *she choked out.* "You'll replace me."

Brian let out a quiet laugh. "Hanna, you sound crazy. This will be good for us,

CHAPTER 13

I promise. Distance makes the heart grow fonder."

She shook her head again, harder this time. "No. I know how this goes. You're gonna meet some hot, model type girl, and you'll forget about me by Christmas."

Brian sighed, reaching into his pocket. "Here," he said, pulling out a small box. Hanna frowned. "What's this?"

"Open it."

With trembling fingers, she lifted the lid, and inside sat a delicate ring, a deep red ruby set in a thin gold band. A promise ring.

Brian took her hand. "I promise you, Hanna Nowack, I'll stay true to you and that someday I will replace this tiny ring with something more permanent."

The tears spilled over. She threw her arms around him, holding on tight as if she could have time to stop. Maybe if she held him hard enough, this moment would never have to end.

* * *

Present Day 2006

Hanna blinked, the memory fading, her fingers twitching nervously. Not all promises lasted, and some returned only to haunt you.

She moved toward the kitchen. It was just her and Caitlyn tonight, quiet and easy. She would deal with Nick later, knowing he deserved the truth.

Her phone buzzed, interrupting her thoughts. Steve Riley's name flashed on the screen.

"Hey, Steve," she answered, balancing the phone on her shoulder as she opened the pantry.

"Just checking in," Steve said warmly. "Are you two doing okay?"

"We're good," Hanna said, comforted by his voice. "Just making dinner."

"Ah, glamorous life," he chuckled lightly. "Everything quiet?"

"For now," she replied, glancing toward Caitlyn. "Thanks."

"Always," Steve replied softly. "I'm just a call away."

"I appreciate it," Hanna said with a faint smile. "Talk soon."

She ended the call and turned back to dinner. She prepared mac and cheese, cheese dogs, and whatever vegetables she had, simple food Caitlyn enjoyed.

As she cooked, her thoughts drifted back to Richard. She was convinced he was hiding something and intended to find out what it was.

Laughter burst from the living room, where Caitlyn sat watching Rugrats.

"No Nick tonight?" Caitlyn asked.

"He's working," Hanna responded softly.

She checked her phone, noting two new voicemails.

Nick's voice filled her ears first. "Hanna, I'm sorry about the other night. Can we talk this weekend? Call me back."

She sighed and deleted the message.

The second message was from Michael. "Hanna, it's Michael. The warden wants you to meet Richard tomorrow. Call me back. How do I—hello? Machine?" The call ended abruptly.

She chuckled softly, knowing Michael would never master cell phones.

After dinner, she planned to start a crime board, pinning everything she had on Richard, and call Rick and Steve for their input.

She drained the mac and cheese and put the hot dogs under the broiler. Cooking should not feel so complicated, she thought.

Her thoughts froze suddenly when she heard soft guitar chords coming from the living room.

Her breath caught in her throat as Brian's familiar voice drifted through the air.

Slowly, she stepped into the living room to see Caitlyn sitting cross-legged, entranced by a home video. Brian sat on the old couch with Caitlyn nestled beside him.

"Daddy, love you more," Brian whispered softly on-screen.

"Mama, that's my favorite part!" Caitlyn giggled.

"Caitlyn, where did you find that tape?" Hanna asked, her voice shaking slightly.

"In the box," Caitlyn replied innocently.

The box had been in the attic. Someone had placed it here.

Her fingers trembled as she picked up another unmarked tape and slid it into the VCR.

CHAPTER 13

The screen flickered, revealing Brian older, sitting alone.

"Hanna, if you're watching this, something happened. I need you to listen. You must move forward, live, and love again. Raise Caitlyn strong. If something doesn't feel right, trust your gut." His voice grew urgent. "Be careful. Someone intended you to see this." He paused, eyes piercing through the screen. "I love you, Hanna. Always."

The screen went black.

Caitlyn stared up innocently. "Who was that man?"

Hanna fought tears. "That was your daddy, Brian. He's with the angels."

Hanna finished dinner mechanically, trapped in memories. Caitlyn mentioned watching the video repeatedly, holding tightly to Brian's memory.

* * *

Hanna brought herself together, trying to compose herself as she walked back into the kitchen. Why hadn't she seen the tape before?

This time of the year always tripped her up. She has always gotten overly emotional around the time of his death.

She drained the mac and cheese and threw the hot dogs in the broiler. She was on autopilot, but she couldn't get the video out of her head. The song. Was the universe trying to tell her something?

Maybe Nick was a bad idea. Should she listen to it?

"Mommy, can we play my song again?"

Hanna turned, glancing at Caitlyn, who sat at the table swinging her legs, completely unaware of the way her words made her mother's breath hitch.

"Sweetie, what song?" Hanna asked carefully.

"The one my daddy in heaven sings to me. I love it."

Hanna asked softly, "Caitlyn, how many times have you watched that video?"

Caitlyn shrugged. "I dunno. Lots."

Hanna gripped the counter, steadying herself. The weight of the moment pressed down on her. Lots. Had Caitlyn been watching that video over and over? Holding onto something Hanna had tried so hard to move past? And why did it feel like, in this moment, she was the one holding onto a ghost?

* * *

Later, after Caitlyn had fallen asleep, Hanna soaked in the tub, her phone nearby. She thought about calling Nick, dependable Nick, but her heart resisted. It still belonged to Brian.

She returned to the living room, replaying their wedding tape. Brian's vows filled the room with promises of everlasting love, and Hanna's tears fell freely.

"Marriage is a sacred bond, a covenant built on love, trust, and commitment. Today, before God, family, and friends, Brian and Hanna come together to make a lifelong promise to one another. The vows they are about to exchange are not just words but the foundation of their future together."

Brian looked into Hanna's eyes. "Hanna, from the day you walked into my life, you became my compass, my constant, my home. I have spent every day since choosing you, and I will spend every day ahead doing the same. You were not just someone I fell in love with; you were someone I chose. Someone I will always choose. I promise to love you the way you deserve to be loved, with honesty, with loyalty, with everything I have. I promise to stand beside you when things are good and hold on tighter when they are not. I promise to make you laugh when you want to cry and to remind you every day that you are my best decision. Life will change us, and the years will pass. We will have days that are easy and days that test us. But no matter how many seasons come and go, my love for you will stand unshaken. If you ask me in ten years, twenty, or when we are old and gray if I still love you, know this: my heart will answer before I can even speak. You are my greatest love, my greatest choice, and my greatest privilege. Always."

Hanna took a shaky breath. "Brian, I have loved you longer than you will ever know. Before we even met, before I knew your name, my heart already belonged to you. I told one person, one time, that I was going to marry you. And the day I finally saw you, I knew I had been right. From the moment we met, you changed

CHAPTER 13

my world. You have been my light in dark times and my shelter in the storm. With you, I feel understood and complete. I promise to stand by you and choose you every day, especially on the hardest days. No matter what life brings, I will be by your side because you are my family, my home, and my heart."

With tears streaming down her face, Hanna slowly ejected the tape from the player, her fingers trembling as she held it in her hands. She traced the edges, the worn label smudged from years of handling. Clutching the tape to her chest, tears spilling as she whispered, "I don't know how to let you go."

* * *

Outside, in the darkness beyond the glow of the house, a figure lingered. The wind howled through the trees, rain misting the air, but the figure did not move. They crept closer to the living room window, where Brian's voice carried through the glass, filled with promises made nearly a decade ago.

Peering through the thin curtain, they watched her. Hanna sat frozen, shoulders trembling, pain etched across her face as she clutched the tape to her chest.

She still loved him. Even now, she still belonged to him.

The watcher's hands curled into fists.

She was supposed to forget.

But soon, she would understand. She had never been alone.

Chapter 14

The next morning, after getting Caitlyn off to school, Hanna decided to call Nick.

Maybe this weekend would be a good time to tell him it wasn't working. She didn't feel the way he did, and no amount of time or effort would change that. He deserved someone who could love him fully, someone who could give him their whole heart. And hers... hers still belonged to a man she had buried nearly ten years ago.

She picked up the cordless phone and dialed.

Nick answered on the second ring, "Hi, Hanna. I was hoping to hear from you last night. How are you?"

She hesitated, "I'm okay."

"You don't sound okay."

Hanna exhaled, running a hand through her hair. "I've just been thinking a lot."

Nick's voice softened. "About us?"

She swallowed hard. "Yeah."

Silence stretched between them.

Finally, Nick spoke, "I know things have been complicated. I know you're still processing everything. I meant what I said, Hanna. We have a future. I love you, I really do."

Her throat tightened.

"Nick"

"Just tell me one thing." His voice was firmer now, edged with something she couldn't quite place. "Do you still think about him? Do you still think

CHAPTER 14

about Brian?"

Hanna closed her eyes. She could lie and tell him what he wanted to hear. That Brian was in the past, that she was ready to move forward with him. But that was she couldn't do it. She didn't want to lie to him; he was a good man and deserved better. "Nick..." She forced herself to say it, to be honest, "I don't think I've ever stopped."

The silence that followed was deafening.

Nick let out a slow breath. "I see, I understand now."

Hanna hesitated, "Nick, I don't want to hurt you."

His voice was tight. "But Hanna, you already have."

She pressed her fingers against her temple and said, "Nick, this isn't fair to you. You deserve so much more."

"No." His voice cut through the line, sharp and final. " No, don't do that. Don't tell me what I deserve because what I deserve, Hanna, is the truth."

She exhaled, closing her eyes. "I gave you the truth, I have been honest, I have never led you under false pretenses or led you on. I can't give you what you're looking for."

Nick didn't respond right away, but when he did, his voice was much quieter. "So that's it, then?"

Hanna swallowed against the tightness in her throat. *"Yeah, I guess it is."*

"Okay then."

It was barely more than a whisper, and then the line went dead.

Hanna set the phone down on the counter, staring at it for a long time, the weight of the moment pressing down on her.

It was done, and she had made her choice. She looked out the dining room window, and just beyond the tree line, she saw something, a shape; it wasn't moving. She couldn't make out if it was a person or an animal. Hanna's caught her breath, her heart hammering in her chest. She jumped when a deer ran through her yard; she turned, and whatever was there before was gone. Maybe it was the deer.

With Brian's death anniversary coming up, she decided she would go up to the cabin; the lake would be a nice change of scenery, and no one knew she still had it.

She walked over to call to see if Irene could watch Caitlyn, and the phone rang as she was going to grab it; it was Irene.

She picked it up. "Hi, Grandma."

But it wasn't Irene's voice that answered. It was Lee, and his tone was flat and blunt. "Hanna, Grandpa's dead."

The words hit her like a punch to the ribs.

Her fingers curled around the phone. "What?"

"Went last night, peacefully." Just like that, and with no warning. There is no buildup or soft cushion to land on.

Hanna swallowed hard, trying to breathe past the lump in her throat. "Grandma"

"She's okay, but you should come over." The line went dead.

Hanna stared at the phone, her stomach twisting.

As Hanna grabbed her keys, she glanced toward the tree line one last time. There was no one there. But across the street, Mr. Donovan stood on his porch, frowning at something in the distance. When he noticed her looking, he gave a small wave.

She almost asked him if he saw anything. But she didn't. She barely registered tossing Caitlyn's bag into the car and barely felt herself moving through the motions of getting on the road.

* * *

By the time she pulled up to her grandparents' house, the weight in her chest had settled into something suffocating. She barely had the car in park before she was out the door.

She got to Nowack's place and walked in the door. Inside, the house smelled the same: warm, familiar, like fresh bread and old wood. But something was missing. Grandpa.

Lee stood in the kitchen, arms crossed, expression unreadable.

But it was Irene who drew Hanna's focus. She sat at the kitchen table, hands wrapped around a cup of tea, her eyes distant. I'm not crying or breaking down, just still.

CHAPTER 14

Hanna's voice came out unsteady. *"Grandma."*

Irene looked up, and for the first time in her life, Hanna saw it

The absence. The hollow space left behind.

Irene reached out, and Hanna didn't hesitate. She sank down beside her, gripping her grandmother's hands.

Irene let out a slow, shaky breath. *"He just went, sweetheart. Just... stopped."*

No pain or warning, he was just gone.

Hanna closed her eyes. Not yet. No tears yet. *"What do you need me to do?"*

Irene squeezed her hand. *"Just stay a while."*

Hanna nodded, her throat tight. She could do that. She could be here.

She just wasn't sure how to be here without him.

Hanna looked up at Lee, her voice tight. "Did you call Uncle Stan, Uncle Mac, and Uncle Peter?"

Lee nodded. "Yeah. I left them a message."

Hanna's stomach dropped. "Please tell me that's not how they found out."

Lee shrugged. "I had to tell them, Hanna."

Hanna clenched her jaw, forcing herself to stay calm. She turned to Irene, squeezing her grandmother's hand. "Grandma, I'll be right back."

Irene gave her a small nod, her expression unreadable.

* * *

Hanna stepped outside, the cool morning air hitting her like a slap. She pulled out her phone, dialing Uncle Stan's number.

The call barely rang twice before he answered. "Hello?"

"Uncle Stan."

His voice immediately warmed. "Hanna, how the heck are you?"

She swallowed hard. "Did you listen to the message from my dad?"

"Nah, I saw it was him and deleted it. Why?"

Hanna closed her eyes, gripping the phone tightly. "Oh, Uncle Stan." Her voice broke before she could stop it.

Stan's tone shifted instantly, concern replacing the lightness. "Hanna, sweetie, what is it?"

She exhaled shakily. "I'm sorry, Uncle Stan."

Then, his voice was quieter. "Hanna, which one?"

Her throat burned. "Grandpa."

There was an uncomfortable silence

When Stan finally spoke, his voice was thick. "Did you talk to Mac and Peter yet?"

"No, I called you first."

"I'll call them now. Thanks for telling me, sweetheart. I'll be over in a bit."

"Thanks, Uncle Stan. I'm sorry."

"Me too, Hanna. Me too."

Hanna ended the call, pressing the phone to her forehead for a moment before dialing Michael.

He answered the phone after a few rings. "Dr. Carter."

Softly, Hanna said, "Michael."

"Hanna? Is everything okay?"

She inhaled deeply. "Not really. My grandpa passed away last night. I need to take the week off."

Michael's voice softened. "I'm so sorry, Hanna. Take all the time you need. Your patients aren't going anywhere."

She closed her eyes. "Thanks, Michael."

"I'll see you when you're ready to come back in November."

"Yeah, see you then."

Hanna hung up, staring at the phone in her hands.

It didn't feel real. None of it did. Hanna ended the call, shakily exhaling as she slipped her phone back into her pocket. The weight of it all pressed down on her: Nick, the shadow outside her house, and now this.

Her grandfather was gone. The man who had been more of a father than a grandfather. The one who had always been constant, always there. She felt the loss settle deep in her chest, heavy and unmoving. She wasn't ready for this. Then again, is anyone ever ready to say that final goodbye?

She took a slow breath and walked back inside.

CHAPTER 14

* * *

Lee was still standing in the kitchen, arms crossed, his expression as unreadable as ever. Irene hadn't moved from her place at the table, her fingers slowly tracing circles along the rim of her tea mug.

Hanna sat down beside her and gently placed her hands over her grandmother's. "Uncle Stan is coming. He's calling Mac and Peter."

Irene gave a slight nod, barely perceptible. "Good."

Lee finally spoke. "Are you staying here tonight?"

Hanna hesitated. "I'm not sure yet."

She glanced at the old wooden clock on the wall. Time kept moving, even when it felt like it shouldn't. Even when she wished it would stand still.

Tomorrow, there would be things to handle, decisions to make, people coming in and out.

But tonight, she would stay here. With her grandmother. With her father.

* * *

The family gathered that evening at the Nowack farm. Henry and Irene's sons arrived with their wives, and Peter brought his children, who ran outside to play with Caitlyn.

Despite the somber mood, Caitlyn was happy to see her cousins. She laughed and chased them through the yard, briefly untouched by the weight of grief that pressed down on the house.

Inside, Stan turned to Irene. "Ma, I'll head to Wainwright's tomorrow and take care of the funeral arrangements."

Irene gave a small nod, still trying to take it all in. Her Henry was gone. His health had been unpredictable for years, but you wouldn't have known it from the way he carried himself. He moved through life as if age couldn't touch him, working the farm with the same energy he had in his thirties. But in the end, time had caught up.

Hanna stood by the window, watching the children play, her mind adrift in disbelief. There was so much she had wanted to say to him. So many things left unsaid. Apologies for the ways she had pushed back as a teenager. Words of love she never quite found the courage to speak.

Memories came rushing in—trips to Dairy Queen, the whispered "don't tell your grandma we went" (even though she always knew), the Saturday morning rides to the dump, the way he used to tease her about ants in her pants while pinching her backside and laughing. If only he had truly known how deeply she loved him.

She swallowed hard, fighting the sting of tears. Life would never be the same. Holidays would never feel the same.

He had been everything she had ever wanted in a husband. No man had ever measured up to the pedestal she placed him on.

"Maybe we should order some food," Brenda, Peter's wife, suggested.

Irene gave a small nod, still dazed.

Brenda walked to the phone and ordered a couple of pizzas. When she hung up, she turned to Hanna. "Why don't you come with me?"

Hanna hesitated, then nodded.

"I've got the kids," Peter assured them.

The ride was quiet but necessary. The house felt suffocating and heavy with loss, and stepping away, even for a short time, was a relief.

* * *

When they pulled into the driveway, Hanna immediately noticed the familiar car. Her stomach clenched, and she muttered under her breath, "What is he doing here?"

Brenda followed her gaze. "Nick is h—" She stopped herself, catching the shift in Hanna's expression and the sudden tension in her posture. There was no need to ask. This was not a welcome visit.

Inside, Nick was waiting. He stood in the living room as if he belonged there, as if he had not been told the day before that it was over.

Hanna's pulse quickened. Her hands curled into fists.

The moment he saw her, he stepped forward and pulled her into a hug. "Hanna, I'm so sorry."

CHAPTER 14

She didn't return the gesture. Her voice was low and controlled, edged with anger. "What are you doing here?"

"I was at the hospital when your grandfather came in. I wanted to be here for you and your family."

Her jaw tensed. "That's not why you came. You need to leave."

Sensing the weight of the moment, Irene stepped in. "Hanna."

Hanna met her grandmother's eyes but said nothing. This was not the time for a fight. Not today.

Irene turned to Nick and gave a small, polite nod. "Have a seat."

Nick glanced at her, then back at Hanna, and the slight smirk on his face made her stomach twist.

There was no grief in his eyes, no hint of real sorrow. What she saw instead was harder to name, but it left her uneasy. It was the look of someone who wasn't telling the whole truth. Someone who knew more than he was letting on.

* * *

After dinner, Nick pulled Hanna aside, his expression tense. "Can we talk?" His voice was quieter than usual, almost careful. "Just a minute. Then I'll leave."

Hanna hesitated, then sighed. She grabbed her jacket and glanced at her Aunt Brenda, who rolled her eyes.

Outside, the night air was crisp, the scent of damp leaves filling the air. Hanna crossed her arms, bracing herself. "Nick, I thought I made myself clear."

He was starting to get annoyed. "You don't have to do this alone, Hanna. Let me be here for you."

She shook her head. "You can't force yourself into my life. I don't feel the way you do about me. I'm sorry, but I never will."

Nick exhaled sharply, frustration flickering in his eyes. "I think if you opened your heart, if you stopped putting up this wall, you'd see how good we could be together."

Somewhere in the back of her mind, she knew he was a good man. He had been kind and patient. But there was no spark. No part of her ached for him the way she had for Brian.

She sighed. "Nick, I need space. The more you push, the more I'm going to resent you." She hesitated, softening her voice. "You deserve someone who looks at you the way I looked at Brian."

Something in Nick's face darkened. His jaw clenched, his fists curled at his sides.

"That's it, isn't it?" His voice was tight, bitter. "I'll always be competing with a ghost."

Hanna could feel the anxiety coming over her. "Nick"

"What does he have that I don't?" His voice rose now, sharp with something almost desperate. "Jesus, Hanna, I'm right here breathing, alive, and he's six feet under, rotting."

The slap cracked through the night air before Hanna even realized she had moved.

Nick's head snapped to the side, his cheek burning red where her palm had struck.

For a long moment, the only sound was the distant hum of crickets.

Then her voice, low and firm. Cold. "Get the hell out of here, Nick. You came to do this the day I found out my grandfather died? You inconsiderate bastard!"

Nick turned back to her, eyes wide. "Hanna, I didn't mean it. I was just angry, please."

"No." Her voice didn't waver. "Don't come back. Don't call. Don't make me take alternative actions." She stepped forward, her hands curled into fists. "Get off my family's property. Now."

Nick swallowed hard. His face was flushed with humiliation, anger, and something else she couldn't name.

"Hanna"

The front door creaked open, and Peter stepped onto the porch, his stance casual but his eyes dead serious. "You heard her, Nick. Time to go."

Nick's jaw tensed, and he glanced at Peter, then back at Hanna. His face

CHAPTER 14

twisted in something between regret and resentment.

Finally, he muttered, "Sorry for your loss."

He turned and walked to his car, the gravel crunching under his feet. A moment later, headlights flickered on, and he was gone.

Peter let out a slow breath, watching the taillights disappear. "I didn't know," he said finally, glancing at Hanna. "He seemed like a good guy."

Hanna let out a bitter laugh, rubbing at the sting in her palm. "Seemed is right.

Chapter 15

Nick gritted his teeth, gripping the steering wheel so hard his knuckles turned white.

"Way to go, Nick," he muttered, shaking his head. "That's one sure way to win her over."

He couldn't believe how he had acted. The words had just *come* out sharp, ugly, and cruel. He was angry and frustrated, but damn it, that wasn't how he wanted her to see him.

Except wasn't it?

Nick exhaled sharply, staring at the road ahead. He knew what Hanna saw when she looked at him tonight: the man who lost. And that? That is unacceptable.

Maybe he just needed to give her time and maybe a little space. Let things settle. Yeah, that was it. Once the dust cleared, he could try again. He'd send flowers, maybe write a letter reminding her of everything he had done for her these last five years.

He was the one who stayed and the one who never left. His fingers tightened around the wheel. Why did he say that? Why did he let his temper get the best of him?

If he was going to win Hanna over, he had to be like Brian. That was the key. If he could become the man she had loved, she would finally look at him the way she had looked at her husband.

But God, she made it so damn difficult.

She clung to the past like it was the only thing that ever mattered. But what about now? What about the man who has been picking up the pieces

CHAPTER 15

the last few years?

Caitlyn saw him. Caitlyn loved him, and if Hanna could just truly see that, she would have no choice but to love him too.

Because love wasn't just about the past, it was about who stuck around, and quite frankly, Brian was gone, and he was here.

He knew in the end, Hanna would wear his ring.

He took out his phone. "Deck, it's Nick. Can I stop by? I need some advice." Deck responded, "Sure. I'll put some coffee on."

* * *

Nick pulled into the church parking lot, the looming brick structure of St. Mary's casting long shadows in the evening light. Before he even reached the rectory door, Father Declan "Deck" opened it, a warm but curious smile on his face.

"Nick," Deck stepped aside, smiling. "This is a surprise."

Nick stepped inside, the familiar scent of old wood, candle wax, and incense filling his lungs. Deck had been a priest for over ten years, recently assigned to St. Mary's, a change their mother was thrilled about. She had always wanted at least one of her sons close to home.

Once inside, Deck studied Nick. "Man, you don't look so good."

Nick sighed, running a hand down his face. "Deck... I think I messed things up really badly with Hanna."

"It can't be that bad."

Nick let out a humorless laugh. "Yeah? Well, I lost my temper and told her Brian was six feet under and rotting."

"Nick," he exhaled. "We all say things in anger, but it's how we control those words that matters. There is nothing more dangerous than words."

Nick rubbed his temples, tension rolling through his shoulders. "I don't know how to fix this."

Deck gave him a long look before pouring them both a cup of coffee. "Then maybe the first step is figuring out why you said it in the first place."

Nick stared at his cup, silent because deep down, he already knew it wasn't just anger or frustration. "Why am I so jealous of what she feels? He's been dead for years."

Deck exhaled, his gaze steady. "Nick, if you want her to love you, then you have to accept that she will always love him. Ask yourself, if Brian were still alive, would you honestly be with her?"

Nick opened his mouth to answer but then closed it because he didn't know how to answer that.

"She made a commitment to him, Nick," Deck continued. "In front of God. That's not something to take lightly."

Nick let out a bitter laugh. "You think I don't know that? You think I don't know that I'm fighting a dead man?" His voice dropped, "He's been gone for nearly a decade. I've been there. I was the one picking up the pieces. I was the one making sure she didn't fall apart."

"Nick, you're not just fighting a dead man. You're fighting a ghost. A man who was taken from her. A man she loved, shared a home with, and had a child with. You're trying to erase someone who was never meant to be erased."

"I don't want to erase him."

Deck's voice was quiet but sharp. "Don't you?"

Nick started fidgeting

Deck leaned forward. "She will never be able to love you until you accept that she will always love Brian. That he will always be a part of her, their child, is what sealed that union."

Nick swallowed hard, looking away. Because as much as he wanted to argue, Deck was right.

"Nick, let's look at it this way: if it was you in Hanna's position, and let's say Hanna died, and another woman was vying for your attention and affection, how would you feel?"

Nick thought about it, "I see your point. I wouldn't want to love anyone but Hanna," and then it hit him, "She will never love anyone but Brian, but Deck, how do I change it? I want to show you something." Nick reached into his pocket. He flipped open the velvet box, revealing the ring.

His voice was quieter now, more measured. "Look, Deck. I was going to

CHAPTER 15

give this to her this weekend."

Deck's gaze flicked to the ring. His expression didn't change. Instead, he met Nick's eyes and said, calm but firm, "Brother, she might not ever let him go; she might not ever say yes to you."

And for the first time, Nick felt something cold crawl up his spine. "So, what you're saying, Deck, is that I either accept Brian as part of our relationship… or I lose Hanna forever?"

Deck shook his head. "No, Nick. You have to accept that Brian will always be a part of *her*, not just your relationship but *her life; she loved him*. A piece of her went with him when he died, and a piece of him remains in their child. She may be able to give you part of her heart, but not all of it. The rest will always belong to him."

Nick clenched his fists. "But Deck, I've *been* here. Through the sleepless nights, the screaming, the grief. I've been here for *Caitlyn*. She's been calling me *Daddy* for months."

Deck's expression shifted, his voice calm but firm. "That seems strange, Nick. Hanna let Caitlyn call you 'Daddy,' but she won't give you her heart?"

Nick exhaled sharply. "Hanna only heard it once."

Deck's gaze hardened. "Nick, no, no, no, you should have corrected Caitlyn the moment she said it. Then afterward, you should have talked to Hanna about it. You're *not* her father. You're not even her stepfather. That decision is *Hanna's* to make, not yours. You don't get to decide if it's okay or not. You *crossed a boundary*."

Nick opened his mouth and then closed it. He nervously responded, "I—I never really thought about it that way."

Deck's tone softened. "Look, all I can say is reflect and pray. Ask God to open your heart, to show you his will, but you have to accept too that it might not be his will for you and Hanna to be together. You need to give Hanna some space and let things settle. Once the time is right, talk to her. If you want me there, I'll be here, but you have to accept that she might never look at you as more than a friend."

Nick nodded slowly, running a hand down his face. "That might not be a bad idea, Deck. Thanks… for being a good brother. For helping me see where I went wrong." He swallowed hard. "I love Hanna, Deck. I do. And I *know* we can be happy. I just need to be patient. More accepting."

Deck gave him a measured look. "Patience is good, Nick. Acceptance is better. But understanding? That's what will matter the most."

"Nick, you stay at her house, and she at yours, right?"

"Yeah, occasionally. Why?"

"Where do you sleep at her house?"

Nick couldn't figure out where Deck was going with this. "Usually in the guest room."

"And when she is at your house?"

"In my guest room, Deck. I don't know where you're going with this."

"Nick, you haven't been intimate, which is a good thing, but ask yourself why."

Deck was right; she kept him at a distance. He would kiss her, but it was never a kiss.

Nick got up and let out a slow breath. "Thanks for everything, Deck." He pulled his brother into a hug, the weight of their conversation settling deep in his chest.

As he stepped back, reality hit him like a freight train. He had been such an ass. The way he had treated Hanna, the way he had convinced himself that *because he had been there, he was entitled to her love.* Love and jealousy will make a man do crazy things.

Next weekend, he'd reach out to her. She had mentioned she was on vacation time, and with the hospital giving him the weekend off, they had time. Maybe they could take the train into the city, spend the day together, talk, and figure things out. If they decided it wasn't going anywhere. Then he'd accept that; he wasn't going to push any more, and he wasn't going to try to force something that wasn't there. He realized then that he had been an asshole, and it was time to stop.

No more pushing or forcing his way in, and he would give Hanna the space she needed to grieve Henry. This time, he was going to do things differently. He would be patient; he would let her breathe, let her grieve, and let her settle. Because that's all this was: grief, stress, and bad timing.

CHAPTER 15

She was overwhelmed, and she wasn't *thinking clearly*. Once things calmed down, once the emotions faded, she'd be able to see things for what they were. She'd see him, and when she did, he'd be waiting. He wouldn't hover or push; he would just wait.

Because love wasn't about chasing someone down. It was about being there, being constantly present, and he had been.

Nine years, nine years of standing beside her, of picking up the pieces, of raising her daughter, of raising *their* daughter, if Hanna would just accept it. He knew in time she would. Caitlyn already saw it. Caitlyn already knew. And when Hanna was ready to let go of the past, she'd finally understand what Caitlyn did. Nick wasn't just a man who stayed; he was the only choice left. The right choice and when she realized that... She'd say yes, well, maybe not now and not next month, but next year. Yes, next year, they'd be planning their wedding; he felt it in his bones.

And when the time was right, when she was ready to listen, he'd tell her the truth about Caitlyn. But not yet. Hanna wasn't ready, but she would be; she just needed time, and Nick had all the time in the world.

* * *

Nick arrived home, and for a moment, he just stood there, staring at the space around him. It was too quiet, too empty. This wasn't how it was supposed to be; Hanna should be here.

He let his eyes drift, the edges of reality blurring, until he saw how things would be, how things *should* be, imagining ... *The soft glow of the kitchen light, Hanna standing by the sink, rinsing dishes, her hair loose around her shoulders. She turns when she hears him, her lips parting just slightly, eyes warm,* inviting, just like she used to look at *him*.

Like she did with Brian, a slow, satisfied breath filled Nick's lungs. That's right, Hanna. That's how you should be looking at me.

He *steps forward in his mind, his arms sliding around her waist, pulling her back against his chest. She tenses, but he ignores it, pressing his lips to her neck.*

"Nick," *she breathes, but there's something there, something just beneath the surface hesitation.*

No, wait, she's not supposed to hesitate.

He turns her around, cups her face, and kisses her hard. And when she pulls back, when she raises her hand to slap him, he catches her wrist, his grip tightening. He loves it when she fights him. When she makes him earn it. When she makes him remind her who she belongs to.

The fantasy shifts, the edges warping, twisting, and deepening into something darker. The attic, the room that is under lock and key, no one goes in there.

They would learn each other, and she would fight at first. She would resist because Hanna was stubborn. But eventually, she'd understand.

That he was the only one who truly loved her. That she was *his*, and his jaw clenched. He just had to be patient and wait.

Chapter 16

It had been a week since Henry's funeral.

It was a beautiful service, simple and heartfelt. So many people had come to pay their respects, a testament to the man he was. Henry had touched countless lives.

He was kind, compassionate, always seeing the best in people, and the first to lend a hand to anyone who needed it. Her brother, Kevin, came with his wife, Lindsay. While they were there, they announced they were expecting their first child.

Kevin wanted Hanna back in his life after years of silence. An added benefit? They lived in Florida, a great vacation spot and a chance to escape the harsh New York winters.

Even though Nick had behaved himself, keeping his distance and respecting her boundaries, which threw her off, Hanna couldn't shake the feeling that he was up to something.

But she was too grief-stricken to dig into it yet. Her grandparents had been her anchor after Brian passed.

Without them, she wasn't sure where she would be today

＊

Winter 1997

A month after Brian's funeral, Hanna sat at the kitchen table in her grandparents' house, hollowed out.

Her grandmother, Irene, slid a steaming cup of tea in front of her and said, very quietly:

"You have two choices, Hanna. Live for your daughter... or die trying to be with him."

There was no anger in her voice. No judgment.

Irene didn't wait for an answer.

She simply stood, kissed Hanna's head, and left her alone in the room.

Hanna sat there for a long time, the words circling through her mind.

Die to be with him... or live for Caitlyn.

For the first time in weeks, she moved.

She got up. Took a shower and put on fresh clothes.

She rejoined the living.

As she walked down the stairs, she spotted Henry at the kitchen table, feeding Caitlyn.

He turned and smiled, his voice warm. *"Caitlyn, your mommy's finally awake."*

Hanna crossed the room and wrapped her arms around him.

Henry patted her arm gently. *"It'll take time, Hanna. There's no set amount of time for grief. You take all the time you need. But don't stop living.*

She would.

She would find a way, to live... and live without Brian

* * *

Present Day October 2006

"Don't stop living." That is what Irene was doing now.

The farm felt so empty. With Irene gone to New Haven to be with Peter's family, there wasn't much left tying Hanna to it.

Being away would be good for her. Good for all of them. She left with Peter, heading back to New Haven to be with his family. Being away would be good for her and give her a chance to heal, to surround herself with her youngest grandchildren. And Vermont, this time of year? Well, it was beautiful; she would be able to take it easy and let someone else take care of her for a change.

Lee had taken over the farm, keeping it running, but it wasn't the same

CHAPTER 16

without Henry. Hanna ran her hand through her hair. With Irene away and her own plans to head up to the cabin this weekend, she needed to make arrangements for Caitlyn.

She picked up the phone and dialed Elaine and Tony's number.

Elaine answered on the second ring, "Hanna, darling, is everything okay?"

"Yeah, Ma," Hanna said. "Would you and Tony be able to watch Caitlyn this weekend? I'll be back Tuesday. I just need to get away for a few days. With everything that's happened, I just..."

Elaine cut in, her voice warm. "Hanna, of course we can. Why don't you pick her up Wednesday after school? That way, you don't have to rush back on Tuesday."

Relief washed over Hanna. "That would be great, thank you."

"Why don't we pick her up from school on Friday?" Elaine suggested, "That way, you don't have to worry about driving at night."

Hanna smiled. "I'll send a note to her teacher. Thanks, Ma."

"She's our granddaughter, Hanna. We'll take her anytime."

"Love you."

"Love you too, sweetheart."

As soon as she hung up, Hanna sighed, tension easing from her shoulders. That was settled. She glanced at the calendar. Two days until she left. She figured she should start packing now. Four days at the cabin meant she needed to prepare for anything. The weather this time of year is unpredictable, warm during the day and cold at night.

She pulled out her suitcase and started folding sweaters, mentally making a list of what else she needed. She'd have to stop for groceries on the way up.

Her phone rang, and she looked down at the caller ID.

Nick.

Hanna sighed. *"What now?"*

She answered. "Hello?"

"Hanna, it's Nick. How are you?"

"I'm okay. You?"

"Doing well," he said. " I wanted to call and apologize for everything at your grandma's house It was wrong. I should've respected your space. No excuses. I'm sorry."

Hanna blinked, thrown off by the sincerity in his voice.

She pulled the phone away, staring at the screen to make sure it was really Nick. "Nick… I appreciate that," she said carefully. "Thank you."

"Hanna, it was all me," he said, almost too quickly. "I don't like the way I was acting. It wasn't love. I don't even know what it was."

He hesitated, then added, "I was wondering if maybe we could spend some time together this weekend. Go into the city, get lunch, and talk to figure out if there's still something between us."

"Nick," she started.

"Hanna, please. I just need to hear it from you. Face-to-face. Even if it's goodbye."

Something about the way he said it made her stomach knot.

Still, Hanna forced a polite tone.

"I appreciate it, Nick, really. But I'm going out of town this weekend. I just need some time. It's been a lot."

"Oh. I get it," Nick said. Then, almost too casually, "Where are you headed?"

"Up to Vermont," she said lightly. "To my uncle's."

"Is Caitlyn going with you?"

"Yeah, we're leaving in a few days."

"Well… maybe when you get back. Let's have lunch or something."

"We'll see."

"Thanks, Hanna. And really, I'm sorry."

She hung up, staring at the phone. *He doesn't give up does he?*

That wasn't like him.

He was up to something.

Hanna pushed the thought aside as her eyes flickered to the clock. Caitlyn would be home soon, and she hadn't pulled anything out for dinner. Maybe tonight was a takeout night.

CHAPTER 16

* * *

After dinner, Hanna plopped down onto the floor, pulling the *Disney Scene It* game box toward her. Caitlyn bounced in excitement, her curls bouncing with her.

"You're going down, Mommy," Caitlyn declared, giggling as she set up the game pieces.

"Oh, is that so?" Hanna smirked, raising an eyebrow. "I don't know, kid. I'm the queen of Disney trivia."

Caitlyn gasped dramatically. "No way. I know more than you!"

Hanna chuckled. "Alright, big shot. Let's see what you've got."

Caitlyn grabbed the remote and started the game, her little fingers moving fast over the buttons. The opening theme played, and they settled in, ready to battle.

The first question popped up on the screen: "In *The Little Mermaid*, what does Ariel give to Ursula in exchange for legs?"

Caitlyn shot her hand up. "Oh! Oh! Her voice! She gives her voice!"

Hanna narrowed her eyes. "Are you sure, Caitlyn?"

"Yes! That is my final answer!"

The screen flashed: CORRECT.

Caitlyn jumped up, throwing her arms in the air. "YESSS! One point for me!"

Hanna shook her head, laughing. "Alright, alright, you got that one. But I'm just getting warmed up."

The next question appeared: "What is the name of the teapot in *Beauty and the Beast?*"

Before Caitlyn could even speak, Hanna blurted out, "Mrs. Potts!"

Caitlyn gasped. "Mommy! You didn't even give me a chance!"

Hanna shrugged, laughing, "What can I say? I'm just that good."

Caitlyn crossed her arms, trying to look serious, but the corners of her lips twitched. "Okay, fine, the next question is mine."

The game continued, filled with laughter, playful competition, and exaggerated reactions when one of them got a question wrong. Caitlyn cheered when she won a round and groaned dramatically when Hanna beat her.

"In The Lion King, what is the name of Simba's best friends?"

Caitlyn barely let her mom finish before shouting, "*Timon and Pumbaa!*"

Hanna held up her hands. "Okay, okay! You're on fire tonight."

Caitlyn puffed out her chest. "I'm a *Disney* expert."

Hanna chuckled, grabbing a handful of popcorn. "I don't doubt it."

Caitlyn immediately burst into giggles. "Mommy, do it, the voice from the Lion King!"

Hanna sighed, already knowing what her daughter wanted. She took a deep breath and, in her best *Mufasa* voice, rumbled, "Remember who you are."

Caitlyn collapsed into a fit of giggles. "You sound so silly!"

"You're the one who asked for it," Hanna teased, poking Caitlyn's side until she squealed.

* * *

Unseen beyond the tree line, a shadow stood motionless.

They watched the house, watched her, and imagined what it would feel like to be inside. To be surrounded by warmth and light. To be close.

The flicker of the television cast soft reflections through the window, revealing the outline of a mother and daughter wrapped in laughter. They looked safe. They looked unguarded.

The wind moved gently through the leaves, but the figure remained still.

Soon, she would belong to him.

* * *

Farther back in the darkness, another figure stirred. This one was not focused on the house. He was watching the person who was watching it.

The next move would not simply shift the balance. It would determine who made it out and who did not.

Chapter 17

The past two days had passed quickly, filled with Halloween festivities, and tomorrow morning, she would be leaving for the cabin. After putting Caitlyn to bed, Hanna moved around the house, finishing up the last of her packing. Caitlyn's small pink suitcase sat by the front door, ready to be dropped off at Tony and Elaine's. If she needed anything else, they could always grab it from the house.

She walked back into her room, folding a sweater to tuck into her bag, when a shiver crawled up her spine. The fine hairs on the back of her neck stood on end, a feeling, a distinct, undeniable sense of being watched.

She turned toward the window, heart pounding. The streetlight cast long shadows across the yard, the tree branches swaying slightly in the breeze. Nothing out of the ordinary. But just as she started to turn away, there was a shape, dark and motionless. Her breath caught. She reached for the lamp and flicked it off, hoping to see better against the reflection in the glass. But when her eyes adjusted, nothing. Then something jumped, and she jerked back. A deer. She laughed. "I'm being traumatized by a deer who's going after my strawberries."

Thud. Thud. Thud.

The hard knock on the door made her jump. Hanna took a slow, calming breath and flipped on the porch light.

She rolled her eyes. Nick.

She exhaled sharply, pressing her fingers to her temples before opening the door. "Nick? What are you doing here?"

He lifted the two cups, a familiar boyish grin on his face. "Thought you could use some hot cocoa. I know how nervous you get before long trips."

Hanna hesitated, then sighed. *Damn it, Nick.* He always knew little details like that, the small things she wished didn't matter anymore. She stepped back. "Uh... yeah, thanks. Do you want to come in?"

"Sure, unless I'm disturbing you. You're still not packing, are you?"

"You know me," she muttered. "Just making sure I have everything."

Nick stepped inside and immediately spotted Caitlyn's tiny suitcase by the door. He gestured toward it. "Well, at least Caitlyn's ready."

Hanna nodded. "Yep."

Nick glanced around the living room. The *Disney Scene It* case lay open on the floor, along with a few scattered game pieces.

"Aww, game night?" he asked, bending down to pick up the case.

Hanna blinked, glancing over. "Oh yeah. A few nights ago. Guess we forgot to put it away."

Nick made himself comfortable, walking into the kitchen as if he was family.

Hanna fought back a sigh and thought, Sure, just make yourself at home.

Nick's voice pulled her back "Hanna, I know I said I'd wait until after you got back, but "

She already knew where this was going. She turned to face him, forcing a tired smile. Might as well get it over with; otherwise, he will never quit.

"Sure, we can talk now, Nick."

Nick exhaled, relieved, like he had been holding the words back for days. But he didn't say it, not yet anyway. Instead, he rubbed the back of his neck, hesitating. "Look, I know how you feel about Brian. I know that's not changing."

Hanna blinked. Trying not to roll her eyes, here we go.

Nick's gaze met hers. "I get it. He's always going to be a part of you. And I'd never ask you to forget him."

Nick stepped forward, just enough for her to notice, but not close enough to make her pull away.

"I just need to know, is there any room in your heart for me?"

Her breath caught. *What is he up to?*

CHAPTER 17

"I know he'll always have a piece of your heart. I just want to know if there's a piece left for me too." Her throat tightened. Because that was the worst part. Nick wasn't cruel or some monster; he had been kind and patient. Nick had picked up every shattered piece of her life and helped her when she couldn't even help herself. He had been there, but she never looked at him that way. To her, he was just a close friend. But that didn't change what was missing. Hanna swallowed hard, staring at the floor. "Nick…"

Nick took another step, his voice softer. "I know it's been nine years. I know moving on isn't easy. But you deserve it."

Her head snapped up. "Don't, don't tell me what I deserve."

Nick's expression tightened. "That's not what I meant."

"Isn't it?" She fired back.

He let out a slow breath, shaking his head. "I just… I don't understand, Hanna."

He hesitated, and the words cracked. "Tell me what he had that I don't." Nick swallowed hard, his voice breaking on the words. "Tell me why, after all these years, after everything I've done, everything I've been for you, why is it still him?"

And that was it. That was the moment something snapped inside, causing her to break. Something switched inside of her, causing her voice to shake, but it was sharp, cutting, and very unforgiving. "Because he was my home, Nick."

Nick froze. His breath hitched.

Hanna swallowed hard, forcing herself to keep going, to make him understand. "Brian wasn't just some guy I loved. He wasn't just my husband; he was my best friend, my first love. He was the place I belonged, my feeling of safety and of warmth. I knew that no matter what happened in this world, I had someone who knew me. Who understood me in a way no one else ever could. I could sit in silence with him and still feel heard. I could fall apart, and he'd hold the pieces together before I even knew I was breaking. He was," Her throat was closed. She choked on the words, "He was my home. And you, Nick? Well, you're a house, you're sturdy, and you're standing.

But you're not home, at least not to me."

For a long moment, Nick just stared at her. His hands were trembling at his sides, and then his expression changed. " But, I'm alive, Hanna. I'm here. I stayed."

"I never asked you to," she said softly, shaking her head, tears streaming down her face. "I never asked you to stay, Nick. You did that on your own; I have always been honest with you."

"You're never going to let go of him, are you?"

She blinked. The answer was so painfully simple. "I don't know how."

Nick let out a short, bitter laugh. His hand raked down his face. And then his voice dropped and became cold and almost calculated. "You're still in love with a ghost."

She got up and stepped back from him because his tone became something too familiar; it reminded her of the inmates she worked with, and that terrified her.

But Nick wasn't finished. His lips curled into something that wasn't quite a smirk, and then he threw the grenade. "You think he was perfect, don't you?" Nick's eyes darkened. "You think you knew him, but there was a part of him you didn't, Hanna. A part he never let you see."

She shook her head. "Stop."

"Ask Doug." Nick stepped forward. "Ask your father-in-law, ask Steve; they all knew."

"You know what, Nick?"

Nick's smirk spread. "Brian had skeletons, lots of them, Hanna. You have no idea who you married or even what you married. You think he was all innocent; he was no better than the inmates you work with today."

Hanna could feel the tears filling up her eyes; the room blurred.

Nick let the words sink in, watching her crumble. He walked over and grabbed his jacket. "I'll give you some time, then maybe you'll finally realize what's right in front of you."

And then he was gone. Hanna stood there, shaking.

The sound of the door clicking shut echoed through the silence. She could feel her heart pounding

CHAPTER 17

Nick was wrong. She wasn't in love with a ghost. But suddenly doubt bled in.

Brian had secrets? Doug and Steve knew? The walls closed in, and her hands shook, and for the first time since Brian died, she wondered if she had ever truly known him at all.

* * *

Nick got into the car and *slammed the door so hard the frame rattled.*

His chest *heaved*. His hands *shook*.

And thence *lost it*.

BAM. His fist slammed into the steering wheel.

BAM. Again.

BAM. Again. Harder.

"A house?!" He choked out, his voice raw, ragged, and shaking. "W*hat the fuck does that even mean, Hanna?*"

He hit the wheel again, so hard his knuckles split, pain radiating up his arm. *"I'm not home? I'm just a house?"* His breath was jagged, uneven. "*Who the hell wouldn't want a house?*"

His pulse roared in his ears. His vision blurred with rage. She had to see. She had to fucking see he was everything she needed.

He had stood by her, waited for her, and picked up her shattered pieces when no one else did. Nine goddamn years, nine years, and still it was him. Brian, the fucking ghost, the dead man.

His grip tightened around the steering wheel until his knuckles went bone white, blood smearing across the leather.

His voice dropped to a whisper, shaking with barely contained fury. "He's gone, Hanna." His breath caught. His fingers curled so tight his nails dug into his palms.

He was dead; Brian was fucking dead, buried six feet in the ground. She still breathed for him and, for some reason, still lived inside his shadow. Nick let out a broken laugh, his head tipping back against the seat, staring at the ceiling. He should have known she would never choose him, not while the past still owned her. Not while she still saw Nick as a man who stood in a dead man's place, instead of the man standing right in front of her.

His throat burned, and his ribs ached from the weight of it. She rejected him; she humiliated him. He wasn't going to lose, not like this, and definitely not to someone who didn't even exist anymore.

He exhaled sharply, wiping the blood from his hand onto his jeans, fingers flexing against the leather wheel. Then, slowly, his expression changed. The hurt dulled, and the pain faded, and once it did, all that was left was something cold, sharp, and almost dangerous.

She just needed to see. She needed to understand. He could be home. He would show her, and by the time he was done, *she would never think of Brian again.*

He pulled out of her driveway; he would give her some time to think, and she would come to see. He needed someone to talk to, someone to validate what he was thinking. He knew he told Hanna that if she told him face-to-face, he would let go, but she was a prize; she was a doctor's wife.

She would look good on his arm at events, Dr. O'Sullivan and his beautiful, petite wife with the dirty blonde wavy hair, blue eyes, and shapely frame, and their daughter, the spitting image of her mother. He headed toward Great Meadow Correctional Facility; he knew who he could talk to, the only person who would understand.

Chapter 18

Nick pulled into the Great Meadow Correctional Facility parking lot and checked the time. 9:06 p.m. It was too late for visiting hours; he would need authorization.

He reached for his phone, and he scrolled through his contacts until he found Madeline Alden. They had gone to medical school together, tangled in an on again, off again thing for years. Now, she was prison medical director at Great Meadow, a position of power Nick had used to his advantage more than once.

He pressed send.

The line rang twice before she answered. "Nick?" There was a flicker of surprise in her voice. "It's been a while. How are you?"

"Good," he said smoothly. "Even better if I could see you tonight."

She warmly said, "My door is always open to you."

She was always predictable. He would have to cater to her for a few weeks, and then he would disappear for a while.

"I need a favor first," he continued. "Can you call the prison and authorize me to see Richard Hale? Dr. Nowack forgot to set it up today."

Her tone shifted slightly. "That's strange. She didn't mention anything. Is he okay?"

Nick kept his voice casual and reassuring. "Yeah. Just a routine visit."

"Oh... okay. Sure, I'll call."

"Great, Maddie. I'll see you soon."

But before he could hang up, she hesitated.

"Nick..." Her voice was softer now. "I miss you. Do you think we can finally talk about us?"

Nick exhaled, adding just the right amount of wistfulness to his voice.

"I miss you too, Maddie," he said, then, in a calculated, deliberate way. "And yes. I've realized there's no one for me but you."

"See you soon," and ended the call

That was too easy. Nick leaned back in his seat, watching the dull glow of the prison lights ahead. He'd give Maddie a few minutes to make the call, then he'd head inside.

* * *

After a moment, he stepped out of the car, adjusting the cuffs of his coat as he walked toward the front gate.

The guard on duty barely looked up. "Visiting hours are over. Come back in the morning."

Nick didn't hesitate. "Dr. Alden should have phoned. I'm Dr. O'Sullivan. Here to see Richard Hale."

The guard frowned, then checked the logbook. "Oh, yes. Sorry, Doctor. She just called about five minutes ago." He pushed the log forward. "I just need you to sign in."

Nick took the pen, scrawled his name, then handed it back without a word.

The guard motioned him forward for a pat down. Nick lifted his arms, expression impassive as the second guard frisked him, then nodded.

"All clear, you can follow me."

Nick walked in silence, his footsteps echoing against the linoleum floors. Another guard led him through the dimly lit corridors until they reached a secured treatment room.

The guard gestured toward a chair. "Have a seat. I'll be right back with the prisoner."

Nick sat down, fingers tapping lightly against his knee as he waited. A few minutes later, the door clanked open.

Richard Hale was escorted inside, shackles clinking against the floor. His

CHAPTER 18

grin was already in place as he was forced down into the chair across from Nick, the heavy restraints locking him in place.

The guard glanced at Nick. "I'll be right outside the door."

Nick gave a small nod, but his focus never left Richard

Richard leaned back in his chair, the metal cuffs clinking as he stretched his fingers. His smirk was slow and taunting, like he was savoring the moment.

"Dr. O'Sullivan, what do I owe you for this unexpected visit? You must have played some big cards if you're here this late."

Nick didn't sit. Didn't flinch. He simply met Richard's gaze, voice clipped, "Cut the theatrics, Richard."

Richard's smirk widened. "But Nick, it's all part of the game. Part of the plan."

Nick exhaled sharply, "I need your help, you sick fuck."

Richard tilted his head, amusement flickering in his dark eyes. "Oh, it's about her, isn't it? The doctor. She still won't give herself to you, will she?"

Nick's jaw tightened. "Richard, knock it off."

Richard clicked his tongue, shaking his head. "Tsk, tsk, Nicholas. I'm not the one seeking advice from a convicted killer."

Nick shot up from his chair, pacing. He hated this, hated that Richard could sit there, shackled to a chair, and still make him feel like he was the one trapped. "She called me a house," Nick finally said, voice tight. "She said Brian was her home... and I'm just a house."

Richard blinked once, slow and deliberate. Then, he let out a low, chilling chuckle. "What did you think, Nick?" He leaned forward as far as the chains would allow, eyes sharp. "That she'd fall into your arms after his death? That she'd look at you and forget she ever loved him?"

Nick's hands curled into fists and snapped, "I have been there for her. By her side, helping her raise our daughter."

Richard stilled. His expression flickered, something dark creeping beneath the surface. "Interesting, our daughter?" he repeated, his tone almost... amused. "I didn't realize it had gone to that level." He studied Nick, gaze sharp, scanning him like a puzzle he was piecing together. Then his grin returned, slower this time. "Ah. I see." Richard tilted his head, dragging the moment out, savoring it. "You're going in via the daughter, aren't you?" His smirk grew. "Better; she called you Daddy, didn't she?"

The color from Nick's face, drained.

The reaction was small, but Richard saw it. He laughed softly, shaking his head, "I hit a nerve." His voice was almost delighted. "Manipulation only gets you so far, my dear friend. Look where I am." He motioned to the shackles, the cold steel digging into his skin. "And yet... how is it that you're still on the outside? The truth always has a way of coming out, Nicky." He leaned in, voice dropping to something almost gentle, almost cruel. "Our dear doctor will figure it out; we both know it. The only difference? You just want her to figure it out after. He let out a slow, amused chuckle. " Ahh, interesting."

Nick dragged a hand through his hair. He was already losing his patience. "Richard, stop it. My secrets will stay in the past; she doesn't need to know. I just need to get her to forget about him."

Richard's smirk faded slightly, his dark eyes studying Nick like a puzzle he was figuring out in real time. "I told you," Richard said, shaking his head. "This was always going to be harder than you thought. But no, you didn't listen." He leaned back, chains clinking against the chair. "You can bury a body, but not a ghost, Nicky. He still has a reach beyond the grave."

Nick's hands curled into fists. His voice came out tighter, more controlled. "He's gone, Richard. Dead for nine years, and I am here alive and breathing. I've done everything for her. I've been there. I deserve this, especially after all I've done for her."

Richard tilted his head slightly, amusement flickering in his expression. "And what exactly have you done, Nick?"

Nick ignored him, his voice sharp. "I tried reasoning with her. I even told her she was in love with a ghost. That Brian had secrets, and he wasn't the man she thought he was."

Richard let out a low, breathy laugh. "Where did you think that would get you?" He studied Nick for a moment before shaking his head. "You really thought that would be enough? That she'd fall into your arms? Oh,

CHAPTER 18

Nick, you're delusional." The laugh grew, rolling into something louder, something borderline hysterical. "And I'm the one locked up in here? I'm the one they think is insane?" He let out another sharp laugh, leaning forward, his voice dropping to something colder. "You know what's funny, Nicky?" His eyes darkened. "I'm starting to think you're worse than me."

Nick shot Richard a dirty look.

Richard's grin widened. "You don't use your hands. No, you play mind games. You get inside people's heads, deep into their heads, and then you manipulate them, twisting and pushing them where you want them. It's no different from what I do. It's just," he let out a low, slow chuckle, "more *socially* acceptable."

Nick's temper snapped. "Stop it, just stop it, Richard." His voice must have carried because the guard cracked open the door.

"Everything okay in here?"

Nick inhaled through his nose, forcing control back into his voice. "Yes, sorry. He kept moving his leg when I was trying to examine his knee."

The guard hesitated, then nodded. "Alright, I'll be right outside."

The second the door closed, Richard leaned back in his chair, grinning. "Careful, Nicky," he warned, his voice laced with mock concern. "Or you'll end up in here with me." His smirk deepened. "They'll find out your secrets, and they'll find out about us."

Nick stilled. His entire demeanor shifted. Slowly, he walked up to Richard, his eyes dark, his voice deadly quiet. "No one will ever find out about us, Richard." He let out a small, amused laugh, shaking his head. "And if they did? No one would believe it."

Richard raised a brow, intrigued.

Nick leaned in slightly, his voice just above a whisper. "Do you know why, Richard? Because I'm an upstanding, reputable surgeon from a prestigious family." His voice dropped lower, sharper. "And you? Well, you're nothing but a cold blooded killer from the wrong side of the tracks."

Richard didn't react immediately. Then, slowly, a grin stretched across his face. "Oh, Nicky," he sighed, shaking his head like a disappointed teacher. "You really think that matters? You may have been born with a silver spoon, but let's be honest, you're just as rotten as I am. Tell me something," Richard murmured. "If your daddy hadn't kissed the DeLuca family's ass, would you be standing here right now? Or would you be in here, rotting away next to me? Better yet, how do you explain your time here visiting me? That isn't suspicious, Nicky?"

Nick's jaw tightened and mouthed, "I made my own way; no one owns me, and I got permission from the Prison Medical Director; no one will question that."

Richard's smirk widened as he watched Nick's grip tighten around the edge of the chair.

"Nicky, Nicky, Nicky..." he tsked, shaking his head in mock disappointment. "So many skeletons in that polished little closet of yours. Makes me wonder how long before Hanna starts rattling the wrong ones."

Nick's expression darkened, his breath slow and controlled. "I don't have any skeletons, Richard. Nothing to rattle. Nothing to find."

Richard chuckled, low and taunting. "No, Nick," he mused. "You may not have killed him yourself. But you wanted him dead, you wanted him out of the way, and when he died, I don't remember you grieving." He leaned forward as much as the shackles allowed, eyes locked onto Nick like he could see straight through him. "What was it you said to me after you met her? Hmm..." He tapped his fingers against the table, pretending to think. Then, his grin widened. "Oh, that's right. You wanted Brian's wife, you wanted Hanna, because you wanted her to look at you the way she looked at him." He tilted his head, his tone turning razor sharp. "But she never will, Nick; she knows, just like the rest of us, that you're nothing more than a piece of shit."

Nick's mask cracked, "Fuck you, Richard." His voice was venom. "She will be mine. I haven't waited this long to get nothing from her; she owes me." His voice dropped lower, nearly a growl. "And it's time for her to pay up."

Richard's smirk didn't waver; instead, he spat at Nick's feet.

Richard's eyes gleamed with amusement. "Not if I slip up in one of my sessions with her," he murmured, his voice like silk. "Not if I let something

CHAPTER 18

accidentally slip about someone close to her, someone she shouldn't trust. I bring up our visits and how she owes you."

Nick's rage boiled over. His hand flew out, gripping the front of Richard's jumpsuit, yanking him forward. The chains rattled violently against the chair. "Bastard." His voice was lethal. "I will have you fucking killed if you mess this up for me."

Richard's smile never faded. If anything, it widened. "Go for it," he whispered. "I'm not the one with everything to lose. I'm not out there pretending to play house with a woman still haunted by her dead husband, a man whose death just happened to work out a little too well for you."

Nick stared at him, breathing heavily. His grip tightened for just a second before he released him with a sharp shove.

He turned for the door, his movements stiff with barely contained fury.

As his hand gripped the handle, he looked at the guard. "Take this piece of shit back to his cell. I'm done with him."

The guard nodded, stepping inside.

Nick didn't look back.

But Richard did, and his smirk lingered, his eyes knowing. Because he knew he would never see Nick again.

* * *

Nick got out to his car, his hands hitting the steering wheel. That bastard, that sick bastard. He looked at the time, 9:56. He started the car; he didn't realize he was in there that long, and he headed over to Maddie's.

Nick pulled into the driveway, cutting the engine with a slow exhale. Maddie. He murmured her name, eyes lingering on the house, letting the past settle over him. His thoughts gently wandered to her; she had the kind of beauty that wasn't just seen but felt, the kind that stayed with a man long after she was gone. Sharp, refined, effortlessly striking. She carried herself with an air of quiet confidence, the kind that didn't demand attention but still held it with ease. She was warm in the way fire is controlled and contained but still capable of burning you if you got too close.

She would have been the perfect wife. If Hanna had never existed, maybe she would have been. He could have loved her. He did once love her, back in college, and maybe part of him still did. That could be the reason why he kept running back to her.

Her eyes were piercing, always seeing right inside of him. With her, he got lost, sometimes too lost, and the world never existed, but it wasn't enough; she didn't look at him like Hanna looked at Brian, and he wanted that.

Nick stepped out of his car, climbing the steep steps to her door. He knocked softly.

The door swung open, and there she was, just as he remembered. That was Maddie. God, she was striking. She had a way about her, a presence, an effortless grace that never felt forced. Her golden skin glowed even in the dim porch light, smooth and untouched by time. She had the kind of presence that made men want to stay, not just for a night, but for a lifetime.

She looked at him, her piercing blue eyes meeting his instantly, reading between the lines. There was intelligence there, sharp and unshaken, but there was warmth too, something softer that only a few got to see. She was control and ease wrapped into one, a woman who knew how to handle herself in a world that often tried to break people like her.

Nick had always admired that about her. He could have built a life with her. Maybe in another world, he would have, a world where Hanna didn't exist.

Maddie leaned against the door frame, arms crossed, a slow, knowing smile playing at her lips, "Nick."

Nick loved the way his name rolled off her tongue, like she was savoring the taste of it. She tilted her head, amusement flickering in her eyes. "That was quite the performance on the phone."

Nick played innocent. "What do you mean?"

Maddie let out a soft, knowing chuckle. "Oh, sweetheart," she whispered. She then stepped closer, her fingers tracing lightly down his tie, lingering just enough to make him feel it. "You only ever say things like that when you want something." Her blue eyes locked onto his, steady, unwavering,

CHAPTER 18

reading deep into him. "So, tell me, what is it this time?"

Nick grinned, unbothered. "Maybe I just missed you."

Maddie arched a perfectly sculpted brow. "And in what way?" She let the words linger, deliberate. Her fingers curled loosely around his tie, tugging slightly, just enough to test him. She whispered in his ear, her voice smooth as silk. "I did you a favor, Nick." Her lips hovered just over his skin. "I think you owe me one in return."

He didn't answer; he didn't need to. In one swift motion, he grabbed her by the waist, pulling her against him. His mouth crashed against hers, hard and demanding, meant to remind them both of what they could have been, teasing of what they could become. And for a moment, it almost felt real.

Maddie inhaled sharply against his lips, her body stiffening for half a second before melting into it, her fingers twisting tighter in his tie.

But just as quickly, Nick pulled away. A slow smirk curved his lips as he traced a finger along her jawline, bringing his nose to her nose, teasing another kiss. "I told you," he murmured, his breath warm against her skin. "I just missed you," he smiled at her. "Now, let's go inside and talk about us. About our future."

Maddie smiled something soft and knowing. And just like that, she led him inside.

His plan was coming together nicely; by tomorrow, he would make sure he and Maddie were the talk of the medical community, and he would make damn sure Hanna heard about it, one way or another.

Chapter 19

Morning light filtered through the curtains as Hanna lay still, eyes fixed on the ceiling, Nick's words looping through her mind like a broken record.

"Brian had skeletons, Hanna. Lots of skeletons. You had no clue who you married."

She squeezed her eyes shut, willing the words away.

Was it true? Had Brian hidden parts of his life from her? He was different after that last trip to Chicago. She'd brushed it off at the time, convinced herself she was imagining it. But now… now she wasn't so sure. Nick was manipulative, but was he lying?

Hanna exhaled and sat up, pushing the thoughts aside. She would ask Steve. He had always known more than he let on.

Right now, she just needed space. Four days away, four days of silence, no unexpected phone calls, no unannounced visitors.

Nick didn't, thank God, or else he would have shown up there, but he thought she was going to Vermont anyways. The cabin had always been theirs, her and Brian's place, their retreat from the world.

She zipped up the suitcase and glanced at the clock. Forty five minutes until Caitlyn needed to be up. Enough time for a shower and breakfast.

* * *

Once Caitlyn was off to school, Hanna started loading up the car. She packed her bags first, carefully arranging them in the back of her Subaru Forester, and then secured Caitlyn's booster seat.

CHAPTER 19

As she turned to grab the last bag, Mr. Donovan, her older neighbor, shuffled across the street. "Hanna," he greeted, voice warm but eyes sharp as ever.

"Oh, Mr. Donovan, how are you?" She asked, tucking a loose strand of hair behind her ear.

"Good, good," he said, nodding toward her car. "I see you're going away."

"Yeah, just for the weekend. Would you mind keeping an eye on things?"

"I always do, I always do, my dear." He shifted his weight. "Is your boyfriend going with you?"

Hanna frowned. "My boyfriend?"

"You know, the guy in the BMW. He's here all the time."

Nick. He wasn't here all the time, was he? She forced a neutral expression. "Oh... my friend Nick. No, he won't be."

Mr. Donovan hesitated, his expression darkening. "You should be careful, Hanna. I've seen men like him before." He looked over his shoulder, then back at her. "Men like that don't take no for an answer."

Her fingers clenched around the suitcase handle. A bad feeling, and she had one too. But she just smiled. "I will, Mr. Donovan. Say hello to Mrs. Donovan for me."

As he walked back across the street, a strange unease settled in her chest. What did he mean by all the time? Had Nick been coming around when she wasn't home?

* * *

Hanna finished loading the car and double checked the house. Lights off, everything off, and doors locked. She climbed into the driver's seat, turned the key, and headed toward Tony and Elaine's. Halfway there, her phone buzzed.

Nick, what now? She sighed, deciding to check it once she arrived.

She arrived, and as she was pulling into the DeLuca driveway, she spotted Elaine waiting outside.

Once the car was in park, she grabbed her phone and looked at the message.

Nick: *Have a good time in Vermont. Please give me a call before you leave, if possible. I have news, and I want you to hear it from me.*

A cold shiver ran down her back. She was so glad she didn't tell him where she was going; he might figure it out and show up.

Elaine pulled open the door. "You all set?"

"Yep. Looking forward to the peace."

Tony stumbled outside, rubbing his eyes. "You got everything you need?"

"I do. Thank you both again for watching Caitlyn."

Elaine smiled. "Anytime."

Tony grinned. "I'm gonna teach her about Harley's and see what bad influences I can lead her to, maybe give her some cigars and bourbon, and teach her some poker."

Elaine shot him a glare.

Hanna just shook her head. "I better get going," she said, stretching. "Want to get to the cabin before dark."

"Call us when you get there!" Tony called after her.

Elaine gave her a quick hug. "Be safe."

* * *

Hanna pulled out of the driveway, took a deep breath, and dialed Nick's number.

"Hanna, great of you to call."

"Hey, Nick, I got your message. My coverage is going to be spotty. What's up?"

"I just wanted to tell you to have a great trip and to apologize for what I said. I was having a bad day."

Right, she thought, "Nick. It's in the past."

"Good. Also, I know I've been pressuring you lately, and I'm sorry."

"No need to apologize, I get it."

"I also wanted to let you know I met someone."

Hanna's grip on the wheel tightened. *He met someone? What the hell was*

CHAPTER 19

that last night? "That's great, Nick."

"You might know her, Madeline Alden."

Hanna felt a little tension in her stomach, not with jealousy, not exactly, but with something *unsettled.* Maddie. She *loved* Maddie. She was smart, capable, and kind, and the perfect match for someone like Nick. Still, the words felt strange in her mouth. "Nick, that's amazing! I love Maddie. You two make a beautiful couple. Honestly? I think you're perfect together; you both have so much in common."

Nick swallowed. That was not what he wanted to hear, it was supposed to make her jealous. "Thanks, Hanna. I think so too." The lie was effortless.

"Have a safe trip."

"Thanks, Nick, I really am happy for you and Maddie. I wish I had thought of it; it definitely is a great match."

She hung up, and for a long moment, she just sat there. This changed everything, and deep down, she expected to feel *something, maybe* regret, sadness, or even loss. But all she felt was relief that maybe he would finally back off.

* * *

The forty-five minute drive to Saratoga Lake was easy, the roads winding through rolling hills and thick stretches of forest.

Hanna stopped at the market for groceries, grabbing enough to last a few days. As she pushed the cart to her car, a strange prickle ran down her spine, sharp, sudden, electric. For a second, she felt watched, and she turned, scanning the parking lot. Nothing, just cars, a few people unloading groceries, and a teenager smoking by the curb. Nothing out of place. But still, the feeling stayed, tightening at the base of her neck.

She loaded the bags quickly, slid into the driver's seat, and locked the doors before pulling out of the lot. It was nothing, just her mind playing tricks on her, except it didn't feel like nothing.

* * *

Nestled deep in Saratoga Springs, the cabin sat at the water's edge, hidden away on six acres of private land. A gravel driveway curved through dense pines, leading to the two-story timber retreat, its cedar siding glowing under the setting sun.

The wraparound porch offered two views: to the front, the vast lake stretched toward the horizon, its surface like glass, and behind the house, the forest loomed, deep and unyielding.

Hanna clicked the garage remote, pulling inside. She turned off the car and sat there for a moment, breathing. She was here and looking forward to four days of peace and quiet. She popped the trunk and began unloading her bags, heading up the porch steps. She hit the button to close the garage door and then opened the door leading in. The house looked just as she left it, with the same memories lingering. She needed this weekend and just hoped she wasn't already being followed.

* * *

Stepping inside, Hanna walked into the kitchen. To the right, the great room opened with vaulted ceilings supported by thick, exposed wooden beams. Floor to ceiling windows lined the lake facing wall, framing the water like a living painting.

A massive stone fireplace anchored the room, its hearth worn smooth from years of use. She and Brian had spent countless nights there, curled up in front of the fire, sharing stories and silence.

A leather sectional in a warm, aged brown sat centered around a reclaimed wood coffee table. A simple rug softened the floor beneath them. Built-in bookshelves lined one wall, filled with novels, psychology texts, and a few of Brian's records, ones she still couldn't let go of.

The kitchen carried a quiet elegance, modern but rustic, with dark granite counters and natural wood cabinets. A black marble island stood beneath soft pendant lights. The farmhouse sink looked out over the lake.

Through the sliding glass doors, a wooden staircase led from the back deck down to the dock. The air outside was cool and clean, touched with

CHAPTER 19

pine and lake water.

Hanna headed upstairs. The master suite was spacious and familiar. The bed faced another wall of windows, offering a stunning view of the lake. A stone fireplace and an oversized reading chair completed the room, along with a private balcony where she often sipped coffee in the early morning.

Down the hall, Caitlyn's bedroom sat ready, decorated in soft pastels. Across from it, Hanna's office overlooked the trees. Two guest rooms, one with a lake view and the other with a forest view, were simple and inviting.

The cabin felt too big, too empty without Caitlyn's laughter echoing off the walls. But Hanna needed this time. Space to think. Space to breathe. Space to grieve. So much happened the last month, Grandpa, Nick, Richard, and in a few days, Brian's anniversary, and that got her every time.

Nick's voice whispered through her mind again, insidious and unshakable. "You're in love with a ghost."

Her fingers curled into fists. How could he think they could just pretend yesterday never happened? How did he brush it off like it was nothing? Like, Brian was nothing?

She just kept thinking about his face and how defeated he looked when she said he was just a house; not everyone got a fairy tale.

Maybe a house didn't have to be a home. Nick never lied, and he was always there, even when she didn't call. Caitlyn adored him. Maybe that should be enough.

Maybe this year, she should stop waiting for a ghost to come back to life. Maybe it was time to bury Brian for good. But then again, if she did... would she ever forgive herself?

Chapter 20

Hanna woke to the sound of the soft rustling of trees outside her window; the wind had picked up. The sun had barely risen over the lake, and when Hanna rolled over to look out the window, she saw the leaves blowing through the air and the waves on the lake. She slowly climbed out of bed, the wooden floor cool beneath her bare feet, threw on her robe, and headed downstairs. She went through the motions without thinking, grinding the coffee beans, filling the kettle, and waiting as the rich, dark aroma filled the kitchen.

Mug in hand, she stepped onto the wraparound porch, sinking into one of the Adirondack chairs. The air was crisp, clean, and untouched; the lake was perfectly still except for the occasional ripple. Birds flitted between the trees, their soft morning chatter the only sound breaking the silence.

This was why she loved it here: no expectations and no voices pulling her in different directions. Just the open sky, the endless water, and time to think.

She sat there for a long time, slowly sipping her coffee, letting the warmth seep into her chest.

* * *

By mid-afternoon, she had finished breakfast, tidied up the cabin, and now sat curled up on the couch with a book, something she very rarely got to do. Something light, something easy, and hopefully interesting. But her eyes skimmed over the words without really absorbing them. Her thoughts kept

CHAPTER 20

drifting to Nick. The way he looked at her that night, the way his voice softened just before he left. The way her own voice had wavered.

She exhaled sharply and forced her focus back to the page. By the time she closed the book, the sun had shifted, sending long rays of light streaking through the trees. She needed to move, get out of her own head.

But even as she tried to clear her mind, Nick lingered at the edges of her thoughts. Would it really be so bad? But then again, he was with Maddie now; did she really need to consider anything more? She stopped at a small clearing where the trees opened up just enough to let the lake peek through.

She imagined a different version of her life. One where she didn't fight it, one where she let herself fall, and one where she let Brian go. Brian was everything. But Brian was gone.

She sighed, rubbing her hands over her arms as a cool breeze swept through the trees. Maybe she just needed to stop overthinking. Maybe a house didn't need to be a home. Maybe this was what moving on looked like, but then was she too late?

As the sun dipped behind the trees, casting long golden streaks over the lake, Hanna made her way back to the cabin. The afternoon had been peaceful, too peaceful, maybe. The kind of quiet that left too much space for thoughts she wasn't sure she was ready to face.

Stepping into the kitchen, she pulled a chicken breast from the fridge, seasoning it with a little salt, pepper, and garlic powder before tossing it into a pan. She chopped some broccoli and red bell peppers, letting them sauté in olive oil while the chicken cooked through. The scent filled the kitchen, warm, familiar, and grounding. Simple enough for dinner and leftovers for lunch tomorrow.

Once everything was plated, she poured herself a glass of water and grabbed her laptop from the counter. Work felt like a lifetime ago. She slid into her chair at the dining table, tucking one leg under herself as she opened her email.

Her inbox was full of final thesis submissions from her students, waiting to be reviewed. Normally, she loved this part: the deep dives into research, the dissection of arguments, and watching them come into their own as thinkers.

But tonight? Her focus wasn't there. She cut a piece of chicken and clicked over to her other folder, the one labeled "Richard." That was the real reason she brought her laptop. The FBI reports, the security footage, the last known financial transactions, and everything she had on Richard was compiled here.

She needed to find a pattern. Some small details everyone else missed. Something to get ahead of him. She took another bite of food, barely tasting it as she scrolled through bank statements, intercepted messages, and case notes. Every move Richard made had layers of false leads, dead ends, and distractions. But patterns existed, no matter how carefully someone tried to hide them, and Hanna was going to find his.

She reached for her fork again, eyes narrowing at a transaction flagged from three weeks ago.

That's new. She clicked the file open, her heart picking up speed. Dinner forgotten, she leaned in closer. Maybe, just maybe, she had something

* * *

The food on her plate had long since gone cold. Hanna barely noticed.

Her fingers flew over the keyboard, scrolling through case files, psychological reports, and old FBI notes. She wasn't looking for what Richard had done — she already knew that.

She was looking for what he was still capable of doing.

Even locked up since 1998, Richard had never truly been powerless. People like him never were.

She clicked through prison logs, visitor records, and monitored communication reports. Most of it was routine — legal counsel, required evaluations, and a handful of distant family members.

But then...

She was taken aback by two unexpected names: Henry Calloway, a professor of criminology at a small college in Boston — no legal connection, no family relation — and Dr. Nicholas O'Sullivan.

CHAPTER 20

The anger bubbled up before she could stop it.

Nick.

She blinked and read the name again. No. That couldn't be right.

She clicked on his visitor logs.

Eight visits. Spread over the last six years. The most recent was just a few weeks ago.

Why the hell had Nick been visiting Richard?

Her mind raced, trying to piece together what she had been missing.

Nick had never mentioned Richard. Never once talked about him. Yet he'd gone to see him. More than once.

What the hell was he doing?

This wasn't about Richard moving money or pulling strings. It was about his influence.

His ideas. His ability to infect people, even from behind bars.

And somehow, Nick had been caught up in it.

Nick had told her he wanted her. That he loved her. He said he would always protect her.

Yet he had been visiting Richard for six years, and she had never known.

He could have told her he was meeting with an inmate. That much wouldn't have been unusual.

But why hide it?

* * *

Hanna woke early the next day. She looked out the window, and the lake was calm, the surface smooth as glass.

She went down to the kitchen and started the coffee. She poured a cup and settled at the dining table, flipping open her laptop. Today, she needed a break from Richard; she had work to do.

Final thesis papers from her students filled her inbox, most of them third year criminal psychology students. She took a sip of coffee and clicked on the first submission.

"The Criminal Mind: Psychopathy vs. Sociopathy in Violent Offenders."

A classic study, but always relevant.

The student's argument was clear: sociopaths acted on impulse, their emotions driving them to violence, while psychopaths were cold and calculated, always pulling the strings of those around them without a second thought.

Hanna's grip tightened around her mug, the warmth pressing into her palms. That description fits Richard Hale a little too well. She swallowed hard, exhaling slowly before clicking to the next paper, hoping, just for a moment, that it would be about something else.

"The Power of Influence – How Notorious Criminals Shape Psychological Study."

Her eyebrows lifted. This one explored serial offenders who, even from prison, continued to shape criminal theory, inspire academic studies, and, in some cases… gain followers. She skimmed the introduction.

> *"Figures like Charles Manson, Ted Bundy, and Richard Hale have left an undeniable imprint on criminology, with their cases studied for decades after their convictions. But beyond the academic field, some criminals have been known to cultivate relationships with outsiders, even developing followings, or influencing students and researchers who get too close to their subjects..."*

Then there he was, Richard Hale. Her student had listed him by name. She scrolled down, searching for the cited sources.

Referenced Work: Interviews Conducted by Henry Calloway, Ph.D. Visitor summaries provided by Dr. David Meyers, crimi-

CHAPTER 20

nologist

Her fingers hovered over the keyboard, her mind racing, searching for any possible explanation that didn't lead where she knew it did. But there wasn't one. Nick had lied to her over and over again. He had a secret life, and yet, he accused Brian of having skeletons, and Nick had his own.

He had stood in her kitchen, held her hand, and told her he loved her while keeping this secret buried. She closed the laptop slowly, her pulse thudding in her ears. The cabin felt different now, too still and too quiet; maybe she had made a mistake coming out here.

The walls seemed to press in around her, and the lake outside, so peaceful hours ago, now stretched like a dark, endless void.

She shoved the chair back, grabbed the glass of water from the table, and stepped onto the porch.

What had Nick and Richard talked about? Why had Nick gone to see him, and always after an hour? How long had he been playing her? She took a slow sip of water, staring out at the lake, the surface reflecting the moon in scattered ripples.

Tomorrow was Brian's anniversary; it had been nine years, nine years since she lost him. Since her world had collapsed, and now, on the eve of that terrible day, she was finding out that the one person who had been there for her all these years was not who he seemed to be and had been lying to her all along.

She should go to sleep, but she already knew she wouldn't, with so much going through her mind. Instead, she turned, heading back inside. She left the laptop closed and climbed the stairs, moving through the darkened bedroom, but instead of crawling into bed, she went to the dresser. The small wooden box was right where she left it. She didn't know why she brought it, but she subconsciously put it in her suitcase, almost as if she brought Brian with her.

She hesitated, then slowly lifted the lid. Inside, nestled in the drawer, were her wedding ring and Brian's ring next to it. The man she had never been able to part with, nor would she ever. She ran her thumb over the smooth band, her vision blurring. It had been nine years. Tomorrow, she would wake up to the same day she had dreaded every year since the moment he was gone.

But this time? This time, it felt different because Brian was gone. And Nick… Nick had never really been who she thought he was. And for the first time in nine years, Hanna didn't just feel grief. She felt truly alone.

Chapter 21

With Hanna gone, Nick figured he might as well drop by Maddie's to keep the lie alive. He let out a breath as he reached the door. How much longer could he fake this?

He faked a smile and knocked. Maddie opened the door quickly, smiling like he was the best part of her day. "Nick!" The way she said his name made something twist in him, something soft and familiar. One day, Hanna would say it like that. He kissed Maddie, slow enough to keep her close. "Been thinking about you."

She brushed past him with a smile. "Dinner's ready."

Maddie's place looked like it belonged in a magazine, but not the flashy kind. Everything had its place. Right through the front door was a wide staircase, and just past that, a living room that stretched open with tall windows and a stone fireplace. It was bright but not cold. The leather couch actually looked comfortable, which surprised him a little.

The kitchen? It had one of those massive islands in the middle, the kind you only see in show homes. Dark cabinets lined the walls, and low lights hung over the counter like she'd measured their placement with a ruler. Between the kitchen and dining room was a tucked-away bar she called a butler's pantry, but really, it just looked like her wine hideout.

Upstairs, four meticulously designed bedrooms carry the same polished aesthetic. But the master suite? It was a statement. Deep blue walls. Big windows with shutters. The bathroom had a fancy shower and a soaking tub sunk into stone. Maddie's house wasn't just beautiful. It was controlled. Every piece, every placement, is intentional, just like her.

THE LIES WE WHISPER

She led him into the dining room, where the candles were already lit, the wine poured, and the smell of lamb lingered in the air. She walked him to his chair and motioned him to sit.

He did, watching as she lifted his glass. He took a sip, smiled, and caught the flavors right away: blackcurrant, violet, a little truffle, and that sharp finish of tobacco she always picked for him. He raised a brow. "You know me too well, Maddie. What year?"

Her lips curled slightly. "1996."

He stilled. They were in their second year of med school and had been together for three years. Back when things had been effortless. She had thought of everything tonight.

Maddie disappeared into the kitchen and returned with the main course: roasted lamb, crisp green beans, rosemary potatoes, and a fresh salad. She served him first, then herself, taking the seat beside him. Glass in hand, she lifted it slightly. "To better days ahead," she said, then smirked. "And for dessert."

Nick smirked back, playing along. "What's for dessert?"

"Your favorite, chocolate cream pie."

She still remembered. She always remembered.

Dinner was perfect, just like it always was; conversation flowed, and the wine worked its magic. Once the plates were cleared, Maddie returned with coffee and pie. She leaned back in her chair, watching him, her expression shifting, curious and calculating. Then, casually, "You need a favor, don't you?"

Nick exhaled, setting his glass down. "I need to see Richard Hale's file."

Maddie's eyes sharpened. "See?"

"Not the whole thing." He softened his tone. "You have your laptop, right? I just want to review a few things."

Maddie looked at him. "Nick, we've known each other a long time; you don't do small. What's this really about?"

He ran his fingers through his hair, deliberately letting himself look a little unraveled. "I just—" He shook his head. "I need to understand something. You said Richard fixates on people. He studies them, and I think he's doing

CHAPTER 21

it for Dr. Nowack, and I just want to make sure she's not getting in over her head. Steve and I," he hesitated, then leaned in slightly, voice lower and warmer, continuing the lie, "we just want to make sure she's not getting reeled in."

Maddie's lips pressed into a thin line. "So ask her."

"I did," Nick said smoothly. "She said it's fine and wouldn't tell me what he's been saying, Hippocratic oath and all, and that worries me, us."

Maddie hesitated, her fingers drumming lightly against the table. "I could lose my job over this, Nick."

His voice dropped, soft and coaxing. "I'd never let that happen, Maddie." He leaned in closer to her and began stroking her cheek, bringing his voice to a whisper. "Just one session, Maddie." He kissed her nose, lingering just long enough. "You and I both know Richard is dangerous. If he's trying to get into Hanna's head, I need to know before it's too late. I would hate to lose a good friend."

Maddie swallowed, looking away. Her gut told her to refuse, that something was off, but Nick had always been good at finding the right words. At making things sound reasonable.

Against her better judgment, she sighed. "Fine, let's finish here, and I can get you situated in the study. I just hope I am doing the right thing."

Nick smiled and lightly kissed her lips. "Thank you, Maddie; you're doing the right thing." He kissed her again and gently whispered, "Do you even know how much I love you?"

Maddie felt the weight of those words settle into her chest. Damn him; he always knew just what to say. And even when she wanted to push him away, she didn't.

Because, truth be told? It was hard not to fall when he looked at her like that.

Later, after dinner, she led him toward the study. Just outside the door, she hesitated. "So… are we saying the L word now?"

Nick gave a low laugh. "Maddie, I never stopped."

She pulled him in, arms wrapped around his waist. "I never stopped loving you either."

Once they were in the study, she opened her laptop and started typing in her login. The screen flickered to life.

Nick leaned over, his breath warm near her ear. "When I'm done, let's go sit by the fire. Just you and me. No more waiting."

She smiled at the screen. "I am looking forward to it." And she turned toward the door. Nick caught her wrist and pulled her back, his lips finding hers. As he pulled away, he whispered, "I'll miss you."

She smiled and just shook her head

Nick sat down and started going through the transcriptions from Hanna's interviews, thinking to himself. This is working out perfectly; she's still so naive. He continued searching and finally clicked on the file 'October', and started skimming through the transcripts of Hanna's sessions with Richard

"It's fascinating, really. People respond differently when faced with stress. Fear makes them predictable. But not you, Doctor." Richard said

"I'd say the same about you."

He chuckled. "You think you have me figured out?"

"I think you like to believe you're in control," she said, her tone neutral. "You steer conversations where you want them to go. You play the long game. But the truth is, Richard? You're still in here, in this room, shackled to that chair, while I'm the one who gets to walk away."

"What's wrong, Richard? You don't like it when someone else pulls the strings?"

"Clever, Doctor. I underestimated you."

"I know," she said smoothly. "That was your first mistake."

That is not what he was looking for, he thought to himself. Nick's thoughts drifted to Hanna. He liked what he was reading; she was so aggressive in the sessions, and he loved that about her, and he would love to see that side of her. Nick continued looking and selected another.

Richard responded. "It's funny, you know. It's fascinating to observe how individuals construct their own narratives. Sometimes, the truth is right in front of them, yet they choose not to acknowledge it.

CHAPTER 21

Hanna asked. "And what truth are we talking about?"

He smiled. "That's for you to decide."

"You want me to dig, Richard. To find something hidden in your words. But I don't chase ghosts."

"Maybe you should."

"Why, Richard?"

Richard's fingers idly tapped the metal armrest. "Because the past never stays buried, Doctor. Not really. And some other things? They're just waiting to be found."

"What things, Richard?"

Richard replied in a relaxed manner, "You see, Doctor, that's the problem. You keep looking for things: events, actions, and evidence. You want a puzzle with clean edges, a trail that makes sense. But that's not how the world works, is it? It's never about what. The what only exists because of the who. And who? That's where it gets interesting. You see them every day. You trust them. You need them. And they, well, they need you to stay exactly where you are, blissfully unaware. But if you start asking the wrong questions? If you start digging. You might not like what you find, Doctor. Because the moment you do, you'll realize they are not who you think they are."

"Richard, who is that you're talking about?"

"Look at that, Doctor, we are out of time. to be continued." Richard started laughing.

Nick didn't like what he read; he knew Richard was talking about him. Damn him. He scrolled back, scanning Richard's words again. Look outside the box; someone close to you doesn't want you to find out. Richard is going to ruin everything.

He scrolled back through the transcript. He had to get Hanna away from Richard and make sure she never put the pieces together. She was his; Brian had handled it. And Maddie? Well, that game is nearly finished. But then again, did he need to end things with Maddie? He thought, watching the cursor blink. She's easy, predictable, and accommodating. Maddie never fought but was always up for the challenge. Hanna wasn't; Hanna made things difficult. But Maddie? Maddie never said no. But maybe, yes, maybe he could have both.

He startled a little when her arms wrapped around his neck. She leaned in close, whispering, "So, did you find it?"

Nick turned, offering her a slow, effortless smile before brushing his lips against hers. "Yes."

She smiled, but something in his smile put her off. She placed her fingers on the laptop lid. She couldn't put her finger on it. That nagging feeling, that quiet itch at the back of her mind. Then Nick kissed her, and just like that, it was gone.

Nick's plans were falling into place. Maddie was easy, and Hanna, well, that was inevitable. He just had to decide how to play the final move.

Chapter 22

November 3, 2006

The dream felt so real, so much so that Hanna could still feel the warmth of his skin, the weight of his arm draped across her waist, and the slow, steady rise and fall of his chest.

It was Brian, and he was here, really here; she could see him, clear as day. They were tangled together in bed, the sheets a mess around them, the morning light barely filtering in through the curtains. He was looking at her, not just at her, but into her, that slow, lazy smile tugging at his lips. God, she missed that smile.

"We should have more," he murmured, while his fingers were tracing up her arm, his voice thick with sleep.

She blinked, confused. "More what?"

"More babies," he grinned, nudging his nose against hers. "We should fill this house up. Five bedrooms, Hanna. What the hell are we gonna do with five bedrooms if we don't fill them?"

She laughed softly, rolling her eyes. "Brian."

"I'm serious." He tucked a curl behind her ear, his thumb brushing her cheek. "Caitlyn needs brothers and sisters. Lots of them."

"You just want a football team or a little army," she said, smirking.

He grinned

"Brian!"

"What?" He looked at her again, with that look, the one that had always undone her. "I love you, Hanna. I love our life, and I want

more of it with you."

God, she wanted that too, but something was wrong. A flicker of doubt crept in, pressing against the edges of the dream.

Hanna's brows knitted together as she searched his face. He was too perfect; his dark brown eyes held that familiar warmth, almost too warm and too whole. There was no exhaustion or scars, and not a trace of the bruises from the accident. Not even the faintest shadow of pain. His smile was easy, untouched by the weight of everything that had happened.

But then, the sheets weren't warm anymore. Brian wasn't warm anymore, and a chill crept in. Hanna's breath hitched. No, no, Brian was still smiling, still looking at her with all the love in the world. But her body knew what her mind didn't want to accept.

This wasn't real.

The warmth drained from her face, her blue eyes darkened, and her lips parted, barely able to form words. Brian reached for her, his thumb brushing her cheek, but there was nothing there.

The air around her grew heavy and suffocating, and her hands trembled. Because if this wasn't real, if Brian wasn't real, then she would still be alone, and Brian was still gone. And then, the dream shattered like glass, leaving only cold air and an empty bed. Hanna jerked awake, her chest heaving, the warmth of Brian's touch evaporating like smoke.

Her fingers gripped the blankets like an anchor, her body trembling from something deeper than the cold. It was just a dream, just a dream, but it had felt *so real.* Her skin still burned where he had touched her, and her ears still rang with his voice.

"More babies, Hanna."

She clenched her jaw, forcing out a slow, shaky breath.

No babies and no Brian. She was alone, just like she had been for nine years.

Hanna sat down on the chair on the porch with her coffee. She put her coffee down and wrapped her arms around her knees, staring out at the lake. The wind had picked up, sending ripples across the surface, carrying

CHAPTER 22

the last of the autumn leaves across the water.

It was peaceful, cruelly so. Nine years ago, at this exact moment, she had still been his wife. Nine years ago, she had still woken up to the sound of his heartbeat. Nine years ago, she still believed they had forever. And now? Now all she had were memories and a dream that had torn her apart all over again. The dream bled into memory. Then that night, their last fight.

Hanna squeezed her eyes shut, but it was too late; the memory had her now, it had sunk its claws in, dragging her under.

Why was she doing this to herself?

* * *

November 3, 1997

Brian stood in the doorway, jacket half zipped, helmet tucked under his arm. His face was tight, exhaustion dragging at his features, the sharp angles of his jaw clenched like he was holding something back. His dark brown eyes, usually so full of fire and mischief, were different tonight; they were shadowed. almost guarded, as if he were here, but part of him was already somewhere else. Like he was carrying something too heavy to put down.

Rain clung to the edges of his jacket, the faint scent of leather and the cold night air trailing in with him. His hair was damp and unruly, the ends curling at his temples. He looked like he hadn't slept in days; whatever weight he was carrying had been dragging him down for longer than he'd ever admit. But it wasn't just exhaustion in his eyes; it was something else, something pulling him farther away. It was as if there was something he wouldn't let her see.

"Screw this, Hanna." *His voice was sharp.* "I'm not doing this tonight."

She had stood in the kitchen, arms crossed, nails digging into her skin. The sting behind her eyes burned hotter by the second. "Then when, Brian? When are you gonna stop lying to me?"

The grip on his helmet tightened, and something flickered across his expression, something raw, something unspoken, before he forced it down. But he buried it, just like always. "I'm not lying."

But she knew he was. She could see it in his face, especially in the way his eyes didn't quite meet hers and in the way his body was already half turned toward the door as if he was ready to run. Like he had already decided that leaving was easier than telling her the truth. "Bullshit," *he shouted. A muscle in his jaw twitched. His knuckles whitened around the helmet.* "I have to go."

That broke something inside her because he always left, and they never dealt with anything anymore. He wasn't the same since Chicago; he was hiding something. "You know what?" *Her voice had cracked.* "Go. You're already halfway out the door anyway."

He turned, and then the door slammed.

Then she heard the roar of his motorcycle, and just like that, he was gone. No goodbye, no see you later.

* * *

Hanna sat on their bed, gripping a framed photo of them from their wedding day. Her tears had dried, but a dull ache sat heavy in her chest. She pressed her forehead against the glass. What happened in Chicago? Why was she losing him? Did he not love her anymore? Was there someone else? She didn't know when exhaustion pulled her under, but the next thing she remembered

BANG. BANG. BANG. The pounding on the door sent a jolt through her entire body.

She sat up quickly, disoriented. Brian? She ran toward the door, wiping at her face. "Brian, what the—" *She froze. There were two officers at the door. She knew them: Rick and Michael.*

They were her friends, their friends. Their faces were tight, and they had a serious look on their faces; something was wrong.

Michael's voice was quiet, careful. "Hanna... you need to come with us."

The words didn't make sense. Nausea twisted in her gut. "What? Why?"

Rick exhaled, eyes dark. "It's Brian, Hanna; there was an accident." *The world blurred.* "He was hit tonight while out on his bike; it looks like two cars, the first one didn't stop, and the second one did. He's on his way to the hospital."

Two cars. The words didn't make sense. None of it made sense. Two cars? She turned, moving on instinct toward Caitlyn's room. Her hands shook as she lifted

CHAPTER 22

her sleeping daughter, holding her tight to her chest.

When she got back to the door, her grandparents were at the door; dispatch had called them to get them over to Hanna's. Irene took one look at her, at Rick and Michael behind her, and her expression shattered. "Go, we'll stay with Caitlyn; call with an update."

Hanna barely felt her grandmother's arms wrap around her.

* * *

The bright lights of the ER made her head spin.

She barely made it to the front desk before she heard her name.

"Hanna!" Matt Wheeler, Brian's good friend, rushed toward her.

She ran to him. "Where is he? Is he?"

Matt grabbed her shoulders, his grip firm. "He's alive."

Hanna choked on a breath. Alive.

Matt nodded. "He's banged up, but he's awake, which is a good sign. He's in x-ray right now. Hanna, he's lucky; he has a long road ahead of him."

She barely registered being led down the hall and barely processed the beeps of machines. And then, Brian. He looked awful. His face was swollen and bruised. His lip was split, dried blood crusted near his temple, and his right arm was in a sling.

But he smiled. "Hey, baby." His voice was hoarse and weak. "Told you I was tough."

Hanna's sob tore through her chest as she collapsed onto him, wrapping herself around his good side. "You scared the hell out of me."

Brian winced but chuckled, his fingers threading through her hair. "I know. I'm sorry."

"I don't care about the fight," she whispered into his shoulder. "I love you. I love you so much. I am so sorry."

He pressed a kiss to her hair. "I love you more than anything. And I promise, everything's gonna be okay."

And for the first time in weeks, she believed him. For the first time in weeks, she felt like maybe, just maybe, they would be okay.

***

A few hours later, the doctor came in, "Mrs. DeLuca, can you step out for a few minutes while we take a look at Mr. DeLuca? We just need to do a quick exam." Hanna nodded.

The nurse looked at her. "The coffee machine down the hall has good coffee, better than the cafeteria."

Hanna smiled and walked over to Brian. She leaned down, pressing her lips to his, lingering for just a second longer than usual. "I'll be right back."

Brian exhaled slowly as if he was memorizing the moment, memorizing every detail of her face. His fingers brushed the back of her hand, barely holding on, his thumb tracing her wrist in slow, lazy circles. "Take your time. I think they are going to have me tied up for a while. I love you, Hanna," he whispered. "Always remember that."

She smiled, pressing a kiss to his knuckles. "I love you, too."

And just as she pulled away, just as she turned to leave, he saw it. A single tear slid down his cheek.

She hesitated as if something inside of her was telling her not to go. She turned back and looked at him. But he smiled, small and tired. "Go get your coffee, baby."

She almost stayed, but she didn't; she headed to the vending machine, and the doctor closed the door.

***

She was standing at the vending machine, stirring sugar into the cup, when she heard "CODE BLUE."

Her heart sank, and an uneasiness ran through her. It didn't give room, but a bad feeling came over her. She ran, almost in slow motion, as the hallway blurred as her heart slammed against her ribs. She knew it was him; she could feel it, and then when she arrived at Brian's hospital room door, he saw them. Doctors and Nurses

The beeping of machines and the flat line, and then the doctor called, "Time of

CHAPTER 22

death."

"NO!" Hanna shoved forward, screaming, shaking her head. *No, no, this isn't happening; this is not happening*

She pushed past the nurse, barely hearing the frantic voices around her. The flat line cut through everything, shrill and unforgiving.

"No!" Then, all of a sudden, a pair of strong arms wrapped around her. Tony. He was saying something, but her world was already breaking apart. Her knees buckled, and the walls closed in. His voice was low, and he choked, hearing the pain in his voice. "Hanna, don't."

She fought against him, sobbing. "Brian! No, no, no!"

Her body started shaking. She looked at the doctor to bring him back. "Can someone bring him back?"

The pain was impossible; it was as if her insides were on fire, as if she was drowning; it was every nightmare she'd ever had all at once. The weight of reality crashed into her. It was as if someone sucked the air out of the room, and she couldn't breathe.

She and Tony went down. She collapsed into him, shaking, her body wrecked with sobs that had no sound. He was crying with her. Her world shattered in a split second. Brian was gone, and how would she live without him

* * *

Present Day 2006

Hanna's breath hitched as she pressed the heels of her palms against her eyes. She took a slow sip of coffee, staring at the water, trying to focus on something *other* than the ache in her chest. Every year she relived that moment, minute by minute.

The flashing lights, Michael and Rick standing there, faces pale, eyes dark. *"Hanna, it's Brian. He's been in an accident."*

The hospital had cold walls, sterile air, and her heartbeat in her ears. *"He's lucky to be alive,"* Matt Wheeler had told her.

She had seen him bruised and battered but awake. He had smiled at her. Told her he was okay. He told her he loved her.

She had kissed his knuckles. Whispered, *"I'm sorry about earlier."*
He had shaken his head. *"Don't be." "I love you, Hanna."*
She had left the room. For ten minutes, ten minutes. Long enough for the coffee to burn her tongue. Long enough for them to call it. She fought back the tears. It still hurts; it still feels like it just happened.

Hanna sat by the lake. Every year, she relived it. The lights, the sirens, and that moment, the moment it all changed for her.

"I miss you, you asshole," she whispered, wiping a tear.

She set her coffee down slowly.

Leaves rustled. Silence. Then a flicker, a shadow. She looked over; there was nothing there, the wind was starting to stir, a storm was coming in.

* * *

Back inside, she flipped through photo albums. Brian holding Caitlyn. Brian with his bike. Brian on the couch.

She thought to herself, *how do I let you go? For nine years I have held on to you. Do I really need to move on?*

The wind picked up, and then a crack of lightning.

Then she saw it: movement. Was it a person? She froze; it was a person, with broad shoulders and dark hair.

Her breath caught. "Brian..." No, not possible, she thought to herself. *he's dead*

Then again, she saw the figure. She whispered. "You came back."

She flung the door open, barefoot, rain pelting her, screaming, "Brian!"

She ran, heart pounding. "Brian, wait!"

She reached the lake. Mud clung to her toes. The lightning flashed across the sky.

She spun, searching. "Brian!"

Nothing.

Her knees hit the ground. "Please..."

Hanna looked around, unaware she was shivering from the cold rain, kneeling in a puddle. She looked down. *What am I doing? He's gone.*

CHAPTER 22

She heard someone call her name from toward the house. She looked up just as a flash of lightning hit; someone was on the porch. Someone was watching her.

The lightning cracked again, and she saw who it was more clearly; it was Steve Riley. *What was he doing there?* The panic in her chest loosened, just slightly.

* * *

Steve stood on the porch, rain soaking through his jacket, hair clinging to his forehead.

He didn't shout again. He didn't have to. The sight of Hanna, barefoot and crumpled in the mud, was enough to gut him. She looked so small out there, and something in his chest twisted hard.

He moved fast, but not frantically. He moved like a man who'd carried too many people through too many storms and never once let one fall.

His boots kicked up wet grass and mud, each step purposeful. Even drenched from the rain, he stayed steady, focused.

When he reached her, he didn't scold. He just looked at her, soaking wet and shaking, and said her name like it broke something in him.

"Hanna, are you out of your damn mind? It's freezing. For God's sake, are you trying to kill yourself?"

He stopped in front of her, his broad frame blocking out everything else. Like he was a wall. Like he could shield her from the storm.

She sat crouched on the ground, shaking. Water dripped from her hair. Her sweater clung to her skin, soaked and heavy with mud.

She opened her mouth, but nothing came out. All she could do was look down and cry into her hands.

Steve didn't wait for an answer. He picked her up and carried her to the cabin.

Her body trembled with every step. The adrenaline had crashed, leaving nothing but cold and exhaustion.

At the porch, he pulled the screen door open, carried her inside, and set her down on a kitchen chair.

* * *

The warmth hit her immediately, but it didn't stop the shaking.

Steve ran a hand through his soaked hair, water dripping onto the wooden floor. "What the hell was that, Hanna?"

She sat at the table, her arms wrapped around herself. She couldn't look at him; all she could do was cry. Finally, she swallowed hard. "I-I thought I saw him." Her voice barely made it past her lips.

Steve's expression shifted, something unreadable flashing across his face. He didn't ask who because *he* knew. Of course, he knew. Today wasn't just *any* day. Today was the day she lost Brian; that is why he was there; he knew how it hit her and that she shouldn't be alone.

Steve let out a slow breath, rubbing the back of his neck. "I went by your place earlier and then over to the DeLuca's. Tony and Elaine said you came up here." He walked to the living room, grabbed an afghan off the couch, and put it around her.

She gave a weak nod. "I just needed to be alone."

Steve snorted. "Yeah, well. Looks like that's working out great for you. You're lucky I got here when I did."

She huffed a weak, humorless laugh.

For a second, neither of them spoke. Just the sound of rain hammering against the roof, the distant rumble of thunder rolling through the valley.

Steve's gaze softened. "I get it, Hanna."

She blinked up at him.

"I do." He exhaled. "But Brian's gone." His voice was gentle but firm. "And standing out there in the storm isn't gonna bring him back."

Her throat tightened, and she turned away. "I know," she whispered, looking down, and knowing didn't make it hurt any less.

Steve hesitated, then stepped forward and gripped her shoulders.

"You're freezing, covered in mud, and soaking wet. Why don't you take a shower or a hot bath, then put on some dry clothes? I'm going to run out

CHAPTER 22

to my truck, grab my bag, take a shower, and then we can talk."

She didn't argue or try to fight him. She gave him a small nod and disappeared up the stairs to her room.

* * *

In the bathroom, she stripped off her wet clothes and stepped into the shower. The hot water spilled over her skin, warming her slowly, but it did nothing to quiet the thoughts racing through her mind.

She had seen him. She was certain of it.

Or maybe not. Maybe it was someone else. Maybe no one had been there at all.

She leaned against the wall, closing her eyes.

What was happening to her?

It could have been a tree, a trick of the light, or just her own imagination pulling shadows into shapes. But none of that changed how real it had felt.

She needed to calm down. She needed to stop letting fear take over.

Chapter 23

Steve stepped out of the room across the hall from Hanna's. Her door was still closed. He came down the stairs, cutting through the kitchen and out to the back porch, grabbed a few logs, and fed the fire back to life. Once the flames caught, he pulled out his phone and dialed.

"Steve?" Rachel's voice came through, laced with mild irritation. "I was expecting you hours ago. Are you still at Hanna's?"

His voice dropped low. "I went by her place. It was dark. I stopped at Tony and Elaine's; they said she came out to the cabin."

"You're at the cabin?" she echoed.

"Yeah," he said, rubbing the back of his neck. "Rach, I'm staying. It's not good. I found her outside in the rain, barefoot and confused. Delirious."

"You want me to come out?"

"No. I've got it," he said quickly. "Just wanted you to know I won't be home tonight."

"Is she okay?"

"I don't know." His jaw clenched. "When I got here, she didn't answer. I let myself in. The back door was open. I called for her." He hesitated. "Rach... it's bad."

Rachel was quiet then, "Maybe I should come, just in case. She's my best friend."

"Stay home," he said firmly. "It's pouring, and I don't need another thing to worry about."

There was another pause, but this one lasted longer. "I get it," she said finally, but the edge in her voice was unmistakable. "Just... keep me

CHAPTER 23

updated."

He ended the call and stared at Hanna's door. She wasn't getting better. If anything, she was slipping further. Every year, the grief dug in deeper. And if she didn't talk to someone soon, if she didn't let some of this out, she was never going to move forward.

***

She came downstairs minutes later, wrapped in clean clothes, her hair damp and clinging to her temples. Her eyes were hollow with exhaustion.

The fire crackled steadily. A bottle of whiskey sat on the table, two glasses beside it. Steve gave her a small, knowing smile and poured her a drink without asking.

She took it without a word.

The storm raged outside, but for the first time that day, she didn't feel entirely alone.

She sank into the couch, glancing at Steve. His damp blond hair was darker, his steel gray eyes sweeping the room, sharp, observant, always calculating. They weren't soft anymore. Time had carved them colder. Maybe even harder. And for the first time, she noticed the weight of years she hadn't been there for. He looked older.

He was still the man people called when everything went to hell.

Steve watched her, curled up with the whiskey glass, her face lit by the fire's glow. She looked small and fragile. And for the first time, he admitted what he hadn't wanted to: Brian had been wrong. Hanna wasn't okay. After what he saw tonight, maybe she never would be.

He took a slow sip of his drink, eyes drifting toward the rain streaked window. The storm had calmed, but the shadows outside lingered, thick and unmoving.

"I really thought I saw him," Hanna said suddenly, her voice barely above a whisper.

He didn't speak right away. Just looked at her. Pale and trembling, a haunted look in her face. Maybe she had seen something. Maybe it was grief playing tricks. But that twist in his gut, that wasn't grief.

That was instinct.

He set his glass down. "Hanna," he said gently, "are you sure you saw someone? Could it have just been the grief messing with your head?"

She shook her head, staring into the fire. "I swore I saw someone. At the edge of the woods. By the lake."

He turned toward the window, the storm still humming. "Maybe it was a deer or a bear?"

"No, Steve. I saw a person. I know I did."

He moved to the coffee table and sat across from her. "Who knew you were coming up here?"

Her brows furrowed. "Just Tony and Elaine. Why?"

It was exactly what he feared. They wouldn't have told anyone except him. Which meant if someone *had* been here, it wasn't an accident. Someone followed her.

He stood and crossed to the window. Trees shifted in the wind, but nothing moved beyond them. Still, that didn't mean they were alone.

"What's wrong?" Hanna asked softly.

He hesitated, then lied. "Nothing. Just watching the storm roll over the lake."

He didn't want to scare her. Not tonight. If she had seen someone, it sure as hell wasn't Brian.

But he also knew she wasn't imagining it.

He turned back, crossed the room, and sat beside her. He put his feet on the coffee table, then gently pulled her close. She leaned in without hesitation, resting her head on his shoulder.

He wrapped an arm around her, kissed the top of her head, and let his chin settle there.

"Hanna," he murmured, "you're going to be okay. I promise."

The fire crackled beside them. The storm whispered outside. And Steve held her tighter, hoping it was true, because if she didn't make it through this, he'd have failed her. And Brian.

Moments later, he said softly, "Han… With this weather, I'm going to stay

CHAPTER 23

here tonight. Is that okay?"

She nodded, half asleep already.

Steve reached for her glass and took it from her fingers. She stirred, eyes fluttering, and clutched his shirt as if she didn't want him to leave.

He kissed her head. "I'm not going anywhere."

Chapter 24

Tony, Elaine, and Caitlyn were sitting at the kitchen table, and a stack of UNO cards was lying in the center. All of a sudden, Caitlyn let out a loud giggle as she slapped down a Draw Four.

"Draw Four, Grandpa."

"You're killing me, kid," he said, drawing four cards.

Then the phone rang. Tony turned to look at the caller ID box on the counter: "Sal."

His smile faded, and he looked at the time. Sal never called this late without a reason. "Yeah?"

Sal's voice was low and firm. "Your father wants to see you now, Tony."

Tony straightened. "Is something wrong?"

"He will explain when you get here."

"When?"

"Now would be good."

He set the phone down slowly.

Elaine looked at him, trying to read his face.

Tony nodded. " I've got to run over to my dad's."

Her smile faded. "He's not pulling you back in, is he?"

Tony shook his head. "No."

She smiled, "Good."

With keys in hand, he bent down and kissed Elaine's cheek, then walked over to Caitlyn, ruffling her hair before pressing a kiss to her forehead. As he approached the door, he looked back at Elaine. Of all the days for his father to summon him, it had to be today. Nine years since they'd buried

CHAPTER 24

their son, and this was supposed to be a day of quiet remembrance, not business; he needed to be there for Elaine.

* * *

The ride over was silent, the radio playing low. Something was off. Vince didn't summon people without cause, and certainly not his own son, not anymore. That hadn't happened in years. Not since Tony had "stepped back."

He pulled up to the DeLuca gates, the iron crest catching in the headlights, a golden lion wrapped in ivy and fire. It served as the family's emblem. Old world. Ancient blood. As he rolled the window down, the guard waved him through without a word.

This place wasn't just a house. It was a fortress. Vince had built it brick by brick, not just with money, but with fear, reputation, and alliances inked in blood. Every stone whispered of power, of men who'd vanished, of debts that had been paid in silence.

Tony parked beside Carlo's car and got out. The front door opened the moment his feet hit the gravel.

* * *

David stood there, expression unreadable. Vince's right hand consignee to the old man's kingdom.

"Study," David said, voice low, the way men in their world always spoke when something had gone sideways.

Light from the chandelier glinted off the marble as Tony walked inside. He followed the smell of cigar smoke and tension down the hallway. The study door was open just a crack. Inside, Vince sat behind his desk, fingers drumming against the wood like a metronome of pressure. There was something in his eyes, not command, not certainty, but a flicker of something Tony hadn't seen in a long time.

Grief. Maybe even fear.

Carlo was already seated, arms crossed, jaw set.

Tony stepped in. "Papa, what's going on?"

He followed Carlo's gaze to the folder on the desk, not realizing that everything was about to change.

Vince rubbed his hands over his face and turned to Carlo before speaking in broken English. "I tried to stop it, but, eh, I was too late."

Tony frowned. "Stop what?"

Vince's voice dropped. "Sal did some a dig'in and found out it was Richard. He was behind the killings, and he wasn't working alone."

Carlo leaned forward. "Who else?"

Vince shook his head. "I don't know; it's not the Rossettis, Bianchis, or the Vitale. If they had, they would have asked for something."

Tony looked at Carlo. "So it wasn't one of ours."

Vince's gaze darkened. "This isn't about territory and control. They just want us gone."

Carlo started pacing. "So who was it?"

"Someone outside of the circle," Vince said. "Someone who knows us, our moves, our weak spots. Someone who knew exactly how we'd react."

Tony's fists clenched. "We've been looking in the wrong place."

Vince nodded. "This is personal."

Carlo's voice cracked. "Tony Jr, Joseph, Thomas, and Brian, were they targets?"

Vince looked away. "Yes, that is your task: find out who wanted those boys dead."

Tony froze. "Did you order the hits?"

Vince snapped. "On da boys, no. The woman, *eh,* you think I wanted to? You know what weakness means in this world. I didn't have a choice."

Tony stepped forward, voice rising. "They were innocent."

"So were yer sons," Vince said. "Richard Hale did the work; he justa went beyond what I asked him ta do. Someone else got to him."

Carlo glared. "Who?"

Vince's jaw tightened. "If I knew they'd be dead, but they're still out there." He pushed the file across the desk, toward Carlo. "It's yours now."

CHAPTER 24

Carlo, stunned, nodded his head.

"I built all of this for you, for them," Vince's voice cracked. "And now they're gone. I won't bury another one."

Tony stepped forward, eyes burning. "You're just walking away?"

Vince met his gaze. "Don't mistake grief for weakness; it's time I take a step back. Whoever did this isn't done."

Carlo grabbed the folder. "Neither are we. I will get them, Papa."

* * *

Nick walked through the ER's sliding doors; the fluorescent lights were too bright, and all he could smell was antiseptic. Coffee. Bleach. Routine.

But he wasn't okay.

He'd barely made it back in time. One more minute and he would've been late for his shift.

A nurse glanced up. "Dr. O'Sullivan? You good?"

He gave a tight smile. "Yeah. Long night."

In the lounge, he sat down and rubbed his face; he couldn't shake it. Not what he saw or knew.

A knock broke the silence.

"Dr. O'Sullivan?"

Renee popped her head in. "We need you in the ER. Consultation."

Nick stood. "Thanks."

She lingered. "How was the movie?"

He blinked. Then remembered. The excuse.

"Oh, the movie," he said quickly. "Not what I expected, but it was good."

Renee smiled. "Maybe we can go to a movie together sometime."

Nick's reply came fast, too rehearsed. "Actually, I just got engaged. The other night."

Her face flickered. "Oh. Congrats."

"Thanks."

As he walked past her, the smile dropped from his face.

He hadn't gone to a movie.

And what he saw? It changed everything.

Chapter 25

Steve Riley stepped onto the deck, the wood creaking beneath his boots. The storm had faded to a light drizzle, the air heavy with the damp scent of pine and smoke. The lake stretched out before him, glassy and still, clouds drifting across the pale moon.

He glanced back through the window. Hanna was curled up on the couch, finally asleep, her breathing even. She looked smaller than he remembered, like the weight she carried had hollowed her out in ways no amount of time could repair.

She wasn't okay. And deep down, he knew she never had been.

Steve exhaled and pulled out his phone. He hit dial.

The call connected on the second ring.

"Hello."

"Where are you?" he asked, keeping his tone low.

"Same place I said I'd be. What's going on?"

Steve scanned the tree line. That uneasy feeling in his gut still hadn't gone away. "Just checking in," he said quietly. "Nothing I can't handle."

He ended the call and lowered the phone, his fingers tightening around it for a moment before he slipped it back into his pocket.

* * *

Summer 1997

Brian looked at him, serious in a way Steve had rarely seen.

"I need you to make me a promise," Brian said.

Steve smirked. *"I'm not robbing a bank or killing anyone, so forget it."*
"Ass," Brian muttered. "I'm serious."
Steve straightened. "Alright, man. What is it?"
Brian stared into the fire, then met his gaze.
"Promise me... If anything ever happens, you'll take care of them. Hanna and Caitlyn. Like they were your own."
Steve stiffened. "What aren't you telling me?"
"Nothing. Just... in case."
When Steve hesitated, Brian pushed harder. "I don't trust anyone but you with them."
The firelight made him look older somehow. Worn down.
"I promise, man," Steve said without hesitation.
Brian was far from finished. His voice dropped to a rough whisper. "Raise Caitlyn like your own. I'm not saying marry Hanna but if it came down to it... I'd rather it be you than anyone else."
Steve swallowed hard. "I got you, man."
And he had meant it.

* * *

Present Day 2006

Steve walked back into the cabin, his mind made up. Hanna could not be alone, not with someone watching her. Nick could not protect her. And Steve was not sure he could either. But he had to try.

She would never accept the truth if he said it outright. She was too stubborn for that. So he needed a reason she would believe.

He glanced upstairs. Her place in Cohoes had extra rooms. That would be enough.

He stepped back onto the porch and called Rachel.

"Steve?" she answered, surprised.

"I need your help, Rach."

"You want me to come out there?"

"No. I need you to call Hanna. Pretend you're upset. Say you threw me

CHAPTER 25

out. Make it believable."

She was quiet for a moment too long. "What's going on with Hanna?"

"She thought she saw Brian. But I think she saw someone else. I don't know what kind of danger we're in yet."

"Then tell her that."

"She won't let me stay if I do."

Rachel sighed. "Fine. What do you want me to say?"

"Tell her we fought. Say you need space and don't want to explain it. Just that you asked me to leave, and I needed a place to go."

"Not hard to picture," she said flatly. "We have been fighting nonstop."

Steve rubbed his face. "Are we okay, Rach?"

She gave a short laugh. "You tell me."

He ended the call.

The storm had passed, but the ground was slick and the air still carried a sharp edge. Something felt off.

Steve walked along the porch, scanning the trees. He nearly turned back inside.

Nearly.

Then he saw them.

Footprints. Deep. Fresh. Not his. Not Hanna's.

He crouched and ran his fingers along the edge of one. It was too deep. The stride changed after a few steps, longer now. Whoever had been there started running.

He followed the tracks to the edge of the woods. His boots sank in the mud as his flashlight cut through the darkness. The trail ended at the road, where tire marks were carved into the soil.

Steve stood slowly, his shoulders tight. This was not in his head. Someone had been here.

He pulled out his phone.

"This is Director Riley. I need a forensic unit at Saratoga Lake for footprint and tire analysis. I am sending coordinates now."

* * *

Steve returned to the cabin just as Hanna stepped onto the porch. She blinked, surprised. "Did you go somewhere?"

He shook his head. "Just walked around the porch."

She gave him a look. "Why are you really here?"

He took a breath. "To check on you. And… ask for a favor."

She crossed her arms. "What kind of favor?"

"I need a place to crash. Rach and I are on, um, a break. I thought maybe I could stay with you for a bit." He gave a fake smile. "Maybe take occupancy in one of the spare rooms."

"You can stay here and have privacy."

"And miss the fun of you and Caitlyn? No way."

Hanna sighed. "Fine, you can stay. Just don't turn it into a frat house."

He grinned. "Wouldn't dream of it."

She smirked. "Caitlyn is going to love having you around."

"Think she'd be good at beer pong?" he teased.

She rolled her eyes, but the tension cracked just a little.

* * *

The next morning, Steve and Hanna sat on the porch, coffee cups in hand, watching the lake catch the first streaks of light. Mist drifted low over the surface, and the air carried the crisp scent of wet pine and earth. A breeze rolled in, and Hanna pulled the blanket tighter around her shoulders.

"It's beautiful here," Steve murmured, eyes fixed on the water.

Hanna nodded. "I love it. It's quiet. It gives me room to think."

Steve took a slow sip of his coffee, then glanced over. "Nick didn't come with you?"

She hesitated. "He doesn't know this place exists."

His brow lifted. "Seriously?"

"What?" she said, defensive. "We're just friends. I don't understand why everyone keeps thinking it's more."

Steve set his coffee down, fingers drumming once against the mug. "Rachel said things were" he lifted two fingers "progressing."

CHAPTER 25

Hanna let out a breath, rubbing her thumb against the rim of the cup. "He wants something I can't give him. He expects me to just—" She swallowed. "Forget about Brian. Like it's that easy."

Her voice cracked slightly, and her jaw tightened. "Then Caitlyn called him 'Daddy' the other night. Do you know what he did? He smiled. Like he earned it."

Steve stilled. His gut clenched. "What did you do?"

"I froze. I didn't expect it. But the fact that he didn't even try to correct her? That he just sat there like it was owed to him?" She shook her head. "It felt wrong."

"It was wrong," Steve said, his voice steady but low. "He should've corrected her."

He leaned back in his chair. "Grief hits everyone differently, Hanna. But it shouldn't blind you to what's real. Brian wouldn't want you stuck; he'd want you living. Loving. Finding peace."

She stared into her coffee. "It's not just about Brian."

Steve turned toward her. "Then what is it?"

"I don't know." She exhaled. "There's this… pressure in my chest. Like a warning. Like something's coming."

Steve studied her for a moment. "The gut never lies."

He smirked slightly. "Some of my best cases? Solved by instinct, not evidence."

Hanna let out a soft laugh, shaking her head. "You think that's supposed to make me feel better?"

Steve lifted his mug. "Just saying, your instincts have always been sharp. Maybe it's time you listened to them."

She didn't answer. Just stared at the lake, the golden light spilling across the water. Deep down, she knew he was right.

* * *

Later that morning, Hanna was in her room, folding the last of her clothes into her bag. She zipped it shut, then glanced around the cabin with a long, quiet breath. The solitude had been necessary, but it was time to go.

A knock sounded at the door before Steve poked his head in. "I'll see you tonight, Han."

"Roomie," she said with a smirk. "Caitlyn's going to love having you there."

"Party on."

She rolled her eyes. "Let me grab a spare key for you, just in case I'm not back in time. I have to stop at the prison; one of my inmates asked for a session. Then after I pick up Caitlyn, I'm going to check on my grandma."

"Got it. Do you mind if I hang around here a bit? I need to clear my head."

"Not at all. Just lock up when you leave."

"Will do. Thanks, Hanna."

As she slung her bag over her shoulder, she took another breath. Tuesday. At least the week would be short. But today she had work. And someone to face.

Someone she wasn't sure she trusted anymore.

Chapter 26

Hanna's phone buzzed against the console. She glanced down. *Rachel.*

She answered on the second ring, softening her voice. "Hey, Rach. You okay?"

"I'm fine." But Rachel's tone was clipped and too careful. "Do you have time to meet later? It's only Tuesday, and this week already sucks."

Hanna adjusted her grip on the wheel, reading between the lines. "I'm heading back from the cabin now. I could be there in thirty."

There was a pause. "Maybe a late lunch instead?" Rachel said, and this time her voice wavered.

"Sure." Hanna frowned. "Rach… What's going on?"

"I don't know," Rachel said slowly. "I think Steve's sleeping with someone from work."

The words hit like a slap. Hanna's heart stuttered. "What?"

"I saw him the other night. With a woman. He said it was nothing, but I know what I saw."

Hanna took a breath, trying to keep her voice steady. "Rachel, you know how he is. Work, secrets, and late nights, it's part of the job."

Rachel laughed, bitter and brittle. "Yeah? Then why hasn't he married me after eleven years? He says he doesn't believe in marriage, but maybe he just doesn't believe in it with me."

Silence stretched between them.

Hanna's thoughts drifted to the cabin. Steve showing up. The way he looked at her. The way he didn't even deny Rachel's suspicion when it came up.

"You're taking a break?" Hanna asked carefully.

Rachel's sigh crackled through the line. "Yeah. I told him I needed time. Then he says he wants to stay with *you*."

Of course he did.

"Rachel "

"It's fine," Rachel cut in, her voice flat. "We'll talk later."

"Okay," Hanna said quietly. But the line was already dead.

She exhaled, her hand tightening on the wheel. Is Steve sleeping with someone? That didn't sound like him. But *something* wasn't right. He was hiding something. Rachel might've been wrong about *who, but* not about *that.*

* * *

Steve returned to the house after Hanna had pulled out of the driveway. The air was crisp, still damp from the earlier rain. He took one last look around before stepping inside.

He pulled out his phone and dialed. Tony picked up on the third ring.

"Tony, it's Steve. I need the code for the security room. I want to review some footage."

"Everything okay?"

"Yeah, routine stuff. I'll let you know if it turns into something."

"Alright. The room code is 101726. It's in the blue book, Treasure Island. It's the fifth book on the top shelf."

"Got it. Thanks."

Steve ended the call and went to the bookshelf. Treasure Island, fifth book, top shelf. Just where Tony said.

He pulled it free, and with a faint click, the bookcase shifted, revealing a steel door.

He entered the code. The lock disengaged with a quiet beep.

Inside, the security room was cold and sterile. Monitors lined the walls, cycling through camera feeds inside, outside, in the woods, and in the driveway.

CHAPTER 26

He sat at the desk and pressed play. Hours of footage. Trees. Deer. The lake.

Then motion.

Steve rewound the footage and slowed the playback. A figure appeared on the front porch, standing still, watching Hanna through the window.

She was inside, making dinner, completely unaware that anyone was there.

He zoomed in, studying the grainy image. It was a man, and it definitely wasn't Brian.

Zooming again, he watched as the shadows shifted and faint features began to take shape.

Steve rewound further, back to the night Hanna first arrived. Her SUV pulled into the driveway. She stepped out.

In the trees behind her, just beyond the reach of the camera, something moved.

There was a man there, barely visible, positioned with precision. He clearly knew where the blind spots were.

Steve narrowed the frame and fast-forwarded through several nights. The man kept coming back. Sometimes he stood closer, but he was never caught clearly. He remained just outside the camera's grasp.

His hat was pulled low. His face stayed turned away. His movements were slow and deliberate.

Steve tightened his grip on the edge of the desk.

He went back again, reviewing the footage carefully. The figure never tripped a single sensor, but he always appeared when Hanna was home.

Finally, Steve caught something. The man tilted his head, just slightly.

He zoomed in with care. A jawline emerged. Then the curve of a nose, a partial glimpse of a mouth.

And then he saw it, beneath the ear, a faint scar.

It struck something in Steve's memory. He knew that scar. He just couldn't place it yet.

His fingers hovered over his phone, but he didn't make the call.

Not yet.

Whoever this man was, he knew Hanna. And Steve was going to uncover exactly who he was.

Chapter 27

Hanna pulled into the parking lot, spotting Rachel's car already there.

She sighed, gripping the steering wheel for a second before finally stepping out.

The scent of fresh coffee and toasted bread lingered in the air, mixing with background conversation. A server walked past carrying a tray of steaming soup, the clink of silverware filling the quiet spaces between words.

Hanna spotted Rachel immediately, tucked into a booth near the window, and absently stirred her iced tea.

Even in the dim light, Rachel stood out.

Her electric blue eyes, piercing and sharp, flicked up as Hanna approached, the color almost unnatural against her sun-kissed skin. Her long, chestnut brown hair, usually worn loose, was pulled into a messy ponytail, a few waves slipping free around her face.

She was dressed casually but effortlessly put together in a fitted sweater, leggings, and white sneakers. The kind of outfit that said she'd come straight from work, where comfort mattered more than fashion.

There was a tiredness around her eyes.

Hanna slid into the seat across from her. "How bad was your day? Scale from 'mildly irritating' to 'pass the tequila'?"

Rachel smirked. "Somewhere around 'why didn't I go into vet medicine instead?'"

Hanna snorted. "Humans are the worst."

Rachel sighed. "Seriously. A guy came in convinced he had early-onset Alzheimer's. Turns out he just wasn't drinking enough water."

Hanna raised a brow. "And you didn't strangle him?"

Rachel leaned back. "Only because I'd lose my license."

A waitress appeared, setting down two glasses of water. "You ladies ready to order?"

Rachel barely glanced at the menu. "Turkey club, no mayo."

Hanna smirked. "Make it two."

Rachel arched a brow. "Weren't you gonna get a salad?"

Hanna shrugged. "Long week."

Rachel let out a dramatic sigh. "Finally. She's human."

The waitress jotted down their orders and walked off.

Hanna took a sip of water. "So, what's new? Besides diagnosing dehydration as a brain disease?"

Rachel exhaled, tracing a fingertip over the condensation on her glass. "Not much."

Too quick and too flat. She was waiting for the right moment. Hanna leaned forward. "Rachel."

Rachel looked up, hesitated, then finally sighed, setting her glass down. The lightness in her face faded. Her fingers drummed against the table once, twice, before going still. Then she looked up, her expression serious. "I'm worried, Han."

Hanna stilled. She didn't have to ask who he was. Steve.

Rachel hesitated, then finally spoke. "He's hiding something."

Hanna frowned. "What do you mean?"

Rachel swallowed. "I saw him the other night. With a woman." Her voice was quieter now. "And it wasn't the first time."

Hanna's stomach tightened. "Rachel, he works with women."

Rachel shook her head. "This one is different." She pushed her glass aside. "The way he looked at her... his body language. He was relaxed but also tense. It was like he wanted to be there, but also like he was waiting for something."

Hanna studied her. "Are you sure she's not someone from work?"

Rachel let out a humorless laugh. "Hanna, I've met all of them."

Hanna exhaled. "Did you ask him?"

CHAPTER 27

Rachel looked away, jaw tight. "Kind of. We argued about it."

Hanna let her talk.

Rachel let out a sharp breath. "I wouldn't be so mad if he just married me." Her voice wavered. "I'm the only thirty-three-year-old I know who isn't married. We've been together almost twelve years, Han. Twelve." Her voice dropped. "It's not like I'm asking for a big wedding. Just a justice of the peace, something small." She swallowed hard. "And you know what he says? Why fix what's not broken? We don't need a piece of paper."

Hanna sat there, unsure of what to say.

Rachel laughed, but it was hollow. "I'll never have children. I can't until we're married. We fight about it all the time." She met Hanna's gaze. "It's almost like I'm not good enough."

Before Hanna could respond, the waitress arrived, setting their plates down.

Rachel quickly wiped her cheek, forcing a small, tight smile.

Hanna looked up. "Thank you."

The waitress nodded. "Enjoy."

Rachel picked up her fork, pushing her food around the plate.

Hanna knew she should say something. But for once, she didn't know what.

Rachel wiped at the corner of her eye, quickly composing herself. Then, she looked straight at Hanna. "I told him he had to get out."

Hanna had a feeling of dread; she already knew what was coming next.

Rachel sighed, shaking her head. "I know he's staying with you." She met Hanna's gaze, her voice softer now but edged with frustration. "Maybe you can get it out of him."

Hanna hesitated, then nodded. "That, I will."

Rachel exhaled, nodding once before picking up her sandwich. "How was the cabin? And what's going on with Nick?" Hanna asked, mid-reach for her water.

Rachel's eyes narrowed. "Oh, that's a face."

Hanna sighed. "It's… complicated."

Rachel smirked. "It's always complicated with you."

Hanna huffed a quiet laugh. "No, this is worse."

Rachel tilted her head, intrigued. "Worse than Nick proposing?"

Hanna didn't know how to explain it. But holding it in wouldn't help. So she just dove in. The fight. How Nick kept pushing, acting like she was supposed to just move on, like Brian had never existed, and how he was seeing Maddie. Caitlyn calling him Daddy. The way it had knocked the air out of her left her frozen, unable to correct it. And the way Nick had just grinned like it was his right, and the pressure.

Rachel sat there, listening, expression unreadable as Hanna picked at the edge of her napkin.

"He doesn't say it outright," Hanna murmured, "but I can feel it, like he's waiting, expecting something I don't think I can give him."

Rachel exhaled sharply, shaking her head. "You shouldn't feel like you owe him anything, Han."

Hanna knew that. But it wasn't that simple.

Rachel leaned forward. "And Caitlyn, what did you say to her?"

Hanna swallowed. "I didn't."

Rachel's brow furrowed.

"I couldn't." And that was the worst part. Caitlyn hadn't meant anything by it, and maybe that was what scared Hanna the most. Nick was there, her constant, and now, she couldn't help but wonder, had Caitlyn already started to forget?

Rachel's voice was softer now. "Do you even want this with him?"

Hanna hesitated. She stared at the condensation on her glass, tracing the rim with her finger before finally speaking. "Rachel... I don't love him. Not in the way he loves me."

Rachel's expression didn't change, but she sat up straighter, just listening, hanging on to the words Hanna was saying.

Hanna exhaled. "He's a great guy. He's safe." She shook her head, almost to herself. "Before I left for the cabin, we had a fight. I thought he was being sincere, but..."

Rachel leaned in. "But what, Han?"

Hanna swallowed. "I told him he was a house... and Brian was my home."

CHAPTER 27

Rachel's lips parted slightly, but she didn't speak right away. Jesus, Han." She sat back up, exhaling. "That's, that's everything, right there."

Hanna felt her stomach tighten. But what if that wasn't enough? Her voice was quieter now, like she was speaking the thought out loud for the first time. "But, Rachel... what if a house is okay? I had my once in a lifetime. He's good with Caitlyn. I could settle. I could learn to love him."

Rachel's expression darkened. "Learn to love him? Seriously, Han?" She shook her head. "Don't settle."

Hanna knew Rachel was right. But a small voice in the back of her mind whispered, Would it really be so bad? Would it be worse than being alone?

The rest of lunch was quiet, the weight of the conversation lingering between them.

Once the bill was paid, they made small talk, Caitlyn, about what their grandmothers were up to these days. Safe topics, easy distractions.

But as Hanna climbed into her car, gripping the wheel a little tighter than usual, she couldn't shake the question still echoing in her head.

Would it be so bad to settle?

Chapter 28

The late afternoon sun hung low, bleeding gold across the razor wire lining the perimeter. The prison loomed ahead, a hulking mass of concrete and steel, its shadow stretching long across the cracked pavement.

Hanna cut the engine and sat for a moment, looking at the prison. One session. One hour with Richard Hale. This was another opportunity to learn something valuable from a man who had spent years perfecting the art of giving nothing away.

She stepped out of the car and moved toward the gates.

At the first checkpoint, she swiped her badge. The low buzz of the gate unlocking barely registered through the weight pressing against her chest. The usual procedures blurred together: ID scan, metal detector, and the slow walk through sterile corridors.

Michael waited outside the psych unit, arms crossed.

"You didn't have to come in on your vacation," he said. "You could've pushed him to tomorrow."

Hanna didn't hesitate. "It's fine. Obviously, something's on his mind."

Michael studied her, searching for doubt or hesitation. Finally, he smiled wryly. "Bet you're glad you became a criminal psychologist."

She returned the smile, dry and sarcastic. "Living the dream."

He let out a breath. "Alright. I'll be in the observation room."

She adjusted the strap of her bag. "Let's do this."

Hanna entered the interview room to find Richard Hale already seated. The same steel chairs and the same damn smirk were waiting for her.

She moved deliberately, setting her notepad on the table without opening

CHAPTER 28

it. Control was everything. If she lost it, if she showed even a flicker of weakness, the session was over. Richard would retreat, and she'd have to start from the beginning.

Richard tilted his head. "It's been a few weeks," he said, his voice smooth but laced with something uglier. "I was starting to think you'd gotten scared. I'm thrilled you could squeeze me in."

Hanna's tone stayed even. "I had personal matters to attend to."

Richard drummed his fingers against the table. "Tell me, Doctor… did you think about me while you were away?"

Her stomach tightened, but she stayed neutral. "You think too highly of yourself."

He chuckled. "No, I think it's precisely the right amount."

She leaned in slightly, her voice clinical. "Let's pick up where we left off."

Richard's eyes roamed over her, clinical and dissecting. Then he leaned in, voice dropping. "Want a little foreplay first, Doc? Or should I just drive it in deep?" His smile curled, slow and mocking. "You look like the type who likes it rough."

Hanna didn't flinch. Her voice stayed level. "Do you want to continue, Richard, or should I document that you're too emotionally unstable for this session to proceed?"

A flicker of something dark crossed his face, but it passed. "Doctor, you're turning me on, trying so hard to exert control." He shifted. "Fine. Izzy, then?"

Hanna nodded. "You said she saw you."

Richard's fingers twitched. "Izzy understood me," he murmured. "The way you do. You remind me of her."

Hanna tightened her grip on her pen. "That's not an answer."

"No. But it's the truth."

Silence stretched.

"Izzy died the same night as Tony Jr."

Richard tapped the table. "She was collateral. Wrong place, wrong time."

"That's not what you said before."

"No. It's not."

"You said Tony Jr. screamed."

His smirk faltered. "You've been thinking about this a lot, haven't you?"

Hanna's voice stayed cold. "Tell me why he screamed."

Richard leaned in, whispering. "Are you jealous, Doctor? You want me to make you scream? I could. Right here. Right now."

She let the silence stretch. "Richard, you can either continue this session appropriately, or I'll document that you were too emotionally unstable to proceed today."

Richard watched her.

"The choice is yours. If you want to continue, tell me why he screamed."

His smirk slipped. Anger cracked through. "What do you think, Doctor? Give me your theory."

Hanna flipped open her notepad. "I'm not here to theorize, Richard. I'm here to listen."

"You want me to take you through it? All of it?"

She waited. Then: "But what if the crash didn't kill him? Then we have to ask: what did? Or more importantly… who did?"

"I didn't have a choice," he said. "I loved her. Tony Jr. was a prick. I stood there when she left the room. Watched her get into that car. The prick needed to die."

"What did you do, Richard?"

"I grabbed my knife. Made my way to his car. Slit his throat. Cut it deeply. When I kicked his body, his head came off."

Hanna didn't react.

"He fell. His foot struck the gas pedal. Her scream was the only sound I heard. There was blood everywhere."

"You cared for her. But she was with Tony Jr., and he wouldn't let her go. So you thought killing him would give you her."

His fingers curled against the table.

"You didn't plan the aftermath. When his body dropped, the car lurched. You didn't expect that."

Behind the glass, Michael whispered, "Holy shit," and checked the recorder.

CHAPTER 28

Richard's voice lowered. "How does it feel, Doctor? To sit across from the man who killed your brother-in-law?"

Hanna's breath stayed steady. "It feels like you're finally telling the truth. So you admit to killing him, Richard?"

He smiled. "Is that what you want? You want me to tell you how it felt? Is my confession turning you on?"

Revulsion flickered. She buried it. "Last warning, Richard."

She wrote, *The patient continues to confuse domination with intimacy.*

"Testy today, Doc?"

"I appreciate your acknowledgment of what you did."

His composure cracked. Rage bled through. "Bitch, you're damn right I killed him. He deserved to die. He was DeLuca scum. It cost me the woman I loved, but it was worth it. Even knowing she was carrying my child."

Her heart twisted, but her face stayed blank.

He leaned in. "She's better off dead than being part of that family. And you'll see that too, Hanna. It was the best kill I ever did. Worth it. And baby, I'd do it again."

"That's enough for today, Richard." She stood and headed toward the door, motioning to the corrections officer.

He smiled. "You can count on it."

Chapter 29

Hanna dropped into the chair across from Michael's desk, exhaling sharply. Her pulse was still trying to catch up with what had just happened.

She had done it; she had unraveled Richard Hale. And in doing so, she had uncovered the truth about Tony Jr.'s death.

Her fingers pressed into her temples. "I think I need a drink."

Michael let out a low chuckle, already moving toward the cabinet behind his desk. "Hanna, I should never have doubted you."

She lifted her head just as he pulled out a bottle of whiskey and two glasses.

Her brow arched.

Michael smirked. "For times like these."

He poured a generous amount into both glasses, sliding one across the desk toward her.

Hanna took it without hesitation, curling her fingers around the cool glass.

For a moment, neither of them spoke. The weight of what had just happened still settled heavily in the room.

Then Michael exhaled. "We need to contact the authorities. He just confessed to murder."

Hanna nodded slowly, staring into the amber liquid. Her breath had finally evened out, the adrenaline still lingering but no longer suffocating her.

"I honestly didn't think it would work," she admitted.

Michael leaned back, lifting his glass. "Yeah, well." He took a slow sip.

CHAPTER 29

"You're a terrifyingly good liar when you need to be."

Hanna huffed out a quiet laugh, shaking her head.

She wasn't sure if that was a compliment or a warning. But it didn't matter. Richard Hale had just handed them the truth. Now it was time to make damn sure he never walked free again.

Michael made the call. Local agents relayed it up the chain. Hanna, knowing it was going to be a long night, called Elaine. Caitlyn would stay with them again, and she'd come by shortly. She also asked to speak with Tony.

* * *

An hour later, the door opened.

A woman walked in who didn't just enter; she took command.

She was dressed in fitted black slacks, a dark blazer, and a simple button down. Her badge clipped to her belt, a holster just visible beneath her jacket.

She moved with sharp precision. Practical. Efficient.

Her auburn hair framed a face carved in composure. But it was the eyes that caught Hanna. Green. Piercing. Watching everything.

"Naomi Walker. Senior Agent, FBI." Her voice was smooth and even. No wasted syllables.

Michael shook her hand first. "Agent Walker."

Then she turned to Hanna. Her grip was firm.

"Hell of a thing you did today, Dr. Nowack."

Hanna exhaled. "It's not over yet."

Naomi gave a faint nod. "No. But it will be."

She took the seat across from them. "Walk me through it."

Hanna pushed through the exhaustion. "Hale's smart. Always controlled and doesn't slip."

"But today he did," Naomi said.

"I baited him. Used what I knew about Izzy and Tony Jr. It worked."

Michael nodded. "And it was true."

Naomi turned to him. "I want the full recording."

Michael gestured. "Already queued."

Naomi flipped open a notebook. "His exact words."

Hanna repeated them, her voice steady: "How does it feel to be sitting across from the man who killed your brother-in-law?"

Michael shook his head. "Jesus."

Naomi wrote it down. Her posture sharpened. "This isn't just a confession. It's a taunt."

"He wanted me to know," Hanna said quietly.

Naomi nodded. "And he wanted you to react. But you didn't."

"No."

"That's why he respects you."

Hanna blinked. "Excuse me?"

"You don't let him win. That's why he keeps playing."

Michael crossed his arms. "We need to lock this down."

Naomi raised a hand. "We will. But carefully."

"Meaning?" Hanna asked.

"He confessed to a cold case. That's leverage. But if we rush it, what if he recants?"

Michael frowned. "He won't."

"But we need airtight evidence," Naomi said. "I want to know if there are others."

Hanna's breath caught. "What do we do?"

"We don't just prove he killed Tony Jr." Naomi closed her notebook. "We take down the whole damn network that let him get away with it."

*　*　*

Afterward, Hanna walked with Naomi outside.

"Ever consider the FBI?" Naomi asked. "You'd be a strong addition to CSI."

Hanna gave a tired laugh. "Tempting. But I like staying behind the glass."

Naomi smirked. "You've got the instincts. Most would've cracked under

CHAPTER 29

pressure."

Hanna looked back at the prison. "I've had enough monsters for one lifetime."

Naomi tilted her head. "Doesn't mean they're done with you."

The words settled uncomfortably.

Naomi handed her a card. "In case you change your mind."

Hanna ran her thumb across the embossed print. Naomi Walker, FBI.

"If I ever get tired of therapy and whiskey..."

Naomi chuckled. "Some of us make a career out of both."

She walked off. Michael joined her.

"Are you going to think about it?"

Hanna shook her head. "No." Then, softer: "Maybe."

Michael smirked. "Knew it; it's a good opportunity, Hanna."

As they walked toward the lot, Hanna felt the weight of the card in her pocket.

And for the first time in a long time, she wondered if she'd been fighting the wrong war all along.

Chapter 30

The gravel crunched beneath her tires as the DeLuca house came into view, warm light spilling from the windows like a welcome she wasn't sure she deserved. Before she could put the car in park, the porch light snapped on. The front door creaked open, and Tony stepped out, his silhouette framed in gold.

Hanna barely had the car in park before she was climbing out.

"Everything okay?" Tony's voice was steady, but his brows were knit together in concern.

She swallowed. "Yeah. I have something to tell you before it hits the news."

Tony didn't hesitate. "Come inside."

He led her in, the warmth of the house feeling both familiar and heavy.

Elaine was in the kitchen, drying her hands on a dish towel, when she spotted them.

"Hanna," she said gently. "We just put Caitlyn down. I can get her packed up, or she can stay here."

Hanna exhaled. "Let's keep her here. But… can we talk?"

Elaine's gaze flicked to Tony. "Let's go sit in the living room."

Nothing had changed in this room. Same white paint. The same framed photos line the shelves. Brian's smiling face frozen in time. Tony Jr. still in his graduation cap.

Hanna drew a breath, trying to calm the thrum in her chest.

The house hadn't moved on. And now, it never would.

Tony sat on the edge of the couch. Elaine lowered herself onto the armrest

CHAPTER 30

beside him, her hand resting lightly on his shoulder.

"Okay, Hanna." Tony's voice was quieter now. "What's going on?"

She hesitated. She had played this moment in her head a hundred times on the drive over, but now, sitting in front of them, there was no clean way to say it. She wet her lips.

"I thought this would be easier." A humorless laugh escaped. "Maybe I'm in over my head."

Elaine shook her head. "Just say it, Hanna."

Rip the band-aid.

Hanna exhaled. "Richard Hale confessed to killing Tony Jr. tonight." The words came out fast. Too fast.

Tony froze, not in shock, but in stillness.

Elaine turned to him, her voice barely a whisper. "He… confessed?"

Hanna nodded. "Yes. And…" She forced herself to continue. "They think there might be others."

Elaine's hand flew to her mouth.

Tony stood.

Hanna's eyes followed him. "Tony "

He ran a hand down his face and turned away for a moment, like he needed to lock something down. He couldn't slip. Couldn't let them see the truth.

When he turned back, his expression was neutral. Controlled. "He confessed to you?"

His voice held no edge. No cracks.

Something about it felt… wrong.

Still, Hanna nodded. "Yes. But that's all I can say. Doctor-patient confidentiality."

Elaine let out a sound between a laugh and a sob. "Jesus Christ, Hanna."

Tony didn't move.

Elaine wiped at her eyes. Tony sat there, staring at nothing. It wasn't grief. Not the way it should've been. It was something else, heavier. And then finally, he exhaled.

"I won't say anything," he said, voice steady. "But I'm not so sure I like you being in the same room with that man."

"I'm okay," Hanna said softly. "He's shackled. It's a controlled environment."

Tony shook his head. "Monsters find a way, Hanna."

Elaine exhaled sharply. "I've never understood how you could do this. Sit across from them like they're people."

Hanna didn't respond. She wasn't sure she could. She had spent so long analyzing them, breaking them down, and trying to understand them. But what if Richard Hale was right? What if he wasn't the only one who liked the game?

She pushed the thought aside. Focus. Ground yourself.

She looked back at Tony. "I'm sorry." The words came out too fast, too breathless. "I really didn't think…" She stopped herself. It was hard enough saying it out loud. Because the truth was always difficult, and honestly, she hadn't expected it to work. She didn't think he would actually confess.

But he had.

And now, nothing would ever be the same.

Tony hadn't moved. His knuckles were white where his hands curled in his lap.

Hanna glanced at Elaine. "Do you want me to take Caitlyn? Give you both some time?"

Elaine shook her head, still watching Tony carefully. "No, Hanna. She can stay here. It's a lot to take in." She inhaled sharply and met Hanna's eyes. "I'm glad it came from you."

Hanna nodded. "I'll stop by tomorrow to get her stuff."

She stood. Tony didn't.

Elaine followed her to the door, casting one last glance at her husband before speaking in a low voice. "He'll be okay. He's just… taking it in."

Hanna hesitated. "Are you sure?"

Elaine gently squeezed her arm. "Drive carefully, sweetie."

Outside, the cool night air hit Hanna like a slap. She climbed into the car but didn't start it right away. Her fingers gripped the wheel, pulse still trying to settle.

CHAPTER 30

Way to go, Hanna. She had blurted it out, dropped a bomb, and left them in the wreckage.

But what was worse? The way Tony reacted... or the way he didn't?

She started the engine and pulled away. But deep down, she knew this wasn't over.

* * *

How the hell did Hanna figure this out? His heart thundered, loud and sharp, each second like a hammer against his ribs.

He hadn't expected this, not like this. Not tonight.

It wasn't that he didn't know. He had known for years. But he never wanted Elaine to. And Hanna? She was never supposed to get this far.

She was supposed to keep chasing shadows. Keep looking in the wrong places. Asking the wrong questions.

Instead, she had landed on the truth.

Tony forced himself to stay still. To breathe evenly. To not react the way he wanted to.

Because if Hanna had figured this out...

What else could she find?

The thought sent a sharp pulse of unease through him.

This was bad. Really bad.

She wasn't stupid. If she had connected *those* dots, it wouldn't take much for her to keep digging. And if she kept digging?

She might not like what she finds.

Tony exhaled slowly, clenching his fists finger by finger.

He had to find a way to make sure this was all she found.

Because if she kept going, if she uncovered everything, it wouldn't be Richard Hale she needed to be afraid of.

Tony stood slowly. Every movement controlled. Every breath measured.

In the living room, Elaine was still sitting on the couch, her eyes unfocused, caught in the gravity of what Hanna had said. She didn't notice as he walked into the kitchen. He briefly lost his breath before picking up the phone.

He dialed the number from memory.

A familiar voice answered, low, rough, and calm as ever.

"Carlo."

Tony pressed his fingers to his temple. "Carlo. How are you?"

"I'm fine. What's going on?"

Tony glanced toward the living room, making sure Elaine was still sitting there. His voice dropped lower.

"Hanna was just over. She's been working with Richard Hale."

"And?"

Tony swallowed. "Hale confessed to killing Tony Jr. tonight."

A pause. Then Carlo's voice, sharp and deliberate: "Feds involved yet?"

Tony rubbed a hand over his jaw. "I think so."

"Let's talk tomorrow."

Click.

The line went dead.

Tony set the phone down slowly, staring at it for a long moment.

This wasn't over.

It was just getting started.

Chapter 31

Hanna arrived home and stared at the house. It stood there quietly against the evening sky, its clean lines and understated elegance a stark contrast to the sprawling wilderness of the cabin. Compared to that vast, isolated retreat, this place felt smaller, safer, and more contained.

The crisp white siding, contrasted by deep charcoal trim, gave the exterior a polished but unpretentious charm. A covered porch stretched across the front, framed by simple, sturdy columns. The warm glow from the windows softened the sharp edges of the house, casting long, golden shadows against the dusk.

Inside, the open floor plan made it easy to keep an eye on Caitlyn while still giving them both space to breathe. The great room was cozy rather than sprawling, the furniture arranged for comfort over aesthetics. A plush sectional, well worn but inviting, faced the fireplace where Steve sat, the blue flicker of the television reflecting off the glass.

The kitchen, a few steps away, had bright and practical quartz countertops, simple cabinetry, and a deep farmhouse sink that had seen more late-night dishwashing than home-cooked meals. The small breakfast nook, tucked beneath a row of windows, was where Caitlyn often sat coloring, her crayons scattered across the table.

Down the hall, Hanna's bedroom was calm and uncluttered, a refuge of muted tones and soft textures. The bed was big enough to feel luxurious but never too empty, though there had been nights she'd woken up reaching for someone who wasn't there.

The house wasn't grand, but it wasn't meant to be.

She walked to the door, unlocked it, and stepped inside. "Honey, I'm home," she called out, her voice dry, almost ironic, as she set her bag down.

Steve's voice floated from the living room. "How was your day, dear? Crack any minds?"

Hanna smirked faintly. "Why, yes. I cracked a murder case."

Silence, and then a second later, Steve appeared in the doorway, leaning against the frame, arms folded loosely across his chest.

"You did what, darling?" he asked, a thread of dry amusement in his tone.

She paused, taking in the easy way he stood there, relaxed but attentive. He looked comfortable and casual, but her eyes traced over him like muscle memory, noticing and cataloging rather than marveling. A familiar presence. One that felt anchored.

"Let me put my things down, and I'll tell you about it," she said.

"Where's Caitlyn?"

"She's staying with Tony and Elaine tonight." Hanna glanced at him, her expression dimming with exhaustion. "I'll explain everything in a second. Let me change first."

"You better be quick," he said, offering a half smile. "You can't come in teasing me like that. I want details."

She gave a soft, dry laugh, then disappeared down the hall.

Steve turned toward the window, scanning the street. He had the cameras installed earlier today. Yeah, maybe a little aggressive, but he couldn't be too careful. He used a "gutter company" on paper, but really, it was a necessary precaution.

From her room, Hanna called out, "Hey, do you know Naomi Walker?"

Steve's jaw tightened. "Yeah. She used to work under me before transferring. Why?"

Hanna emerged, pulling her hair into a loose ponytail. "She's part of the story."

They met in the living room, Hanna settling across from him.

"I had a breakthrough with Richard Hale tonight," she said.

Steve tensed. "What kind of breakthrough?"

"He confessed."

CHAPTER 31

"To what?"

"Killing Tony Jr."

Steve froze, his mind shifting into gear. If that confession was on the record, it could collapse more than one secret. He kept his expression neutral.

Hanna's eyes were wide, still riding the rush. "It unraveled fast. He talked about Izzy. Said she wasn't supposed to die. She wasn't wearing her seat belt. after he killed Tony, the car lurched and she…"

Steve rubbed his jaw. "Jesus."

"Yeah."

There was a long pause. Hanna finally added, "Naomi Walker is leading the FBI team. They want me to keep working with him."

"Are you okay with that?"

She hesitated. "I don't know. But I need to see it through."

Steve nodded once. "Be careful."

"I'm always careful."

He didn't correct her, but she wasn't always. And that was the problem.

"She even asked if I'd join the CSI unit."

Steve blinked and hysterically said,. "She did what?"

"She offered."

"You're not thinking about it, are you?"

"Maybe."

"Hanna, that's not the life of a mother, let alone a single mother."

"Thanks for killing my high."

"No, I'm a realist, and I know the life. I have been doing it for almost twenty years, Hanna. No offense, you're not cut out for it."

"Maybe I am."

"Hanna"

She gave him a dirty look and then shifted. "Had lunch with Rachel today."

"And?"

"She's done waiting. Marry her already."

Steve stiffened. "Hanna "

"She's tired, Steve. Would you rather not have her at all?"

His stomach knotted. "Did she say that?"

Hanna didn't answer, not directly. But it was enough.

"It's complicated," he said.

"No, it's not."

He turned away, silence filling the room. "Hanna, there is more to it than what you know. I don't like being pressured."

"I know." Then she looked at Steve. "Before I left for the cabin, Nick said something. That I didn't really know Brian. That you did."

Steve's eyes darkened. "Brian didn't have secrets. Nick is trying to mess with you."

"Well, it worked," Hanna admitted. She sighed. "I should've known better."

"If anyone has skeletons, it's Nick. Not Brian. Something's off about all of this."

"You don't look convinced," he said after a pause.

"I want to be."

She left and returned with the tape. "Watch this."

Brian's voice echoed from the screen. "I did what I had to do to keep you safe."

When it ended, she turned to Steve. "What did he mean?"

Steve shook his head. "I don't know. Maybe just preparing for the worst. I wish I had an answer."

She deflated slightly. "I'm overreacting again."

"Hanna, you're letting Nick get to you. I swear to you, Brian loved you. He wanted to make sure you were taken care of in the event something happened to him."

She nodded slowly. "I think I need a shower."

Steve laughed, "Yeah, me too; you got a stank."

She got up and hit him. "You're an ass."

"But a cute one." He gave her a grin.

She shook her head.

Steve watched her disappear down the hall, the doubt still heavy in the room.

Chapter 32

Steve stepped outside, the cool air biting against his skin.

He needed to call Rachel, but he knew once he did, he'd be tied up for a while. First, he had to call Tony.

He pulled out his phone, dialing quickly.

Tony answered on the second ring. "Yeah?"

Steve exhaled slowly. "It's me. I just talked to Hanna."

Tony sighed heavily on the other end. "I did too, earlier. Wasn't ready for it, Steve. Wasn't ready for her to find out. Hell, I just found out myself." He paused, then "I'm scared of what else she's going to dig up."

Steve's grip on the phone tightened. "Exactly." His voice dropped lower. "Is it true? Vince stepped down?"

Tony's voice was quieter now. Almost resigned. "Yeah. It's true."

That changed things. More than Steve liked.

Tony continued, his voice harder now. "Can you meet with me and Carlo? We've got something you need to see."

"How's tomorrow?" Steve asked.

"I'll call Carlo. I'll set it up."

Steve almost let him hang up... almost.

"Tony. One more thing."

"What?"

Steve exhaled sharply, scrubbing a hand down his face. "The agent tonight. Naomi Walker. She tried to recruit Hanna."

Silence. Then Tony's voice came back colder, clipped like a blade. "We can't let that happen."

"If she keeps pulling at threads, she's going to dig up things better left buried. For all of us."

"Let's meet tomorrow, Steve."

Steve hung up without saying another word.

He stared out across the quiet street.

Tony was right. If Hanna didn't stop, she kept pushing. She might not like what she found. None of them would.

Steve peeked in the window to see if Hanna had come back; she still must be in the shower.

He paced for a minute, running a hand through his hair.

He didn't want to start a fight. And he didn't want to throw Hanna under the bus either.

But he hated that Rachel was going to Hanna about the marriage thing. It didn't sit right.

Finally, he composed himself, pulled up Rachel's contact, and hit Send.

Rachel picked up on the second ring. "Steve?"

"Rach, are we okay?" His voice was low, rough around the edges. "I mean... are we really okay?"

Rachel heard it instantly: the uncertainty.

And damn if she didn't like it.

For once, *he* was the one worrying about losing *her*.

"I don't know," she said, keeping her tone unreadable.

Steve exhaled sharply. "Rach, I love you. Only you. There's only ever been you." His voice softened. "Is this really about the marriage thing? Because if it is... if it'll make you happy, I'll do it. I'll buy you the biggest damn diamond out there. I'll suck it up and marry you."

Rachel cut him off, smirking a little. Desperation looked good on him. But she didn't let him off that easy.

"Then what, Steve?" she asked, her voice even. "We sign a paper, and suddenly everything's fine?"

Steve blew out a breath that sounded more like a growl. "If that's what you need, yeah. We can go to the JP tomorrow and settle this."

Rachel stayed quiet, letting the words sit heavy between them.

CHAPTER 32

Finally, she sighed. "It's not about a piece of paper."

Steve rubbed his hand over his jaw, his frustration bleeding through. "Then what is it, Rach? I'm standing here telling you I'll do whatever it takes to fix this."

And that was the problem.

He always *fixed* things with money, with reassurances, and with promises he barely understood himself.

Rachel swallowed hard, her voice softening. "I don't want you to marry me because you think you have to."

Steve's voice dropped lower, almost raw. "I don't. I want to... because it's you."

Rachel closed her eyes, fighting the ache in her chest.

Damn him.

She *wanted* to believe him.

"Steve," she said quietly, "I think some time apart is what we need. You have to figure out what you want. Not what you think will fix it. Not because you're scared of losing me."

"Rach "

"Steve." She cut him off, firmer this time.

He stopped. Fell silent.

Rachel pushed the lump down in her throat and kept going. "You shouldn't marry someone because you're afraid. You should marry them because you can't picture the world without them. Not because you're afraid of change."

"I don't want to lose you," he said again, softer now, almost like a confession he couldn't take back.

Rachel's chest twisted painfully. God, he was making this so much harder than it had to be. "Then prove it."

She hung up before she could hear him say another word. For the first time in a long time, Rachel felt something heavy lift from her shoulders, a sliver of control she hadn't realized she'd lost, and she liked it.

Steve stared down at his phone for a long moment, his hand tightening around it.

Then he tipped his head back, staring up at the empty sky.

The night pressed in around him, thick and endless, but his mind raced. He loved and wanted her. Even needed her. But marriage?

Marriage had always felt like a prison sentence he didn't deserve, and now, she was giving him a deadline.

Twelve years. She never wanted marriage before; why now?

He shook his head slowly, something colder settling in his chest.

Maybe he should do it. He felt he had no choice anymore.

* * *

Across the street, tucked into the shadows beyond the dim reach of the streetlight, a figure stood motionless, watching him. Steve had no idea he wasn't alone. He turned and walked inside, closing the door behind him with more force than necessary.

* * *

Hanna looked up from the couch, fresh out of the shower, her hair damp and curling slightly at the ends.

The second she saw him, her eyes narrowed.

Steve's whole body was tense, his shoulders wound tight like he'd just come back from a war and lost.

"Everything okay?"

Steve let out a bitter laugh, running a hand through his hair. "I told Rachel I'd marry her." He exhaled hard. "She told me we needed time apart. That I can't just… fix things."

Hanna's lips parted slightly, but she didn't speak right away.

Oh, Rachel. That's smart. Make him work for it.

But Hanna knew it could go either way; it could force Steve to fight harder, or it could backfire completely.

She stood and crossed the room, pressing a hand lightly to his arm. "Why don't I make us a drink," she offered, voice low, "and we can figure the rest

CHAPTER 32

out?"

Steve exhaled sharply, his head dipping forward, weariness bleeding out of him.

"I don't want to lose her, Han."

Without thinking, Hanna pulled him into a hug, wrapping her arms around him, not romantically, but grounding.

The comfort he didn't know he needed until he was there, holding onto her like a man trying not to drown, was a relief.

Outside, in the shadows beyond the window, the figure stiffened.

The sight of them, that closeness, that easy touch, ignited something ugly.

The figure's breath hitched, fingers twitching at their sides, nails digging into their palms.

Too close. Acting too familiar. She's mine.

The words snarled silently through his mind, thick and jagged.

The warmth inside the house, the way she leaned into him. It wasn't just wrong; it was a betrayal.

Inside, Hanna murmured something low, something Steve barely caught, but it was enough.

His shoulders sagged, the tension momentarily draining from him.

The figure outside shifted, inching closer, something feral unfurling in his chest.

He didn't even notice the branch beneath his foot until it snapped with a sharp *crack*.

Inside, Steve's head snapped toward the window, instincts kicking in like a live wire under his skin.

He froze, listening. From the corner of his eye, he noticed movement and a blur in the tree line.

A deer bolted through the brush, startled by the sudden sound.

Steve exhaled, tension bleeding off his shoulders.

Just a deer.

Still, the unease clung to him like smoke.

He turned back toward Hanna, but his jaw stayed tight, his mind turning slow and wary.

***

Outside, the figure watched from the shadows, breath shallow, muscles coiled tight.

He lingered for a moment longer, long enough, then melted into the darkness, vanishing between the trees like smoke.

***

Thud. Thud. Thud.

Hanna froze mid-step in the kitchen, her fingers tightening around the counter.

Steve was already looking at her.

Neither of them moved.

There was another thud, three solid knocks against the door, louder this time.

Hanna took a step forward, but Steve shook his head once, silent. He moved to the door, flipping on the porch light.

The moment he saw the figure standing there, Steve's blood pressure spiked.

Nick. What the hell was he doing here?

Steve unlocked the door and yanked it open. "Nick."

Nick shifted on the porch, clearly surprised to see him. His hands were shoved deep in his pockets, his stance uneasy, like he wasn't expecting Steve to answer.

"Steve," Nick muttered, glancing past him into the house. "Uh, is Hanna here?"

Steve's jaw flexed. "Yeah. You wanna come in?"

Nick hesitated. "Rachel, here too?"

Steve smirked. "Nope. It's only me and Hanna tonight. Hanna and I are

CHAPTER 32

having a slumber party. Wanna join us?"

Nick's lips pressed into a thin line. He didn't like that.

Still, he stepped inside, stiff and cautious. Steve shut the door behind him, watching him soak in the room, the dim lighting, the warm, lived-in feel, and the way Steve moved like he belonged there.

Hanna walked in from the kitchen, holding two drinks. She blinked when she saw Nick. "Oh. Nick, hey." She lifted a glass. "Want a drink?"

Nick hesitated. "Sure."

He didn't want one, but he wasn't about to say no.

Steve exhaled and leaned back against the couch, casual as hell. "You look uneasy. Everything okay?"

Nick's shoulders loosened slightly, but his hands stayed buried deep, his fingers curling into fists.

Because Hanna was supposed to be his. Not Steve's; why was he even there?

Hanna returned a second later, handing Nick a drink before dropping onto the couch.

Right next to Steve, and then his hand brushed casually against her thigh.

Nick's fingers tightened around the glass.

"So," Nick said, forcing lightness, "how was Vermont?"

Steve's head snapped toward Hanna. *Vermont?*

She barely flinched. "It was good. My grandma was delighted to see us."

Steve narrowed his eyes but said nothing.

Nick turned the glass in his hands. "Did Caitlyn have a good time?"

"Yeah. The best."

Steve studied her, then Nick.

Nick studied them.

The tension in the room twisted tighter.

Nick sat stiffly in the armchair, gripping his drink like it might anchor him. He watched Steve lazily sprawl across the couch, his body too close to Hanna, too familiar.

Nick didn't like that. He didn't like it at all.

Finally, Hanna broke the silence. "Anything going on at the hospital? How's Maddie?"

Nick exhaled, seizing the distraction. "Busy. I had three surgeries today and five more scheduled for tomorrow. Maddie's good. Things are progressing nicely. I really like her."

Hanna nodded politely. "Good. I'm really happy for you two. You make a perfect couple."

Nick's eyes sharpened. "What about you?" he asked, tilting his head. "Anything good happening at the prison?"

Steve watched him carefully.

Hanna didn't blink. She kept her voice casual. "Actually, I was going through the visiting logs on one of my patients."

Nick didn't move, but something flickered, a hair too fast.

Steve saw it. His mouth curled slightly. This was about to get good.

"I saw that you visited him," Hanna said evenly. "Eight times over the last six years, and one a few weeks ago."

Steve's gaze shifted to Nick.

Nick's fingers curled tighter around his glass. "Oh really?" he said lightly. "Which one? I see many patients there."

"Richard Hale."

Nick forced a chuckle. "Not sure if I know him. Maybe I consulted on something."

Steve clocked the lie immediately.

"Richard never had surgery," Hanna said calmly.

Nick's glass clinked lightly against the table as he set it down. "Maybe I checked in on someone else."

"It wasn't a medical visit," she said.

Nick leaned forward, elbows on his knees. "Hanna, I don't know him."

"Are you sure?"

Nick's smile flickered. "I think I'd remember somebody like that."

"You signed in," Hanna said quietly. "Dr. Nicholas O'Sullivan. Visitor."

Nick shifted

He knew he was in a tight spot.

CHAPTER 32

Steve tilted his head lazily, arms sprawled wide across the couch, relaxed, watching.

Nick smoothed a hand over his shirt as he stood. "Didn't realize the time. I'm due over at Maddie's." He shot Hanna a look. "Can we talk outside?"

Hanna hesitated. "Sure."

Nick nodded, cutting a glance at Steve.

Steve smirked and waved lazily. "Catch ya later, Nick."

Nick didn't smile back.

Hanna followed him out the door, letting it shut behind them.

Steve waited until the door shut before flipping open his Ultra Mobile PC and queuing up the outside mic. Because if Nick thought he was going to get Hanna alone, he had another thing coming

* * *

Hanna folded her arms across her chest, tilting her head slightly. "What's up, Nick?"

Nick exhaled slowly, stepping a little too close. His presence loomed, tense and uneasy.

"I don't like this," he muttered.

She frowned. "Don't like what?"

"Him. Acting like he owns the place. Acting like you two are…" Nick's jaw clenched. "Like you're together."

A slow prickle crawled up Hanna's spine.

"Nick, where the hell are you getting this?"

"Hanna, wasn't he Brian's best friend? And isn't he dating your best friend?" Nick shook his head, the words spilling out faster now. "I watched him with you. He's too flirty. He wants more than friendship."

Hanna stilled.

Her voice, when it came, was low and firm. "Nick, nothing is going on with Steve. I would never do that to Rachel. Or Brian." She exhaled tightly.

"That's how Steve is. You'd know that if you ever bothered to be around my friends."

Nick scoffed. "Always goes back to Brian, doesn't it?"

Something inside her snapped.

"What is your issue with Brian?" she demanded, her voice like a blade.

Nick's mouth curled into a grimace. "Who said I have an issue?"

"You just did," Hanna said, her voice steady and deadly calm. "The way you said his name. Like it disgusted you."

Nick swallowed hard. He didn't answer.

Hanna exhaled, the tension bleeding out of her shoulders.

Suddenly, she felt tired. Tired of this, tired of him.

"Nick, you said you had plans with Maddie. I think it's best if you go."

Nick's face shifted, and for the first time that night, he looked shaken.

"Hanna, don't be mad. I'm just trying to protect you. He wants something more from you."

"Nick," Hanna said, her voice final, "you don't know what you're talking about."

Nick hesitated. His eyes searched hers, like he was hoping for something, anything.

"We can talk tomorrow, Hanna. Just… think about what I said."

Without waiting for an answer, he turned and walked to his car.

**

Inside, Steve sat motionless, fingers hovering over the trackpad of his Ultra Mobile PC, listening to every word.

Little spitfire, he thought, a slow smile curling at the edges of his mouth.

Damn, Hanna could handle herself.

But he didn't miss the way Nick's entire demeanor shifted when Brian's name came up.

The way he tried and failed to pull Hanna back, like she was something slipping through his fingers.

Like he was losing control.

CHAPTER 32

And Steve wasn't stupid.

Nick was lying about Richard Hale.

And if he was lying about that, what the hell else was he hiding?

Outside, Nick yanked open his car door a little too hard.

Hanna stood there, arms crossed, not moving, not chasing him.

Not this time.

Nick hesitated at the door frame, like he might say something, might try one last desperate play.

But he didn't.

He got in the car and drove off, tail lights flashing red into the night.

Hanna exhaled, scrubbing a hand over her face before stepping back inside.

* * *

Steve clicked the screen closed as the door swung open.

She stood there for a moment, shaking her head like she couldn't even find the words.

"What the hell was that?" she finally said.

Steve leaned back against the couch, arms folding lazily across his chest. "That's what I'd like to know."

Hanna dropped onto the couch beside him.

Without thinking, Steve threw his arm around her shoulders, pulling her in close.

"It's going to be okay," he said, his voice low and certain against the uncertainty pressing at the edges of the night.

Hanna leaned into him, but inside, a small voice whispered something else.

Will it?

Chapter 33

Great Meadow Correctional Facility

Meanwhile, that same night, Richard sat in his cell, leaning back against the cold, unyielding wall. The dim light overhead flickered, casting jagged shadows across the concrete floor.

He exhaled slowly, savoring the moment, the weight of his victory settling deep in his bones. He had done it; he was leading Hanna in. His plan was unfolding exactly as expected. A slow smirk curled at the edge of his lips as he ran his fingers through his disheveled hair, brushing against the faint bruises along his jaw and rubbing the stubble that was coming through.

This was the price of the game, the price for making it believable.

He was letting Hanna think she was in control. That she was the one playing him, but she had no idea that this was his plan all along.

Every word, every glance, every hesitation he had fed her exactly what she needed to hear. He laid breadcrumbs for her to follow, drawing her closer, dropping hints in each session, wrapping her in the illusion that she was the one holding the power, opening Pandora's box. The part about Tony Jr. is brilliant. She took the bait, playing right into his hands.

His fingers drummed against his knee, slow and methodical. He could almost hear her footsteps in the halls of the prison and could imagine the look in her eyes when she finally realized the truth.

By then, it would be too late. He had played this game before, and this was one game he never lost.

His mind drifted back to his first kill.

It wasn't the path he had wanted; no, he wanted more out of life. Not

CHAPTER 33

then. Maybe not even now.

But choices had been made. Lines had been crossed. Once you stepped into the dark, there was no turning back, and the DeLuca made sure of that.

He could still see her face, smell her perfume, Frankie Bianchi, her silk robe pooling around her like spilled ink, and feel her breath hitching as she whispered that final, desperate plea.

"Please, don't do this."

* * *

February 1992

The cold drizzle had turned the Brooklyn alley into a slick mirror of black pavement. Richard Hale followed Lucas through the dimly lit passage, his pulse a war drum in his ears. Sweat gathered beneath his leather gloves; he was nervous, and the weight of the gun at his side was unfamiliar and wrong.

He was only eighteen, a kid playing a man's game.

Luca Romano, a seasoned DeLuca enforcer, moved with practiced ease, barely sparing Richard a glance.

"You sure you're ready for this, kid?" His voice was low, rough, indifferent, and relaxed.

Richard swallowed hard, nodding once. His throat was too tight to speak, his stomach a coil of knots; he was nervous, he did not want to do this.

Francesca Bianchi, the mistress of Frank DeLuca's was tucked away in a modest apartment, protected by Frank's name. But Vince Sr. saw her as a distraction, a liability, and liabilities needed to be taken care of.

The door creaked open, spilling warm light into the hallway. The air was thick with vanilla and cheap perfume.

Frankie lounged on the couch, barefoot, a silk robe slipping from one shoulder. Her copper-red curls framed sharp cheekbones and sun-kissed skin dusted with freckles. Her golden hazel eyes flicked between Luca and Richard, amusement curling her lips until it didn't.

She studied Richard, her expression shifting.

"Frank sent you?" She scoffed, her voice smooth as silk, though a flicker of

doubt cracked through the act.

Luca shook his head. "Not Frank. Vince."

The color drained from her face.

Richard gripped the gun, his fingers trembling. It felt heavy, too heavy, he thought to himself. Was it too late to turn back and run?

She wasn't a threat. Just a woman, who was now scared, pleading for her life. His hands were shaking as she backed away.

"Please," she whispered, barely audible. "I won't say a word."

His pulse roared. His breath turned shallow. He wasn't sure he could do this.

He was only eighteen, barely a man, just a scared kid with a gun in his hand.

Luca stepped closer, his voice dropping to a whisper.

"You don't do this, Vince will find someone else who will. And next time? Maybe it's you bleeding out on this floor."

The words settled deep, coiling in Richard's gut like lead, his life or hers.

He raised the gun, his hands shaking, his eyes filling with tears.

Frankie's lips parted. Her breath hitched.

"Please," she said again, softer this time, her golden eyes locked onto his searching. For mercy. For hesitation.

But mercy wasn't a choice.

He shut his eyes and pulled the trigger.

The shot shattered the silence. She crumpled, silk pooling around her as the crimson stain spread across her chest.

The room shrank, suffocating. Richard stared at her motionless body, his chest heaving, ears ringing. What did he just do?

Luca clapped a hand on his shoulder. "Good job, kid; the first one's the hardest, but memorable."

Richard didn't answer. He didn't feel anything; he just stared at the body on the floor and the pool of blood surrounding it.

Too damn young to be playing this game, and in that moment he realized there was no going back now.

Luca wiped down the doorknob and nodded toward the exit. "Let's go."

Richard followed, stepping over the body without looking down.

Outside, the rain had turned to sleet, cold and relentless. He lifted his face to

CHAPTER 33

the sky, letting the freezing drops numb his skin.

He had just become a killer. And Vince Sr. would do everything in his power to ensure he remained one.

* * *

Present Day 2006

Richard sat in silence, rubbing the rough stubble on his chin, eyes locked on something far beyond the room, some memory only he could see.

Hanna thought she was the one digging for answers, peeling back the past layer by layer. She had no idea she was walking straight into the truth he had buried deep, right where he wanted it.

His fingers twitched, almost involuntarily, an old habit. The sensation of the wheel beneath his grip. The hum of an engine purring in the rain. The low fog that blanketed the road that night.

Routine. That was always the weakness. People clung to it like a lifeline, never realizing it made them predictable. And predictability? That made them easy.

He tilted his head back, exhaling a slow, steady breath as a smirk touched the corner of his mouth.

It had been smooth and clean, almost beautiful in its simplicity. There were no witnesses or questions, just a tragic moment in time, written off by everyone who needed to believe in accidents. Everyone believed what they saw or thought they saw, and that was the best part. They never looked deeper or pulled at the thread, and once he was finished, Hanna wouldn't either.

A smile came to his face; she still thought she was in control. That made it all the more satisfying. She was solving a puzzle she didn't even know he'd built for her. The pieces were scattered now, distant and harmless. But soon, very soon, they'd start clicking into place, one by one.

And when they did? She'd see the full picture. He had been writing the story all along.

Richard's smile widened, the kind of smile that never reached the eyes.

The game was far from over. He knew secrets about her deceased husband, truths concealed in silence, shadows, and blood, and that was what made it enjoyable for him; everything was coming together, and when she least expected it, he would strike.

Chapter 34

The next morning, Nick ran harder than he typically did. His feet pounded against the pavement, each step a desperate attempt to outrun the weight of the night before. The cold air sliced through his lungs, sharp and punishing. He welcomed the burn. He deserved it. He needed it.

He could still see it. Still feel it.

Last night had unraveled like a slow motion nightmare, one he couldn't wake from. The words. The looks. The moment it all shattered.

The argument had started like any other: sharp words, controlled anger, and tension simmering beneath the surface. But then it had cracked, spiraled, and turned into something else. Something *final*.

He could still hear her voice, the way it trembled despite the fire behind it. The way she looked at him was like she was seeing him for the first time, and she didn't like what she saw.

And then she was gone.

Just like that.

Now, the pounding of his feet against the pavement was the only sound that made sense. He pushed harder, trying to chase the silence, trying to outrun the guilt.

But no matter how fast he ran, last night stayed right behind him.

What was Hanna doing digging into Richard?

Nick had forgotten he had even met with him, at least, that's what he told himself. It had been nothing. A footnote. A moment that meant less than nothing. He had to make Hanna *see* that. But how?

Every time they talked, they fought.

Every time he tried to reach her, she pulled away.

And now, the thought that had been gnawing at him for days settled in his chest like a stone.

Was she really considering him?

His breathing was ragged, his strides lengthening as if running harder could chase that thought from his mind. He had to show her. Had to make her see that he could be the man she needed. That he could be *understanding*. That he was *better* for her than anyone else.

Better than Brian.

His jaw clenched. Brian was a ghost, a relic from her past, and yet he still haunted them. He was the comparison Nick could never seem to shake, the shadow that always lingered just out of reach. The person standing in the way of Hanna

And now there was Steve. Steve wasn't a real threat, but he also never missed an opportunity to question him. Always watching him with a detective's eye, waiting for him to slip, to show some fatal flaw.

Nick couldn't *get rid* of him, not without raising questions.

But maybe he didn't have to.

Maybe he had to *befriend* him.

Pull him in. Make Steve *see* how good he was for Hanna. Make him believe that Nick was the better choice. That he was the only one who could give her what she needed.

And then the plan started coming together.

Later that day, he'd call Steve. Ask him to go out for drinks. Act like nothing has changed. Keep it light and casual, just two guys talking.

And then, little by little, he'd work his way in.

Gain his trust.

Make Steve think *he* was the one coming around, that *he* was the one seeing Nick in a new light.

And when that happened, when Steve *trusted* him, when Hanna *chose* him There would be no one left standing in his way.

Nick arrived home, stripping off his sweat-drenched clothes as he stepped into the shower. The hot water hit his skin, washing away the morning's

CHAPTER 34

run, but it did nothing to clear his mind.

He had to word it right. Make it seem natural, almost casual.

The last thing he needed was to make Steve suspicious. If he pushed too hard or asked the wrong questions, it would set off alarms. No, he had to ease into it, make it seem like nothing more than a friendly conversation.

Hey, Steve. I thought we should grab a drink and clear the air.

No. Too forced.

Man, I feel like we always get off on the wrong foot. Let's grab a drink.

Better.

Nick let the water run over his face, eyes closed, replaying every possible way the conversation could go. Steve wasn't an idiot. If he caught even a hint of manipulation, this would blow up before it even started.

He had to be careful. I had to make Steve *believe* this was his idea.

By the time he stepped out of the shower, he had the perfect approach. He toweled off, grabbed his phone, and exhaled slowly before dialing.

The game was already in motion. Now it was time to play it right. Nick finally had the right approach.

He finished getting dressed, rolling his sleeves up just enough to seem relaxed but not too casual. He needed it to look effortless, like he wasn't trying at all.

Grabbing his phone, he took one last breath.

Make it sound natural. Make it sound easy.

He pressed the send button. The line rang once. Twice.

Then Steve picked up.

"Nick?" The hesitation in his voice was there, guarded as always.

Nick let out a short chuckle, just enough to sound genuine. "Yeah, man. Look, I was thinking... I feel like we always get off on the wrong foot. How about a drink? No tension, no bullshit, just two guys talking."

There it was, and Nick held his breath.

Then Steve sighed. "Alright. Where?"

Nick leaned against the counter, staring out the window as the sun dipped lower in the sky. "How about Hudson & Vine? Laid-back, not too crowded. I'll grab the first round."

"Tonight?"

"Yeah. Eight work for you?"

Steve hesitated, and for a second, Nick thought he'd say no. Then, "Fine. See you at eight."

The call ended.

Nick smirked, slipping his phone into his pocket. The game was already in motion. Now it was time to play it right.

* * *

Hanna stepped out of the shower, wrapping a towel around herself as steam curled through the bathroom. The hot water had helped clear her mind at least a little, but there was still a weight pressing at the back of her thoughts.

Something about last night still didn't sit right.

She sighed, brushing the fog from the mirror and staring at her reflection. No answers there. Just tired eyes and a lingering unease she couldn't quite shake.

With a deep breath, she grabbed her clothes and got dressed, her stomach grumbling as she stepped into the hallway. The faint smell of coffee and something sweet filled the air.

Hanna frowned. *Steve's cooking?*

That was… unexpected.

When she entered the kitchen, she found Steve standing near the coffee maker, staring at his phone in shock. He didn't even notice her at first.

"Good morning," she said slowly. "I think. You okay, Steve?"

Steve blinked like he was snapping out of a trance. "I just got the strangest, most unexpected phone call."

Hanna grabbed a mug and poured herself some coffee. "Okay… and?"

He exhaled, shaking his head. "I'm going to have drinks with Nick tonight."

Hanna froze mid-sip. "Wait, what?"

"Yeah." Steve looked just as confused as she felt. "Nick, and he wants to have drinks tonight."

CHAPTER 34

She stared at him, trying to process. "Nick called you?"

"Yep."

"And you said *yes*?"

Steve set his phone down on the counter. "I think I blacked out for a second because somehow, I did."

Hanna set her mug down, crossing her arms. "That makes no sense."

Steve huffed a laugh. "Tell me about it." Then, like the last thirty seconds of conversation hadn't happened, he turned to the stove. "Oh, do you like pancakes?"

Hanna blinked. "Uh… yeah?"

"Good, because I made a shitload." He gestured to the absurdly large stack of pancakes on the counter. "Didn't realize a box made this many."

She arched a brow. "You made the whole box?"

Steve shrugged. "Yeah… isn't that how it's done?"

Hanna chuckled, shaking her head. "Only if you want to be eating pancakes for days?"

Steve groaned. "Fantastic! Well, grab a plate because I am *not* doing this alone."

Hanna smirked, reaching for the syrup as she sat down across from him.

For a few minutes, they just ate, the conversation easy and natural, too natural.

"So, what's on your agenda today?" Steve asked, cutting into a pancake like this was some kind of routine breakfast they always had.

Hanna wiped some syrup from her fingers. "I need to go to the office for a few hours. Just catch up on paperwork and check in with a few clients."

Steve nodded as if he already knew that. "Figured. You were at your desk late last night."

She tilted her head. "And you? What's your plan?"

Steve poured more coffee into both their mugs, sighing. "I've got a meeting downtown at noon, then probably back to the office for a few hours before," he shook his head. "Before I meet Nick."

Hanna raised a brow. "Right. *That,*" she smiled.

Steve made a face, then took another bite. "You know, I think this might be the first time I've voluntarily made plans with someone I'm 99% sure I don't trust."

Hanna smirked. "Only 99%?"

"Eh, I'm giving myself a 1% margin for error. Gotta leave room for surprises."

Hanna rolled her eyes, but before she could reply, something about the whole moment made her stop.

They were sitting at the table, drinking coffee, talking about their plans for the day, and giving each other updates like a married couple.

Steve must have caught it, too, because he suddenly looked up at her, fork halfway to his mouth. "This is… weird, right?" he asked, squinting at her.

Hanna burst out laughing. "Oh, *so* weird."

Steve chuckled, shaking his head. "Just making sure we're on the same page."

Hanna smiled, taking another sip of coffee. "So… you won't be home for dinner tonight? Caitlyn and I should do something on our own?"

Steve nodded, still distracted by the absurdity of their conversation. "Yeah, probably best. Not sure how long this thing with Nick will go."

Hanna tapped her fingers against her mug. "Do you know what time you'll be home? Should I wait up, or will you just wake me when you get in?"

Steve froze mid-chew. He blinked at her like he'd just short-circuited and smiled.

Hanna realized it at the same time he did and smiled back.

Steve swallowed hard. "Okay, yeah. This is getting *really* weird."

Hanna cracked up, covering her face with her hands. "God, we sound like an old married couple."

Steve shook his head, grinning as he reached for more coffee. "Well, at least one of us realized it before we started arguing over grocery lists."

Hanna smirked. "Give it time."

They both laughed, shaking off the strange moment, but as Steve went back to eating, Hanna couldn't shake the nagging feeling that something about Nick's invitation was off, and she had a feeling tonight would prove

CHAPTER 34

her right.

Chapter 35

That same day, Hanna pulled into the prison parking lot, staring in awe at the imposing structure that loomed in the distance. It was a fortress, cold and unyielding, its towering gray stone walls stretching high into the sky, crowned with razor wire that glistened under the dull afternoon sun. Guard towers stood at the corners, watching, waiting, their windows dark and unreadable. Even from the outside, the presence of authority was suffocating, the thick, reinforced walls designed not just to keep prisoners in, but to keep the world out.

Beyond the entrance, the main building rose like a monolith, its weathered brick and steel gates a stark reminder that once someone entered, they rarely left the same. The barred windows, barely large enough to let in a sliver of light, were like dead eyes staring back at her.

She parked, turning off the engine but not moving right away. A row of transport vans lined the side of the lot, waiting to take inmates to court dates or transfers. Officers patrolled the perimeter, rifles slung over their shoulders, their presence as routine as the air that hung thick with control.

The sign near the gate read *"Great Meadow Correctional Facility—New York State Department of Corrections."* The bold, black letters stood stark against the faded concrete wall, a silent warning of what lay beyond.

Hanna exhaled sharply and stepped out of the car. *Why would she want to give this all up? It's the glamorous life,* she chuckled. Being an agent would get her out of the tall stone walls and into the light.

The sound of steel gates buzzing open echoed in the distance as a group of visitors were let through: families, lawyers, and people who had business

CHAPTER 35

with the forgotten men inside.

She adjusted her coat, then looked down as she felt the familiar looseness at her ankle. One of her sneakers had come untied.

Squatting down, she looped the laces quickly, double knotting them this time. As she did, she let her eyes drift upward, scanning the bleak walls of the prison, the heavy gates, and the guards watching from above.

It was magnificent, in its haunting way, an architectural feat designed for one purpose: confinement.

No matter how many times she came here, it always felt the same, as if she was standing on the edge of a place that swallowed people whole.

She finished tying her shoe, stood up, and squared her shoulders.

The walls weren't meant to intimidate her. But they sometimes did.

Hanna stepped toward the gate, where a guard stood waiting, his expression neutral but familiar. She reached into her pocket and handed over her ID badge. He barely glanced at it before scanning it under the flickering fluorescent light.

"Morning, Doc," the guard said, handing it back. "Didn't think we'd see you today."

"Just checking in," Hanna replied, slipping the badge back onto her lanyard.

He nodded once. "You know the drill."

She stepped toward the security checkpoint, where another guard gestured her forward.

"Feet apart, arms out," the female officer instructed.

Hanna complied without hesitation.

The pat-down was routine and quick but thorough. The press of hands against her arms, down her torso, along the waistband of her pants. A firm sweep over her ankles before the guard finally stepped back.

"All clear."

Hanna lowered her arms as the second gate buzzed open, the steel locks clanking loudly as they disengaged. She stepped forward, the cold, sterile air hitting her the moment she crossed the threshold.

Inside, the walls seemed even taller, the ceiling lower.

Now, she just had to remind herself why she kept coming back.

Hanna walked down the long, sterile corridor, her sneakers barely making a sound against the polished concrete floor. The fluorescent lights overhead buzzed faintly, casting their usual cold, artificial glow. It was the kind of place where time didn't feel real, where the days blurred together, measured only by the sound of cell doors locking and unlocking.

She reached her office, slipping her ID badge from around her neck and swiping it against the reader before unlocking the door. The handle clicked, and as she pushed it open, she caught movement from the corner of her eye.

Michael. He must have heard her.

"Morning, Hanna," he greeted, stepping toward her.

"Morning," she replied, setting her bag down on her desk.

Michael glanced over his shoulder, making sure they were alone before lowering his voice.

"Davidson's awake."

Hanna's breath hitched for half a second, but she masked it quickly.

Michael leaned in slightly. "I was waiting for you before going down to the med bay to talk to him."

Hanna exhaled, rubbing the back of her neck. She had been dreading this moment, but it was inevitable.

She nodded. "Alright. Let's go."

Without another word, they turned and headed down the hall.

Hanna and Michael walked briskly through the corridors, the air thick with the faint scent of antiseptic and something stale, something that never quite left these walls. The med bay was tucked away near the far end of the facility, past a security checkpoint and behind a set of locked double doors.

When they stepped inside, the sterile white walls and harsh overhead lighting did little to make the space feel inviting. A few cots lined the room, some occupied by inmates in various states of recovery, while a glassed-in nurse's station overlooked it all.

A nurse at the counter looked up as they approached.

"We need to see Liam Davidson," Michael said, flashing his badge.

CHAPTER 35

The nurse, a woman in her late forties with graying hair pulled into a tight bun, gave a tired nod. "He's conscious. A little groggy, but he's stable." She glanced toward the far cot, separated by a thin curtain. "Try not to agitate him. He's been in and out since last night."

Hanna gave a reassuring smile. "We'll keep it short."

The nurse sighed. "I'll hold you to that."

* * *

They made their way over, Michael pulling the curtain back slightly to reveal Liam lying in bed, propped up by thin pillows. His arm was bandaged, and his face looked a little worse for wear, bruises darkening along his jawline, evidence of whatever had happened before he ended up here.

Davidson's tired eyes flickered up, locking onto Hanna. A slow smirk tugged at the corner of his lips.

"Well, well," he rasped. "Doc."

Hanna stepped closer, hands slipping into her coat pockets.

"Hey, Liam."

His smirk didn't fade. "You making calls within the walls now?"

Hanna didn't flinch, keeping her expression even. "Sorry, I missed our sessions."

"No worries," he muttered, shifting slightly. "Not like I had anywhere to be."

She glanced at the monitors beside him, checking the slow but steady beep of his heart rate. "Are you doing okay?"

Liam let out a rough chuckle. "Been better." His gaze sharpened slightly. "You gonna tell me what happened?"

Hanna glanced at Michael before turning back to Liam.

"That's what we were hoping you could tell us. What do you remember?"

Liam was hesitant. "Alright. Here's what I remember."

Hanna and Michael exchanged a glance but remained silent, letting him speak.

"The morning started like any other. Same routine. Got up, grabbed breakfast, and stayed clear of the usual trouble spots. I wasn't looking to start anything and wasn't expecting anything. But then things got... off."

Liam frowned, his fingers tapping absently against the bed sheet.

"I was heading back from the yard when I felt it, the kind of quiet that doesn't belong here. You learn to pick up on things in a place like this. Who's watching you? Who *isn't* watching you? And that morning? It was wrong. Too many eyes, not enough movement. Like something was waiting to happen."

Hanna felt her anxiety going into overdrive.

Her mind flashed back to another place, another time. A different morning, a different silence. The day Brian left.

She hadn't understood it then, the way everything had felt *too still, too off*. But afterward, when the shock faded, she realized the truth her instincts had *known*. Even if she hadn't wanted to listen.

Now, sitting across from Liam, she felt that same unease curling in her gut.

"I made it about halfway down the tier when I heard footsteps, too fast, too close. Before I could turn around, someone grabbed me. Felt like two guys, maybe three. They weren't just trying to rough me up, either. This was different. This was planned."

His voice dropped slightly.

"One of them had something. I felt it scrape against my ribs, but I twisted just in time. That's when I got hit. Hard. The side of my head sent me to the ground."

Liam reached up, pressing gingerly against the bruise along his jaw.

"I remember someone saying something quick and low, like a warning. 'Stay down. Stay the hell out of it; stop sticking your nose where it doesn't belong, or something quick.' I didn't get a good look at their faces before I blacked out, but I know one thing for damn sure."

He met Hanna's gaze, his eyes cold now, steady.

"This wasn't random; it hit a nerve with someone. Michael said

Liam gave a humorless smirk. "Yeah, and I got the memo loud and clear."

Hanna crossed her arms, her mind already piecing things together. "You

CHAPTER 35

said they weren't just trying to rough you up. So what *were* they trying to do?"

Liam exhaled sharply, eyes flicking to the side like he was weighing whether to say it out loud.

For a second, she thought he was going to defect. He shifted slightly and exhaled through his nose, but he still hesitated to answer them.

Michael stepped forward. "Liam. We don't have time for games."

Liam let out a dry chuckle. "Games? But, Doc, you have to understand this *is* the game."

Hanna's skin prickled.

There was something in his voice, something laced beneath the words. A hint of knowledge. A buried truth.

She kept her stance steady, her voice calm. "Liam. Who sent them?"

He finally looked at her, really looked at her, and that uneasy feeling in her stomach deepened.

"Oh, I've got a few ideas," he admitted, his voice quieter now.

Michael tensed beside her. "And?"

Liam's lips quirked slightly, but the amusement didn't reach his eyes.

"Let's just say… I stuck my nose where it didn't belong. And some people aren't too happy about it."

Hanna felt her heartbeat pick up slightly. *Some people.* That phrase carried weight in a place like this. It meant more than just inmates. It meant people outside these walls. People with reach. People who *could* get rid of someone and make sure they stayed gone.

Michael exhaled sharply. "You're going to have to do better than that, Davidson."

Liam's smirk faded. He shifted again, wincing slightly. "Have you ever heard the phrase 'it's better to let sleeping dogs lie'?"

Hanna didn't answer. Because suddenly, she wasn't thinking about Liam at all.

She was thinking about Brian. About the way he had warned her before he disappeared. The way he told her not to push, not to dig too deep. The way he had looked at her the last time she saw him, like he *knew* something was coming. And now, sitting in this cold, sterile med bay, listening to Liam skirt around the truth, she felt it again: the moment *before* everything goes wrong.

Michael sighed. "If you don't want to help yourself, that's your choice."

Liam tilted his head slightly. "Oh, I never said I didn't want to help myself."

Hanna narrowed her eyes. "Then tell us what you know."

Liam's smirk had returned, but this time, it was different. Less amused and more calculated.

"Maybe I will." He exhaled, then met her eyes. "But not yet."

Hanna clenched her jaw, but before she could push further, the nurse's voice cut in from across the room.

"Alright, that's enough for now. He needs rest."

Michael cursed under his breath, shaking his head. "We'll be back."

Liam just smirked. "I'll be here."

As Hanna turned, she caught something, just a flicker, a moment.

Liam's expression shifted as they walked away. For the briefest second, his face hardened, flat, unreadable. A mask slipping into place. And then, just as quickly, it was gone. Like he knew something and was just *waiting for the right moment*. Hanna didn't like what she was feeling: *dread*.

As they stepped back into the hallway, Michael exhaled sharply. "I don't like this."

"Neither do I," Hanna murmured.

Michael gave her a sideways glance. "Where do we go from here?"

Hanna's fingers curled into fists at her sides. "We find out exactly what Liam was poking around in," she said. "And we'll do it before *they* come back to finish the job." she paused and then "I need to stop by and see Maddie; I will catch up with you.

Michael nodded, "See you back on the other side."

* * *

Maddie was the kind of woman who demanded attention without asking for it. Striking, yes, but it was more than that; she was deliberate. Every

CHAPTER 35

move, every glance, and every carefully measured word had a purpose. She exuded control in a way most people only pretended to, and it made Hanna wonder just how much Maddie really knew.

"How are you, Hanna?" Maddie asked, folding her hands neatly on the desk.

"I'm good. And you, Maddie?"

"I'm well." A polite, practiced smile. "I meant to stop by, actually, to make sure you got what you needed from Nick's visit with Richard."

Hanna kept her expression neutral. There it was. The confirmation she needed. She already knew Maddie had been the one to authorize Nick's visit, but hearing it out loud was different. The casual way Maddie said it, like it was nothing, like it wasn't a problem at all, sent something uneasy curling in Hanna's gut.

She needed to be careful. She needed to dig without making it obvious she was looking. Hanna forced a thoughtful expression, leaning back slightly. "You know, I haven't had time to catch up with him yet," she said, choosing her words carefully. "I assume it was just a standard psych eval?"

Maddie's expression didn't change. "Something like that."

Something like that, a flicker of something beneath Maddie's composed exterior.

Hanna tilted her head slightly. "Nick didn't mention anything to you about the session?"

Maddie's head tilted. "No," she said smoothly. Then, a calculated tilt of her head. "But I'm curious myself. Mind if we call him?"

Hanna thought to herself this was even better than she expected; wait until she tells Steve. She smiled, "Sure, that would be great."

Maddie picked up the phone, dialed Nick's number, and put it on speaker. A few rings. Then, "Dr. Nicholas O'Sullivan."

"Hi Nick, it's Maddie," and before she could say she had Hanna with her Nick cut her off.

"Maddie," Nick's voice shifted, immediately smoother. "I've been thinking about you all morning. Last night, and..."

Before he could finish, Maddie cut in, her face turning red. "Nick." Her voice sharpened. "I have Dr. Nowack here; she was following up on your visit with Richard a few weeks ago. She's looking for the psych report you owe her."

Then there was silence. Nick felt the heat rise up his neck, his shirt suddenly too tight, his heartbeat too loud.

No. No, no, no. Hanna wasn't supposed to know; she was digging. Steve must have put her up to this, and Maddie, his Maddie, was helping her.

A bead of sweat rolled down his temple. Nick swallowed, forcing a strained chuckle. "Oh. Right. The report. Of course."

But it was too late. Hanna had already heard the hesitation; she knew.

Nick swallowed hard, scrambling. Think, think. "I—I left it in her mailbox," he lied, forcing his voice to stay smooth. "Did she not get it?"

Hanna didn't blink. Didn't flinch. "No, Nick," she said, her voice calm, even. Too even. "I didn't."

Nick's stomach dropped.

Then Maddie chimed in, and the floor beneath him cracked wide open.

"All documents, physical and digital, are logged," she said smoothly. "There's nothing, Nick."

Maddie was questioning him too now? He exhaled through his nose, forcing himself to sound unbothered. "Maybe… I forgot to put it in the box," he said quickly, forcing out a sheepish chuckle. "Honest mistake. Dr. Nowack, I can meet you in an hour to go over my results."

Hanna didn't react right away. And that was when he knew she was playing him. She would rather not see him alone. She didn't trust him. "Oh, sorry," she said lightly, "I have an appointment. Maybe later."

Nick felt it, the walls closing in. He licked his lips, forcing a breath. "Okay."

Hanna stood. Cool. Composed. In control. "Thank you both," she said, nodding to Maddie.

Maddie smiled, easily, almost friendly. "Let's grab lunch soon."

Hanna nodded. and lipped soon and waved

Then, she was gone.

Nick exhaled, forcing his muscles to loosen. He had almost-almost, pulled

CHAPTER 35

it off.

Then, Maddie joined back on the phone "Nick," she said smoothly, her voice quiet. Dangerous. "Do you want to tell me why you met with Richard Hale?"

"I told you, Maddie."

"No Nick, You didn't; you told me Hanna asked you to. I think you're up to something. I am done. We are over," and she hung up

Nick just sat in his chair, thinking, *How was he going to get out of this one?*

* * *

Hanna walked back to her office, took out her phone, and sent Steve a text.

"Nick told the Prison Medical Director that I asked him to stop in and see Richard the other night; we called him and he about cracked

She hit send. She glanced at her calendar. Two more appointments, and then she could go home.

11:30 – Gideon Marks

12:45 – Elias Mercer

After that, she was done for the week. No more, Richard, not until Monday. The thought settled in her chest with an odd mix of relief and anticipation. Their sessions were unsettling, yet she was eager to continue.

Her gaze drifted to the business card she had tucked into the corner of her desk: Naomi Walker. She picked it up, running her thumb over the embossed lettering. The offer still lingered in her mind, tempting her. *The money would be good. The work... different.* But was she ready to step onto the other side?

The clock on the wall read 11:22; it was time to move. She slipped the card back into her purse and grabbed her notepad. Gideon Marks was waiting.

* * *

Steve Riley arrived at the DeLuca manor around 11:55 a.m., rolling to a slow stop in front of the iron gates. The estate loomed behind them, imposing, untouchable, an empire built on old money and even older power.

But this wasn't Vince DeLuca's empire anymore.

Vince had stepped down.

Now, Carlo DeLuca ran the family.

Steve wasn't sure if that made this meeting better or worse.

The security presence was impossible to miss. Cameras tracked his every move, and the two guards stationed by the gate were armed, their postures rigid with vigilance. Nothing happened here without the family knowing about it first.

One of the guards approached his window, hand resting on the strap of his rifle. His face was unreadable, but his body language was clear: no one got through these gates unless they were meant to.

Steve rolled down the window, keeping his movements deliberate.

"Name?" the guard asked, voice clipped and professional.

"Steve Riley. I have a meeting."

The guard studied him before lifting his radio. "Riley's here."

A burst of static, and then a calm but firm voice responded.

"Let him in."

The iron gates groaned open, revealing the long, tree-lined driveway leading to the manor.

Steve exhaled slowly, gripping the wheel as he drove forward. His phone buzzed, and he looked at it, a message from Hanna. *Fuck, I will have to deal with this later*, he thought to himself.

The DeLuca estate was the kind of place that carried the weight of generations. It wasn't just wealthy; it was controlled. Every detail, from the towering oak trees to the symmetrical gardens, screamed precision.

The circular driveway wrapped around an ornate fountain, water cascading in perfect rhythm, its presence more decorative than inviting.

And then there was the house itself.

A mansion that could have been lifted from the hills of Italy, with stone columns, sprawling terraces, and ivy climbing up the walls like it had been there for centuries. But beneath all the beauty, Steve saw the truth.

CHAPTER 35

This wasn't a home.

It was a stronghold.

He parked, stepping out just as another guard approached. Unlike the men at the gate, this one had a pistol holstered at his hip instead of a rifle. More discreet, but no less dangerous.

"Follow me," the guard instructed.

No small talk. No hesitation.

Steve adjusted his jacket, his mind already working through the possibilities of why he was here.

The moment he stepped inside, he felt it. A shift in power.

Vince DeLuca had been the kind of leader who operated in the shadows, calculated and methodical.

Carlo? Carlo was a different animal. The house reflected that change. The DeLuca estate had always been controlled, but now it felt colder. Less like an untouchable dynasty and more like a kingdom preparing for war.

The polished marble floors still gleamed. The chandeliers still cast their golden glow. The walls still held their expensive paintings. But the silence had changed.

Steve followed the guard down the long hallway, past doors that concealed more power moves than he wanted to think about. Finally, they stopped in front of a set of large, double doors.

The guard knocked once.

A voice from inside called out, "Enter."

The doors swung open.

* * *

Carlo DeLuca sat behind the large mahogany desk, his posture relaxed but unreadable. He wasn't his father, Vince, but he was still the man in charge.

Tony DeLuca stood near the window, arms crossed, his face shadowed in the dim light. He wasn't looking at Steve, not yet.

Because this time, Steve had been the one to make the call.

Carlo finally spoke, his tone measured. "Glad you could make it, Steve."

Steve gave a small nod. "Didn't seem like a meeting I could skip."

Carlo smirked slightly, but it wasn't amused.

"I felt this meeting was important," Carlo continued. "We all care about Hanna. We all care about protecting our secrets." He let the words settle before adding, "If she keeps digging, she might find something she doesn't like."

Steve exhaled slowly, glancing at Tony, who still hadn't spoken.

Then Carlo shifted his gaze, his voice cooling.

"How did she get Hale to crack?"

Steve straightened slightly. "She dug. Went through past files and police reports and started putting things together."

Tony finally moved, turning his head slightly toward Steve.

Steve met his gaze and kept going.

"I think what tipped her off was Izzy," Steve continued. "She died the same night as Tony Jr. That didn't sit right with her."

Silence stretched between them.

Then Steve added, "Now my former partner, Naomi Walker, is on the case. The same one who helped us all those years ago."

That got Carlo's attention. His eyes flickered with something unreadable.

Tony's jaw tensed slightly. "And?"

Steve hesitated, then exhaled. "I don't think she remembers. But I may have to meet with her to tell her."

Carlo drummed his fingers once against the desk. "To control the narrative."

Steve gave a single nod. "Exactly."

Carlo didn't answer right away, but the way his fingers stilled against the desk told Steve he was considering the risks.

Finally, Tony spoke again, his voice lower now.

"Good. I don't know how much more Elaine can handle."

Steve's brows furrowed slightly.

Tony exhaled sharply. "She just moved back in. I wasn't expecting Hanna to show up last night and tell us she got Richard to confess to Tony Jr.'s murder."

CHAPTER 35

Steve blinked. "She told you in person?"

Tony nodded. "Yeah." His tone was clipped. "She wanted us to hear it from her first before the news reported on it."

Carlo leaned back slightly. "How did Elaine take it?"

Tony's jaw tightened. "Not well."

Steve exhaled slowly. Of course, she didn't. Elaine had been through enough. Losing Tony Jr. had nearly broken her. And now, hearing the truth after all these years? That wasn't something Elaine would recover from easily.

Tony sighed, rubbing a hand over his face. "Look, I know Hanna meant well. She thought she was doing the right thing. But that doesn't change the fact that this is bringing everything back."

Carlo studied Tony for a moment, then turned back to Steve. "We don't need Hanna pushing Elaine over the edge," Carlo said. "We need this handled quietly."

Steve's throat tightened slightly, but he nodded. "I'll take care of it."

Carlo smirked slightly. "I know you will."

Steve met his gaze, but there was no satisfaction in his expression. "Did you ever work with Hale?" His voice was steady, but there was a weight to the question. "Will he crack on with the others?"

Carlo's smirk faded. His fingers tapped once against the desk with a silent hesitation. Then, finally, "I don't know." He exhaled, his expression darkening slightly. "And that has me worried." Silence stretched between them.

Steve added, "I am staying with Hanna. I didn't want to bring this up on the phone, but… someone is watching her."

Tony and Carlo exchanged a look, their postures stiffening. Carlo was the first to speak. "What do you mean, watching her?"

Steve leaned forward, lowering his voice. "The night I went out to the cabin, I found her outside in the storm. She was convinced she saw Brian."

Tony's brow furrowed. "Brian's dead, Steve."

Steve nodded. "Yeah. That's what I told her. But I checked the tree line. Someone was there, watching her. I could feel it." His jaw tightened, his fingers tapping against the table. "It wasn't just paranoia. I know what it's like to be watched, to be hunted. This wasn't random."

Carlo's face darkened. "You see who it was?"

"No," Steve admitted. "But I know how these things work. They were careful, stayed just out of sight, but left just enough behind to let us know they were there."

Tony exhaled sharply, dragging a hand down his face. "Jesus Christ. Any idea who?"

Steve hesitated. "That's what I don't know. And that has me worried."

Carlo's voice was low and measured. "You think it's connected to Richard?"

Steve locked eyes with him. "I think it's connected to Richard, yeah." He let the weight of the words sink in before adding, "And if I'm right? Hanna's in more danger than she even realizes."

Tony's fists hit the table. "Then we don't wait. We find out who the hell is out there before they make a move."

Carlo nodded. "I'll start making calls. If someone's watching Hanna, we'll know who soon enough."

Steve exhaled, glancing toward the window, his mind already racing through the next steps.

"I think whoever is watching her is waiting," Steve responded

Carlo looked up, his voice cool, steady, and final. "Yeah. And when they move, we'll be waiting, too."

Chapter 36

After Hanna's last session, she walked down to her office and grabbed her things. Her mind was all over the place. She closed her office door, peeked into Michael's office, and said, "See you tomorrow." He waved. As she walked to the car, her thoughts were all over the place: Richard and Davidson. Were they connected?

She climbed into the car, started it, and put it into gear, her fingers tightening on the wheel as she headed toward Tony and Elaine's house to grab Caitlyn's things. Her thoughts then went back to Naomi and a job with the FBI. It was so enticing, no more walking into a dungeon; it felt so refreshing yet challenging. But could she do that to Michael? They had been working together for so long, and with the cuts, he would be short-staffed, but maybe her leaving would allow one of the team to come back, and at the same time, she would stop worrying about whether her time was up. Every year, it seemed, the state cut more and more psychological services in the prison. Maybe she would reach out to Naomi to find out more about the position and the requirements. The only resistance she had to possibly taking the position was that she didn't want to be gone too long from Caitlyn.

As she pulled onto the long driveway, she noticed Tony's car was gone. He was usually home around this time. Maybe out playing golf.

Frowning, she parked and shut off the engine. Before she could knock, the white door swung open to Elaine smiling, "Hi Hanna, are you hungry?"

Hanna shook her head politely as she stepped inside, the familiar scent of garlic, basil, and slow-cooked tomatoes wrapping around her like a blanket.

She followed Elaine into the kitchen, where a pan of manicotti sat on the stove, across from a pot of homemade red sauce.

"Are you doing okay, Mom?" Hanna asked, watching Elaine stir the sauce.

Elaine let out a small sigh before nodding. "Yes. Just taking it in. I'm still processing everything about Tony Jr. I won't lie, it was a shock. But I'm glad the person responsible is behind bars."

She reached for a clean plate and grabbed a serving spoon. "Tea? Or how about just a little something to eat? I made some manicotti, or if you'd rather, I can pack some up for you to take home.

Hanna smiled. "I'll take some to go." The best part of having an Italian mother-in-law was that Elaine never let her leave empty-handed. Sometimes, *too* much.

Elaine smirked, already pulling out a container. "I'll throw in some garlic rolls too. Made those fresh this morning."

Hanna laughed. "Are you trying to fatten me up?"

Elaine fired back. "You're looking a little thin. I'll pack some for Steve, too. Sad about him and Rachel."

Hanna glanced up, curious. "What do you mean?"

Elaine set the tea down in front of her. "I spoke to Rachel's mother this morning." She hesitated for a moment before softening her voice. "It's nice of you to let him stay with you; I don't like you being alone in that house."

Hanna forced a smile, stirring honey into her tea. "It's nice having a roommate, but Mr. Donovan keeps a close eye on the house. On the people coming and going."

Elaine hummed, satisfied for now, before sitting across from her. "Now, Hanna, tell me what else is going on in your life?"

Hanna exhaled. *So much for a quick visit.*

A few hours later, Hanna glanced at the clock.

Caitlyn's bus would be here in forty-five minutes.

She apologized to Elaine for losing track of time, gathered the packed food, hugged her, and hurried out the door. It had been almost a week since she'd last seen Caitlyn. She was going to be *thrilled* when she found out Steve was staying with them.

CHAPTER 36

***

Hanna pulled into her driveway twenty minutes before the bus came. She carried the food into the kitchen and then took Caitlyn's belongings to her room, her heart already racing with anticipation.

Moments later, the front door burst open.

"Mommy!!" Caitlyn's blonde curls bounced as she ran to Hanna.

Hanna scooped her up, squeezing her tightly. "I missed you, squirt. Tell me all about your time with Grandma and Grandpa."

Caitlyn beamed. "Well, we played Uno and you know what?"

"No," responded Hanna.

She whispered, "Grandpa cheats!" as if he were in the room, "And then Grandma made all kinds of noodles. She even let me help!"

Hanna laughed. "Well, maybe you and I can make some this weekend."

Caitlyn's eyes widened. "We have a field trip coming up; we're going to the science museum! Can I go?" She dug into her backpack and pulled out a crumpled permission slip.

Hanna took it, scanning the form. "Of course. Two weeks from Friday, I might be off that day; you might get lucky, and I will be able to chaperone."

Caitlyn gasped. "Really? That'd be so neat!"

Hanna smiled. "Why don't you go put your things away?"

As Caitlyn sprinted down the hall, she suddenly stopped outside Steve's room, peeking inside.

"Mama, do we have a visitor?"

Hanna called back, "Uncle Steve is staying with us."

Caitlyn's face lit up. "Really! and she pulled down her arm. "Yes!"

She and Steve had a unique relationship; he was like a big kid, so it felt like Caitlyn was having a play date. Hanna wondered why he hadn't become a dad; he would have been so good at it.

"When will we be home?" Caitlyn asked.

"Late, sweetie, he is going out with a friend," she chuckled to herself

***

Nick arrived at Hudson & Vine. He walked in and noticed Steve wasn't there yet. Good. That gave him enough time to collect his thoughts and prepare for how the night would progress.

He grabbed a table near the bar. Thinking to himself that this was his only chance to turn things around. He didn't want Steve to see him as Doug's bratty little brother anymore. He wanted him to see him as an equal, a man worthy of Hanna, and he knew Steve was his way back in.

Moments later, the door swung open. Steve. The moment he spotted Nick, he thought to himself. *Here we go; hopefully, this will be short.*

Forcing a smile, he walked over. "Hey, Nick."

Nick leaned forward slightly. "Steve, hi, I'm really glad you could make it. I'm hoping we can use this time to resolve some things and get on a good path."

Steve kept his expression neutral, but his mind was already elsewhere. *I should have had Hanna bail me out. Why didn't I think of that before? She should have thought of it.*

"What are you having?" Nick asked. "I have the first round."

Steve sighed. "Whatever stout they have on tap."

"Great. I'll be right back."

As Nick walked away, Steve pulled out his phone and typed a quick message to Hanna: *Save me in forty-five minutes; call or text.*

Then, glancing up, he saw Nick flirting with the bartender.

Steve rolled his eyes and pulled his phone back out.

Make it thirty instead. He put his phone back into his pocket. Steve exhaled and rubbed his temple.

Thirty minutes. I just have to survive thirty minutes. He said to himself, watching Nick,

Nick returned, setting the beers down on the table, smiling. "Nice bartender," he said casually, taking a sip. "She's currently studying to be a nurse, and we had a good conversation, giving her pointers on how to ensure she gets a good floor at the hospital."

Steve smirked. "You get her number?"

Nick scoffed, shaking his head. "There's only one woman for me, and

CHAPTER 36

that woman is Hanna."

Steve didn't even blink, but his grip on his glass tightened slightly. "You don't say, 'Wait, what happened to that doctor you were seeing, Maxine, Maddie something,'" he muttered, wiping his mouth.

Nick leaned back, giving a relaxed shrug. "That is over, and I don't mean it like that, Steve." He made an uneasy chuckle. "I care about her. She's the kind of woman a man could build a life with."

Steve's expression didn't change. He just kept drinking his beer. His eyes were on Nick, watching his body language.

Nick kept going, playing it smoothly. "You get it, right? Like you and Rachel. How long have you two been together?"

Steve took a sip of his beer before answering. "Is there a point to why we're out tonight?

Nick exhaled, as if this was all just a friendly misunderstanding. "Come on, Steve. Can't two guys just have a drink?"

Steve leaned forward slightly, resting his forearms on the table. His voice was calm and measured. Dangerous. "Cut the bullshit, Nick."

Nick stilled.

Steve tilted his head. "I know what this is."

Nick forced a smile. "What do you think this is?"

Steve didn't blink. "You want me to tell Hanna you're a good guy? That you've 'changed.' That she should give you a chance." He let that hang for a second before adding, "And you think I'd actually go along with that?"

Nick chuckled, shaking his head. "Man, you really think I'm that calculated?"

Steve didn't answer. He simply took another sip of his beer.

Nick exhaled, setting his glass down. "Look, I get it. You're protective. You have always been. That's good; that's why Hanna trusts you."

Steve watched him. Waiting for the next line of bullshit

Nick leaned in slightly, lowering his voice. "But you're not her keeper."

Steve's jaw flexed, but he stayed silent.

Nick kept going. "At some point, you have to let her make her own choices. You really think Brian would want you standing in the way of her happiness?"

Steve went completely still.

For the first time, Nick felt a shift. It's a subtle, dangerous shift.

Then, Steve smiled. "You're right, Nick," he said smoothly, swirling his glass. "I do think Hanna should make her own choices." He leaned forward. "And that's exactly why I won't tell her to choose you; like you said, I need to let her make her own choices ."

Nick's fingers tightened around his beer, but his face remained neutral.

Steve smiled again, slower this time. "You know what I see when I look at you?"

But this time, Nick didn't answer.

Steve's voice was quiet, yet razor-sharp. "You know what I see, Nick? I see a guy who can't handle the fact that Hanna already made her choice." He took a slow sip. "And it wasn't you."

Nick forced himself to stay relaxed, but inside, his pulse was pounding.

Steve set his beer down, his gray eyes locked onto Nick's, unflinching. "You can play whatever game you want. Try to get inside her head, twist things however you like." He leaned in just slightly. "But it won't work on me."

Nick exhaled slowly, masking the irritation creeping into his chest, and he smiled, the way he always did when he knew the game wasn't over. "Steve, that's not what I'm trying to do." His voice was calm, easy. Convincing. "I understand," he murmured, lifting his glass in a casual toast. "I'm not trying to pressure Hanna into anything. I just want us to be cordial, maybe even friends. So things aren't as tense as they were last night."

Steve didn't respond. He just looked at Nick sipping his drink with no emotion.

Nick could almost hear the gears turning in his head. Good, that meant he was thinking about it. Nick exhaled, shaking his head like a man who just wanted to put the past behind him. "Look, I know you don't like me. And maybe I haven't given you much of a reason to; I probably wouldn't like me either." He met Steve's gaze, steady. "But I'm not the enemy here; I really am not."

CHAPTER 36

Steve took a slow sip of his beer, just watching him.

Nick pressed on. "Hanna and I, we've had our fair share of arguments. I get that. But I care about her, Steve. And whether you like it or not, I'm going to be in her life, whether it's just as a friend or as something more."

Steve's jaw tensed just slightly; he liked this game; it was a challenge. Nick did it subtly, but no doubt about it, it was a challenge, and Steve loved challenges.

Nick didn't push. Not yet. He leaned back instead, giving the illusion of letting go. "Look, man, she respects you, and the two of you have a close friendship," Nick continued. "I respect that, I really do. Steve, I'm not asking for a ringing endorsement, just..." He shrugged. "Maybe we should stop assuming the worst about each other and give each other a chance."

Steve set his beer down and smiled, the unfriendly kind of smile. "Nick," he said, voice smooth and measured. "I don't assume anything about you."

Nick arched a brow.

Steve leaned forward slightly. Not aggressive, just unshakable. "I know exactly who you are. I've seen it before. I deal with guys like you for a living."

Nick held his gaze, fingers tightening slightly around his glass. This wasn't going the way he wanted. Steve wasn't supposed to be this hard to break.

"Cordial," Steve repeated, his tone almost amused. "Friends." He let that sit for a moment as if he were actually considering it. Then he smirked. "Sure, Nick. I'm game. We can be friends."

Nick didn't like his tone. Steve was supposed to be willing and not mock him. Nick had underestimated him, and he needed to find a way to turn this around.

He forced a chuckle. "Look, man, I don't want bad blood between us." He kept his voice light and easy, the way someone trying too hard to be casual does. "I really want to try. I know we both have our... thoughts about each other, but maybe we can put that aside and find something in common, some kind of common ground. I really want to make the effort for Hanna."

Steve grinned, but it wasn't friendly. "Okay, I'll bite," he said, taking a slow sip of his beer. "What do we have in common?"

Nick kept his posture relaxed, though inside, he was recalculating.

"You like football?" Steve asked.

"Not really," Nick admitted.

Steve shrugged. "How about baseball?"

"No."

Steve smirked. "Nick, this isn't going so well. Do you like any sports?"

"Golf."

Steve nodded, considering. "Golf? Yeah, I don't like golf."

Nick took a slow sip, resisting the urge to grit his teeth. Steve was toying with him, and he didn't like it one bit

"Okay," Steve continued, "TV shows. What do you watch?"

Nick hesitated, choosing his words carefully. "I don't really watch much TV, but I like Grey's Anatomy and a show called Supernatural. It's in its second season. It's really good."

That actually made Steve stop and think. "I haven't seen either," he admitted. "But Supernatural sounds interesting. What's it about?"

Nick smiled. There it was, his opening. "It's a horror fantasy show about these two brothers, Dean and Sam Winchester, who hunt demons, ghosts, and other supernatural creatures across the country. It's the first show I've seen that blends urban legends and classic horror themes with a monster-of-the-week format. They often portray themselves as FBI agents."

Steve took another drink, nodding. "Interesting. So, every week, they kill a monster?"

"Yeah. Last week, they went after H.H. Holmes."

Steve's expression shifted. "The serial killer, the dead serial killer?"

Nick grinned. "Yeah. And they killed him."

"No shit," Steve muttered, and he was actually intrigued.

Nick could feel it, the shift, the crack in Steve's wall. He pressed a little more. "It's on Thursdays. I usually have it on. Maybe one night we can grab some beers and watch."

Steve took that in, studying him.

Nick had no idea if this was actually working.

CHAPTER 36

Then, Steve nodded. "You know, Nick, I think I might take you up on that."

Nick smiled. His strategy was actually working. He would have never expected a TV show to be the thing to break the ice, but Steve was biting just like he planned. He lifted his glass, taking a slow sip.

Across from him, Steve watched him carefully, finishing his beer. Inside, Steve looked at Nick and thought, I'm going to get you, you sick fuck. I will play you at your own game. He set his empty glass down and smiled. "Another beer, Nick?"

Nick grinned. "Yeah, I could use another one, thanks."

"Sure, no problem, I'll be right back." Steve got up, slapped Nick on the back hard, and headed to the bar.

Nick watched Steve at the bar, feeling the thrill of progress. They were bonding.

At the bar, Steve pulled out his phone, and Nick frowned slightly, watching him. Who was he texting?

A minute later, Steve returned, sliding Nick's beer across the table.

Nick picked up his glass. "Everything okay?"

Steve barely hesitated. "Yeah, man. Just gotta get back to Hanna's. Something happened with the kitchen faucet."

Nick frowned, feigning concern. "Want me to tag along? I'm a pretty good plumber."

Steve shook his head. "Nah, I got it. But thanks." He stood up, grabbing his coat. "Hate to do this to you, but I gotta run. Your beer's paid for."

Nick nodded slowly, forcing a grateful smile. "Thanks, man."

Steve clapped him on the shoulder a little too firmly and walked away. "Catch ya later."

Nick watched him go, a slow frown creeping onto his face. Something felt off.

Steve wasn't leaving because of a faucet. He was up to something. Nick took a slow sip of his beer, watching the door swing shut behind him. This is far from over.

Chapter 37

Steve arrived back at Hanna's house, shutting the door quietly behind him. The faint scent of hot cocoa lingered in the air.

As he walked down the hall, he peeked into the kitchen and spotted her at the table, laptop open, working on her case study, fingers flying over the keyboard. She was so focused, she didn't even hear him come in.

Steve smiled at the amateur mistake and moved as quietly as he could. He walked up behind her, resting his hands gently on her shoulders before leaning down to press a quick kiss against her cheek.

"Honey, I'm home," he teased. "Miss me?"

Hanna jumped and spun around, glaring. "What the hell, Steve? You scared the crap out of me! Keep it down; Caitlyn's sleeping!" She eyed him suspiciously. "Are you drunk? And what's with the kiss?"

Steve chuckled, dropping into the chair across from her. "Not drunk. Just had a good night."

She folded her arms. "Uh huh. What was so good about it that you needed me to lie about a broken faucet?"

Steve smirked. "Well, wifey, Nick thought he could convince me you should give him another shot."

Hanna blinked, then burst out laughing. "You're kidding."

"Nope." Steve leaned back, grinning. "Apparently bonding over sports and TV shows was supposed to seal the deal."

She rolled her eyes. "Did you bond?"

"Sure. I played along. I wanted to know what he's up to."

Hanna rubbed her temples. "Oh my God. This guy."

CHAPTER 37

Steve's voice softened, serious now. "He's not giving up, Hanna. Not yet. But whatever game he's playing, I'm not letting him win."

Her mouth lifted in a small, grateful smile.

Steve slapped her thigh playfully. "Anyway, tell me about busting him at Maddie's."

Hanna smirked, leaning back "Oh, it was beautiful. I stopped by Maddie's office, and she brought up the visit. He was there a few weeks ago. I told her I never received the report, and she decided to call Nick. It couldn't have gone any more perfectly. So she called him on speakerphone. Once she got him on the phone, she barely got out, 'Hi, Nick, it's Maddie,' before he cut her off, all smooth and charming, telling her he'd been thinking about her since last night."

Steve raised an eyebrow, smiling. "His Maddie?"

Hanna nodded, jaw tightening, "He didn't even realize I was there."

Steve chuckled darkly. "And when he did?"

"He panicked," Hanna said, satisfaction dripping from her voice. "Maddie cut him off, told him I was there, and followed up on his psych report from his visit with Richard a few weeks ago."

"Damn, Hanna," Steve said, impressed.

She smiled, then continued. "He hesitated. That half second of silence before he scrambled to cover? That was all I needed. He tried to lie and said he left the report in my mailbox."

Steve snorted. "Classic."

"I let him think he had a way out, and then Maddie, bless her heart, sealed the coffin shut."

Steve leaned in, "What'd she do?"

"She told him all documents, both physical and digital, are logged. That there was nothing in the logbook."

Steve let out a low whistle. "Damn. He knew he was caught."

"Oh, he knew," Hanna said. "And I played him, to let him think he still had some control. He offered to meet in an hour to 'go over' his results." She chuckled. "I told him I had an appointment, that it might be later."

Steve let out a sharp laugh. "Damn. You left him twisting in the wind."

"Now I just need to figure out why he met with Richard."

"Hanna." Steve's voice dropped. "Leave it alone."

"Why?"

"I already have my hands full with everything else going on. Just let Naomi figure it out." He paused. "Seriously, Hanna, please let it go."

"I just really want to know," Hanna really wanted to dig; she wanted to know why he visited him all those times.

Steve studied her. "Do you really think Richard will tell you the truth?"

"No," she admitted.

"Then let it go," Steve repeated, his voice firm. "Nick's caught, and he knows he's caught. That's punishment enough for now. We'll wait and see what his next move is."

Hanna was still disappointed. "I guess you're right."

Steve smiled. "Hanna, I'm always right."

She rolled her eyes and smacked him upside the head. "Ass."

They both laughed.

* * *

Later that night, Steve sat on the back porch; he got up and went to the ledge, the old wood creaking beneath his boots. The porch light cast a warm glow behind him, but he stayed outside, perched on the edge like a sentry.

Inside, faint sounds drifted through the walls, the crackle of a TV show Hanna had probably fallen asleep watching.

But Steve didn't move. His breath came slow and steady; clouds rose into the cold air. His hand brushed the side of his jacket, where his sidearm rested snug against his hip. Just in case.

They didn't know it, not really, but Hanna and Caitlyn were the closest thing he had to a family.

His holidays. He enjoyed his Sunday dinners immensely. His life.

His thoughts shifted to Caitlyn, fiery, funny, and fierce. Everything he would've wanted if he'd ever had kids of his own.

CHAPTER 37

And then his mind drifted back to a promise made long ago.

* * *

November 3, 1997

Brian lay propped in the hospital bed, bruised and pale, bandages wrapping his ribs and a dark cut above his brow. The steady beep of the monitor was the only sound until Steve stepped in, hands shoved in his jacket pockets.

"You look like hell," Steve said, managing a half smile.

Brian let out a weak laugh. "Feel worse. Like I went ten rounds with a semi."

"They say you're gonna be okay."

Brian shrugged. "So they say. My body says otherwise."

Silence stretched between them.

Steve leaned against the wall, arms crossed. He hated hospitals. Hated seeing Brian like this, hooked to machines, color drained from his face.

Then Brian turned toward him, his voice quieter. "If I don't make it..."

"Don't start with that," Steve cut in, jaw tensing.

"I mean it." Brian's tone didn't waver. "If something happens, I need you to promise me. Take care of her."

Steve looked away, swallowing the lump rising in his throat. "Brian, come on."

"I'm serious." Brian's eyes locked on his. "You've always had her back. If I can't... you have to."

Steve exhaled slowly, the weight of those words pressing down on him. "You're not dying."

"Maybe not. But just in case..." Brian winced, adjusting slightly. "She's strong. She'll get through it. But she's gonna need someone who doesn't run."

Steve hesitated.

"I don't trust anyone else," Brian added. "Not with Hanna. Not with Caitlyn." The room fell still.

"I promise," Steve said, his voice rough. "Like I did before. I'll protect them. I'll raise Caitlyn like she's mine."

Brian smiled faintly, then coughed. The tissue he picked up took on a red hue.

"You want me to get a nurse?" Steve asked, already stepping forward.

Brian waved him off. "They said this might happen."

Steve didn't sit. Couldn't. He just stood there, watching his best friend fade a little more around the edges.

Brian looked up, his voice low. "If I don't make it, don't just protect her. Don't let her get lost."

Steve nodded once. "She won't be alone. I'll make sure of it."

Brian's eyelids fluttered as the pain began to pull him under again. "That's why I asked you. You're the only one I trust."

* * *

Present Day 2006

Steve sat alone on Hanna's porch, staring out at the trees as the quiet settled around him. The memories came whether he wanted them to or not.

He had kept that promise to Brian, and he always would. He had shown up for Caitlyn when it mattered. He was there for pancakes on Sundays, for school projects and field trips, and for the dances and the birthdays. He had been a steady presence in her life, just like he said he would be.

Rachel had tried to understand. She came around sometimes. She smiled when she was supposed to. She made an effort, at least in the beginning.

He did love them. Maybe not the same way Brian did, because no one could, but enough to protect them with everything he had. He only wished Rachel could see that.

He sighed and dragged a hand down his face. *Fuuuck.* Rachel had been the mistake that stayed. What began as a night of drinks and sex had stretched into twelve years of something he could never quite define. She kept showing up, and he kept letting her in.

He liked her. She was beautiful and smart. She knew how to work a room and looked good on his arm. She was a great date to a formal event. But he wasn't in love with her. Not really.

She was a comfort. A familiar bed. A distraction. A relationship that became a routine because walking away had always felt harder than staying.

CHAPTER 37

He didn't want to lose her. But he sure as hell didn't want to marry her either.

The door creaked open behind him. Hanna stepped out, a blanket draped over her shoulders. She placed a gentle hand on his back.

"You okay?" she asked softly.

Steve smiled up at her. "Yeah. Just getting some air."

"Can I join you?"

"Of course."

He grabbed a chair for her, and she settled in close.

"You looked deep in thought," Hanna said.

"Just thinking," Steve replied.

"About?"

He chuckled low. "Why I shouldn't get married."

"Steve!" she scolded, laughing.

He shook his head, more serious now. "No... maybe you're right. Maybe it's time I gave her it all."

He looked up at the sky. "Hanna."

"Hmm?"

"What if she's not the right one?"

Hanna hesitated. "I'd say after twelve years... she probably is."

"I guess," he said quietly. "But what if she isn't?"

She turned toward him, earnest. "Then don't do it, Steve. Don't let us pressure you. You have to do what feels right for you and for her. Otherwise...you'll both be miserable, like my parents were."

Steve didn't answer.

The porch went quiet again, filled only with the soft rustle of wind through the trees and the far off hum of a highway.

After a moment, Hanna spoke. Her voice was low. "When I was thirteen, my mom used to take me to the mall with her friends. Said it was our day out, just us girls."

Steve glanced over but stayed quiet.

"She'd give me a hundred bucks and tell me to go wander. To go buy something. Encouraging me to go hang with my friend's." Hanna paused, wiping a tear from her cheek. "At first, I thought she really wanted to spend time with me. Like it was our thing. But she didn't want to bond. She wanted me gone long enough to sit in the food court with her boyfriend, her boyfriend who was six years older than me."

Her voice didn't shake, but something in her eyes did.

"She made it feel like freedom. Like she trusted me. I thought it was special, you know? That she believed in me and wanted a relationship with me. But it wasn't that. I was a cover story. A built-in excuse. So my father didn't know she was screwing around."

Steve's jaw tightened.

"And when she left, that was it. No calls. No visits. Nothing. She was off chasing the teenage dream she never got to live. I don't think she ever wanted to be a mom. I think she just wanted to feel wanted."

Steve reached for her hand.

"My dad wasn't much better. He didn't want us because he loved us. He wanted to win. He thought if he had the kids, she'd come back. It was all a game. And we were just the middle piece. Kevin was smart; he didn't buy into it. But me?" Her voice caught slightly. "I just wanted to feel loved. I thought maybe it was finally my turn. That I mattered like Kevin did."

She looked down at their joined hands.

"I used to take whatever I could get. Even if it hurt. Even if it wasn't real. Just to feel like I mattered."

Steve squeezed her fingers gently. "Hanna… I didn't know. I didn't realize how bad it was. I never really questioned why you lived with your grandparents. You do matter, and I know you mattered to them."

She smiled faintly, but it didn't quite reach her eyes. "Then promise me something."

"Anything."

"Don't marry someone because it's been twelve years. Or because people expect it. Marry someone who sees you, Steve. Who really sees you for you. Because if you do it for the wrong reasons… it's the kids who suffer."

Steve sat quietly. He didn't know how to respond, not really. The words were too heavy, too honest. He never realized how bad it was for her.

CHAPTER 37

After a moment, he stood and reached for her hand. "Let's go inside," he said quietly.

He helped her up, and together they walked toward the house. As they stepped through the door, Steve cast one last glance toward the dark horizon.

He had made a promise, and he was going to keep it.

* * *

Outside the Window... A figure stood in the shadows, watching her, watching them.

Steve's effortless confidence and the way he moved through Hanna's home like he belonged there. He caressed and kissed her, and she allowed him to do so. They were too comfortable and getting too close.

His hands curled into fists, jaw tightening. She was supposed to need him, not Steve; she was supposed to see what was right in front of her. Instead, she sat there, laughing, trusting Steve, as if he was the one who could protect her. It seemed as though he was the one who truly understood her. Did she love him? His thoughts raced; they were always touching each other, and the way he looked at her and she at him.

He gripped his fists tighter; if she wasn't going to see on her own that he was better than Steve, then he'd have to show her.

Moving silently, he walked to the mailbox, slipping a single plain envelope inside, with her name written in sharp, deliberate letters:

HANNA.

A slow smirk curled his lips. She would understand soon enough. She would see who truly belonged in her life. Who truly had her best interests at heart. As he disappeared into the night, one thought pulsed in his mind like a heartbeat.

Let the games begin.

Chapter 38

The next morning, Hanna walked in on Steve feeding Caitlyn pancakes.

"Mama, Uncle Steve made pancakes! Look at all of them!" Caitlyn's gray eyes widened with excitement, still puffy from sleep but sparkling with delight.

Hanna grabbed her coffee, taking a slow sip as she crouched beside Caitlyn's chair, nuzzling her lightly. "That he did," she murmured, breathing in the soft, sleepy warmth of her daughter. "Good morning."

"Morning, Mama." Caitlyn grinned, taking a big bite of pancake.

Steve glanced over. "Pancakes?"

"Not today, but thank you." Hanna settled into a chair, savoring the rare moment of peace. She liked having Steve here; the house felt less hollow, and truthfully, so did she. It never felt like this when Nick was around. Back then, it had always been tense, uneasy.

Steve leaned forward, smiling, elbows resting on the table. "What's the plan today?"

"I have a spelling test and gym," Caitlyn announced proudly.

Steve narrowed his eyes at her. "Did you study for your test?"

Caitlyn scoffed, giving him a confused look. "Do I look like someone who doesn't take spelling seriously?"

Steve and Hanna exchanged a look of amused surprise before breaking into smiles.

"You do look like someone who likes to slack," Steve teased.

Caitlyn slowly turned her head toward him, mouth open in mock outrage.

CHAPTER 38

"I bet you didn't study in school either! You *look* like you didn't know how."

Hanna almost choked on her coffee, laughing.

Steve grinned. "You're lucky I like you," he said, ruffling her hair.

After Caitlyn finished her breakfast, Hanna hurried her to get ready. They barely made the bus; they were caught up in their laughter and morning fun. For a moment, Hanna let herself wonder if this was what life could have been like if Brian hadn't died.

Shaking the thought away, she grabbed a few bills and headed out to the mailbox. She opened the metal door and froze.

A single envelope sat inside. Her name was scrawled across the front.

A chill crept up her spine.

Slowly, she pulled it out, the paper feeling foreign in her hands, wrong somehow. She turned back toward the house, walking faster.

She threw open the door. "Steve!" she called, her voice sharper than she intended.

Heavy footsteps thundered down the hall. Steve appeared instantly, his eyes locking onto the envelope trembling in her hand. His whole expression shifted, hardening.

He took it carefully by the corner. "Don't touch it anymore," he said firmly.

Disappearing into his room, he returned seconds later pulling on plastic gloves. "Get me a freezer bag," he ordered, his voice low and controlled.

Hanna grabbed one from the kitchen, her hands shaking.

Steve carefully slid the envelope into the bag, then pulled out the letter. His eyes scanned the words. His jaw clenched.

"What does it say?" Hanna asked, her stomach twisting.

Steve hesitated. "You don't need to hear this, Han."

"Tell me," she insisted. "I have a right to know."

He exhaled, clearing his throat before reading:

Hanna,
You don't see me, but I see everything.

> *I saw you last night the way you leaned in close with the warmth in your touch, I see the quiet comfort you find in him. The way he looks at you like he could keep you safe. But he can't.*
>
> *I wonder, did you feel it? Do you feel my presence, does it get your heart racing?*
>
> *You move through your life thinking you're in control, that your world is predictable, that the people around you are enough. But you forget. I don't need an invitation. I am always there, watching and waiting for you. Hanna I am closer than you think, a lot closer.*

Hanna gasped, cold dread sinking deep into her bones. "I'm being watched?"

Steve's expression went steely. He stepped forward, voice low and unwavering.

"Nothing will happen to you," he said. "I promise."

He sealed the letter carefully in the bag.

"What about Caitlyn? Is she safe?" Hanna's voice cracked.

Steve grabbed her shoulders, steadying her.

"Hanna, listen to me. I promise, nothing, and I mean nothing, is going to happen to you or Caitlyn. Not on my watch."

But for some reason, that didn't make her feel any better.

Steve exhaled sharply, already shifting back into action. "Go get ready. I'm taking you to work. You're not going anywhere alone today."

Hanna nodded, too numb to argue, and turned down the hall.

***

As soon as she disappeared into her room, Steve stepped outside, dialing his phone.

"Hi, it's Steve. We have a problem," he said quietly. "Someone left Hanna a threatening letter. I think we need to move Caitlyn out for a couple of days until I figure out who's behind it. Call me back."

He tucked the phone away and swept the yard with his eyes. The grass

CHAPTER 38

was still damp from the morning dew, but near the edge of the property, he spotted subtle impressions in the ground. Someone had stood there, watching.

Steve crouched low, running his fingers through the dirt, searching for anything: footprints, cigarette butts, fibers. But there was nothing.

Whoever it was had been careful. But not careful enough.

Steve stood and pulled out his phone again.

"Agent Matteson, it's Director Riley. I'm bringing in an envelope. I need a team to check the yard and do a full sweep. I'll text the address."

"Copy that." Matteson asked. "What am I walking into?"

Steve's jaw tensed. He scanned the empty yard one last time. "This wasn't some punk screwing around. Someone left a message. I want to know who."

"We'll be there."

Steve ended the call and stood for a moment, letting the cold settle into his bones. Whoever had come here believed they wouldn't be noticed. They believed Hanna was exposed, that Caitlyn was unprotected. And as much as he hated to admit it, a part of Steve feared they might be right.

For a second, doubt gnawed at him, a sharp, unwelcome thought.

How could he protect both of them? How could he keep them safe when the threat was already this close?

A wave of fear rose in his chest, sharp and sudden, like the weight of a promise cracking under pressure. It felt like failing Brian, like betraying the vow he had made to protect them as if they were his own. Now he was chasing shadows, following footprints through the dark. He clenched his jaw and pushed the fear down. This time, he would not fail. Not while he was still standing.

Steve sent the address to Matteson and slid his phone back into his pocket. Whoever had been standing outside that window believed they had the advantage. They were wrong. Steve Riley didn't back down from threats. He confronted them head-on.

Chapter 39

The ride to the prison was quiet; all Hanna could think about was that letter, Steve couldn't promise she would be OK.

"What time is your last appointment?" he asked.

Hanna pulled her planner out of her bag. "It's a long one today, 2:30."

"I will be back here by then; do not come out until you get my call that I am here, and Hanna, I promise you, I will not let anything happen to you."

Hanna nodded; it still did not make her feel better. "I will see you at 2:30. Thanks, Steve."

Hanna got out of the truck; it felt as if Steve was just as shaken up. She was hoping that Steve and Rachel would settle things but now felt that this was only going to get in the way.

Hanna headed to her office, checked in, and the pat-down was quick today. She turned on her light and set her things down at the desk. First appointment today, Richard. She got her things together and headed down to the interview room.

Hanna stepped into the room, the heavy door clanking shut behind her. The air was stale, thick with the scent of old sweat and metal. Richard sat in the single chair, his wrists and ankles shackled, the chains rattling slightly as he shifted. His head was tilted back against the cold concrete wall, eyes half-lidded, a lazy smirk tugging at his lips as he watched her approach.

"You look tired, Hanna," he murmured. "Not sleeping well?"

She ignored the bait. "How are you today, Richard?"

His smirk deepened. "Now that's sweet of you. But we both know you don't really care."

CHAPTER 39

She crossed her arms. "I wouldn't be here if I didn't."

Richard let out a low chuckle, shaking his head slightly. "You're here because you think there's something left to salvage. A little piece of my soul that hasn't rotted away yet." His gaze locked onto hers, sharp and calculating. "Am I right?"

Hanna didn't answer. She wouldn't give him the satisfaction.

Richard exhaled through his nose, rubbing his jaw where the bruises were still faintly visible. "I've been thinking about her."

Hanna narrowed her eyes. "Who, Richard?"

"Marcia." His voice dipped lower, thoughtful. "The third one."

She waited, giving him space to talk, knowing he wanted to drag it out, to savor every second.

"She shouldn't have been there," he continued. "She was nothing but a woman standing in the wrong place at the wrong time. And you know what the worst part is?" He lifted his gaze, something almost wistful in his expression. "She thought she could beg her way out of it."

Hanna clenched her jaw.

Richard laughed under his breath, shaking his head. "Begging never works, does it? She tried, though. So many promises, so many desperate little words." He sighed. "I almost felt bad for her, well, almost."

Hanna took a step closer. "And yet you killed her anyway."

His eyes darkened. "Of course I did."

The silence stretched, thick and suffocating. Then Richard's entire demeanor shifted. His smirk vanished, his head tilting slightly. The chains rattled as he leaned forward as much as they would allow, his voice lower now, harsher.

"Men aren't as easy as women."

The change sent a slow chill crawling up Hanna's spine, but she kept her expression neutral. "What do you mean?"

Richard's lips twitched, not a smile, but something else, something predatory. "Their screams are different; they are, let's say, worse. Women scream with desperation and fear. But men?" His gaze darkened, flicking up to hers. "Men scream like they still think they can fight."

The room felt smaller and even a little colder.

"Thomas DeLuca," Richard murmured, his voice almost reverent. "Now, *he* was interesting."

Hanna stiffened.

Richard watched her reaction, the corner of his mouth lifting again. "You ever hear a man scream, Hanna? I mean, really *scream*? Not the panicked kind, not the 'please don't kill me' kind. But the kind that comes when they *know, know* they aren't getting out of it?"

She didn't answer.

Richard chuckled; the sound was low and unsettling. "Thomas screamed higher than any woman ever did. I took him piece by piece. I wanted to see how loud he'd get." His fingers flexed slightly against the cold metal of the shackles. "And he didn't disappoint."

"Richard, was it because you wanted control? Or was it that you found enjoyment in the screams?" Hanna asked, still trying to control her emotions

Richard's grin widened. Slowly and deliberately, he let her question hang between them for a moment; he wanted to feel her reaction. His fingers began to drum against the metal of his shackles, his gaze never leaving hers.

"Control?" he echoed, tasting the word as if it amused him. "Is that what you think this was about, doctor?"

Hanna didn't blink. "Well, isn't it?"

Richard exhaled through his nose, tilting his head slightly. "Control is predictable and calculated. But this..." His voice dipped lower, almost thoughtful. "This wasn't about control." His eyes darkened, his expression shifting in a way that Hanna couldn't quite place, something that had made her grip tighten into fists at her sides. "It was more about curiosity."

A slow chill crept up her spine, but she refused to let it show.

Richard leaned forward as much as the chains allowed, his voice softer now, almost intimate. "I wanted to see, Hanna, to know how far a man like Thomas could go before he broke, and I mean really broke, before he realized that the name and the bloodline meant nothing." He took a second to continue to savor the memory. "And you know what I learned?"

CHAPTER 39

Hanna swallowed hard but kept her face unreadable. "What?"

Richard smirked. "Men will say anything, do anything, but in the end? Men, women, they all scream the same."

The words hung heavy in the air between them.

Hanna steadied her breathing, fighting against the unease curling in her gut. "And did you enjoy it, hearing them scream?"

Richard tapped a finger against the chair, the smallest flicker of amusement in his gaze. "Now, that's the real question, isn't it?" He leaned back, stretching his fingers as if savoring the feeling of movement despite the chains. "What answer do you want, Hanna?"

"I want the truth, Richard. I can't help you if I don't know it."

He chuckled, shaking his head. "No, you want *your* truth. The version of me that fits into whatever box you've built in that head of yours." He let the silence stretch before he added, "I'll tell you what, though…if you want to know whether or not I enjoyed it," his voice dropping to something just above a whisper, "well then, Doc, you already know the answer, don't you?"

Her stomach turned, but she forced herself to hold his gaze.

Richard smiled. "See, you're learning. I told you, we aren't that different."

Hanna exhaled sharply, pushing away from the wall, her body screaming at her to leave. But she couldn't, not yet. She was intrigued and wanted to know more and dig deeper.

Richard, with his eyes fixed on her, watching her take it all in, "Now Tony Jr., he didn't scream, but then again, I didn't give him a chance to; I took his head right off. He never saw it coming. Izzy screamed, but she screamed because she didn't expect this from me."

Hanna forced her shoulders to stay squared, even as a sickening weight settled in her stomach. She wouldn't give him the reaction he wanted.

Richard leaned back against the chair, the chains rattling slightly as he moved. His grin was slow, almost lazy, but his eyes were something else, black pits that swallowed the dim light of the room.

"Tony Jr.," he repeated, voice as smooth as silk, "didn't even get the chance to scream. One clean stroke, and it was over, my most perfect kill." He made a flicking motion with his fingers as if wiping something away. " It was quick and, frankly, quite efficient. One would say it was almost merciful the way I did it, don't you think?"

Hanna clenched her jaw but said nothing, watching his eyes and his body language.

Richard's smirk deepened. "But Izzy? Oh, *she* screamed." He let out a low chuckle, shaking his head as if reliving the moment. "Oh, she screamed because she never saw it coming. It wasn't about pain, no, that scream was because of pure betrayal. She didn't expect that from me, of all people?" He clicked his tongue. "That one stuck with me; I think I lost her before that accident took her."

"So you do compare your kills, correct, Richard?" Hanna questioned.

He lifted a brow, amused. "Wouldn't you? I mean, think about it, it's no different than you collecting experiences or a little girl collecting dolls. You tuck them away for a while, and then when you need to feel something, you pull them back out?" He leaned forward slightly, chains clinking. "Now, tell me, Hanna… what do *you* collect? Wait, you seem like the type of person who collects letters and rereads them when you want to relive a memory, is that right?"

She ignored the question. "And what does this do for you? Reliving and categorizing them?"

Richard let out a slow breath, tilting his head as if considering her words. "It reminds me," he said, voice sharp and cruel, almost thoughtful, "that every single one of them belonged to me in their final moments, that I took their last breath."

The words slithered down her spine, settling like ice in her veins. Hanna inhaled through her nose, forcing her pulse to slow. "Richard, I think you want me to react, maybe even flinch, but that's not going to happen."

Richard's lips twitched. "I know," he murmured. "That's what makes this so much fun, but, Doc, I do promise you, by the time we finish together, I will get a reaction out of you."

She exhaled slowly, locking her gaze onto his, changing the direction of the conversation. "You said choices were made for you and that you never wanted this, but yet you sit here bragging about it. "

CHAPTER 39

His eyes flickered, just for a second.

Hanna pressed on. "So which is it, Richard? Were you a victim, or did you enjoy it? It can't be both."

He went still, and for the first time, the smirk disappeared completely.

Then, slowly, Richard leaned back, a small, quiet chuckle escaping his lips. "Oh, Hanna, darling," he murmured. "You're finally asking me the right questions."

The hair on Hanna's neck stood up; she had to get through five more minutes with him. "OK, Richard, if I am asking the right questions, then answer me: were you the victim? Because from where I am sitting, you enjoyed it too much to be the victim."

Richard's smirk didn't return this time. Instead, he studied her, his head tilting just slightly, his fingers tapping against the cold metal of the shackles. The silence stretched, thick and suffocating, wrapping around them like a noose. Then, finally, he exhaled through his nose, almost as if he was disappointed. "You still think those are separate things," he said, his voice lower now, almost gentle.

Hanna forced herself to hold his gaze. "A victim doesn't have a choice, Richard. You did; you *chose* to kill and take those lives."

He chuckled, shaking his head. "Did I? Do you really think I had a choice, Hanna?" His fingers flexed, slow and deliberate. "You think I walked into this life? That I wanted it, that I chose to be born to a woman who gave a rat's ass about me or a man who would not acknowledge me as his son?" He leaned forward as much as the chains would allow. "Let me tell you something: when a gun is put in your hand, when the first order is given, it's not a question of whether you'll do it, it's a question of when, *a*nd if you hesitate, you become the example." His voice cracked as he said, "So no, Hanna, I had no choice."

Hanna's jaw tightened. "So you're saying you killed to survive."

"At first," Richard murmured, tilting his head, watching her reaction. "That's the part you want to hear, isn't it? That I was just another scared kid trying to make it out alive?" His lips curled, the darkness creeping back into his expression. "But here's the part you don't want to hear." He leaned in, his voice dropping to a whisper. "I stopped being scared a long time ago."

Richard let the silence drag, savoring the moment. "You want to believe there's some tragic story that explains all of this. Something that makes it easier to swallow. But the truth, well?" He exhaled, shaking his head. "There *is* no clear line between being a victim and being a monster. You cross it once, and suddenly, it doesn't exist anymore."

Hanna said softly, "So you enjoyed it."

Richard's grin returned, but it was smaller this time, more controlled. "I learned not to care." His eyes darkened. "And once you stop caring, you start wondering what else you can do."

Hanna kept her face unreadable.

"Ah, look at that, our time is almost up, isn't it?" Richard mused, tilting his head toward the clock. "Tell me, Hanna, did you get what you came for, or did you want to stretch this out further?"

She stood slowly, steadying her breathing. "I think that is enough for today."

Richard chuckled under his breath. "Until next time, *dock tour*."

Hanna turned toward the door.

And just before she left, his voice followed her, low and taunting.

"Hey, doc, next time, ask me which one I liked the most; that one will put your panties in a bunch."

* * *

She couldn't shake the chill, so she quickly walked into Michael's office and plopped into the chair in front of his desk.

"Sure, make yourself at home," he said.

"Michael, you have to listen to this," she said, handing him the tape player. He rewound the tape player over and over again, his fingers steady despite the way his jaw tightened. The audio crackled softly, Richard's voice spilling into the room like a slow-moving toxin.

"*Men aren't as easy as women. Their screams are worse... Thomas DeLuca*

CHAPTER 39

screamed higher than any woman. I took him piece by piece, seeing how loud he'd get."

The color drained from Michael's face. He pressed stop. The silence that followed was heavier than any sound.

He looked up at Hanna, puzzled at first, but she caught the slight tension in his shoulders, the way his fingers curled slightly into fists.

"I'm impressed you stayed so calm; I would have been sick to my stomach by then," he finally said.

Hanna exhaled, running her fingers through her bangs. "I am not going to lie. It was tough and a little unexpected."

Michael leaned back in his chair, rubbing a hand over his face. "We thought we knew how bad he was." He gestured to the tape. "Turns out, we had no idea, but I can't stop thinking, is he playing us?"

Hanna nodded and brushed off his statement, "I think we need to bring Naomi back in. It seems Mr. Hale is admitting to a lot more than we thought. What was strange is he admitted to it like it was nothing."

Michael didn't hesitate, and he picked up his phone, already dialing. "I'll get her here within the hour."

Hanna forced herself to sit still, but her leg bounced under the desk. Michael noticed. "He got to you, didn't he?" he said quietly.

She looked up at him, eyes sharp. "He wanted to," she paused, "maybe a little."

Michael sighed, running a hand down his face as he studied her. The tape sat between them, its presence heavier than either of them acknowledged.

"I think we need to assign another therapist to this case, Hanna," he said finally, his voice measured but firm. "This is really getting too close to home, and I don't like where it is headed."

Hanna shook her head. "No, I want to see this through; I have to see it through. I honestly think he'll continue to open up to me; he is setting me up for something. I promise I am okay." She leaned back in the chair. "Michael, I *need* the distraction right now. I have a lot going on outside of work."

Her mind drifted back to the letter she and Steve had found that morning.

The words kept replaying in her mind, carving themselves into her thoughts like a whisper she couldn't shake.

"You move through your life thinking you're in control, that your world is predictable, that the people around you are enough. But you forget..."

She still didn't know what unsettled her more: the words themselves or the fact that she didn't know *who* had sent them.

Michael studied her before finally nodding. "Hanna, it's still against my better judgment," he said, his voice quiet but firm. "But I trust you; just swear to me you will jump off of it the minute it gets to be too much."

Hanna swallowed, nodding. "Then trust me when I say I need to finish this."

Michael leaned forward, elbows on his desk, eyes locked onto hers. "Then don't let him inside your head, because once he's in, I am afraid he won't leave."

She nodded again, but even as she said it, she wasn't sure if it was already too late.

Chapter 40

Steve sat in his office, looking down at the footage in front of him. He tried focusing, but his thoughts went to Hanna and to Rachel. He took out his phone, dialed Rachel's number, left a voicemail, and hung up. He called a hundred more times but did not leave a message. His head rested on his hands. He missed her. He had a duty to protect Hanna, but he loved Rachel, and his life was with her.

He looked at the footage again. There he was, the same figure that he had seen at the cabin. He looked again, and in the distance, was that?

He zoomed in as far as he could; there was another one. He began to feel this was bigger than he thought.

There was a knock at his door that startled him. A young man, maybe early twenties with dark brown hair, walked in. "Sir, if I may,"

"What do you have?" Steve asked, "Sir, we found three sets of prints from different shoes. If you examine the prints, you will see that they belong to three different people. The Trace Evidence Unit is working with footwear impression examiners, and we should have something back later today."

Steve nodded his head, and the young man headed toward the door. "Wait," he pulled a video out of his drawer. "Take this to FAVIAU and have them examine it. There is a person on this; have them check for another." He handed him the tape.

"Yes, sir." He left the room.

Steve went back to the recordings.

"I'll get you, you bastard," he muttered, staring at the image on the screen. He took out his phone again and tried calling Rachel.

This time, it rang.

She answered on the second ring.

"Steve?"

"Rach, where have you been? I've been calling you all morning."

"Steve, I don't have any messages."

There was a brief silence. "I didn't leave any." He said, ashamed, "Can you meet me at the park for lunch?"

"I don't know, Ste… "

"Please?" he cut in, his voice quieter this time.

"Okay. I'll meet you."

"Rach, I'll see you at noon."

"Bye, Steve."

The line went dead.

Steve packed up; before heading to the park, he had one important stop.

* * *

Steve sat on the bench at the park, his knee bouncing, fingers wrapped tight around the small box in his pocket like it could anchor him. He'd rehearsed the words a thousand times, but now, with Rachel minutes away, his mind was blank.

It had only been a week, but it felt longer. Seven days without her voice, without her beside him in the quiet. He missed her. He did. But somehow, it all felt heavier now. Messier. Not just absence, but something else. Something unsettled.

He'd spent too much time with Hanna. Enjoyed it more than he should have. More than he was willing to admit out loud.

This wasn't supposed to be a forever break. He wasn't walking away. He couldn't.

But the ring in his pocket didn't feel like certainty anymore.

It felt like a question he wasn't sure he wanted answered.

Pressure. He hated pressure.

But he didn't want this to drag on either.

CHAPTER 40

She'd forced his hand. He didn't have a choice.

He looked up at the sound of heels on pavement, and there she was. Rachel. Beautiful, familiar, and unsure.

She stopped a few feet away, arms crossed like a barrier. "Okay, Steve. I'm here. Talk."

He stood and took a breath. "Rach... I've been miserable without you."

She looked as if she didn't quite believe him. "Steve "

"No. Let me say this." He stepped closer, gripping her hand. "I was an idiot. I didn't realize what I had. I don't want to lose you."

He held her gaze. "I've been thinking... and the truth is my life doesn't make sense without you. At least... I *don't think* it does."

Her fingers curled around his, instinctively.

"I still love you," he said quietly. "I want to believe we're still us."

But the truth was he didn't *know*.

Before she could respond, he leaned in and kissed her. Desperate. Hopeful. Maybe even afraid.

She flinched barely but then leaned into him, matching the kiss with her ache.

When he pulled back, he didn't let her go.

Instead, he knelt down.

Her breath caught. "Steve..."

He pulled the box from his pocket and opened it. The ring sparkled in the fading light.

"I love you," he said. "Be my wife. Be with me."

The silence was too long. And maybe that should've told him something. Finally, Rachel nodded. "Yes."

He forced a smile and slid the ring onto her hand. Her fingers trembled. She stared at it, then looked up. "Steve... are you *sure*?"

He didn't hesitate. "I am."

But maybe he said it too quickly. Maybe he had to. "Let's get married. Today."

She gave a breathy laugh. "I can't; I have patients."

"Tomorrow, then."

She kissed him, soft and uncertain. "Let me enjoy this first, okay?"

He nodded.

"I love you," she whispered.

"I love you too."

But the way she looked at him… it wasn't all joy. It was something else. Like she was hoping this could be enough. Like he was, too.

"Does Hanna know?" she asked.

He shook his head. "No. I stopped at the jewelry store on the way here."

"Spontaneous," she said, but her tone wasn't teasing. It was quiet and careful.

"Can you come by Hanna's tonight?"

"You're not coming home?"

He wanted to; he wanted nothing more than to go home. "I wish. She got a letter this morning."

Rachel gasped. "Where is she now?"

"I dropped her off at the prison."

Her expression twisted. "What about Caitlyn? Who would do this to them?"

"Caitlyn's going to Tony's."

Rachel hesitated. "What if we brought her to our house?"

Steve shook his head. "I can't put you in harm's way. I'd never forgive myself."

She nodded, understanding, but it didn't mean she liked it. "I should go," she said softly.

"I love you," he told her.

She nodded again, more slowly this time. "I love you."

As she walked away, she pulled out her phone, thumb hovering over Hanna's name. The voicemail picked up. "Hanna… he proposed. I don't know what you said to him, but thank you."

She ended the call but didn't put the phone away.

Her gaze drifted to the ring on her finger. It sparkled in the fading light, so beautiful, so right. But her chest tightened.

Chapter 41

Hanna had the house to herself. It was her turn to host Thanksgiving, and this year would be different without her grandparents; Henry was gone, and Irene was staying in Vermont with Peter. Caitlyn was with Tony and Elaine, and Steve was off with Rachel, doing wedding things. It gave her time to sit with her thoughts and try, unsuccessfully, to make sense of everything.

From the other room, her phone rang.

She ran in quickly and glanced at the screen, Nick.

Her thumb hovered. Every instinct screamed *Don't answer.*

Despite her better judgment, she rolled her eyes and answered.

That was her first mistake.

"Hanna?" His voice was tight. Anxious.

She forced a smile, gripping her mug tightly. "Hi, Nick. How are you?"

"I'm..." he exhaled. "I was wondering if we could talk. Would it be okay if I came over?"

Her stomach twisted. With Steve not home, she wasn't sure she wanted to be alone with him, but there was something in Nick's voice. It wasn't smug or demanding; it was almost... broken.

"Fine. You can come over."

"Is now good?" he asked quickly.

"Sure."

"See you soon."

* * *

Fifteen minutes later, Nick stood in her doorway.

His clothes were wrinkled, his hair slightly damp from the evening mist, and his hands stayed buried in his pockets. He looked nothing like the polished doctor the world knew. His eyes were red-rimmed, not from lack of sleep alone; she could tell he'd been crying. That much was clear.

Hanna's concern spiked, chased quickly by a ripple of unease. Something was off.

"What is it, Nick?"

He stepped inside slowly, his movements awkward, uncertain, like a man carrying too much and not sure where to put it down. His eyes flicked around the room, then back to her.

"I need to tell you something," he said, voice low. "Something I should've told you a long time ago."

She tilted her head, cautious. "Okay. Come sit down."

They moved to the living room. He dropped into the armchair with the weight of someone much older than he was. She took the couch across from him, her muscles already tensing.

"Can I get you water or something?"

He shook his head. "No. I'm okay."

She nodded once. "What's going on?"

Nick leaned forward, elbows on his knees. He looked at his hands as if they might hold the answers he didn't want to say out loud.

"It's everything, Hanna. All the things I kept hidden because I thought if you knew the truth, you'd walk away for good." His voice cracked slightly. He didn't look at her yet.

Hanna waited, still, her heart thudding slowly in her chest. "What did you do, Nick?"

He dragged a hand through his hair and let out a bitter laugh. "I was jealous, Hanna. I've been jealous since we were kids. The first time I saw you was at that party, the one where you were talking to Jason Murphy. He grabbed your arm, and I started walking over, but then Brian walked in. That was it. I saw the way you looked at him, and I knew."

He looked up, his eyes pleading. "Brian only dated certain girls. I figured

CHAPTER 41

once you realized that, you'd move on."

"Go on," Hanna said, her voice quiet but steady.

Nick took a deep, uneven breath. "After high school, I waited. I really thought maybe I had a chance. But then you left, and when you came back, you were married to him."

His voice broke as he continued. "Then he died, and I thought that maybe it was finally my turn. I believed you'd realize I was the one who had always been there."

He leaned forward, his elbows on his knees, his voice hollow. "But you still looked at him like he was everything. You held on to him like he might somehow come back. I couldn't figure out how to make you see me."

Hanna didn't speak. She sat frozen, barely breathing. For a moment, she felt the ache of sympathy claw at her chest.

But then something shifted. The sorrow cracked, and heat rose in its place.

"You thought it was your turn?" she asked, her voice low but sharp. "You waited for me to break so you could step in?"

Her hands curled tightly in her lap. "You watched me lose him, watched me fall apart, and you still believed what? That you deserved me? That I should be grateful you stuck around?"

Nick's face twisted in pain. "It's not like that."

"Then what is it like, Nick?" she asked, her voice sharp and trembling. The betrayal was too much, cracking something open inside her.

She stepped back, her pulse racing, every word cutting deeper than the last.

"You looked at my grief and thought it was your opportunity. You believed that if you stayed close long enough, I would forget the man I loved and eventually fall into your arms?" Her anger burned hot and fast. Tears welled in her eyes, but she refused to let them fall.

Nick looked at her, his expression pained. "I thought that if you really saw me, if you gave me a chance, I could make you happy."

Hanna approached him slowly, her steps measured. She lowered herself in front of his chair, her eyes locked on his. Her voice dropped to a gentle whisper. "Nick, what did you do?"

He swallowed hard. "Oh God, Hanna." His voice cracked as he tried to steady himself. "I watched you. At first, it didn't feel wrong. I told myself I was looking out for you, making sure you were okay. I needed to be close, to remind you I was there."

His hands trembled as he continued. "Sometimes I followed you. More than I should have. I put a tracker on your car so I'd always know where you were." He paused, shame settling over him like a weight. "When you said you were going to Vermont, I checked. I saw you were still in New York. I panicked. I thought something was wrong, so I drove to the cabin."

He looked down, his voice barely audible. "You saw me. You ran toward me, and I got scared. I panicked and ran back to my car."

Hanna stood up suddenly, her hand covering her mouth as the weight of his words settled over her.

Nick's eyes widened. "No, Hanna, please don't look at me like that. I never meant to scare you. I just... I didn't know how to stop. That's why I came tonight. You had to know."

She didn't respond. She couldn't. The man standing in front of her wasn't declaring love. He was unraveling something darker. This wasn't affection. it was obsession.

"And then you found out about Richard," Nick continued, his voice barely above a whisper. "I never thought that would happen."

He rubbed the back of his neck, unable to meet her eyes. "He and I have known each other since we were three. After graduation, we drifted apart. Life took us different places. But a few years ago, he called out of nowhere and asked me to visit."

Hanna's pulse quickened. She didn't move, but her fists tightened at her sides.

"I didn't tell you because I didn't want to risk... losing what we had," he said. "I went at night. Maddie let me in. I told myself it was just a visit, just catching up, but it was more than that."

His jaw tensed. "The last time he called, he sounded off. He said he needed to talk, that it was important. So I went back. But he wasn't in a

CHAPTER 41

good place. Something in him had shifted, and I couldn't handle it. I told him to leave you alone, that you'd been through enough. I begged him."

He finally looked at her, eyes heavy with something that almost resembled guilt. "I thought I could protect you. I thought my silence was helping."

She stepped forward, her voice sharp with disbelief. "Then why didn't you tell me? You wanted something real with me, but you kept secrets. You lied. That's not love. Love requires honesty. Trust."

Nick's voice came out hoarse. "Hanna, we've known each other our whole lives. I thought I could protect you. I thought I could handle it."

She shook her head, tears brimming in her eyes. "You knew who he was. And you still went. You still chose to hide it from me."

Nick reached toward her, his face twisted with desperation. "I swear, Hanna—"

"No," she said firmly. "I think you need to leave."

His head snapped up, panic flashing in his expression. "Please. Don't do this. I know I made mistakes. I know I hurt you. But I love you. I really love you."

Her voice trembled, but her words didn't falter. "No, Nick. You don't love me. You love the idea of me. You love the control. You think you deserve something just because you stayed close."

His breathing grew uneven, desperation cracking through his voice. "Please, Hanna. I'll change. I'll do whatever it takes. Just don't shut me out."

She held her ground, her voice quiet but steady. "You made this choice, Nick. Not me. I need time to process everything, and you need to leave."

Nick pushed to his feet, then sank to his knees in front of her, tears streaming down his face. "Hanna, I'm begging you. Please."

She turned her face away, her expression breaking. "Nick... please. Just go."

He reached for her again, pleading. "Hanna, don't do this. We can talk through it. I love you."

They didn't hear the front door open.

Didn't hear the heavy footsteps until they were already in the room.

Steve stood in the doorway, eyes sharp, jaw tight.

He took in the scene: Nick on his knees, Hanna standing rigid, arms wrapped around herself like she was holding something in.

"What the hell is going on?" His voice was low and dangerous. "Nick. I believe I *just* heard Hanna ask you to leave."

Nick looked up at him, broken. "Steve, please."

Steve didn't move. His gaze didn't waver.

Nick hesitated.

Steve adjusted the cuffs of his sleeves, his voice deadly calm. "I'm not asking again, Nick. Get the fuck out."

Nick's breath hitched. Then he slowly got to his feet. "I- "

Steve took a step forward.

Nick flinched. "I'm going, I'm going." He turned to Hanna. "I'm so sorry, Hanna."

She said nothing.

Nick looked at her one last time. His eyes begged for anything.

But Hanna turned away.

That broke him. His shoulders fell. Then, with eerie calm, he smoothed his face, wiped his eyes, and walked to the door.

He closed it quietly behind him.

Steve locked the door, then stood at the window, watching Nick's car disappear down the drive. Only when the taillights vanished did he turn back to her.

"You okay?"

His voice had softened, but it still carried an edge, nodding automatically, "Yeah," even though she wasn't sure it was true.

In two steps, Steve crossed the room and pulled her into his arms.

She went without resistance, burying her face against his chest.

The smell of cedar and clean fabric hit her nose, comforting and grounding. She clung to him, trying to anchor herself against the storm still raging inside.

Steve ran a hand slowly down her hair, murmuring, "You're safe now."

But Hanna's mind was a mess of guilt, anger, and heartbreak.

CHAPTER 41

How do you forgive that?

How do you forgive the manipulation, the lies, and the belief that someone had a right to you because they had waited long enough?

Tears blurred her vision.

"I thought I knew him," she whispered against Steve's chest.

Steve tilted her chin up gently. His thumb brushed her damp cheek. "You knew who he wanted you to see," he said. "Not who he really was."

Hanna blinked, her throat thick. "I feel like an idiot."

"You're not," Steve said firmly. "You're human.

He led her gently to the couch, his hand at the small of her back like he was guiding something fragile.

He smiled, soft but sure. "Sit. I'm going to get you some water."

Hanna sank into the cushions, her hands still trembling.

Steve disappeared into the kitchen and returned a moment later, handing her a glass of water.

He lowered himself onto the couch beside her, close enough to offer comfort but careful not to crowd her.

She took a small sip, grateful for something to do with her hands.

Steve waited, giving her space to breathe. Then, his voice low and steady, he asked, "What happened, Han?"

She stared down at the glass. "He..." Her voice cracked. She swallowed hard, forcing herself to meet Steve's eyes. "Nick's been following me. For months. Maybe longer."

Steve's expression didn't flicker, but his hands curled slowly into fists on his knees.

"He admitted it," Hanna said, the words tumbling out faster now. "He put a tracker on my car. He followed me to the cabin. He... he's been watching me, watching Caitlyn. He knew where I was even when I lied about it."

Steve's jaw tightened. His voice stayed calm, but there was an edge underneath it. "Did he ever touch you? Threaten you?"

"No." Hanna shook her head quickly. "Not physically. He thought..." She broke off, emotions crashing over her in waves.

Steve leaned closer, his voice low and grounding. "Take your time. I'm here."

She pressed the heels of her hands against her eyes. "He thought if he just stayed close enough and waited long enough, I would choose him. That I'd finally realize he was the one who was there when Brian wasn't."

Steve's mouth pressed into a rigid line. "Son of a bitch."

Tears slipped down Hanna's cheeks. "I should've seen it. I should've known."

"No," Steve said, his voice sharper now. He reached over and gently took the glass from her shaking hands, setting it aside. He knelt down, grabbing her hands. "You're not the one who crossed the line. He did. He's the one who twisted loyalty into obsession. Not you."

Hanna dragged in a ragged breath. "I feel like I gave him hope without even realizing it. Perhaps I leaned too heavily on him during my grief and failed to notice what it was becoming."

Steve shook his head. "You leaned on a friend. You placed your trust in someone you believed was looking out for your best interests. There's no crime in that, Han. The crime is him using it to manipulate you."

She dropped her head into her hands. "It just feels like everything's broken."

Steve hesitated for a moment, then moved, pulling her into his arms again. She collapsed against him, tears soaking into his shirt.

He tightened his hold around her, protective and fierce, and kissed her head.

"We'll fix this," he whispered against her hair. "I don't care how long it takes. We'll fix it."

Steve let her cry for a few more minutes, not rushing her, holding her.

When her breathing finally started to slow, he leaned back slightly, keeping his hands firm on her arms so she couldn't retreat fully.

"We need to report this," Steve said quietly, his voice calm but certain. "Tonight. Before he has a chance to spin it, or worse, escalate."

Hanna stiffened, pulling back enough to look at him.

"No."

Steve frowned. "Hanna "

CHAPTER 41

"No." She shook her head hard, wiping her face with the sleeve of her sweatshirt. "I just want it to be over, Steve. Please. If we report it, it drags everything back up. The investigators, the questions, the court dates. Caitlyn."

Her voice cracked, and he caught her hand again before she could fold into herself.

"You're thinking about everyone but yourself," he said, his thumb brushing her knuckles. "You're thinking about him, protecting him, and he doesn't deserve it."

"I'm not protecting him." Her voice wobbled. "I'm protecting *us*."

Steve exhaled, struggling against every instinct that told him to push harder.

"If he tries anything again," he said, steel edging his words, "we do it my way. No hesitation. No second chances."

Hanna nodded, exhausted. "Okay."

Steve's jaw tensed, but he softened his voice for her.

"For now, we get you safe. We have installed cameras, locks, and alarms. If he so much as blinks in your direction wrong, I'll bury him in paperwork so deep he won't breathe without permission."

That pulled a watery laugh out of her. "Sounds aggressive."

"Good," he said. "You deserve aggressiveness right now."

She gripped the glass of water he handed her, calmer now. "Thank you," she whispered.

Steve squeezed her hand again. "We're family, and we will get through this, Han. One step at a time. Together."

Chapter 42

Steve arrived at the office on Monday morning and looked at the stack of papers; it was never-ending. He picked up the phone and called down to the agent handling Hanna's case, "Any update on that letter, as well as the footprints and video footage?"

The voice on the other line said, "Yes, sir, I was about to bring them up; I just received them this morning."

"Great, I am here now; you can bring them up."

Moments later, there was a knock at the door.

"Come in."

Agent Collins stepped inside, a thick folder in one hand, an evidence bag in the other.

Steve's gaze flicked to the bag first, then the letter.

Collins shut the door behind him and tossed the folder onto the desk. "Thought you'd want this in person."

Steve leaned back, eyes steady. "That bad?"

Collins smirked, but it was humorless. "Try frustrating as hell." He sat across from Steve, resting an elbow on the armrest. "Let's start with the footprints."

Steve flipped open the folder. The enhanced footprint analysis was clipped to the first page, complete with detailed measurements and comparisons.

"Male, approximately six foot to six two, between 190 and 210 pounds," Collins said, voice flat. "Deep heel strike, weight evenly distributed, had controlled movement. Whoever this guy is, he's trained."

CHAPTER 42

Steve's fingers drummed against the desk. Hmm, trained, measured, and precise, that doesn't sound like shit face.

Collins continued. "They could have possibly been law enforcement, military, or maybe even private sector."

Steve nodded, keeping his expression neutral. Nick didn't fit the profile perfectly, but he already knew it was him.

Collins continued. "Then there's this."

He slid a still image from the security footage across the desk.

Steve picked it up, and he froze. It was Nick; maybe the fucker knew he was closing in on him. The posture, the scar beneath his ear, and the way he stood was too relaxed, almost too calculating.

Steve inhaled slowly, schooling his features. "You enhance this?"

Collins nodded. "We did the best we could. The guy's careful; he knows exactly how to avoid a clean shot." He leaned forward. "You recognize him?"

"Hard to say," Steve lied smoothly.

Collins didn't seem convinced. "C'mon, Riley. You've been in this business long enough. You're telling me this guy doesn't look familiar?"

Steve met his gaze, steady, unwavering. "I'm telling you, I don't throw names based on grainy images."

Collins held his stare for a moment, then sighed, leaning back. "Fine. Let's move on."

He pulled out the evidence bag and set it on the desk. Inside, a white envelope sat untouched.

Steve didn't move. "Prints?"

Collins shook his head. "Nothing, not even smudges."

"DNA?"

"Clean, as if it came straight out of a lab."

Steve exhaled slowly. "And the handwriting?"

Collins smirked, but nothing was amusing about it. "Here's the fun part: it's useless." He tapped the bag. "No distinguishing markers. No matching samples in any database. Whoever wrote this? They've either altered their style, or they've never had anything documented."

Steve studied the envelope. There were no prints or DNA and no traceable handwriting, almost like a ghost. Whoever did this wanted them to know they were untouchable.

Collins leaned forward, arms resting on his knees. "You still think this is about Richard Hale?"

Steve didn't answer; he knew Nick had a connection to Richard, but there was more, there was something else, and neither one of them was talking.

Collins handed Steve the folder. "Sir, this is a dead end; it's gone cold, sir."

Steve nodded, "Thanks, Collins."

Collins walked out the door, closing the door behind him.

Steve exhaled sharply, running a hand down his face.

Think, Riley. Think. Who the hell was pulling the strings?

He shook his head. Dead end. A dead fucking end. The only positive? The cameras at Hanna's place were still up.

Nick had already confessed to watching her. The footage placed him there that night, but it didn't show him putting the envelope in the mailbox. That was the problem. Was there someone else?

Steve should hand this over to the authorities, along with Nick's confession, but he was respecting Hanna's wishes. She felt that Nick had already punished himself enough. But if Nick stepped out of line again, Steve would be waiting, and he would fuck him up before he turned him in.

He leaned back in his chair, fingers drumming against the desk. The note. That was what kept gnawing at him.

Nick had admitted to stalking, but had he written it? If not, who had? With Nick's confession, he couldn't really stay with her anymore. The excuses had run out. And truthfully? He wanted to go home. He missed waking up to Rachel.

Still, the cameras would stay hidden in the gutters. He'd have an alarm installed at Hanna's house and tell her it was just to ease his mind.

But something wasn't sitting right. There was someone else. Steve could feel it. And at some point, they'd slip up. And when they did, he'd be ready.

Chapter 43

December 2006

Hanna sat in her office, sorting through files, finalizing things before heading away for the holiday. The clock on the wall ticked steadily, filling the quiet space as she flipped through paperwork.

Her phone rang. She picked it up, pressing it to her ear. "Dr. Nowack."

A familiar voice crackled through the line. "Doc, it's Brad down on the block. Richard Hale asked me to reach out and said he wanted to see you."

Hanna frowned, gripping the receiver a little tighter. Hale never initiated. Not like this.

"Did he say why?" she asked, already reaching for her notebook in the drawer.

"Nope. Said it was important."

Something about it unsettled her. Hale didn't ask for things; he orchestrated them. And if he wanted to see her, it wasn't for conversation.

Still, she kept her voice even. "Alright. Bring him in thirty."

"No problem, Doc."

The line went dead. Hanna set the phone down, tapping her pen against the desk. A request like this? Unprompted?

It wasn't like him. And that's what made it dangerous.

***

Thirty minutes later, Hanna walked into the room and sat down in front of Richard, already waiting for her. The room was cold. Lifeless. But the air between them was thick, heavy, already charged with something unspoken.

Richard sat across from her, shackled but completely at ease. The fluorescent light overhead flickered once, casting shadows across the sharp angles of his face.

Hanna held his gaze. "Richard, you wanted this session. What is it you wanted to talk about?"

Richard stared at her, dark eyes filled with something unreadable. "Doctor, maybe I wanted to spend a little time with you before you wrap up for the holidays."

She kept her expression neutral. "Richard, is there a specific reason you wanted to meet?"

His lips curled slightly. "You ever wonder, Doctor," he mused, voice smooth, almost conversational. "What happens when a job isn't finished?"

She didn't move. "What job, Richard?"

Richard leaned back slightly, exhaling as if amused by her restraint. "The one that should've been done a long time ago."

His fingers curled around the chain between his wrists, absently toying with the links. "You see, Hanna, people like to think monsters are born." His voice was almost lazy, like he was telling a story he'd recited a hundred times before. "They tell themselves it's in the blood. That there's some gene, some defect, something that makes us different from the rest of them." His lips twitched, his gaze pinning her in place. "But that's a lie."

The chains rattled softly as he leaned forward, his voice dropping to a near whisper. "Monsters aren't born. They're made. And they are made by monsters worse than the ones they create."

Hanna felt it then, the shift in the room.

Richard tilted his head slightly, eyes gleaming under the dim light. "I was created, Doctor. I was molded, cut down, and rebuilt into something useful. Useful to those who needed my services." He started tapping one finger against the steel armrest, slow and deliberate.

"It started with a fire. I was fourteen. My stepfather was a drunk. The kind of man who liked to break things: furniture, plates, ribs, noses… even arms. But I made sure he wouldn't do it again. Locked the door and walked

CHAPTER 43

away while he burned alive inside."

His voice was calm, almost too calm, and it made her skin crawl.

"I thought no one knew," he said quietly. "But I was wrong." He paused, his fingers tapping a slow rhythm against the metal. "Someone knew. He always knew."

"Who, Richard?" Hanna asked carefully.

He smiled. "The one who always knew." Richard's eyes darkened. "And he waited. Let me believe I was free. Let me think I was the one pulling the strings. Then, just when I believed I was truly free, he found me."

His smirk disappeared. "And he made me an offer. One I didn't have a choice to refuse."

Hanna's grip on her pen tightened. "Richard, you would have been out in two years. You might not have received any time if your mom had come forward."

Richard shook his head, jaw clenching. "No. I never had a choice. I was so young, I didn't know any better." His fingers flexed. "Then I was told, 'Do this job for me, Richard, and I'll make sure no one ever finds out what really happened.'"

His stare locked onto hers, unblinking. "And that's how men like me are made, Doctor. It has nothing to do with power or ambition. But with a threat. A threat that leaves them with their back against the wall."

Hanna didn't look away. "And you took it."

Richard chuckled. "Of course, I did. I was young and stupid. Thought it was a game." His hands flexed again. "The first few times, I had a 'trainer.' Someone who showed me the ropes. Told me what to do and forced me to do it." His voice darkened. "Do it, or die myself." He took a deep breath. "The first few were sloppy. I wasn't a killer; I was a kid without choices. But I learned, and I got better and more precise, and eventually, I stopped caring. It was as if my emotions left and all that remained was an empty shell."

His smile faded. "And when I was finally ready? He gave me my first solo job."

Hanna swallowed hard. "And?"

Richard's expression remained blank. "She ruined everything. She made me rethink it all." His voice was almost thoughtful, like he was speaking about another lifetime. "I wanted out, and I was planning to leave. I was going to take her somewhere no one could find us."

He inhaled deeply as if remembering a scent long gone. "But that wasn't how the story ended."

Hanna already knew the answer.

"She died thinking I loved her." His fingers clenched under the table. "And I lived knowing I was the one who put her in the ground." Then Richard leaned in, so close she could see the faint silver streaking through his dark hair and the slight twitch of his jaw.

His voice softened to a whisper. "After she died, that ended what was left of my humanity. I followed instructions. I killed women, and I killed men. I did it all without remorse. It became a job."

A slow smirk. "You were on my list, Doctor. You were supposed to be dead."

She looked at him.

Richard drank it in, savoring the moment, his eyes gleaming with something dark and unbreakable. "You were my twenty-nine."

The words settled between them. Richard leaned back in his chair, the chains rattling softly. "And yet... here we are."

Hanna took a moment. "Richard, what stopped you from making me number twenty-nine?"

Richard exhaled slowly, the smirk lingering on his lips as he studied her. The chains between his wrists clinked as he rolled his shoulders, as if considering the question, as if the answer itself was something he hadn't decided until now.

Finally, he spoke, his voice smooth and deliberate. "Maybe I hesitated."

Hanna said nothing.

Richard tilted his head slightly. "Or maybe someone talked me out of it."

Hanna, on instinct, said, "Nick?"

Richard's smirk widened, but there was no humor in it; it was something cold and calculating. He let the silence stretch, his dark eyes watching her

CHAPTER 43

like a puzzle he'd already solved. Then, he exhaled, shaking his head slowly. "No, Doctor."

Hanna's stomach clenched. Richard dragged his tongue over his teeth, tapping his fingers against the chain between his wrists. "Nick didn't stop me. He tried. But it was him."

The weight of his words settled over the room like a slow building pressure, heavy and unshakable.

Hanna forced her voice to stay steady. "Then who?"

Richard smiled, but there was something wrong about it, something hollow. "You did."

Hanna didn't move. Didn't blink.

Richard leaned forward slightly, his voice dropping to something quieter. "It was you, Hanna."

His eyes never left hers, watching for the moment his words sank in. Then, for the first time, his smirk faded. "It wasn't Nick." His voice was smooth and deliberate. "It wasn't a call. It wasn't a job gone wrong." He tilted his head slightly, as if studying the memory from a different angle. "It was me... watching you."

Hanna's breath hitched, but she kept her expression still.

Richard's gaze darkened. "I saw you with your daughter. I watched her cling to you, like she was afraid you'd disappear too."

His words struck like a blow to the ribs because he had been there. He had seen her at her weakest, and he had been holding a gun.

Richard exhaled slowly, shaking his head. "You had lost. She had lost." Then, he leaned back slightly, dragging his tongue over his teeth before finishing, "And for a moment... something came over me."

He had seen her grief; he had seen Caitlyn's grief, and something inside him had stalled. Richard Hale, who had executed twenty-eight people without a second thought, had looked at her and faltered.

His fingers curled around the chain between his wrists. Then, he exhaled, shaking his head. "I think that is all for today, Doctor. I gave you a lot to think about."

Hanna's grip tightened around her pen, but her face remained neutral.

She wouldn't let him dictate this. Not today. "Richard, I'd like you to go on." Her voice was steady, unwavering. "We have time."

Richard smiled, slow and deliberate. Not because he was amused. "No, Doctor." He shook his head, tapping one finger against the table. "Some stories are best kept for another day."

He gave a low laugh, then his eyes locked onto hers. "But I promise you, our next session will be a tell-all. And I'll make sure you never forget it."

Hanna held his gaze, searching for the right words to keep him talking to regain control.

But Richard saw it. Her fingers twitched slightly, but she didn't push again. Without another word, Richard turned his head slightly, his gaze shifting toward the heavy steel door. "Guards! I'm ready."

The sudden shift was so abrupt, so unnatural, it made the hairs on Hanna's arms rise.

The guards barely had time to react before the heavy door swung open, their boots echoing across the floor as they moved toward him.

Richard stood smoothly, effortlessly, stepping back from the chair as if he had already mentally left the room. The chains between his wrists rattled as they latched onto his cuffs, securing them before leading him toward the exit.

But as he shuffled down the hallway, his voice rang out, "Merry Christmas, Doc."

The words were light, casual, almost friendly.

Hanna was left sitting in the cold, empty room, with a pen that felt too light in her grip.

And a name she knew she'd never escape.

* * *

Hanna kept what she had heard that morning from Steve; it was their day, and she would rather not spoil it; she would mention it another time. She showed up at the courthouse just in time; Steve and Rachel had chosen to keep it simple: a small, intimate ceremony, the two of them, and a couple

CHAPTER 43

of witnesses. There was no grand celebration or lavish party. It was a commitment, sealed with a signature and a kiss. Only Hanna and Doug were present.

Hanna wasn't surprised. Steve and Rachel had never been ones for spectacle, and with everything that had happened over the past year, a quiet wedding made sense.

Hanna watched as Steve took Rachel's hands. His expression was gentle, but something about it felt distant, as if he was trying too hard to be present. Rachel looked up at him, searching his face, her smile flickering just a second too late. Whatever they were sharing, it wasn't certainty. It was hope. Perhaps even fear played a part. When the officiant pronounced them husband and wife, there were no grand gestures, no overwhelming emotions, just a simple, contented happiness that radiated between them.

Afterward, the four of them went out for dinner, raising a quiet toast to new beginnings. Hanna sat back and watched as Steve laughed at something Rachel said, noticing that his shoulders were finally relaxed for the first time in weeks. Maybe he was trying. Maybe he was convincing himself.

And for the first time, she let herself believe that maybe, one day, she would find hers too.

Chapter 44

It had been a few weeks since Nick's confession, and while Hanna had started to let go of the initial shock, the anger still lingered. Some days, it was a dull ache, a reminder of the betrayal. Other days, it was sharper, like an old wound reopening. But life didn't stop, and she found herself moving forward, piece by piece.

Things were finally getting back to normal, and with Christmas around the corner, there was lots of decorating to do. Caitlyn was in the living room, decorating the tree. Hanna walked in with hot cocoa. "You're doing a great job."

Caitlyn was standing on her tiptoes, carefully placing an ornament on one of the branches, her face lit with excitement. "Do you really think so, Mommy?"

"Yes, I do; it looks beautiful."

"Mama, do you think Grandpa Lee will like the tree?" Caitlyn asked, stepping back to admire her work.

"I think so," Hanna replied.

"And Grandpa Tony and Grandma Elaine?" Caitlyn added, taking a careful sip of her drink.

"They will love it, sweetheart."

Caitlyn beamed, setting her mug on the coffee table before returning to the tree and adjusting a red ribbon. Hanna watched her daughter, warmth filling her chest. This was the first Christmas when things finally felt settled.

This was the first Christmas Caitlyn would be spending with Lee. Hanna

CHAPTER 44

couldn't remember the last Christmas she had spent with her father, but this year, he was trying. He called every couple of days, asking what Caitlyn wanted, making sure everything was set. It was unexpected, but Hanna couldn't deny how much she appreciated the effort.

A commercial flickered on the TV in the background, a bright red banner flashing across the screen:

"Three more shopping days until Christmas!"

Caitlyn gasped dramatically, turning to her mother. "Mama, did you see that? Christmas is in three days!"

Hanna chuckled. "I know, sweetie. Better get those last minute lists ready."

Caitlyn giggled, turning back to the tree, humming along to the Christmas music playing softly in the background.

※ ※ ※

Christmas morning 2006

Snow dusted the ground outside as the warmth of the house wrapped around Hanna like a familiar embrace. Snow for Christmas, a nice treat. In the living room, the fireplace crackles softly in the background.

Tony and Elaine sat comfortably on the couch, watching Caitlyn intently as she opened a small early gift, a tradition they had started this year. She tore into the wrapping paper, revealing a set of books, her eyes lighting up with excitement.

"Thank you, Grandma! Thank you, Grandpa!" She beamed, running over to hug them both.

Tony chuckled, squeezing her tight. "Merry Christmas, sweetheart."

Elaine wiped a tear from the corner of her eye, her face filled with warmth. "You're growing up too fast, Caitlyn," she murmured, brushing a hand through her granddaughter's hair.

Nearby, Lee sat watching, a quiet observer in a family that was still unfamiliar to him. His hands were clasped together, his posture stiff, but his expression soft.

THE LIES WE WHISPER

But Caitlyn, in all her excitement, wasn't letting him just sit there.

She bounced on her heels, her hands clasped together. "Grandpa Lee! Can I open yours now? Can I?"

Hanna turned her head, slightly surprised. "How do you know Grandpa got you something?"

Caitlyn grinned. "He asked me last week what I wanted. He kept calling to make sure I didn't change my mind." She looked at Lee expectantly. "So, can I?"

Lee let out a small chuckle, shaking his head. "Go ahead, kiddo."

Caitlyn practically dove under the tree, pulling out a large box with a silver bow. The tag, written in Lee's shaky but careful handwriting, read: To Caitlyn, Love, Grandpa Lee.

She ripped into the paper, her breath hitching the moment she saw the familiar American Girl logo.

"No way! No way!" she shrieked, opening the box in a frenzy. And there she was, the exact doll she had wanted. Complete with a crib, tiny clothes, and accessories. Caitlyn's eyes shined as she turned to Lee. "You got it! You remember, Grandpa Lee, this is amazing!"

Lee smiled, rubbing the back of his neck. "Took me three stores to find it, but yeah. I remembered."

Without hesitation, Caitlyn ran to him and threw her arms around his waist. "Thank you, Grandpa Lee! This is the best Christmas ever!"

Lee froze for just a second, as if unsure of what to do, but then his arms slowly came around her, holding her close.

Hanna swallowed past the unexpected lump in her throat as tears flooded her eyes. She hadn't known what to expect from Lee this Christmas, but this? This was more than she could ever have imagined.

Caitlyn pulled back, already clutching the doll to her chest. "And I get to spend Christmas with you, too! My first Christmas with my Grandpa Lee!"

Lee exhaled, glancing at Hanna as if searching for reassurance.

Hanna gave him a small smile. "Looks like you're officially in, Dad."

Lee scoffed, shaking his head, but there was something soft in his eyes. "Guess I am." and he gave a big smile

CHAPTER 44

Caitlyn didn't wait for more. She grabbed her doll's crib and started setting it up near the tree, already chattering away about all the exciting things she and her new doll were going to do together.

Tony and Elaine exchanged a quiet glance, both smiling as they watched their granddaughter.

Hanna leaned back on the couch, letting it all sink in. The glow of the Christmas lights flickered across Caitlyn's face as she played with her doll, while Lee watched, still caught between disbelief and wonder. Tony and Elaine were laughing at something Caitlyn said, their voices blending into the soft hum of the evening. A slow breath slipped from Hanna's lips, warmth spreading through her chest. It wasn't perfect. It never would be. But it was hers, and maybe that was enough.

Chapter 45

February 2007

Nick parked in the same spot he always used, just off the side of the road where the trees thickened and the motion light above the garage couldn't catch him. The black hoodie helped him disappear into the shadows, something he appreciated more than he liked to admit. He preferred it that way. the stillness, the quiet hum of night, the sense that he could be close enough to see without ever being seen.

He stepped out of the car slowly, careful not to slam the door, letting it click shut with just enough pressure to keep it from echoing across the yard. Gravel crunched beneath his boots as he made his way down the path he knew by heart, the one that curved through the edge of her property. Hanna's house stood just ahead, lights warm in the windows, everything inside familiar in a way that made his chest ache.

It had been three months since he'd last seen her face. Three months since that night, since the fight, since she told him to stop calling. He knew he'd gone too far. He shouldn't have said the things he said about Brian. He shouldn't have raised his voice or cornered her with his feelings. But that didn't mean she had to cut him off completely. Not after everything they'd been through. Not after all the time they'd spent building something real.

He paused at the edge of the yard and looked toward the dining room window, just as he always did. A light was on. She passed by, holding something, maybe a blanket or a book, as she disappeared down the hallway. He glanced at his watch. Just after nine. She was probably putting Caitlyn to bed, the same way she did every night, the same way he used to be there

CHAPTER 45

for.

His chest tightened with the memory.

He had missed Christmas. He had missed New Year's. He wasn't there when Caitlyn opened her presents or when Hanna made cinnamon rolls and danced barefoot in the kitchen like she used to. He should have been there. He belonged there. Once, he had been part of it all. And now, he stood outside looking in, as if he had never been welcome at all.

Keeping to the shadows, he moved around the back of the house, where the lights were off and the curtains didn't reach the edges of the windows. He knew this route. He had studied it. Just a gap in the curtains, barely wide enough to see through, but enough to remind him of everything he had lost.

He stepped in closer. Through the narrow opening, he saw the edge of her bed, the soft glow of a lamp, and Hanna standing near the dresser. She was brushing her hair, her sweatshirt loose over her frame, her face turned slightly toward the mirror. She looked tired, but not in a way that made her seem worn out. She looked soft. Like the version of her that used to curl up beside him on the couch and fall asleep during movies they had watched a dozen times.

He missed her and everything about her. The warmth of her skin, the way her voice dropped when she was exhausted, the way she smiled at Caitlyn in the mornings when she thought no one was watching. He had been there for all of it. He had held her hand when she cried and stood beside her when she felt alone. He had waited because he loved her through everything.

And now she looked at him like he was a stranger, like none of it had ever mattered. The long talks, the quiet nights, the way they had carried grief side by side, it was as if all of it had lived only in his mind. But he knew better. He knew what they were. He knew what they could still be. They hadn't been just friends. There was always something deeper, something unspoken that lived between them, even if she never said it aloud. Even if she was trying now to forget.

She would forgive him, maybe not today or tomorrow. But eventually, she would. She had to.

Because no matter what she told herself, no matter how angry she was, no one else could ever love her the way he did.

Chapter 46

March 2007

The winter months had quickly passed, the snow began to melt, and spring was approaching; everything was finally settling down. Everything was good, things were finally peaceful, and she had a good feeling about today; something in her gut said today was the day she would find Richard's humanity.

Hanna settled into her chair, her tape recorder running discreetly in her pocket. She had sat across from Richard Hale too many times to count. She knew his game by now: leading her down a path, dangling answers out of reach, and then, as she got close, yanking the rug out from under her. But this time? This time, she was ready.

Richard smirked, the shackles around his wrists clinking as he leaned forward. "Doctor, always a pleasure. I must say, I'm surprised you're still coming back for more, but then again that is why your a criminal psychologist, isn't it. " He tilted his head, eyes gleaming with amusement. "But then again, we're alike in that way, aren't we? We see things through."

Hanna didn't react. She wouldn't give him the satisfaction: "Where do you want to begin today, Richard?"

"No foreplay? That's a shame; it's the best part." He sighed dramatically, shaking his head. "Alright then, I guess we will get busy. Let's talk about Vicki and Kristy."

Hanna's neck stiffened. "Okay, Richard. Who are Vicki and Kristy?"

Richard's smile widened. He lived for this, the dance and the torment.

THE LIES WE WHISPER

But today, he had something special in store for her.

"Why, Doctor, I never thought you'd ask," he drawled, his tone smooth, calculated. Inside, he was savoring every second of the control he had over her. Vicki and Kristy were the appetizers. He had something bigger planned for dinner.

Hanna held his gaze, her face unreadable. She wouldn't let him win. "Alright, Richard." She leaned back, folding her arms. "Let's hear it."

Richard tapped his fingers lazily against the metal armrest. "Two beautiful, delicate things. They resembled identical dolls, sharing the same long legs and soft voices. Even the way they carried themselves." He smirked. "Like they knew they were meant for something more."

Hanna stayed still. "And what were they meant for?"

Richard replied. "That's the tragedy, isn't it?" He leaned in, his voice dropping to something lower, something colder. "They thought they were meant for a life of comfort. Of luxury." His eyes gleamed. "But really? They were temporary possessions. Pieces in a game they didn't even know they were playing."

Hanna's fingers curled into her lap. "And you decided to take them off the board."

Richard clicked his tongue. "No, no, no, Doc. You give me too much credit." He lifted his gaze, locking onto hers. "I didn't choose them. Someone else did because they too were a distraction that needed to be taken out."

Cold slithered down her spine. "Who?"

Richard's smirk didn't falter, but something in his eyes flickered for a second. There was a fleeting glimpse of something more profound. Something is rotting.

"The same kind of people who choose everything, Doc., the same ones who ordered all twenty-eight of them." His smirk intensified, and his voice was barely audible. "The ones with money are the ones who hold all the power."

Hanna clenched her jaw. "Richard, I know you want me to beg for the answer. Tell me, who has all the power?"

CHAPTER 46

Richard sighed, tilting his head almost pityingly.

"You're not ready for specifics yet, Hanna. But you're close. So close, you can almost taste it. He leaned forward, his voice dropping into something darker, something that curled under her skin. "The answer won't come from me." His eyes gleamed. "It'll come from someone you trust." The smile was slow and deliberate. "Be careful, Doctor. Not everyone in your life is who they seem. Some are much, much more dangerous than I am. Think, Hanna, think about who it could be."

Her head began to ache; tonight was unlike any other night. He was being both callous and calculating, and usually it is one or the other.

"Richard, let's stop with the games, or you can go back to the block."

Richard sat back, watching her, his smirk slow and deliberate, preparing for what was coming next. "Hanna, sweetheart." He tapped the metal of his shackles. "I do have something for you, something that will stay with you for the rest of your life. This is what our sessions have been building up to.

Hanna took a deep breath, refusing to show weakness. "And what is that, Richard?" She was becoming tired of this game.

Richard's eyes gleamed. "A gift."

Annoyed, Hanna hastily said. "What kind of gift, Richard?"

He grinned, slow and razor sharp. "Closure."

Hanna fired back. "Closure for what? What would I need closure for, Richard?"

Richard's fingers drummed against the arm of the chair. "For him."

Hanna's chest tightened. "Who is him, Richard?"

Richard nodded. "A man with a family, a man who had a young wife and a newborn daughter." He tilted his head. "A man who had everything. Who thought he had time."

Hanna watched him, studying him; she wasn't sure she liked where this was going or what he was implying. She thought about getting up and leaving the room, but still, she stayed. She had to.

Richard leaned forward slightly. "I waited for him, you know."

"You waited for whom, Richard?" He was toying with her; she needed to keep control and figure out who he was talking about.

"I knew he'd come that way," Richard continued. "Same road. I just sat and waited, every night waiting. I knew he liked coming that way, especially on his motorcycle." Richard's eyes glinted. "Routine makes people predictable, and that predictability is what makes them easy to take down."

Hanna questioned. "What did you do, Richard?"

Richard let out a small laugh. "The wait came to a close, and the right time came, and I struck. I applied the brakes with great force."

Richard stretched his fingers. "Most people consider death to be a moment. It's a single event." His smile was slow and taunting. "But it's not; it's a process."

"Who did you wait for, Richard?" Hanna was trying to figure out where he was going with this.

Richard whispered, savoring every word, "I struck Brian DeLuca so hard, I swear I could hear his bones crunching on impact."

Hanna's body tensed as she struggled to conceal her growing feelings for him. The pain was eating her from the inside.

Richard teased. "He flew like a bird. My windshield cracked, and there was blood on my car." Richard smiled. "I got out of my car, and you know what happened next. He didn't just scream like his brother; no, Doc, he gurgled instead. He gurgled like a drain clogged with blood. I waited there to see if he would beg."

Richard giggled, high and childish. "But he didn't. What a waste."

Hanna tightened her grip around her pen; she did not like where this was going

"And then?" Richard ruthlessly smiled, shaking his head like it was a fond memory. " He closed his eyes and lay there lifeless, no movement; I was sure he was dead. But I didn't check; I couldn't risk getting caught." His smile widened. "Imagine my surprise when I found out he actually survived the impact." Richard leaned in slightly. "But you know what made it perfect, Doc?"

Hanna was uncertain about wanting to hear the answer, but she decided to engage in the conversation. "Please, Richard, share what made it perfect."

"He suffered." Richard's smirk was cold and detached. "And he made

CHAPTER 46

everyone around him suffer before finally dying in the hospital, letting his young wife watch his life exit his body."

Hanna stared at him, stunned. He was toying with her. She was losing control of the session, and she needed to get it back.

Richard looked at her; he knew he was getting to her. "Sweetheart," he whispered, almost fondly. "You're not a doctor in here, Hanna. You're just another widow trying to stitch yourself back together. Now tell me, did you cry, Hanna, or did you scream when the life left him? You screamed, I bet loudly. I wish I had been able to hear it."

Hanna couldn't say anything; she couldn't tell if he was telling the truth or lying. He got to her; she wanted to scream and cry out, and she wanted to kill him right then and there.

Richard grinned and the continued, harsher "Hanna, you're trying to sort it out, figure out if I'm lying, but I promise you, I'm not. I hit your husband with the intent to kill him, to do to him what I did to all the others. The fucker deserved it, but darling, I didn't do it alone; oh no, someone else worse than me pushed the buttons." His voice softened as he said, "I requested you because I knew I could fuck with you and break you down. Based on the look on your face, I have, haven't I?" His smile widened. "How does it feel to sit across from the man who stole your world, your life, your love?" Leaning in. "Payback's a bitch, princess."

She looked at him, looking for the words to say.

Richard calmly, "I'm not a monster, Hanna. I'm a mirror. I show people what's already rotten inside. Your husband? He was rotting. Just like you."

The words hit like a gunshot. Hanna stood so fast her chair screeched against the concrete floor. She turned for the door and ran. As she ran, she heard Richard yell. "Give my regards to the dead, sweetheart. I imagine they're still screaming," he said as he laughed a soulless laugh.

* * *

She didn't stop, she didn't look back, and she needed to get away.

Michael was walking down the hall when he saw her running. He ran after her, and she stopped at the door, crying

Michael caught up to her

She looked at him. "He killed Brian." She was sobbing, shaking uncontrollably as she handed him the recorder.

Michael didn't hesitate. He took the recorder from Hanna's trembling hands, his grip firm; she was falling apart right in front of him.

She wasn't just crying; she was reliving that moment all over again.

Michael pressed play, his expression darkening as Richard's voice slithered through the tiny speaker.

"I struck Brian DeLuca so hard, I swear I could hear his bones crunching upon impact... Like his brother, he didn't scream; he flew. Then he lay there, lifeless, not moving. I was sure he was dead. Imagine my surprise when I found out he actually survived. However, his survival was short lived. It went better than I could have imagined. He suffered. He made all those around him suffer."

Michael's jaw tightened as his hand that gripped the recorder went white knuckled.

He looked up at Hanna, her face pale, her entire body trembling as she tried to hold herself together, but she was *gone*, trapped inside Richard's words, inside a truth she had never been ready to hear.

Michael's voice was low and steady. " Shh, Hanna, it's going to be OK; take a deep breath for me."

She couldn't; all she could do was relive that moment with Richard.

"I knew I should have pulled you out of this," he muttered, his voice thick with frustration at her, at Richard, and at himself.

Hanna wiped the tears from her eyes and forced out the raw and broken words. "Richard Hale killed Brian; he killed my husband."

Michael took a deep breath and closed his eyes for a moment. He had suspected the truth after learning about Tony Jr. and Thomas, but hearing it confirmed was a different experience altogether. *Knowing* it? That was a different story.

Hanna shook her head, her entire body still trembling. "He, he *knew* what he was doing, Michael; he planned it; he waited for him." Her voice cracked.

CHAPTER 46

"Brian never had a chance."

Michael tightened his jaw, gazing down at the recorder with a sense of urgency.

Chapter 47

Michael led Hanna to his office and gently sat her down in his chair. He then pulled out the whiskey and two glasses, handing one to Hanna before looking at her and saying, "I will be right back." He gently closed the door and walked into Hanna's office

He took Naomi Walker's card out of his wallet and dialed it. After a few rings she answered, "Agent Walker."

"Agent Walker, this is Dr. Carter, Great Meadow Correctional Facility. Richard Hale just confessed to another murder."

Agent Walker was silent for a moment, and before she could respond, "He confessed to killing Brian DeLuca. I think you need to come down here, and if you could bring Agent Riley with you."

"I will arrive within the hour, and I will send a message to Agent Riley asking him to meet me there."

Michael urgently "Tell him what I told you, and let him know that Hanna was alone in the room with Richard when he spoke to her.

"I will see you soon."

Michael hung up the phone; he was afraid of what this was going to do to her. She just came face to face with the man who destroyed her life.

Michael looked down, gripping the edge of Hanna's desk as the weight of what had happened settled in his bones. Richard had done a lot of terrible things. But this? This was different; this was personal, and not only for Hanna, but for all of them.

He stared down at Naomi Walker's card for a long moment before tucking it back into his wallet. His mind was already racing ahead to what this

CHAPTER 47

would mean for the case, for the investigation, and for *Hanna*.

Especially for Hanna. She had sat opposite that monster for months, listening, analyzing, and striving to maintain control while Richard engaged in his twisted games. And today he won.

* * *

November 8, 1997

The weight of the air in the church was suffocating, thick with grief so heavy it felt like it could crush her where she sat. Hanna barely registered the soft murmurs of condolences, the rustling of tissue against the fabric, and the steady hum of the organ playing a hymn she couldn't name. She couldn't remember who was there and who wasn't there.

She sat in the front row, her black dress clinging to her like a second skin, her hands clasped so tightly in her lap that her knuckles had gone white. She was watching what was going on, but nothing was registering; she was numb, she was out of tears, and she hadn't slept in days.

Beside her, Tony and Elaine sat stiffly, grief carved into their faces, Tony's arm wrapped protectively around his wife as she dabbed at her eyes with a trembling hand. Another son lost; Elaine, normally a strong woman, was broken, almost frail, another piece of her heart ripped out.

Henry and Irene, her grandparents, were on the other side of her, their faces lined with sorrow, holding each other as though they could absorb the pain together. Her uncles and aunts filled the pews behind them, their presence a silent wall of support. But Hanna felt alone, even with all the people around her. The one who comforted her and was her strength was lying in the brown coffee in front of her.

The church was packed with friends and family, people from the police force and fire department, and even those she barely knew but who had come anyway, filling every row, standing along the back, offering their respects. The sheer number of people didn't make it any easier.

She heard the soft voice of the priest speaking, the familiar cadence of scripture, the gentle reassurances about life after death, about Brian being at peace, but it all felt distant. Rachel grabbed her hand and squeezed it.

Steve sat behind her, his expression drawn, his jaw clenched so tightly it looked painful. Doug sat a few rows back, his hands folded, his face unreadable. Rick sat beside him, staring straight ahead, and even Doug's brother, Nick, was there, his presence unexpected.

Hanna had only met him once before, but that day, he had been so kind. His words were soft, his touch gentle on her arm as he squeezed her shoulder, offering quiet comfort when she thought she had none left.

She barely remembered standing at the pulpit, her voice shaking as she spoke about Brian, the husband, the friend, the man who had been her entire world. She had made it through, but she hadn't been able to look at the casket, hadn't been able to say his name without feeling something inside her fracture.

It was a beautiful service. She didn't remember the procession to the burial site, nor sitting in the chair next to the casket that sat above the open ground.

The cold air bit at her skin as they lowered the casket into the ground; she got up, caught. By Steve, she wanted to be in that casket with him, but when the casket hit the ground, the finality of it stole the breath from her lungs. Her heart went to the grave with him, and she would never love another man as long as she lived. She would never let another man touch her; she would be Brian's until the day she met him on the other side.

She stood in silence, held up by Steve; he whispered, "I promise always to take care of you."

But the minute the dirt hit the coffin, she felt it, the realization that he was gone. No, not in theory, not in grief, but forever.

* * *

Present Day 2006

Michael clenched his jaw, running a hand over his face before turning back toward his office.

When he opened the door, Hanna hadn't moved. She was still sitting in his chair, the whiskey untouched in her hand, her fingers wrapped around the glass so tightly he thought it might shatter. Her eyes were unfocused, staring at nothing.

CHAPTER 47

Michael sat down across from her, leaning forward, his voice careful. "Naomi and Riley are on their way."

Hanna blinked but didn't look at him, uncertain whether she heard the words he said.

Michael hesitated. "Do you want to talk about it?"

For a moment, he didn't think she was going to answer.

Then, quietly, her voice barely above a whisper, "I thought I was ready to hear it."

Michael leaned back. "Hanna, no one is ever ready for that, you know that."

Hanna finally looked at him, her expression unreadable. "He enjoyed it," she said, her voice flat and empty. "He enjoyed every second of it."

Michael didn't argue, because she was right.

She let out a bitter laugh, with tears streaming down her face "And he knew. He knew I would be the one to start piecing things together, the one to walk into that room. He waited for this moment. He's been waiting *for* me."

Michael watched her carefully. "Then we don't let him win, Hanna."

She looked at him, something unreadable in her eyes. "He already has."

Michael's stomach turned. He knew he should have pulled her sooner. But before he could respond, there was a knock at his door, and Naomi Walker entered, her expression unwavering. Behind her, Steve followed, his eyes immediately locking onto Hanna.

The moment Hanna saw Steve, she bolted toward him, sobs wracking her body. "He killed Brian," she choked out, gripping his jacket like it was the only thing keeping her upright.

Steve wrapped his arms around her, holding her tight. His gaze snapped to Michael, sharp with unspoken fury. How the hell had he let this happen? She should have never been in that room alone with that monster

Hanna's mind kept drifting back to the day it all became so final, as if she was reliving it all over again.

Steve walked her over to her office and sat her down. So Michael could speak with Naomi.

THE LIES WE WHISPER

* * *

Michael looked at Naomi, rubbing the side of his face. "I should have pulled her months ago. I wasn't sure if I should call you or the local office; I just knew that Agent Riley needed to be here."

Naomi's expression darkened. "You were right to call me. This case isn't about Hanna. If Hale's talking, it means he's ready to burn everything down, and we need to be ahead of it."

Michael walked over to his desk, grabbed the recorder, and then placed it in Naomi's hand.

Naomi slipped the recorder into her jacket pocket. "I need the video, too. Sound is one thing; seeing her face when he said it? That's another."

Michael nodded. "Come with me."

They walked in silence down the corridor, the weight of what just happened pressing down with every step. The hum of the security lights overhead felt louder than usual.

Michael scanned his badge at the control room door. The officer inside barely looked up.

"We need the footage from Interview Room three," Michael said, his tone clipped. "Timestamp starts at 3:17 p.m."

The officer nodded, pulling it up. The screen flickered for a moment, then Hanna was sitting across from Richard, composed and calm. At first.

Naomi leaned in. "Play it."

They watched in silence as the conversation unfolded, Hanna's face slowly draining of color, her fingers tightening around her pen, her body starting to lean back just slightly as Richard's voice dug in deeper.

Then came the moment.

Naomi watched as Hanna visibly froze, neither blinking nor shifting. She just stopped.

Michael said quietly, "That's when he said Brian's name."

Naomi didn't respond. Her eyes were locked on the screen. "Rewind it. I want to hear it again."

The officer rewound the tape.

CHAPTER 47

Richard's voice crackled through the speaker: "I got out of my car, and you know what happened next. He didn't just scream, just like his brother didn't; no, Doc, he gurgled."

Hanna didn't move. On the screen, she looked like a statue. But Naomi saw it: the twitch in her jaw, the flicker in her eyes, the way her pen stopped moving.

Naomi muttered, "She went somewhere else."

Michael nodded. "She didn't come back until she ran."

Naomi straightened. "I want a copy of the material pulled now. If he was performing, we need to know who the audience really was, and most of all, I want to know who is pulling the strings."

* * *

Hanna sat still, her expression distant. Steve could see it, she shouldn't be alone tonight.

"Listen," he said gently. "Rach is out of town. Why don't you come over to my place, or I can stay with you? I really don't think you should be alone tonight."

"No, it's okay," she replied quietly. "I feel like such a burden. It's time I start standing on my own and stop leaning on everyone else."

"Hanna," he said firmly, "I'm not taking no for an answer. It would make me feel better if I stayed. We can go back to your place if that makes you more comfortable."

She hesitated, then gave a small nod.

A knock sounded at the door. Naomi peeked in.

Steve looked at Hanna. "Give me one second, then we'll head out."

He stepped into the hallway, closing the door gently behind him.

Naomi's voice was low. "How's she doing?"

Steve met her gaze. "How do you think? Her patient just confessed to killing her husband, the man she's been grieving for nine years."

Naomi nodded. "Take her home. I've got the audio and the video."

Steve narrowed his eyes. "What aren't you telling me?"

Naomi paused before answering. "Richard mentioned someone else. He said he didn't do it alone."

Steve ran a hand through his hair. "Who?"

"I don't know yet."

"Damn it. We need to talk to him."

"You need to take her home and get some food in her. It's my case, Steve. Let me handle it. Just take care of your friend."

He bristled. "Naomi, don't make me pull rank."

She raised an eyebrow. "Seriously, Riley? Don't go there. I know you care about her, but if you go back in that room, your emotions are going to take over. Be the friend she needs right now. I'll keep you in the loop."

Steve exhaled sharply. "I hate when you make sense."

Naomi smiled and rested a hand on his shoulder. "That's why we're friends. Now take her home. I'll call you when I know more."

"Be careful."

"Always, Riley."

***

Naomi returned to Michael's office while Steve went back to Hanna so they could go home together. She looked at Michael. "Can you get Hale brought down? I need to question him."

"Do you think it's a good idea?"

"Michael, you know the procedure."

Michael picked up his phone "This is Dr. Carter. I need Hale to be brought back to room two."

The voice on the other end "We will have him there in fifteen."

Michael hung up and looked at Naomi. "They are bringing him down to room two. Do you want me to sit in with you?"

Naomi shook her head. "I will only need the footage of the interview. Can you make sure it records?"

Michael nodded. "Shall we go?"

Chapter 48

Naomi walked into Room Two as they were shackling Richard to his chair. He looked up and smiled.

"You're not the pretty doctor I was expecting. But damn, a redhead. Finally, an attractive woman."

The corrections officer walked out, shaking his head. "Good luck," he muttered.

Naomi sat down across from Richard. "This interview is being recorded. I am Special Agent Naomi Walker with the FBI."

Before she could finish, Richard cut in. "This escalated quickly. Let me guess, you want to talk to me about the pretty doctor."

"Mr. Hale, you've confessed to a few cold cases."

"Ah, the DeLuca boys. Don't tell me you're interested in them." Richard smiled. He was going to enjoy this. She looked too confident in that black suit. He loved redheads. She'd be fun to break.

"Mr. Hale."

"Darling," he interrupted, "let's use first names. Call me Richard. What can I call you?"

"Agent Walker."

His smile widened, his voice low and deliberate. "A woman who likes authority. You're turning me on."

Naomi didn't flinch. She knew exactly what he was doing. If he wanted to play, she'd play. She leaned forward, resting her elbows on her knees, letting his gaze land where she wanted it.

"Richard, I like you. Work with me, and maybe I'll give you what you want."

He licked his lips, eyes drifting lower. "You're a feisty one. Do you know what I'd do to you if these cuffs weren't on?"

Naomi gave a tight smile. "Let's talk about what you said to Dr. Nowack."

"I said a lot of things. I bet she's crumbling in her office right now. She wanted to play and got burned. But you, no. You enjoy this. You get off on it, don't you?"

"You told her someone else was pulling the strings. Who is that, Richard?"

He leaned back and looked her over. "Oh, that. He's worse than I am. More vindictive."

"Can you tell me who?"

His tone changed. "Can you promise me protection from the DeLuca's?"

Naomi sat back and crossed her legs. Her voice stayed calm. "You cooperate fully. Names, dates, evidence. Then we'll talk about placement. But nothing is promised until I know what I'm dealing with."

Richard tilted his head. "You know I'm a dead man. You'll need to offer more than that. I know how this game works."

"I'll file the transfer the moment you give me something solid."

He leaned in closer. "I want a night with you. Forget the transfer. Let me have you before they take me out."

Naomi stood and slowly walked behind her chair. Her tone didn't change. "Who is pulling the strings, Richard?"

He chuckled. "Someone close. He's in the shadows and knows everything about the DeLuca's. You should be looking at them. Why is Vince DeLuca free while I'm the one sitting in this chair?"

Naomi leaned over the chair. "Vince hasn't killed anyone."

"That's a lie. He's killed more than I have. He hired me to take out those women. Then someone found out and turned it on him. Vince thought he had all the power, but the real threat was already beside him."

"Do you have proof?"

Richard smiled. "You want paperwork? I don't keep records. You toying with me, bitch?"

Naomi walked back around to the front of the chair and sat down again.

CHAPTER 48

"I want to help you, but I need something I can use. I think the man you're protecting has what I need. Give me his name, and I'll bring down the DeLuca's."

Richard narrowed his eyes. "I know your game. I know my fate. I accepted it when I confessed. I'm going to help you the same way you're going to help me."

Naomi remained still. "How's that, Mr. Hale?"

"I'm not. But I will give you this. The person pulling the strings is closer than you think." He paused, then his voice turned sharp. "This is over. And you? You're not even my type. My time is limited, and I don't owe you anything."

Naomi kept her voice steady. "You help me, I help you."

"No. I wouldn't touch you. Take your offer and shove it. I wouldn't help you if you were the last woman on earth. Now get out of my sight."

* * *

Steve walked Hanna through the door of her house, to the living room, and onto the couch. He looked at her. "I will be right back."

She looked at him and nodded.

He walked out to the back porch and dialed Tony.

"Steve, can I call you back?"

"I need a minute; it's not good."

"What is going on?"

Steve put his hand on his forehead and looked down. "Richard confessed."

"To what exactly?"

"To killing Brian while he was in a session with Hanna."

Tony's voice changed, becoming harsh. "Where is Hanna, Steve?"

"Home. I am here with her now. Can you keep Caitlyn tonight? I am going to stay here with her."

"That is fine. I think she was spending the night anyways." There was a silence, then, "Steve, don't do anything," Tony demanded. "I will take care of Richard."

"Tony," Steve started to say.

"Steve, this one time I need you to stay out of the way. Just take care of Hanna."

Tony hung up.

Steve looked at the house and wondered when it would all end. She had been through so much.

He walked back in, slid his boots off, and went to the living room. She was still where he left her.

"Do you want some water?"

She shook her head. "No."

He sat beside her and pulled her close, holding her like it was the only thing he knew to do.

"We'll get through this," he said softly. "We always do."

He kissed the top of her head, letting the silence settle between them.

She rested against him without a word.

After a moment, he spoke again, his voice quiet. "You've got people who love you. You don't have to carry this on your own."

Chapter 49

Two Weeks After Richard's Confession

Hanna sat at her kitchen table, fingers curled around a cup of tea, long since gone cold. The house was quiet. Too quiet. Caitlyn was asleep in her room, and for the first time in weeks, she was alone.

Elaine had stayed for a few nights, fussing over her like she was a child again, making sure she ate, making sure she slept, and making sure she didn't spiral too far down the hole Richard had shoved her into.

But eventually, she sent Elaine back home, insisting she was fine. But that is when Lee showed up. He was there the very next morning, saying, "I'll stay on the couch," he'd said simply, like it wasn't up for discussion.

And she had let him.

Not because she needed someone to protect her Richard was locked away, and ghosts didn't walk through front doors, but because for the first time in a long time, she didn't want to be alone.

She had spent so many years burying her past, telling herself that the wounds had healed. But Richard had ripped them open with one confession. Lee had missed so much, but now he was the one sitting with her in the ruins, and that was enough.

"I'm sorry," he had said one night, his voice gruff, uncomfortable.

She had looked at him, her fingers tracing the rim of her glass. "For what?"

"For everything," he admitted. "For not being what you needed."

Hanna nodded but said nothing. What more could she possibly add? But the fact that he was there with her seemed to be enough; she accepted him for what he could give her, and it wasn't much, but at that moment, it was all she needed.

They may not have hung out all the time, but they talked constantly, and she began to understand the man and that he gave what he could, what he knew how to give, and deep down she loved him for it.

Lee and Kevin never really patched things up; they would talk, but there was nothing there.

The important thing was that Lee was there now, and that was more than she could say about most people.

Hanna exhaled slowly, glancing at the clock. It was late. The house was empty again. Elaine had gone home, and Lee was snoring on the couch. She offered him the guest room, but he wanted the couch. And for the first time since Richard's confession, she didn't feel like she was drowning.

Maybe she would never get the full truth. Maybe there were still pieces missing, things she would never know.

But she was still here, and that had to count for something.

* * *

Great Meadow Correctional Facility

The prison was silent. Lights out had come and gone, leaving only the dim, flickering glow of the security bulbs humming in the hallways. Richard Hale lay on his cot, staring at the ceiling, hands folded neatly over his stomach.

His last conversation with Hanna played on a loop in his mind. The way her face had paled, the way her fingers had curled against the table as she held herself together. He had broken her. He was sure of it, and that final seed of doubt he'd planted about Nick? Hell, that was a bonus.

Nick had been such a disappointment; he became weak, almost too emotional when it came to Hanna. He let guilt eat at him, let her turn him into something soft. A man like that didn't deserve to win.

Richard smirked. He wondered if she was done with him or just taking a break before coming back for more. She was too stubborn. They always came back. Either way, he had done what he set out to do: tear her apart

CHAPTER 49

from the inside. The soft metallic click of his cell door unlocking barely registered.

Richard didn't turn his head; he didn't shift on the mattress. He knew the corrections officer was owned by the DeLuca's; most of them were. The money was a quiet supplement to a government paycheck.

The cell door creaked open. Two men stepped inside, moving like ghosts, silent and efficient.

Richard smirked. "It's about time."

The first man, broad-shouldered, his face unreadable under the flickering light, reached behind him and locked the door, not that it mattered.

The second, leaner, quieter one knelt beside the cot, his voice low, almost amused. "The fact that you knew we were coming makes you smarter than we thought. You were dumb to talk, Hale. Enough with the chatter," he nodded to the other man and then back at Richard, "Carlo and Tony sent their regards."

Richard finally sat up, stretching his arms. "Of course I did. I knew the minute they found out I killed Thomas, but I knew I sealed the deal when I confessed to Brian and even Tony Jr. Plus, your boss knew I was starting to talk; it was only a matter of time before I exposed them all."

The first man shrugged his shoulders. "That makes this easier."

Richard chuckled; he didn't beg or bargain. He had made peace with this long before they stepped into his cell; it took them long enough. "Let's not waste time," he said, smirking. "Do what you came to do."

The taller man cracked his knuckles before stepping forward, pulling Richard off the bed, and turning him around with his back to him.

Richard closed his eyes; he always knew in the back of his mind it would end like this. Men like him never died in their sleep. He inhaled deeply, knowing it would be his last, and when the moment came, it was fast. A sharp crack echoed in the small cell, his spine twisting unnaturally. His body sagged instantly, dead weight. Richard Hale's lifeless body fell to the ground.

The other man moved quickly, tying the sheet in place and looping it around Richard's neck with practiced ease. Afterward, they stepped out of the cell, moving like ghosts, leaving nothing behind but silence.

Moments later, the same CO came back to the cell, barely looking as he turned the key, locking the door; just another night, just another shift.

Chapter 50

The next day, Hanna arrived at the prison a little after eight.

She had spent the entire drive trying to convince herself that today would be different. That the weight pressing against her chest wasn't real. That she was finally done letting Richard Hale live in her head, in her memory, in her breath.

But the moment she stepped through the front doors, she knew something was wrong.

Michael Carter was waiting for her near the security checkpoint, his expression tight, his face drawn.

"Hanna," he said, his voice softer than usual.

She stopped in her tracks. "Michael? What is it?"

He exhaled, rubbing a hand down his face. "It's Richard," he said. "He's dead."

The words didn't land right away. They hovered there, strange and disjointed.

Hanna blinked. "What?"

Michael's jaw tightened. "They found him in his cell this morning. It looks like suicide. They said he used a bed sheet."

The floor tilted slightly beneath her. Hanna swallowed, trying to will her voice into something steady. "No."

Michael hesitated. "There was a note." He reached into his coat pocket and pulled out a small evidence bag, holding it up for her to see.

Inside was a single torn scrap of paper. Three words, written in Richard's familiar, looping scrawl.

I'm sorry, Doc.

Hanna's stomach ached as she stared at the note, the ink smudged in places, the finality of it heavy in the air.

Richard Hale was gone.

She sat with the silence, unsure what to feel. Grief tugged at one corner of her heart. Relief settled in another. And beneath both, there was something colder, something that felt unfinished.

Michael watched her closely. "You okay?"

She nodded, though she wasn't. Not really. But what else could she say? "Yeah," she murmured. "I'm fine."

Even as the words left her mouth, she recognized the lie. She could always hear it, especially in her own voice.

* * *

Later that morning, Hanna sat in her office, staring at her laptop.

The sunlight filtered through the blinds, spilling across her desk. It should have made the room feel warm, alive. Instead, it felt distant. Disconnected.

The cursor blinked at her like it was waiting for something meaningful. Something heavy.

But she only typed what was required.

Deceased. Cause of death: suicide.

She sat there for a long moment, her fingers hovering over the keys, then slowly closed the laptop like it was something fragile.

She reached into her purse and pulled out Naomi Walker's card, the corners curled, the ink slightly faded, and dialed.

"Agent Walker," came the voice on the other end. Clipped. Professional.

"Naomi. It's Dr. Hanna Nowack."

"Hanna," Naomi said, her tone softening just a touch. "How are you holding up?"

CHAPTER 50

Hanna looked out the window. A leaf tapped softly against the glass. "I'm... managing," she said. "I just wanted to let you know. Last night, we found Richard Hale dead in his cell."

There was a pause, short but deliberate.

"Yes," Naomi replied. "We got the file this morning. Looks like he took the easy way out."

Hanna closed her eyes. "Do you really believe that? That it was suicide? He didn't seem like someone who would give up. Not when I saw him. Not after everything."

Naomi was quiet for a moment longer this time. When she finally spoke, her voice was low, measured, and deliberate. "With someone like Hale, you never really know. Especially when they're at the end. Men like that don't follow patterns. They create their own."

"I don't think his story was finished," Hanna said quietly.

Naomi didn't answer right away. "I read through his file again after the report came in. He had been closing loops, one at a time. Tony Jr. Thomas. The women. And then you." She paused. "You were the last one, Hanna. He requested you for a reason. Once he confessed to you, once he gave you what he thought was the final blow, he was done. You were his last chapter."

"It didn't feel like closure," Hanna whispered. "It felt like he was still playing a game. Like there were still pieces left on the board."

Naomi exhaled, and Hanna felt her stomach twist at the sound.

"You're probably right," Naomi said. "But none of us really understand men like him. Not fully. Once their humanity is gone, all that's left is instinct, the hunger, and finally the control. Sometimes, when the game's over, even the predator lies down."

Hanna was quiet, her thoughts running faster than her heart.

"I guess you're right. Thanks for taking the time to talk."

"Hanna, have you thought about our conversation?"

"I have," Hanna said softly. "Can I have a little more time? I promise I'll have an answer soon."

"Of course," Naomi said. "Take care. And if you need anything, call me."

"Thanks, Naomi."

Hanna hung up and set the phone down slowly.

She looked around her office. The walls that used to make her feel strong, the desk that once gave her purpose. Now everything felt smaller. Quieter. Dimmer.

She stared at her hands for a long moment. Then up at the ceiling. Then at the corners of the room, where the shadows still lived.

She had come here believing she could help someone. She believed she could uncover their humanity and bring it back into the light.

But maybe Brian had been right all those years ago.

Maybe the monsters weren't hiding behind the bars. Maybe she didn't belong here anymore.

There was a knock on the frame of her office door.

She looked up.

Steve stood there, holding a brown paper bag in one hand and a familiar smile that didn't quite reach his eyes.

"Figured you hadn't eaten," he said. "Double cheeseburger. Extra fries."

Hanna blinked, caught off guard. "Did you just bring me lunch?"

"I got one for myself too," he said, stepping inside. "Didn't want you clogging your arteries alone."

He set the bag on her desk.

She looked at it. Then at him. And something in her chest shifted, just slightly.

"I wasn't hungry," she murmured.

"I know." He reached into the bag, pulled out a burger and fries, and set them in front of her. "But I was in the area and figured it might be fun to have lunch with my friend Hanna… in a prison psych unit."

She laughed and shook her head.

He pulled out his own burger and sat down in one of the chairs across from her.

She smiled as she unwrapped hers. "In the area, huh?"

"Actually, yeah," he said, grabbing a fry. "Had to pick up some paperwork."

She took a bite, then raised an eyebrow. "This is really good. Where did you get this from?"

CHAPTER 50

"It's from that place Caitlyn loves, the one with the patio lights and milkshakes as big as her head."

Hanna smiled, softer now. "She would eat there every day if I let her."

Steve grinned. "Last week she told me she wants to open her own burger place when she grows up. She said she'll pay me to taste-test everything."

"She told me the same thing," Hanna said, laughing quietly. "Said I could handle the therapy for sad people who can't get their orders right."

Steve chuckled. "That kid might actually run the world one day."

"She already runs mine," Hanna said without thinking, her voice barely above a whisper.

Steve didn't respond. He just nodded, letting the silence stretch between them, the kind they'd long since made peace with. Then he took another bite of his burger.

"Other than that," he asked casually, "are you doing okay?"

She gave a small nod. "Just trying to get back into a rhythm."

Steve glanced away for a second before clearing his throat. "Rachel mentioned you've been keeping to yourself lately."

Hanna's smile flickered. "Yeah… I guess I needed to."

He didn't push. "Just making sure you're okay. You know I am here anytime you need me."

She looked up at him. "I know. I just didn't want to intrude. You two are still settling into being married."

Before she could finish, Steve cut in gently, "Hanna, you're family. My family. You call when you need me, or just call for the hell of it."

Her smile returned, softer this time, the weight in her chest lifting just slightly.

Steve crumpled his wrapper and tossed it into the trash can across the room. He raised his arms like a kid hitting a game winner. "Score!"

She let out a little chuckle and shook her head.

Then he stood. "I hate to eat and run, but I've got a mountain of paperwork and a meeting I need to prep for."

Hanna stood too and crossed the room. She wrapped her arms around him. "Thanks for lunch, Steve."

He kissed the top of her head. "Don't mention it. See you later, Han."

She watched him as he walked out the doorway, his footsteps fading down the hall. For a long moment, she didn't move.

Then she sat back down at her desk, opened her laptop, and finished the burger in front of her. The warmth of it grounded her, if only for a moment.

Her thoughts shifted back to the day ahead: the reports waiting to be filed, the sessions still on the calendar, and the loose threads Richard had left behind.

She didn't have all the answers. But for the first time in a long time, she didn't feel like she was drowning in questions either. There were still shadows in the corners. But she could see the light again too. And for now, that would have to be enough.

Chapter 51

April 2007

A month had passed since Richard's suicide. Hanna sat on her front porch, fingers loosely curled around her phone, watching Mr. Donovan try and fail to teach his grandson how to weed. It wasn't going well. The poor kid yanked out one of Mrs. Donovan's flowers, and Hanna shook her head with a soft chuckle.

Her gaze drifted back to her screen.

Nick's name.

Her thumb hovered above the call button.

Part of her urged her to leave it alone. Let it be. Move forward without stirring old wounds. But that wasn't who she was. Forgiveness, for her, had never been about forgetting or excusing; it was about release. About reclaiming the peace that resentment stole.

She exhaled slowly. "Steve is going to kill me," she muttered under her breath.

Still, she pressed send.

The line rang twice before he picked up.

"Hanna?" Nick's voice was cautious, his tone edged with hesitation. She heard it in the pause between words, the weight behind her name, like he wasn't sure why she was calling or if he wanted to know.

"Hi, Nick," she said softly, tucking a loose strand of hair behind her ear. "I was wondering if you'd want to come over. I-" She paused, choosing her words carefully. "I'd like to talk."

There was a stretch of silence. Only the sound of his breath on the other end.

Then finally, "Okay. I'll be there in about fifteen or twenty minutes."

She nodded instinctively. "Great. See you soon."

As the call ended, she let out a breath she hadn't realized she'd been holding.

This wasn't a second chance. It wasn't a do over. It was a way to end things the right way on her terms.

* * *

When Nick arrived, Hanna was already at the door. She offered a small, careful smile and stepped aside.

"Come in," she said softly.

He paused at the threshold before stepping inside. His movements were slower than she remembered, measured, almost hesitant. She wasn't sure if it was nerves or something else, but it stood out.

The scent of fresh coffee filled the kitchen. Without speaking, she grabbed two mugs, filled them, and slid one across the counter toward him.

As she looked up, she noticed how tired he seemed. Still Nick, but worn down. The sharpness he used to carry had faded. His shoulders slumped slightly, and a drawn tightness framed his mouth. There was a quietness about him she hadn't seen before.

She wrapped her hands around her mug. For months, she had been angry, furious even. But sitting here now, with silence stretching between them and the years hanging in the air, all she felt was a heavy kind of sorrow. Maybe even regret. She broke the quiet. "How's the hospital?"

Nick rubbed a hand over his face and took a sip from his mug. "Busy," he said, with a faint, wry smile. "A resident almost put a cast on the wrong leg last week."

Hanna let out a soft laugh. "That would've made for a hell of a lawsuit."

"Wouldn't be the first," he replied with a shrug.

She shook her head, smiling faintly. It had been a long time since they'd talked like this.

CHAPTER 51

Nick shifted in his seat. "What about you? How's work?"

Her expression dimmed. "Complicated, as always." She hesitated. "It feels different with Richard gone."

She noticed the flinch, small but unmistakable.

"I don't know how to feel about it," she admitted. "Relieved, maybe. And guilty for feeling that way." Her fingers tightened around the mug. "I really believed that I could help him. That there was something left to reach."

Nick didn't answer at first. He just nodded once. She didn't press. She knew what Richard had meant to him once, maybe still did, in some quiet, shadowed part of himself.

She set her mug down and folded her hands on the table. "Nick."

He looked up.

"I know it wasn't easy for you to open up. And I'm sorry for my part in everything."

He frowned, shaking his head. "You don't have to—"

"Let me say this," she interrupted gently, holding up a hand. "I should've been more honest. I know I led you on sometimes, and that wasn't fair."

His brow creased, his mouth drawing into a hard line.

"You didn't do anything wrong," he said quietly.

"I did," she said. "Not on purpose. But I did." She hesitated, then reached across the table and laid her hand over his.

He went still under her touch.

"I don't want to erase what we had," she continued. "We were friends. You were there for me when I couldn't stand on my own. And Caitlyn... she misses you."

She saw his throat move as he swallowed.

"I want to try again," she said softly. "As friends. But only if we're honest with each other."

He looked down at their hands, then back at her. "What does that mean?"

"No more secrets," she said. "If you ever feel that pull again, if your feelings start to change, I need you to tell me. No surprises. No games."

Their eyes met. His eyes were tired, but behind them was something unspoken, something vulnerable and real.

"I don't deserve your forgiveness," he said after a long moment.

Her smile was quiet, tinged with sadness. "Maybe not. But you have it anyway."

He nodded once, slowly. "I'll try."

* * *

A few nights later, Nick pulled into Hanna's driveway. From the porch light, she could see his grip tighten on the wheel before he stepped out. She wasn't sure if he was nervous, but he moved like someone trying not to make a wrong move.

He knocked lightly before stepping inside. The house smelled of roasted chicken and garlic, warm and familiar. He hadn't even made it through the doorway before Caitlyn came running. "Nick! You're staying for dinner, right?"

Hanna was in the kitchen, wiping her hands on a dish towel. She glanced over her shoulder. "I told you he was," she murmured, her expression soft as she met Nick's eyes. "If you still want to."

He nodded. "Wouldn't miss it."

It felt oddly natural the way he stepped into the kitchen and started helping her without asking. The way Caitlyn chattered nonstop about her day, science projects, books, and the class clown who tried to eat glue. Nick listened like he He used to listen with his full attention, like what she said truly mattered.

Dinner was easier than she expected.

They moved around each other with a kind of quiet rhythm, as if the months of silence had never happened. As if nothing had broken.

She found herself watching him and the way he smiled at Caitlyn, the way his hands moved when he passed a plate, and the way his fingers brushed lightly against hers. It should have felt strange, but it didn't. Not exactly.

She was still guarded and still unsure, but she missed his friendship. Everyone deserved a second chance, even if Steve thought it was a bad idea.

When Nick noticed her hesitation, he didn't press. He simply let things

CHAPTER 51

be.

Maybe that was why she didn't pull away.

They laughed over old stories while Caitlyn added her usual dramatic flair, and for the first time in a long while, Hanna wasn't holding her breath.

She met Nick's gaze across the table and didn't look away.

After dinner, she poured them each a cup of coffee while Caitlyn grabbed a deck of cards from the drawer.

"Nick, play with me?" she asked, already shuffling.

He grinned. "What are we playing?"

She gasped. "You forgot? We always play Crazy Eights after dinner!"

Hanna smirked. "You don't have to. She just likes winning."

Nick leaned in and whispered loud enough for Hanna to hear, "She's just mad because she always loses."

Caitlyn giggled. "You're both going down."

They played for nearly an hour. Caitlyn dominated. After her third win, she threw her arms up triumphantly.

"I am the Queen of Cards!"

Nick shook his head. "Remind me never to bet money against you."

Hanna leaned back, watching them with something warm and unfamiliar curling in her chest.

It felt like something real.

Eventually, Caitlyn yawned and rubbed her eyes.

Nick stood before she could protest. "Alright, kid. Time for bed."

She clung to him sleepily. "Will you stay until I fall asleep?"

He looked at Hanna. She nodded.

"Of course," he said.

"Will you read to me?"

"Always."

Hanna leaned in the doorway as Nick read aloud, his voice low and steady. Caitlyn clung to every word.

"I missed you, Nick," she murmured, eyes half closed.

Nick's voice caught. "Missed you too, kid." He kissed her forehead and smoothed her curls before standing.

When he turned, Hanna was still there, watching quietly. Their eyes met.

As they walked back down the hallway, the house felt still. Not empty, just settled.

Hanna leaned against the counter.

"Tonight was nice," she said softly.

"Yeah," Nick replied, his voice quiet.

She paused for a moment, then added, "I missed this."

He didn't respond right away, but his eyes softened, and the tension in his posture faded.

Without another word, she stepped forward and wrapped her arms around him, this time without holding back.

For a moment, he stood still, caught off guard.

Then he returned the embrace, his arms coming around her with steady ease. There was no tension, no hesitation. A familiar and safe warmth settled between them.

When she pulled back, she looked up at him. "Stay for a cup of coffee?"

His smile came slow, unforced. "Of course."

They sat together long after the coffee had gone cold, the conversation light and easy. They spoke about work and Caitlyn's latest school antics. Nothing important, yet somehow it all mattered.

It wasn't dramatic. It wasn't heavy. It was simple and familiar, the kind of closeness that felt like it had always been there.

Nick wondered if they could find their way back to something better than before. Not the version shaped by bad timing and missed chances, but something real and lasting. She called it friendship, but maybe that was just to protect them both, to slow it down until she was ready to call it something more. He knew she couldn't live without him. That he was what she wanted all along. He knew if he was patient, she would call, and she did, and now here they were, and tonight proved it.

Chapter 52

June 2007

It had been two months since that night in Hanna's kitchen, since they'd quietly agreed they were better as friends. Things with Nick gradually started feeling comfortable again. They'd settled into familiar routines, spending evenings laughing over movies or casually chatting on the porch. It felt natural, free of tension, their friendship cautiously restored. Steve wasn't entirely convinced about Nick's return to their lives, making it clear that if Nick slipped again, there would be consequences.

Hanna felt happier and lighter than she had in years. She suspected Nick might still quietly hope for something more, but for now, she enjoyed the gentle rhythm of friendship they'd rediscovered. It felt safe and easy, and she saw no harm in simply letting things unfold naturally.

Hanna walked back to her office, checking briefly on Caitlyn, who was absorbed in her book. At her desk, she glanced at Richard's open case file. Her task was to summarize any observable behavior that might have hinted at suicidal intent. She'd carefully reviewed all notes and recordings from their sessions, finding nothing overtly alarming. Yet the official conclusion still didn't sit right; Richard had displayed no clear signs. She knew as a therapist she shouldn't rely solely on instinct, but something about the neat simplicity of Richard's death continued to nag at her.

Her eyes drifted to Naomi Walker's business card beside the file. The FBI offer was enticing, but she'd always prioritized Caitlyn over career moves. Relocating to Virginia felt drastic, yet part of her craved a fresh start.

She carefully considered her options for a long moment, then reached for her phone and called Naomi.

"Agent Walker," Naomi answered warmly.

"Naomi, it's Hanna Nowack. I've considered your offer carefully. I'm interested, but I can't leave Caitlyn for long stretches."

Naomi responded quickly. "Hanna, the role is flexible. You'd work mostly from home, with occasional brief trips for interviews, just days at most."

Relief flooded Hanna. "Really?"

"Yes," Naomi confirmed. "But relocation to Virginia, near Quantico, is necessary."

Hanna hesitated briefly, still conflicted. But perhaps leaving New York was exactly what they needed. "I'll take the job, Naomi. Caitlyn and I could both use a fresh start."

Naomi sounded genuinely pleased. "Wonderful. I'll connect you with my realtor, David. He's fantastic."

"Thanks, Naomi."

Ending the call, Hanna felt cautiously hopeful, even though Richard's death continued to trouble her. The unease remained, a persistent reminder that perhaps things weren't as straightforward as they seemed.

**

Nick checked his watch, excitement mixed with nervous anticipation. He'd spent days planning dinner at Citrine, carefully choosing every detail. He wasn't entirely sure when his feelings had shifted again, but seeing Hanna relaxed and happy around him had reignited his hope. Yet, a nagging unease lingered. She still wore that ring around her neck, hidden beneath her blouse. He pushed the worry aside. Hanna seemed happy, and tonight he'd finally show her they could be more than friends.

He reached into his pocket, fingers brushing the small velvet box, then took out his phone and dialed the restaurant.

"Hello. I'd like to make a reservation for tonight at 6:30. Party of six, under the name O'Sullivan."

"Certainly, we look forward to seeing you tonight," the hostess replied

CHAPTER 52

warmly.

Nick hung up; the reservations were set. Nick exhaled slowly, gathering his courage. He dialed Hanna's number next.

It rang twice before she answered cheerfully. "Hi, Nick!"

"Hey, Hanna," he said casually. "I made reservations for 6:30 at Citrine. Is it okay if Doug and Alison join us? You can invite Steve and Rachel too."

She paused briefly, then replied warmly, "Sure, I'll call them." She hesitated slightly. "Nick, I'm really glad we're doing this, glad we're friends again."

"Me too," Nick said, a smile spreading on his face. "The last few months have been great." He exhaled slowly as the call ended, convinced things were finally turning in his favor. He knew after tonight, she would be his. Next year at this time Hanna and Caitlyn would be living with him; they would be a family.

* * *

Hanna lowered her phone, smiling softly. Tonight would be nice, comfortable even. Things felt settled again, stable. Richard's death had shaken her deeply, making her realize she'd clung to the past too long. It was time to embrace the present.

She dialed Rachel next, her mood positive until Rachel answered hesitantly.

"Hey, Hanna." Rachel's tone was strained.

"Are you and Steve free tonight? Nick made dinner reservations at Citrine."

Rachel hesitated. "Citrine? Fancy. Are we celebrating?"

"Just dinner," Hanna said lightly.

"We should be able to make it."

"It will be fun; I haven't had a night out in a long time."

Rachel paused again, taking a breath. "Hanna, I think I made a mistake."

Hanna's brow furrowed slightly. "What's going on?"

Rachel sighed, her voice lowering further. "Things with Steve haven't been great lately. I thought us getting married would change it, you know, Steve."

Hanna's stomach tightened in surprise. She hadn't noticed any issues before now. "Oh no, Rachel, what is going on?"

"I don't even know," Rachel admitted softly. "Maybe we rushed and should have really thought about it. I feel like we are trying too hard." She paused. "And, Hanna, there's something else. I accidentally met someone. It just happened."

Hanna inhaled sharply, genuinely taken aback. "Rachel, I won't judge you, but this is big. Why didn't you tell me sooner? Why don't we cancel dinner and you come here and we have a girls night?"

"I was trying to ignore it," Rachel said miserably. "Look, let's not ruin dinner tonight; you deserve the night out. Can we maybe talk tomorrow?"

"Are you sure? We can skip dinner if you need to."

"No, let's go."

"Caitlyn is staying with Elaine and Tony; why don't you come over in the morning?"

"That works, listen Steve just got home. See you tonight."

Rachel hung up abruptly, leaving Hanna deeply unsettled. She hadn't suspected Rachel and Steve had issues, let alone something so significant. She forced herself to temporarily set aside her worry and dialed Elaine.

Elaine answered on the second ring, her voice warm as always. "Hello, Hanna."

"Mom," Hanna said gently. "Would you be able to take Caitlyn tonight? Nick invited me to dinner."

There was a brief pause, a subtle shift in Elaine's tone. "Dinner with Nick?"

Hanna quickly clarified, keeping her voice casual. "Yes, at Citrine. It's just dinner, Mom. Steve and Rachel will be there, too. Nick knows we're only friends."

Elaine's voice softened slightly. "Of course, sweetheart. We'd love to have Caitlyn. We'll see you soon."

CHAPTER 52

"Thanks, Mom," Hanna replied, relieved. "See you shortly."

She ended the call, feeling a mild twinge of unease at Elaine's subtle reaction, but brushed it away quickly.

Chapter 53

Nick arrived right on time.

Hanna opened the door and offered him a gentle smile. Her gaze drifted over his neatly pressed shirt and deep green tie. For a brief moment, she paused, noticing something strained beneath his polished exterior.

"Hanna, you look stunning," Nick said warmly.

She nodded, brushing a stray hair behind her ear. "Thank you. Come on in; I'll grab Caitlyn so we can go."

Turning toward the hallway, Hanna called out softly, "Sweetie, it's time to go to Grandma and Grandpa's!"

Tiny footsteps echoed rapidly down the hall as Caitlyn squealed with delight, launching herself into Nick's arms.

He laughed, scooping her up and spinning her around. "Hey, kiddo! Miss me?"

"You saw me two days ago, silly!" Caitlyn giggled.

"Two whole days?" he teased. "It felt like forever."

Hanna smiled and reached for her purse. "Ready to go?"

"Ready," Nick said softly, gently ruffling Caitlyn's hair as he set her down.

***

The drive to Elaine's was filled with Caitlyn's laughter and Nick's playful teasing as he sang along dramatically off key to the radio. Hanna, however, felt unease creeping into her chest. Nick had been oddly insistent that everyone join tonight. The tightness in her stomach made her wonder if

CHAPTER 53

he was planning something.

When they reached Elaine's house, Hanna lifted Caitlyn from the car and guided her up the porch steps.

"Thank you for this," Hanna said quietly, hugging Elaine.

"Always, sweetheart. We're here anytime," Elaine responded warmly.

Hanna knelt, pressing a gentle kiss to Caitlyn's forehead. "Be good, okay? See you tomorrow."

Caitlyn smiled brightly. "Promise."

Back in the car, silence replaced laughter, broken only by the faint hum of the radio. Hanna stared quietly out the window, her chest tight with uncertainty.

* * *

At Citrine, they spotted Steve and Rachel pulling into the parking lot. Hanna joined Rachel as they headed toward the restaurant entrance, keeping their conversation intentionally light.

Rachel leaned closer, whispering discreetly, "We need some time to talk alone later."

Hanna nodded in agreement.

Trailing behind, Steve watched Rachel whisper to Hanna. Unable to hear their conversation clearly, he glanced toward Nick, noticing his intense gaze fixed on Hanna. A quiet suspicion twisted in Steve's gut. He didn't trust Nick.

Inside, Nick spoke confidently to the hostess. "O'Sullivan, party of six."

They were led to a warmly lit table already occupied by Doug and Alison, who greeted them with cheerful smiles.

"Took you long enough," Doug teased.

Hanna returned a polite smile and took her seat, noticing immediately when Nick settled a bit too close beside her. Discreetly, she shifted her chair to reclaim personal space.

Dinner flowed smoothly, conversation filled with laughter and comfortable banter. Doug and Alison shared affectionate exchanges while

Steve entertained them with vague, intriguing stories about his recent case. Rachel lightly teased him, though her laughter seemed forced.

Throughout dinner, Hanna grew increasingly uncomfortable with Nick's subtle touches. His hand brushed hers repeatedly, each contact lingering too long, pushing unspoken boundaries. They were friends, nothing more, and she felt trapped by his closeness.

The evening felt eerily perfect, unsettlingly so, leaving Hanna anxious, waiting for something to shatter the facade.

She should have trusted her instincts.

As dessert plates were cleared, Hanna straightened and spoke up, breaking the quiet.

"I have an announcement."

Silence quickly filled the table as everyone turned toward her.

"I've accepted the position with CSI," she announced gently. "I'm moving to Virginia."

Shock gripped the table, freezing Nick mid-movement. Rachel's eyes widened, confusion evident.

Steve finally broke the quiet, his voice gentle yet strained. "Congratulations, Hanna. Are you sure this is what you want?"

She nodded firmly. "Yes. Absolutely."

Rachel managed a faint smile. "Well, then. Let's toast to Hanna's new chapter."

Before they could celebrate, Nick cleared his throat loudly, drawing all eyes toward him.

"I wasn't sure when I'd do this, but…" He hesitated briefly, visibly nervous as he reached into his jacket pocket and produced a small velvet box.

Hanna's heart pounded sharply, panic rising. "Nick…"

He ignored her hesitant tone, confidently flipping open the velvet box to reveal a glittering ring. "Marry me, Hanna. We belong together. What we've built is special, and I love Caitlyn like she's my own. Please, marry me."

He slipped the ring onto her finger as if the decision were already made, his eyes bright with expectation.

CHAPTER 53

Hanna froze, her heartbeat roaring in her ears. She stared down at the ring, feeling its weight as panic rose in her chest. Her lips parted, but words wouldn't form. She was trapped between obligation and instinct, her mind scrambling to find clarity.

Before she could respond, another voice shattered the strained silence, steady and familiar, cutting straight through her heart. "I wouldn't do that if I were you."

Hanna's heart stilled. Her breath caught as she slowly turned toward the familiar voice. Her eyes locked onto a face she knew intimately, a face she had seen only in her dreams.

"Brian?" she whispered, her voice shaking with disbelief. Her fingers pulled free from Nick's grip, trembling slightly. Her mind rejected what her eyes plainly saw.

Rachel gasped, her hands tightening on Hanna's shoulders. "Oh my God."

Hanna barely heard Rachel. Her vision blurred as memories flooded back. Brian lying lifeless in a hospital bed. She had touched him; she felt the cold stillness of death. But here he was, alive, standing before her.

Steve's angry voice broke through sharply. "I told you I was handling this."

Hanna spun to face Steve, her voice shaking with betrayal. "You knew? You knew he was alive?"

Rachel turned angrily toward Steve. "You bastard! You watched her suffer and said nothing?"

Steve ignored Rachel's anger, eyes locked intensely on Brian, thoughts racing to contain the situation.

Meanwhile, Nick remained frozen on one knee, stubbornly ignoring Brian's presence. "Hanna," he pleaded tightly, "don't let him ruin our future. Look at me, not him."

He reached out toward her, but she drew back instinctively, her gaze locked unwavering on Brian.

Everything else faded away.

Brian stood calmly, watching her, his expression gentle and unchanged by time. His familiar crooked smile slowly appeared, warming her from the inside out.

In a quiet, tender voice, as though no time had passed at all, Brian spoke the two words that filled her with both joy and disbelief.

"Miss me?"

Epilogue

June 1986

Hanna quietly slipped from the hallway, desperate for an escape. The laughter spilling from the backyard was too loud, too forced. These dinners had turned into a charade, a staged performance where everyone pretended her parents' divorce wasn't a fresh, ugly bruise pressing against her chest.

She no longer fit neatly into either of their worlds. Maybe she never had.

Her mother seemed interested in her only when it meant twisting the knife in her father's heart. Her father barely acknowledged her existence unless it was to remind her how inconvenient she had made his life.

Sometimes Hanna wondered if either of them had ever truly wanted her or if she was just the reason they felt obligated to stay. First, the reason they got married. Then, the reason they fell apart

Outside on the back porch, the evening air was softer. The glass door muted the noise inside, cloaking her in a quiet, gentle solitude.

Her grandfather Henry sat on the old wooden swing, a glass of sweet tea resting loosely in his hand as he watched the sky fade from vivid blue into gentle gold.

"Are you hiding, sweetheart?" His voice was soft and understanding.

Hanna shrugged. She hadn't planned on talking, but the words tumbled out anyway, raw and aching. "Grandpa… I don't think I ever want to get married. Or fall in love."

Henry turned slowly toward her, his eyes thoughtful. "Is that so? Where's this coming from?"

She wrapped her arms around herself tightly, as if trying to hold the fractured pieces inside. "What's the point? People lie. They leave. They make promises they never keep."

With quiet patience, Henry set down his glass and gently patted the empty spot beside him.

Hanna hesitated briefly, then climbed onto the swing, tucking her feet up and curling close to him.

He nodded gently, his gaze fixed somewhere distant, somewhere beyond their backyard. "You're right. Some people do lie, and some walk away. But love, the real kind, isn't about perfect promises. It's about who stays when things get tough. It's about finding someone who makes you feel safe and wanted. Someone who loves you simply because you exist."

She rested her head softly against his shoulder, feeling the comforting roughness of his old cotton shirt against her cheek. Tears burned at the edges of her eyes.

"Do you really think that kind of love exists?" Her whisper was fragile, almost afraid to hope.

Henry smiled, the lines around his eyes gentle and warm. "I do. And someday, when you find it, Hanna, you'll know. The right person won't want to fix or change you. He'll see you, all of you, and cherish every bit. He'll be the one still holding your hand when the storms come."

Hanna closed her eyes, letting his words settle into her heart.

If she ever allowed herself to fall in love, it would have to be with someone gentle. Someone who was honest and never left. Most of all, someone who loved her the way her grandfather always had.

Family History

The DeLuca Family

Anthony "Tony" DeLuca was the son of Vincenzo DeLuca, the powerful head of the DeLuca crime family, and Rosalinda "Rosa" DeLuca, the elegant but iron-willed matriarch who pulled strings from the shadows. Vince and Rosa had four sons: Carlo, Tony, Frank, and Little Vinny. From the start, all of them were expected to carry on the family legacy.

But Tony wanted something different. He didn't crave power or fear. He wanted a life that didn't involve bloodshed. A quiet life. A normal one.

What no one knew was that Tony made a deal with the feds. It was a dangerous move, one that could get him killed if it ever came out. But in a world like his, nothing stayed secret forever.

To strengthen his empire, Vince arranged for Tony to marry Elaine Moretti. She was a Mafia princess, half Italian and half Polish, the daughter of Chicago's crime boss Giovanni Moretti. Gio saw marriage the same way Vince did, as a way to build alliances. Just like Gio's father had married him to Katarzyna Kowalski, a Polish Mafia heiress, he expected Elaine to play her part too.

With Vince in charge of New York and Gio controlling Chicago, the DeLuca-Moretti alliance became nearly untouchable. Together, they ruled both the Italian and Polish underworlds. It was a bond sealed by family and impossible to break without blood.

On October 9, 1965, Tony and Elaine were married in a wedding that looked more like a coronation. There were movie stars, politicians, and Mafia royalty. Even a senator, a congressman, and the Secretary of State were there.

But Elaine didn't love Tony. She never had.

Her heart belonged to Stefan Wójcik, a hitman who worked for her father. Gio never thought Stefan was good enough. He wasn't an asset; he was a risk. So Elaine did what she was told. She married Tony. And she regretted it every single day.

Their marriage was cold and distant. Built on duty, not love. It brought resentment, heartbreak, and years of silence. But it also brought two sons.

Brian DeLuca was born on February 10, 1970, and Anthony Jr. came three years later, on August 17, 1973.

Tony had other children too. Ones born from affairs. They were kept quiet, raised in the shadows, supported financially but never acknowledged. Over time, Elaine grew colder. Angrier. The betrayals wore her down. She separated from Tony, but divorce was never really an option. Not in their world, where the only way out was death.

* * *

The O'Sullivan Family

Seamus O'Sullivan and his wife, Kathleen (Kate to everyone), immigrated from Sneem, County Kerry, Ireland, in 1954. Seamus was 21. Kate was 18 and fierce in the kind of way that made survival look effortless.

They arrived with nothing. Kate took work as a seamstress, while Seamus enrolled at Fordham Law and bartended at The Black Rose Tavern by night, serving up shots to tired working men and the occasional mob enforcer.

One night changed everything.

Salvatore Ricci and Domenico Russo were talking through a legal problem at the bar. Both worked for the DeLuca family. Seamus overheard, offered some quick advice, and helped them avoid real trouble.

Dom reported back to Vince DeLuca, who called Seamus in and made him an offer: full tuition, a house for him and Kate, and a steady income.

In return, Seamus would offer legal guidance and, once licensed, serve as the DeLuca family's personal attorney.

Seamus said yes. And from that day on, the O'Sullivan's were theirs.

With Mafia backing, Seamus built a strong, respected legal career. He and Kate had five children, each one smart, driven, and expected to succeed.

Liam O'Sullivan, born March 12, 1961, became a lawyer and eventually moved out west, determined to forge his own path, far from the family's obligations.

Brigid "Birdie" O'Sullivan, born November 2, 1965, carved her way into the legal world with grit and fire. She eventually left New York and made a name for herself in Washington, D.C., refusing to let her family ties define her.

Declan O'Sullivan, born January 4, 1968, shocked everyone by becoming a priest. Quiet and thoughtful, he always seemed to carry the weight of things others refused to name.

Douglas O'Sullivan, born August 17, 1970, followed closely in his father's footsteps. He stayed local, took over the family law practice, and kept the O'Sullivan name firmly rooted in New York.

Nicholas "Nick" O'Sullivan, born May 9, 1972, was the outlier. He became a doctor instead of a lawyer, chasing redemption through medicine and always trying to outrun the family shadow.

To outsiders, the O'Sullivan's were a picture of the American dream.

But Seamus knew better. Because once you take a favor from the Mafia, they own you for life.

* * *

The Nowack Family

Henry and Irene Nowack arrived at Ellis Island in 1945, survivors of Nazi-occupied Poland. They carried with them only what they could salvage: memories, grief, and a quiet determination to start over. They settled in

Cohoes, New York, surrounded by a strong Polish-American community that reminded them of home.

Henry found work on the railroad. Irene took a job at Harmony Mills until motherhood became her full-time calling. Together, they built a modest but steady life and raised four sons.

Stanislaw "Stan" Nowack, born September 15, 1950, followed in his father's footsteps and worked the rails. He was quiet, dependable, and calm, just like the tracks he helped lay.

Born on May 19, 1952, Ludwik "Lee" Nowack never conformed to conventional norms. He chafed at rules, rejected expectations, and ran from anything that tried to pin him down. A job at General Electric gave him a way out, but the darkness he carried always seemed to follow.

Marek Nowack, born May 25, 1954, found steady work at Ford and built a life out of routine and reliability. He kept to himself but was always the one who showed up when it counted.

Piotr "Peter" Nowack, born October 25, 1960, broke the working-class pattern and became a dentist. Clean-cut, polished, and proud, he represented everything his parents had hoped America could offer.

The Nowack's weren't flashy. They didn't chase power or money. They chased survival, and later, stability. But not every son escaped the weight of the past. Some wounds don't heal they just find quieter ways to live.

* * *

The Wójcik Family

Jan and Helena Wójcik met aboard a ship fleeing the Nazi invasion of Poland in 1939. Strangers when they boarded, they arrived in America as something more. Together, they built a life in Cohoes, New York, where they raised six children in a home filled with structure, sacrifice, and high expectations, but not much warmth.

Born on January 9, 1947, Andrzej "Andy" Wójcik assumed the role of the eldest, bearing the weight of the family's hopes. Responsible, steady, and serious from a young age, he never questioned the path laid out for him.

Wojciech "Jack" Wójcik, born November 3, 1949, was strong, loyal, and protective of those he loved. He didn't say much, but when he did, people listened.

Kazimierz "Kaz" Wójcik, born July 17, 1951, had a fire in him that no one could tame. Reckless and bold, he lived fast and played by his own rules, even when it cost him.

Jadwiga "Hattie" Wójcik, born September 26, 1953, took on the role of the enforcer. Stern and unsentimental, she believed control was safer than vulnerability.

Rebecca Wójcik, born April 17, 1956, was the family's quiet rebellion. Starved for affection in a household that rarely gave it, she sought love wherever she thought she could find it.

Sophie Wójcik, born September 22, 1957, was the youngest and often overlooked. The baby of the family, she learned early how to disappear, how to listen more than speak, and how to survive without being seen.

Jan and Helena believed in legacy. They groomed the boys for their futures. The girls were groomed for marriage. However, the hidden reality was that the Wójcik children were brought up to endure, not to dream.

***

The Beginning of the End

Rebecca Wójcik met Lee Nowack at Sokołowska's Bar in October of 1972. Her sister Hedwig took one look at him and shook her head.

"That one's trouble," she warned.

Rebecca smirked. "No chance."

Lee approached with that crooked smile and too much confidence. "Wanna dance?"

"I don't know," she said, eyeing him. "You look like trouble."

"I am," he replied. "But I'm also the best dancer here."

That night led to drinks. Drinks led to six weeks. And six weeks later, Rebecca was pregnant.

An out-of-wedlock pregnancy was a scandal. Her father lost his mind. Lee's parents didn't give him a choice.

"Man up," they said. So he did.

They were married on March 3, 1973, angry, reluctant, and already falling apart. They smiled through gritted teeth and posed for pictures like they believed it.

Four months later, on July 3, their daughter was born. They named her Hanna. Held her for photos. Said all the right things. But behind closed doors, everything was already unraveling.

Rebecca felt trapped. Lee turned to the bottle. They thought maybe another child would fix it, or at least distract them long enough to pretend.

Kevin was born on December 15, 1975.

Instead of saving the marriage, he exposed every crack. Lee drank more. Rebecca simmered in resentment, bitter over the life she never chose. Her friends were out living. She found herself stuck with a man she detested and children she struggled to love.

Lee resented her for it. Rebecca despised him for everything.

The marriage turned bitter, then violent.

Hanna became the scapegoat. Blamed for everything. Kevin, the golden child, carried their hopes. The only real love Hanna ever felt came from her paternal grandparents, Henry and Irene, who did their best, in the quiet moments, to protect what little they could.

* * *

By 1985, at thirteen, Hanna had already learned not to expect much. Her parents didn't give affection; they gave silence, blame, and the occasional bruise. She kept her head down, stayed quiet, and made herself small.

Then she saw him.

He was a sophomore walking through the middle school halls like he owned them, probably on some errand or skipping class. She didn't know his name. Not then. Just that he moved through the world like it didn't scare him. Hanna watched from the edges, unnoticed. But she remembered him.

Two years passed. In 1987, she finally met him. She was a freshman. He was a senior. What started as friendship became something more. Something slow and safe. Brian DeLuca didn't ask for anything she wasn't ready to give. He just stayed.

He became the air she breathed. Her anchor and, most of all, her home.

They built a life out of laughter and hope, one she never thought she deserved.

On May 17, 1996, their daughter Caitlyn was born. For a little while, Hanna had everything she never thought she'd have.

And then, on a single night on November 3, 1997, she lost it all. With Brian gone, the girl, who had learned to survive alone, had to do it all over again.

A Note from the Author

Thank you so much for reading *The Lies We Whisper*. Writing this book was one of the most personal experiences of my life. It was shaped by grief, by resilience, and by the quiet strength it takes to begin again when the world no longer feels familiar. I poured my heart into these characters, and it means so much to me that you chose to spend time with them.

Hanna's story is one of survival and healing. It is about learning to trust again after everything has been broken. If her journey stayed with you, if you felt something in the quiet moments or held your breath during the hardest ones, then I am truly grateful. That connection between a story and a reader is the reason I write.

As an independent author, I rely on readers like you to help stories like this reach others. If you connected with the book, or even if you didn't, I would be incredibly thankful if you took a moment to leave a review on Amazon or Goodreads. It does not have to be long or fancy, just honest. Every single review makes a difference.

If you are wondering what happens next, I hope you will stay with me. Hanna's story isn't over yet.

And if you ever want to drop me a note, you can find me on Facebook or Instagram, or just send a message to info@sophiazane.com. I'd love to hear from you.

With all my thanks,

Sophia Zane

About the Author

Sophia Zane is a psychological thriller author with a passion for exploring the darkest corners of the human mind. Her stories are shaped by years of experience in the mental health field, drawing inspiration from countless interviews, observations, and personal insights into trauma, survival, and resilience.

    She lives in a quiet town in Virginia with a spirited crew of rescue animals. When she's not writing, she's wandering local trails, devouring true crime documentaries, or getting lost in a good book. Her work is deeply personal, quietly intense, and always driven by the question: *What makes someone break?*

You can connect with me on:
- https://www.sophiazane.com
- https://www.facebook.com/sophiazanes
- https://www.instagram.com/sophiazanebooks

Also by Sophia Zane

Coming Soon

Beyond the Truth
Book Two in The Lies That Bind Us Series
　　Still reeling from past betrayals and haunted by unanswered questions, Hanna Nowack is desperate to protect the fragile peace she's built for herself and her daughter. But when new threats emerge and old secrets refuse to stay buried, Hanna is forced to confront the truth she's spent years trying to forget.

　　As danger creeps closer and her carefully guarded world begins to unravel, Hanna must navigate a tangled web of loyalty, loss, and deception, where every choice has a cost and some truths may be too devastating to face.

　　In this gripping continuation of *The Lies That Bind Us* series, *Beyond the Truth* delivers a powerful story of survival, resilience, and the haunting consequences of the past.

Printed in Dunstable, United Kingdom